# THE WORLD THAT REMAINS

## EVERGREEN BOOK 2

## MATTHEW S. COX

DIVISION ZERO PRESS

# CONTENTS

# DUST SETTLES

H ope the day would stay quiet kept Harper in a reasonably good mood—after all, she hadn't had to kill anyone in almost four months.

The first week of March rolled in with unusually warm weather, making a plain white T-shirt and jeans comfortable, at least during the day. Up in the hills, the nights still turned quite cold. An unending chorus of tweets and trills filled the air from birds in the surrounding trees, a background accompaniment to the soft scuff of her sneakers on the road that meandered among the houses southeast of the former Evergreen Middle School, which had become the town's primary school. The nice breeze almost even let her smile, but Harper doubted she would ever truly feel happy again, not after having watched her parents die.

Dad's Mossberg shotgun hung heavy on her left shoulder, providing a sense of security as well as a constant reminder of losing him.

The area south of the school surrounding the Hiwan Golf Club had become more familiar to her than the neighborhood she'd lived in before the war. Townspeople had spent the past few weeks reclaiming the overgrown golf course for additional farmland since it already had a usable network of irrigation sprinklers. Planting corn, carrots, and potatoes there got off to a faster start than the huge swath of open land west of Route 74. Of course, having crops growing in a place surrounded by homes made the town council discuss the chances people might help themselves to vegetables unnoticed.

However, everyone living in those houses—with the exception of a few holdouts who refused to evacuate when the Army came through—had children attending the school. Anne-Marie Kirby, the 'town manager,' had assigned people with children to homes nearer the school so the kids didn't have to walk multiple miles each day. No one seemed terribly bothered by the idea that parents with kids might grab an extra bit of produce. And, if it became a problem, they could always post a guard at night.

So far, Walter Holman, the head of the Evergreen Militia, hadn't said anything to make her worry they'd reassign her elsewhere. Patrolling around the houses for half a day had become boring as hell, but whenever she started disliking it, she thought about fleeing her parents' home, desperate to keep those men from grabbing her little sister.

No, boredom could be good.

She'd take boredom any day over running for her life—or having to shoot someone.

"It's so quiet…" Harper gazed up at the sky, enjoying the lack of trouble, though she could definitely do without all the walking around. "Not like anyone has phones to call for help. Guess we gotta be out here for people to find."

Walter still let her go home as soon as the children left school. Cliff Barton, the ex-Army Ranger-slash-mall-cop who she'd mostly adopted as a father, didn't return until around six or as best she could guess by daylight. A few places in town had working mechanical clocks, though her house didn't. She hadn't even looked at a working clock since the morning Dad dragged her out of bed, mere minutes before nukes went off close enough to hear. Her old alarm clock had forever burned the glowing red numbers 5:49 into her psyche. One instant, she complained at him for pulling her out of bed when she still had ten minutes to sleep, the next, she'd been too terrified to say a word.

So, yeah… boredom felt great.

She swiped a few strands of her hair off her face, glancing to her right at houses going by. Harper knew which ones on South Hiwan Drive had people living in them, and which were empty. All the places there on Augusta had been assigned. Here and there, residents waved as they spotted her. She returned their greetings, managing a bright—if not fully sincere—smile whenever someone looked at her.

Not that she had any issues with the people, but smiling came too close to happy and felt disrespectful to her parents, to her sister Madison, her friends, and the whole life she might have led if not for idiot politicians. No one really knew how many had died, but it had to be a heartbreakingly large number, and not just in the USA. In the weeks after the blast, her family had heard rumors that Colorado Springs had taken a direct hit from 'a big one,' which had likely been true. However, Roy Ellis, one of the militia who had been a police officer before the war, mentioned that smaller warheads came down much closer to Denver than she thought. The destruction around Lakewood, her old home, didn't come from the nuke that hit Colorado Springs, but from smaller ones with a fraction of the power.

No, the blast that roared like the fury of an ancient primal god, so loud she expected her house to be ripped off its foundation, had more than likely been from a multi-warhead weapon that landed within four miles. Roy had possibly been trying to make her feel better when he said if one as big as the one that hit Springs landed on Lakewood, she wouldn't have even known what happened... but he'd only freaked her out more.

All things considered, she *could* feel lucky if she allowed herself to. She'd managed to get Madison out of there, away from the 'blue gang' and to the safety of Evergreen. She'd even found Cliff as well as Jonathan Chen, a boy Madison's age who'd been staying with him already. More recently, Lorelei Frost had joined them. The brittle six-year-old had somehow survived on her own for some time after the nuclear strike, but nearly starved before being brought to Evergreen by a nineteen-year-old named Tyler, who Harper had started to like. The child had been in rough shape, so malnourished she lacked the strength to walk for a while... but she survived—and now, had *too* much energy. The girl had befriended Madison and Jonathan in the short time Harper had been friendly with her adoptive dad. Unfortunately, Harper's nagging feeling that something wasn't quite right with him proved true. He'd fled town, no longer welcome here. That left Lorelei without a caretaker, so Cliff had brought her home.

They'd formed something of a new family unit, though Harper still couldn't think of Cliff as Dad. He occupied a place somewhere between older brother and protective uncle she couldn't quite name. Maybe he had, in fact, become a father figure. In truth, he hadn't been required to give a crap about her, or Madison... or even Jonathan, but he had. Accepting him couldn't insult her real parents. It wasn't as though she ran away from them to be with this guy. No, they'd both died trying to protect their kids. If anything like ghosts or an afterlife existed and her parents still had any sort of awareness, they would undoubtedly be relieved she and Madison had him looking out for them.

*Do adopted kids ever truly accept their new parents as 'mom and dad,' or do they always feel half an arms' length away?*

Lorelei hadn't said much of her birth parents other than an occasional remark about her mommy not liking her or always being angry. She hadn't at all spoken of a father, so it made sense why she attached herself to Cliff as 'daddy' so fast. She also considered Harper more like a mother than an older sister. Then again, the girl seemed to love *everyone,* possessed of an almost eerie contagious happiness that verged on pathological.

Harper kicked a rock into the dirt, wondering how her mother would feel about her having shot people to death. During the gang's attack on her old home, Mom had killed a couple men, too. As had her father. They'd probably accept what she had to do to protect herself and Madison. Not like she'd gone off on a killing spree, randomly shooting people for the lols—she'd only killed when necessary to defend herself or Madison. If her parents mourned anything, it would've been how the world had changed so much that a seventeen-year-old went from worrying about getting into college to worrying about surviving to see tomorrow.

At the end of Hearth Drive, she cut north to walk across the former golf course loaded with hundreds of small cornstalk sprouts and made her way toward Island Drive, a little pocket of homes in the midst of the fairways. The roads here mostly formed loops around a once-pleasant little suburban community. It bothered her how well she'd come to know this place over the past few months, more so than home. Not since she'd been seven or eight years old and played with some friends did she really spend time outside there. After that, she and her friends would either be inside with electronics, at school, or driven to some organized activity far removed from her neighborhood. She hadn't really ever gone exploring on foot much past a block or two in any one direction. Her house might have been a small island for as little contact as she'd had with neighbors.

*Wonder how many golf balls went through windows here before? Who'd want to live* this *close to a golf course?*

That thought made her chuckle, though it soon turned into a sad sigh. Dad got a set of clubs for Christmas a few years ago, even though the man hadn't played often at all. Mostly, it made her think of the holiday itself, and of the overly somber Christmas her new family had shared here in Evergreen not long ago.

Neither she nor Madison had expected anyone to care about holidays after the world lit itself on fire, but lo and behold, people made do with improvised holiday trees. Cliff had constructed a rather sad one out of branches he'd stripped from trees slated to become firewood, lashing them together with wire and decorating the pitiful 'tree' with red soda cans. The town council assembled a pile of toys scavenged from every unoccupied house within the city limits as well as sending the semi back to Walmart specifically to gather toys, stuffed animals, and such.

Everyone age five or older got to select one gift for each family member they had. No one bothered with wrapping paper since it seemed a waste of resources—and they didn't have any. She'd been pleasantly surprised at Madison not complaining at receiving only one gift each from her, Cliff, Jonathan, and Lorelei. She'd even started crying when Harper gave her a ballerina doll, since she'd been hoping for a different gift: her big sister not dying. The girl had even offered to give up any and all gifts for Christmases yet to come if only Harper would stay alive. Upon receiving the toy, Madison broke down, thinking a jinx had been cast.

Fortunately, Harper soothed her by whispering that she broke the rules and gave her *two* presents.

She still worried about her sister's mental state. For the past few months, Madison had acted ambivalent to her dead iPhone; however, she reclaimed it to stash in the bedroom the girls shared. While she no longer carried it around believing their parents or her friends would call, she wouldn't allow Harper to toss it.

*Hope she just wants it as a keepsake. Mom gave it to her for her ninth birthday.* Harper smirked. *One year after getting it, it's dead. I wonder if the extended protection plan covers thermonuclear EMP.*

She'd gone into the holidays dreading Madison would mention their parents on Christmas Eve, knowing it would bring a storm of tears… but her little sister hadn't said anything about them. Tears did happen when Lorelei asked about Tyler, hoping he was okay, warm, and had food, wherever he'd gone. The child had no idea how close she'd come to being killed. For reasons that only Tyler would ever know, he hadn't attacked her the night he turned violent. Since he'd been the one to find Lorelei half-starved and bring her to Evergreen, the town had made him her official guardian. The child lived with him, and no one would have been able to do anything in time to stop him if he decided to 'save' her.

Yet, despite what could have happened to her—and what he tried to do to Madison, Lorelei worried about Tyler. Harper did feel a bit of pity for him as he would most likely have been alone on Christmas—if he even remained alive two weeks after fleeing Evergreen. Still, having empathy for his situation didn't mean she wanted him around.

Harper let out a guilty sigh. Tyler hadn't asked to have his particular problems. He couldn't help what his brain did when deprived of medicine the world could no longer produce. To distract herself from misplaced feelings that she'd done something wrong by essentially kicking him out of town, she contemplated if any Third World countries survived the war and might still have real hospitals and doctors and pharmacies. Would the murderous shitheads who launched the nukes have tossed them around the whole globe, determined to incinerate as many people as they could, or had there been some manner of strategy involved? If the US, Russia, China, Korea, the UK, and/or whoever else got into a pissing contest, would any of their leaders randomly throw nuclear weapons at random small nations?

Then again, who knows what kind of chaos went on since no 'superpowers' remained intact. For all she knew, war still might be raging in Central America or Africa or parts of Europe as previously weak countries that escaped the worst of the nuclear bombardment asserted themselves without fear of what the superpowers would do in response.

Assuming, of course, the nukes hadn't burned it all.

Harper reached the end of the baby cornstalks and slipped between trees among the houses on Island Drive. While walking the loop, she thought about the friends she hadn't seen in what felt like forever: Christina, Renee, Darci, Andrea, and Veronica. She'd known Christina since kindergarten, the girl living only a few houses away from her. Darci had to be miserable if she remained alive, since finding marijuana these days would be hard.

*Dar is so laid back...* Harper pictured her friend sitting on the old couch in her basement bedroom, smoking a bong. A blast wave tore the house off its foundation, exposing the basement to the sky... and Darci merely saying, 'oh, bummer.' The mental image made her want to laugh as much as cry.

Not one of her friends had showed up in Evergreen, though roughly thirty people had filtered in over the past several months, all former residents. They had been evacuated by the Army soon after the bombardment amid fears of fallout drift, and moved to a 'settlement camp' somewhere to the north. Harper asked some of them about her friends, but none of the new arrivals had seen them. She hated not knowing what happened to her crew, girls she'd spent so much time with, even if they had treated her as a charity case. Except for Christina and Renee, the others took pity on poor socially challenged Harper and dragged her around to places, forcing Introvert Prime to go out and have fun. Renee, timid as she was, had little problem with people. She merely jumped at every shadow and couldn't handle even tame horror movies. Every time they'd gathered for a sleepover from age ten until recently, Renee always had a nightmare and woke everyone up screaming if they watched any movie or TV show even remotely scary.

Speaking of nightmares, Madison had been having them lately as well. Her sister acted almost normal during the day, especially when her friend Becca came over to hang out… but she'd developed a habit of waking up in the middle of the night, yelling for Mom. More and more, Harper suspected she'd definitely seen the thug climbing in the kitchen window stab their mother to death. Perhaps she'd been cowering away from that sight when the other one shot Dad, but… maybe she sat there stunned and watched everything.

Doctor Hale, or Tegan as she'd asked Harper to call her, said Madison had mentally regressed in response to trauma, acting like a younger child. Fortunately, she appeared to be on the mend, and for the most part during the day, had almost gone back to her old self. She hadn't quite gotten her 'bubbly' personality back yet, perhaps never would. A bubbly girl who giggled at everything belonged in a world with hot running water, food that came from a grocery store, movies, video games, and Starbucks… not the nuclear Wild West. According to Tegan, who'd done a few therapy sessions with Madison, her kid sister remained morbidly terrified something bad would happen to Harper.

Maybe that's why Walter let her do half-shifts and stay home with the kids after they got out of school. Either that, or the militia still considered *her* somewhat of a child and gave her light duty. Still, everyone in the militia remained obligated to respond to emergencies so it didn't really matter where she happened to be in town if a major event occurred. Her siblings—both biological and adopted—needed her, so she didn't mind the easy patrol schedule.

Also, Tegan mentioned that having one of Madison's friends—Becca—

show up in town alive and safe with her parents both in good health had offered a desperately needed scrap of normalcy that helped pull her out of the defensive shell she'd constructed. For now, Harper loved that she could go home with the kids as soon as they got out of school.

Madison would implode if Harper stayed away from her for any length of time. Jonathan, strangely enough, had taken the deaths of his parents, surviving the war, and forming a new family all in stride. At times, she worried about him for behaving too normal. She'd never seen him cry over losing his mom and dad, both killed by rioting survivors who blamed anyone who looked remotely Korean for the war. Though, he had been with Cliff for at least a month before she met them, so maybe he'd gotten all his tears done with already.

And Lorelei... that little girl simply loved everyone. Perhaps her overabundant cheerfulness would also help Madison.

It might even help Harper.

She reached the road that led to the school, but with at least two hours left until the kids got out, she sighed and continued walking down the road, keeping an eye on the neighborhood.

# 2

# NOT THE WORST PLACE

C ompetition shooting had been Harper's version of soccer, gymnastics, or dance class since age nine.

Late that afternoon, after walking the kids back from school, she stood in the yard behind the house on Hilltop Drive they'd been assigned, holding a bow with a camouflage paint scheme. Laughter and cheering filled the air from the front yard where the children—her siblings plus Becca—tossed a Frisbee around.

Despite her familiarity with shooting, she'd never touched a compound bow until recently. The militia had recovered quite a number of them from the Walmart at her suggestion, figuring that with the collapse of the nation's infrastructure, bullets would eventually all run out. A bunch of the guys had presses to reload cartridges, but that didn't mean powder, primers, or slugs fell from the sky. Eventually, they'd have only bows, knives, and swords left to protect the town. Though she still had a healthy stock of 12-gauge shells, 246 at last count thanks to a few successful scavenging trips the militia conducted, she felt no rush to use them up.

For the past few weeks, she'd been throwing an hour or so at a time every couple days at familiarizing herself with firing a compound bow. Using one felt wonky compared to the shotgun. The much slower-moving arrows fell in a sharper arc that sometimes required she aim at a spot well above her target so the arrow would fall onto it at range. She didn't think the bows would be terribly good choices for anyone to carry around Evergreen while trying to be cops. Picturing pre-war police running around with bows proved too ridiculous a thought. She'd have laughed if not for the worry that if she ever wound up carrying that bow on patrol, a bad guy could jump on top of her before she could fire a single arrow.

A stack of boxes and a sheet of scrap plywood up against the base of a tree forty feet away served as a target. Some of the arrows they'd taken from the store had points that resembled pencils more than traditional arrows, 'target heads' as Cliff called them. While they *could* be used as weapons, they weren't intended to shoot anything other than targets. Hunting arrows had bladed points. Those, she didn't fire for practice. Besides, the target heads withstood repeated strikes better than the razor tips would. She also didn't have any of those, as they remained in the militia storage area to be issued as needed when the bullets ran out.

Harper loaded an arrow, drew the cord back, sighted, and let go. Her shot hit the target, but high left… not where she'd been aiming. In Cliff's opinion, that she had been able to consistently hit the target board—even if it didn't bulls-eye—after only four or five hours of attempting meant she 'was a natural.' Dad once said the same thing about her and shotguns, though the firearm had never felt as awkward as the bow.

Going shooting had been a bit more than a simple hobby, but nothing she ever intended to make any sort of career out of. Madison adored her dance classes far more than Harper had ever been into going to the range with Dad. He hadn't been a 'prepper,' merely thought his daughters should learn how to protect themselves.

Little did either of them know how much she would need those skills.

She tried not to think about having killed people, especially the close-range ones that sometimes haunted her dreams. She tried even harder not to think about how she could shoot dangerous people without much hesitation anymore. How had she gone from wanting nothing more than to sit in her room and read to being the only thing standing between Madison and horribleness?

It seemed as though she'd gone in an instant from stressing about scoring high enough on the SATs so she could get into a good college to stressing about starving to death. The two months she'd huddled in the basement with her parents didn't feel like something that had really happened.

Harper sighed at the memory, glancing down at the bow in her hand.

*These things might work to defend the town or something, but not for crap like Tommy beating his wife.*

That thought made her think about the gang who killed her parents. Would they keep expanding, claiming territory, eventually reaching Evergreen? Could they be an aberration? How many gangs like them had popped up in the country as a whole?

She loaded another arrow, pulled the cord back, and tried to picture the way the last arrow flew. After a second's concentration to aim, she let her two fingers snap forward. The arrow plunged into the plywood about a fist's width from center.

"Hey, not bad," said Cliff from the back door.

Harper lowered the bow, frustrated and feeling like a failure. She hadn't consistently missed bulls-eye on a range since she'd been ten. "These things are impractical."

"No tool is impractical if it's the only one you have." He walked over to stand beside her. "It's impractical to drive a nail with a frying pan when you have a hammer. But if you don't have a hammer, and that nail's gotta go in…"

"Yeah, I get it. I'm just not used to this. But"—she held it up—"are we going to wind up carrying these around town on patrol?"

He scratched at his beard, which he'd been trimming with a combat knife. "Ehh… probably not. When we run out of bullets, it'll be a hand-to-hand game."

She cringed.

"Don't worry too much. We're working on that." He patted her shoulder. "Besides, cops cheat."

"Cheat? How? We don't have Tasers either."

"I mean cheating as in there's usually like nine cops jumping on one guy." He grinned. "'Course, that would kinda necessitate changing up how we do things. No more individual patrols. At least two-person teams."

She picked up a third arrow and nocked it. "It's been pretty quiet since Tommy. Do you think it'll stay that way?"

"Way I figure, most people are still a bit shell shocked at the war. Rearranged a lot of priorities. Folks tend to come together and help each other when facing a serious outside threat. We're still in that survivor mode here, everyone clinging together for support. If we have any real issues, it's gonna be from new arrivals."

Harper raised the bow, drawing the cord back. She stared down the length of the arrow at the little colored posts on the spar above her left hand. They corresponded to range, needing to use lower posts for a more distant target. As best she'd been able to tell, the orange one worked out to be the most accurate for the present distance to her target. She lined it up with the bulls-eye and let go of the arrow. The shot went about four inches south of center and a little left. "Grr. Damn."

"Heh." He clapped her on the shoulder. "Bit of that competitive streak coming out."

She smirked, mostly for his being right. Part of her bristled at not hitting the center every time like she could do with a gun. But she also secretly hoped that if she could train herself into a master archer, the town would make her some kind of 'defender' like the snipers at the bus wall. That sounded less dangerous than working as a 'cop' inside town. She no longer thought of it as 'pretending' to be a cop. Somewhere over the past three months—when she didn't wake up and find this reality all part of a strange, horrible dream—she'd come to accept the militia as real and her implied authority as at least somewhat genuine.

"Yeah, a bit." Half grinning, she picked up another arrow and aimed, letting all the air out of her lungs before loosing the shot. That time, she landed the arrow within three inches of the dot at the middle of the plywood.

"You're getting the hang of it. This time next year, you'll be able to slice a mole off a black bear's ass at fifty yards."

She shook her head. "I wouldn't shoot a bear. For one thing, it's an animal. For another, an arrow would probably only make it angry."

He laughed.

"Umm, Cliff?"

"Hmm?"

She faced him. "I was thinking that bows would work better like to defend the town… but that also got me worrying that we might *have* to defend Evergreen."

"Mm-hmm…" He raised an eyebrow.

"Those creeps who attacked us in Lakewood… do you think they're like just a weird one-off type thing or are thugs like that going to be all over the place? Will bandit armies or whatever come after us?"

"You've been watching too many movies." He winked. "If shit like that's going to happen, it won't be until after we're old or gone. Still too much of society left in people."

Harper rolled her eyes. "Tell that to the blue gang. If they went crazy, others will, too. Denver isn't—uhh *wasn't* that bad a place. Like New York is way worse for crime. Was."

"Well, you know that old thing about what happens when a plane is crashing."

She tilted her head.

"I guess not." He held up his hands as if gripping a melon. "See, there's this thing where a bunch of people are on a plane and the pilot says they're gonna crash and everyone's gonna die. So, with the last like five minutes they all have left to live, they go bonkers. Drinking all the booze, screwing in the aisles, all inhibitions straight out the window."

"Eww." She cringed. "Wild sex and drinking sure sounds like the blue gang."

"The shock of civilization being reshaped so severely overnight broke some people. Maybe those idiots figured they were going to die soon, so they stopped caring about decency. Others have been bad all along. And, you put an average person in a ridiculous situation... they do what they have to do in order to survive. Bet some of them 'went with the flow' out of self-preservation when they got forcibly recruited. You know that whole Milgram experiment?"

"Umm, no."

Cliff pinched the bridge of his nose. "What did they teach you kids in school?"

"Umm, chemistry, physics, math, English, social studies, Spanish..."

He sighed. "Maybe if they hadn't dropped civics, we wouldn't be in this mess."

"Huh? The milligram thing was civics?"

"*Mil*-gram." He laughed. "And no, not really civics. Okay, you do know about World War II right?"

"Of course."

"Okay. After it ended, a lot of people wondered how ordinary people could do ghastly, unforgivable things. Many of the Nazis were just like anyone else before the war, neighbors, family, friends... There's even some photos of concentration camp workers smiling and hanging out on breaks like they're ordinary office staff. So, this guy Milgram sets up an experiment to test people's capacity to blindly obey a person in a position of authority. He gets a volunteer and sticks them in a chair, then brings in a test subject and orders them to push a fake button next to a dial. The volunteer pretends to suffer shocks at increasingly high voltages while begging the test subject not to hit the button again. The scientist tells the test subject it's okay, just hit the button, and turns up the voltage. Most test subjects obeyed the person they thought of as an authority figure, even when they believed they were causing great pain to the actor pretending to be electrocuted."

"Wow, really?"

"Yeah. So, you get some random guy captured by those blue idiots, they threaten to kill him if he doesn't do what they say, and he just falls in line. Does atrocious things because he's been ordered to. At first, they're afraid of being shot for disobedience. Then, maybe they get a taste for violence and are caught up in the fray."

She looked down. "Does that mean we killed innocent people?"

"Nope." He grasped her shoulders until she made eye contact. "When someone runs at you, Maddie, Jon, or Lori with a weapon and intention to hurt, they give up being considered innocent. If they surrender and you still shoot them, *that* you should feel bad about."

Harper exhaled in relief. "Okay. So, do you think there are more gangs like that? Will bandit armies attack us?"

"I suppose it's an outside possibility, but I don't see it happening. Most people just want to live and be left alone. I don't believe we're in any real danger of roving bands of warring tribes or anything. Shit like that *might* happen eventually, but not for several generations until there's no one left alive who remembers the modern world. Like, if humanity fails and society reverts to like feudalism."

She nodded, ran to the target to retrieve her arrows, and fired them again one after the next. Her grouping improved a little, but hitting a giant piece of plywood that stood still didn't mean she'd be any use in a real fight with a bow yet. Although her competitive streak reared up and made her want to practice more, barring an unlikely event like a large-scale skirmish where a small army attacked Evergreen, she wouldn't run out of shotgun ammo any time soon.

Though, such an attack wasn't impossible.

"Grr." She hurried to the target to retrieve the arrows again.

"Don't stress out over it." Cliff smiled, watching as she nocked an arrow and took aim again. "You'll get the hang of it. Like anything else, it's just a matter of repetition. No need to drive yourself nuts over it. No trophies to win."

Harper zeroed in on the target, concentrating on a spot about the size of a quarter. She loosed… and came within an inch of where she wanted to put it. Four arrows later, her grouping improved—slightly.

*Ugh. This is going to take forever. Guns are so much easier.*

"Bullets, chocolate, and coffee," said Harper, staring at the bulls-eye.

"What?"

She turned her head toward him; wind draped her hair over her face. "Stuff that will all be gone soon. Arrows, we can probably keep making."

Cliff groaned. "The day we run out of coffee is going to be a true tragedy for humanity."

"I don't think humanity, in general, will run out of coffee." She walked to the target again to collect arrows. "Just the humanity in this country. The places where it grows will still have it."

"It would almost be worth the walk down to Colombia." He smiled.

"Hah. Speak for yourself. I'm staying right here." She fired all five arrows again, taking her time and managing approximately the same grouping. "Ugh. Still not plating them all."

"Plating?"

"Getting them all in a circle the size of a plate."

"Oh. Could be a bum arrow."

She shook her head. "Nah. I'm just not that good with this thing yet and it's frustrating me. A poor craftsman blames their tools... something my dad used to say."

"Wise man." He collected the arrows for her. "So, staying here... that mean you like this place?"

"Evergreen's okay. Maybe there's nicer places out there, but there's definitely worse." She nocked and fired an arrow while barely thinking about it—and nailed the edge of the black dot at the middle of the board. "Dammit."

"Dammit? You hit the bulls-eye."

"Yeah, but I just kinda shot. Didn't even think about much. Just let it go. Ugh. Maybe that means I'm missing because I'm *over*thinking."

"Well..." He gestured at the target. "Keep doing whatever you didn't do."

She tried another reflex shot, but it went high, already ruining the 'plate.' Grumbling, she slowed down for the last three arrows of the set and got them within five inches of the first one.

Cliff nodded. "Lot better than last week. You'll get it. Anyway, you're starting to look ready to snap that thing over your knee. Want to work on the jiu-jitsu some more and burn off some of that energy?"

"Okay." She set the bow on the tiny back porch and returned to stand near him.

For the past few months, he'd been teaching her a number of self-defense techniques, mostly arm-lock takedowns, pain compliance holds, and a few leg sweeps. Today, he grabbed a nine-inch stick to approximate a knife, and used it to go over various disarming techniques in the event someone tried to stab her.

After an hour or so of that, they practiced leg sweep takedowns. She lunged in, grabbed his shoulders, and tried to hook his right leg with hers while pushing backward on his upper body. He held his ground.

"You're going too light, like we're demonstrating."

She locked stares with him. "We *are* demonstrating."

"No, we're practicing. Demonstrating is just showing you the mechanics of the motion. Don't break my ankle, but put a little more into it. If you need to do this for real, you shouldn't hold back at all."

"Okay."

Harper darted in again and swept his leg, easing him over onto his back. The takedown felt a bit fast, but also like he rolled with it, letting her put him on the ground. She glanced at her hands, clutching two fistfuls of his sleeves by his armpits. "How does it work if the guy doesn't have a shirt on?"

Cliff placed his palms flat on her shoulders. "Push. If you can make them overextend past their balance point, they're gonna go over backward. Even if you can't fully sweep the leg, preventing them from taking a step back can make the difference."

They reset and tried it a few times, alternating between Harper doing the sweep and receiving one. With each repetition, the energy level increased almost to the point it felt like a real fight. Despite the speed and force Cliff used to fling her to the ground, his expression remained a complete picture of calm. The sixth time she landed flat on her back, she grimaced, but didn't let herself whimper at the soreness in her side or shoulder. Cliff didn't look like he'd put all that much effort into throwing her. Rather than feel pissed at him for getting too rough, she became angry at herself for being too soft and delicate.

"Again," said Cliff.

Harper sprang to her feet and faced him. She imagined she'd been cornered by one of the blue gang and had two choices: win or wind up without pants. With that mindset, she rushed in and committed to the technique at full strength. For the first time since he started teaching her hand-to-hand skills, she felt like he hadn't *let* her put him on his back.

"Oof," said Cliff. "That's what I'm talking about. You don't have to be bigger or stronger if the other guy doesn't know what he's doing. It's all about leverage."

She grabbed his hand and helped him up. "Sorry."

"Don't apologize. That's what I've been trying to get you to do from the start. Now, in a real situation, you'd go from that toss into a wrist lock. Try to force them over onto their front." He wiped his chin with his thumb. "Or if you're in Afghanistan doing a clandestine mission, after you knock someone down, it's a great opportunity for knife work."

"Ack." She cringed.

He patted her on the shoulder. "No, I'm not going to demonstrate that. The Evergreen Militia isn't going to be conducting any black ops missions." He winked. "Just dealing with thieves, rowdy drunks, or idiots."

"Right."

They resumed sparring. The twelfth time Harper landed hard on her back, her body waved a white flag. The mere thought of sitting up hurt.

"Ow," she muttered, gasping for breath. "I think I'm done."

"All right. We should both get some water."

She peered up at him from the ground, squinting a bit at the sun behind his head. "You know what's really messed up?"

"I can think of a lot of things that would qualify as 'messed up.'" He set his hands on his hips, his breathing also rapid, but not as fatigued as hers.

"Sometimes, it feels like a relief not to be stressing out over college or worrying about what kinda career I want. It's almost relaxing now with everything so different." She gazed up at the clear, blue sky, a fringe of green from trees at the edges of her vision.

Cliff offered a hand.

She grasped it. "I mean, if I could, I'd deal with high school and college all over again ten times to get my parents back and un-break the world, but... yeah."

He pulled her to her feet. "Don't feel guilty about appreciating the relaxed pace of life." He tossed a small towel to her. "It's not exactly relaxed."

"I know. We're back in the Old West... carrying guns everywhere. No medicine, no technology." She dabbed sweat off her face and forehead. "But, I dunno. Whenever I stop being miserable, I feel guilty about it. So many people died. I have no right to think going back in time might not be a horrible thing."

"There's no need for you to feel guilty about not being miserable all the time. That's a dangerous way of thinking that'll lead you to a dark place. Yeah, plenty fine to be sad, but don't let it eat you up.

"Okay… I'll try." She followed him into the house.

He ran water from the kitchen sink into two large glasses before handing her one. "Could be, humanity just reached a breaking point and needed to turn the dial down. Past few years, things have been getting crazier and crazier. Everyone was always angry at everyone else, or offended at every little thing. Hating each other for bullshit. No one talked to anyone; they screamed. One side shouted their ideas, the other side shouted their ideas, and no one *heard* a thing."

"Yeah." She gulped down half her glass in one breath.

Cliff pointed at the window. "Look at that sky. Not a plane or contrail in sight. It gets pretty quiet now. So dark at night."

"You think we'll really be okay here?" She ran more water into her glass and chugged a few mouthfuls.

"Could be." He winked. "It ain't the worst place we could've ended up."

# 3

# RELATIVE NORMAL

Dinner consisted of canned ravioli—again.

At least these two cans had been cheese ravioli, so Madison didn't spend the entire time she ate with a glum face. Harper hated forcing her vegetarian sister to eat meat, but she would rather do that than watch her starve. As Cliff had so indelicately put it back in January, 'vegetarianism is a first-world problem.'

That, of course, had started the first real argument of her new family.

Madison yelled that being a vegetarian wasn't a 'problem,' and lots of people in other countries avoided meat. She claimed 'half of India' had been vegetarian—though Harper had no idea where she'd gotten that statistic from. Cliff had come close to barking at her, but managed to keep himself calm long enough for the outburst to remind Madison of fighting with Dad and switched her from screaming to sobbing.

After that, a truce had developed. Cliff no longer picked on vegetarianism being impractical in a world where not having anything to eat at all had become a real possibility. For her part, Madison begrudgingly ate meat whenever they had no other choice. Though the farm's chicken population thrived, roughly half the meat consumed in Evergreen still came from hunting, and it had been getting rarer lately. Food, in general, had become lean. In fact, that Madison's protest of eating meat had scaled back down to only a sad expression and no hesitation about eating it concerned Harper. The past couple weeks, she'd been constantly hungry, never eating enough to feel satisfied. The only times she stopped feeling hungry was when worrying made her sick to her stomach. Madison and the other kids had to be the same way, though none of them complained about wanting more food.

They all knew they had no choice.

Most nights when the girls cuddled up with her in bed, the faint growls of their stomachs sang them to sleep. Madison accepting meat—when it happened to be available—with barely a whiff of protest broke her heart.

After dinner, Cliff tended to the dishes while Harper headed out to the cinder block grill in the backyard. Two large metal pails of water she'd set on the fire about an hour ago gave off steam but fell short of a boil. The same fire that had heated dinner would give her a hot bath. It took every ounce of strength for her to carry one pail into the house and down the short hall to the bathroom, a task complicated by oven mitts.

She upended the steamy water into the tub she'd filled before sitting down to eat. Leaving the water in the tub for a while let it warm up to the house temperature since it came out of the pipe icy cold. Dumping the heated water into it right away resulted in a tepid or merely cold bath. She filled the pail again and brought it out to the grill, then carried the second near-boiling pail in and added it to the bathtub.

That done, she stepped into the bedroom she shared with her two sisters. Both girls sat on the edge of the bed, ready for a bath with only towels on.

"Okay, it's ready," said Harper. "You two can go in first."

The girls stood at the same time and padded out to the bathroom at the end of the hall, a mere six feet from the bedroom door. Harper set the pail down, dropped the oven mitts on the floor next to it and poked her head into the bathroom, knowing Madison wanted her to hover close for security.

Lorelei dropped her towel and tested the bathwater with one foot.

Madison spun to stare at Harper, drawing a breath as if to yell 'get out!' like she might have done back home in the normal world if her older sister had barged in on her. Caught off guard, Harper braced for the shouting, but her little sister relaxed.

"I'm okay," said Madison in a calm voice. "Thanks for being worried."

"Ooh. It's warm," said Lorelei. She shifted her weight onto her left leg, pulled her other leg over the tub edge, and stood with both feet in the water making soft squeals and gasps.

Harper smiled, forcing herself not to cheer at her sister no longer being so terrified of everything that she refused to have a closed door between them. The girl wanting privacy for a bath felt like another step back to normality. "Okay."

"Wait." Madison eyed the steam wafting up from the tub. "It's still okay if you wanna share it to save firewood. I remember saying we could do that. Not *demanding* you stay with me like I'm some little kid, but... I don't wanna kill trees."

A trace of pleading in the girl's eyes made Harper think her sister wanted her to stay close more than she admitted. Maybe she only acted like it didn't bother her and still feared separation, even if they remained in the same house.

"Up to you," said Harper.

Lorelei bent to touch the water with her hand. "Ooh. Warm."

Harper bit her lip at the tiny child's prominent ribs. She'd improved quite a bit in three months, no longer looking like a refugee from a war zone. Still, Lorelei appeared quite obviously underweight. *Need to take her to the doc again just to make sure.*

"Yeah, c'mon. Water's getting cold." Madison smiled. "If we ever have normal hot water again that doesn't need fire, we should take our own baths. But, it's okay to share so we save wood."

"Where's Jon?" asked Lorelei.

Madison blushed.

"He's gonna take the next bath. There's not enough room in the tub for all of us at once," said Harper.

"He's a *boy*," rasped Madison in a whisper.

Lorelei looked over at her with a 'so what?' expression.

"I'll go after you guys," called Jonathan from his room. "Don't waste more wood. I can use the same water. Don't care if it's hot as long as it isn't freezing."

"Okay," said Harper, stepping into the bathroom and closing the door.

Madison dropped her towel and entered the tub. "Ow. It's too hot."

"Don't add more water. It'll cool off too fast anyway." Harper slipped out of her clothes, then eased herself into the water, adoring the hot bath *far* more than the icy one she'd had on the way to Evergreen.

She sat at the back end of the tub, Madison in front of her, Lorelei closest to the drain. The six-year-old played with a plastic duck more than washed herself while Madison soaped up. Harper basked in the wonderful heat, waiting her turn for the soap.

Bathing had become a once-a-week event, except for a point in February where the pipes froze and they went two weeks without one. Her mind wandered off to the past, specifically how she'd never thought much of showering before, sometimes taking two in one day. Memories of her old bathroom back home played across the tip of her mind. She remembered weird, random things like the scratch on the side of the sink cabinet she caused as a four-year-old trying to roller skate in the house. Or Mom's pulse-jet showerhead. Or the multicolored seashell soaps her mother put everywhere. Even the little white toilet brush holder Mom bought on that one trip to Target felt like a cherished artifact that had been stolen from her.

Daydreaming of her old life brought with it a crash of sorrow at losing contact with her friends. Scenes of hanging out in her room, or Christina's pool, or going to the movies with them, tormented her. Renee's face came to mind from one time they'd gone to McDonalds when they'd all been eleven. The girl had stuck French fries up her nose while crossing her eyes. A remembered chorus of giggles almost made Harper cry.

Renee could be dead, as could any of her old crew. Not knowing the truth let her mind fill in every imaginable horror from a giant chunk of concrete falling out of the sky and crushing them to the blue gang getting their hands on her friends and doing horrible things. Harper hated that she assumed the worst possible scenarios. The Army might have found them all and brought them somewhere safe. Maybe Christina, Renee, Andrea, Darci and Veronica sat around together at some survivor camp, crying over losing *her*.

*Yeah right.*

Madison twisted toward her and offered the soap. "Here."

"Thanks, Termite." Harper proceeded to lather up.

Lorelei splashed at the water in front of her.

"This is kinda weird, sharing a tub… but the world is weird." Madison picked up the plastic bowl floating beside her and poured water over her hair. "We shouldn't kill more trees than we really have to, even if it is embarrassing."

"Snot barrasing," said Lorelei. "It's bathing."

"Kids used to all share baths a long time ago," said Harper. "Like back when people still rode horses."

Madison held her arms out to the sides. "I don't see any cars, do you?"

"Horses?" chirped Lorelei. "I like horses! Can we ride a horse?"

"Maybe." Harper buried her face in the foamy washcloth.

"I like baths, too," said Lorelei. "I didn't have them before."

"Whoa." Madison paused in dumping a second bowl of water over her head to rinse shampoo. "Like, ever?"

"Nope," chirped Lorelei.

Eyes closed under a layer of soap, Harper felt around for the bowl. Someone—probably Madison—handed it to her. "Why not?"

"I dunno," said Lorelei. "Mommy never put me inna tub before. It's good 'cause it's fun and not too much water. I can't swim."

Harper pictured Mila Cline, the nine-year-old creepy girl, quoting the statistics of how many people each year used to drown in bathtubs. The idea of that kid saying such a thing struck her as simultaneously probable, awful, and darkly funny.

*Lori doesn't talk much about her parents. What kind of kid never had a single bath?*

Madison and Lorelei discussed horses while Harper rushed the rest of cleaning herself. She got out of the bath first, dried off, and wrapped herself in the towel before taking a knee beside the tub and teaching Lorelei how to bathe herself.

The girl didn't seem interested in doing much more than playing.

"Come on, get clean," said Madison. "Trees died for this bath. Don't waste it."

Harper chuckled.

A little while later, Harper plucked Lorelei out of the water and dried her off. All three wrapped themselves in towels, then hurried across the hall to the bedroom where they finished drying off and changed into their nightgowns. Harper's nightgown had a bit too much transparency for her to feel comfortable going outside, but in the near dark, it covered her well enough for a brief excursion. She stepped barefoot into her sneakers and hurried to collect the refilled pail she'd set over the fire before taking her bath. It hadn't quite become as steamy as the first two since the fire had died down, but it remained far warmer than the water sitting in the tub.

She lugged it into the house and poured it into the tub to heat the water for Jonathan, then stuck her head into his room. "Tub's all yours."

"Cool." He set his book down and headed into the bathroom.

Harper went to the living room where Cliff occupied one of the recliners, reading. Madison and Lorelei sat on the floor in front of the sofa, playing with dolls. A little less than an hour of light remained. In this new life, darkness defined bedtime… for everyone.

"You know," said Cliff without looking up from his novel, "in olden days when the entire family used the same bathwater, the father would go first, then the wife, then the kids from oldest to youngest. Ever hear that saying 'don't throw the baby out with the bathwater?'"

"Don't throw me out," said Lorelei.

Harper and Cliff chuckled.

He peered over the book at her. "No one's throwing you out."

She grinned at him.

"Umm, yeah." Harper moved around the sofa, sat, and pulled her feet up under a thin blanket. Instead of going for her book, she decided to watch 'sibling TV.' "Everyone's heard that phrase."

"Know where it came from?"

"No, but I have a feeling I'm about to find out." She raked her fingers at her damp hair.

"By the time the youngest kids got to the tub, the water could often be so dirty it was literally possible not to notice a baby in it."

"Eww," said Madison. "And why would anyone put a baby underwater?"

"It's just a phrase." Harper shrugged. "And I second that eww. I'd rather take a cold bath than get into water that's too dirty to see through. The point of a bath is to get clean, not add more grime."

Cliff chuckled.

"How did people make soap back then?" asked Harper.

"Good question." Cliff scratched at his beard. "There's gotta be a book about that somewhere."

"Wow, the master of useless trivia doesn't know something." Harper raspberried at him.

"Careful, young lady." He wagged the book at her.

Laughing, Harper reclined into the sofa under the blanket, comfortable enough that she risked falling asleep right there. Madison hadn't been much of a doll person, at least after eight. Though, video games had been more to blame for that than anything else. Sitting there watching her sister play dolls with Lorelei put a giant smile on Harper's face. Madison appeared to be having fun, even if the 'girl who outgrew dollies' mostly did it for the little one's benefit.

*She's almost back to normal. Well... whatever counts for normal anymore.*

Jonathan walked in wearing long pajama pants, no shirt. He flopped on the couch beside Harper and resumed reading *Huckleberry Finn*. It surprised Harper that she sat there doing nothing but being with her family and *didn't* feel bored. No television, no *Fortnite*, no hours-long conference phone call with her friends. No constant stream of text messages about who dated who or which teacher did what annoying thing that day.

Between the jiu-jitsu that afternoon and a hot bath, her muscles had turned into Jell-O. Other than the lack of electric lights, the moment felt so mundane, she forgot she'd left the shotgun in the bedroom, leaning against the wall by the bed. Not until Cliff closed the book and suggested everyone go to sleep did she twitch with dread and look around in a rapid search, as if the Mossberg might randomly appear in arms' reach.

Jonathan stuck a bookmark between the pages and yawned.

"Now that's the look of an E-1 who lost their rifle," said Cliff, grinning.

"Oops." Harper cringed at the glaring reminder that her life had *not* returned to normal.

He patted her on the head while walking by on his way to the back bedroom. "Not that big a deal. We're all home and I'm here. You should probably keep it nearby whenever you're the adult in the room."

She couldn't quite tell if she should feel relieved or scolded, and got up without a word, following her sisters to the bedroom they shared.

# FAMILY TIME

The next day, heavy rain saturated Evergreen.

Mayor Ned hadn't changed his rule about rain, so everyone stayed inside to enjoy a rainy Friday. Madison bounced out of bed, cheering the weather the way she used to cheer snow. It seemed bizarre to have rain close school, but then again, everyone remained worried about radiation.

According to Doctor Khan and Doctor Hale—who Harper thought of as Tegan—the danger of radioactive fallout at this point should be minimal. At the last full town meeting, which had a hair over a thousand people in attendance, Doctor Khan announced that fallout radioactivity decayed much more quickly than what would linger at the site of a ground detonation. After five weeks, (and it had been more like five months), fallout would be negligible. Detonation sites, however, could remain dangerous for closer to five years.

Still, Ned advised people to avoid rain for the time being just in case. No one would get in any real trouble for going outside, but planting the seeds of fear provided sufficient motivation.

Board games, toys, books, and a brief 'dance class' kept everyone busy. Lorelei had become quite close with Madison and Jonathan, to the point that whenever one of them left the room to use the bathroom, she'd stare longingly at the hallway as though she worried they wouldn't come back.

Twenty minutes into playing the *Busytown* board game, Madison dashed off to the bathroom. Lorelei looked up with such a heartbroken expression, Harper pulled the girl into her lap and held her. In an instant, she switched from pouting to grinning.

*What happened to you before Tyler found you?* Harper smiled back at her outwardly, though inside, she roiled with worry. No one had any idea where the girl had lived before the war, at least no one able to tell her. Tyler hadn't returned to Evergreen, and wouldn't if he wanted to remain out of jail. Lorelei didn't seem to know the name of the city she came from, having only ever referred to it as 'Mommy's house.'

Holding her still felt like Harper cradled a bundle of sticks wrapped in a blanket. At least the girl had no qualms about eating, scarfing down anything put in front of her without complaint. The only time her contagious happiness ever showed a dent was if she wound up more than ten feet away from another person.

*She lost her parents, then Tyler... who knows what happened to her out there after the bombs. Poor kid has to be terrified of being abandoned.* Harper tickled her under the arm, making her giggle. *Maybe she's just super affectionate. Still too darn skinny.*

Madison ran back into the room and took her seat to resume the game. Lorelei bounced and cheered at her as if she'd been gone for weeks. The six-year-old struggled to play, needing a fair bit of coaching to take her turn and understand the rules. Harper couldn't tell if the girl simply didn't care if she 'did well' at the game, being happy to spend time with her family regardless of who won. Perhaps six was too young for that particular game, or maybe Lorelei had some type of developmental issue. Despite having platinum blonde hair, the child didn't live up to the stereotype of blondes. She seemed more... perpetually distracted than unintelligent.

*ADD?* Harper bit her lip. *I really need to bring her back to Tegan, uhh, Doctor Hale.*

Lorelei cheered again at Jonathan making a simple move, but her cry of excitement broke into coughing.

"Aww, she's sick," said Jonathan. "Now we're all gonna get sick."

Harper froze in a panic. Tiny, malnourished child plus nuclear war equaled radiation poisoning. She'd be more vulnerable than most due to her health and lack of body mass. But the attack had happened in September, and they'd gone eight days into March. If Lorelei had received a dangerous dose of rads, she'd have already died or at least gone bald. As far as anyone knew, the worst she'd experienced had been nearly starving.

Tyler had found her lying in an alley, ready to close her eyes and just give up.

Despite what he tried to do to Madison, she couldn't hate him. Without his meds, he'd become an entirely different person. She hated *that* guy, not the man he'd been before, a man who saved the life of a little girl he'd never met before.

Lorelei hardly seemed like a kid who had lived through a horrible event. She smiled all the time, giggled at everything, had limitless energy, and hadn't—at least that Harper had seen—ever cried. The closest she'd come was when Harper told her that Tyler had to go away. But as soon as Lorelei understood he didn't want to leave her and *had* to go, she bounced back to her normal self.

The cough didn't sound particularly loud or worrisome, so maybe she'd merely caught a cold or sucked up some dust. They only had a fireplace for heat and the girl had a weird relationship with clothing... as in she sometimes simply appeared to forget it. Or wore only a shirt, or only pants, or only socks, like she grabbed whatever happened to be right in front of her then went on about her day. It didn't appear to stem from any overt objection to clothing as a concept, more like she had the attention span of a goldfish and zero shame. Madison had taken on responsibility for ensuring her little sister got dressed properly.

Much to Harper's embarrassment, her parents had often reminded her she once had a similar mindset insofar as deciding clothing was for losers. Of course, she'd only been three at the time and grew out of it by five. That made Harper circle back to the worry that Lorelei might have some manner of developmental delay. Or, maybe they'd merely adopted a thrice-removed cousin of Luna from *Harry Potter*. The girl certainly appeared to exist on her own wavelength well apart from the rest of the world.

A sudden, astoundingly loud, thunderclap shook the house.

Jonathan's face paled and he stared up at the roof.

Madison screamed, crawled under the table, and started bawling.

Lorelei glanced up with a 'wow, that was loud' expression, and brushed it off.

It took Harper a second or two to convince her heart to get back to work. She'd gone from 'the shotgun just fell over and went off right behind me' to fearing another nuke had detonated. Judging from Madison's scream-crying, her little sister also assumed the nukes fell again.

Cliff peered under the table. "Easy, kiddo. Just thunder."

Shaking, Madison looked at him, twitching when another—much softer—thunderclap rolled overhead. Still trembling, she emerged from under the table and took her seat again, leaning against Harper, who put an arm around her.

When they'd taken cover in the basement the morning of the attack, the distant nuclear explosions hadn't been as loud, as abrupt, or as brief as the thunder of a minute ago. Harper closed her eyes, her brain putting her right back there. A silent nuclear flash had made the small basement windows glow too bright to look at. She'd huddled against her parents as a slow-building roar grew from a rumble like a distant truck passing to an earth-shaking growl. Hurricane-like wind blasted over the house soon after, along with a continuous pelting of debris that persisted for several minutes.

She would never forget that sound as long as she lived.

"Sorry for being a chicken," whispered Madison. "It's only thunder."

Harper squeezed her. "It's okay. I flinched, too."

"It's nothing to be ashamed of," said Cliff in a soothing voice. "You all lived through bad times. Stuff like that leaves a mark. There's a lot of vets who can't handle loud noises. Fireworks, thunder, guns… grown men break down."

Madison nodded at him, wiping her face with her hands.

A knock rattled the front door.

"Ooh, someone's in trouble," singsonged Lorelei. "Outside inna rain."

Cliff got up and went to the door. He pulled it open, revealing Carrie Rangel, their next door neighbor and occasional babysitter. Her husband had been in New York when the nukes hit, and most likely got vaporized. She stepped inside, pulling a dark green poncho hood down off her strawberry blonde hair. The woman had to be on the younger side of mid-thirties to Cliff's forty, but Harper couldn't help but picture them together. She smiled to herself at the idea, especially given the woman risked going out in the rain.

"Hey," said Cliff. "Must be important if you broke the law, going out in the rain."

"Pff. It's not a law, it's a guideline. And maybe I got tired of rattling around that house alone. Besides…" She lifted the poncho out of the way and handed Cliff a big plastic container. "I brought cake."

"Yay!" yelled Jonathan.

"Yay!" shouted Lorelei after him; her exuberance melted to confusion.

"What's cake?"

Madison kept quiet, still resting her head on Harper's shoulder.

"How do you not know what cake is?" Jonathan blinked. "It's only the greatest thing in the world."

Cliff pointed at him. "That would be coffee. Cake is a close second."

"Nuh-uh." Jonathan shook his head.

"Cake, huh?" Cliff held the container up to examine. The haze of a translucent lid reduced the form of a plain white cake to a blur.

Carrie removed her poncho and hung it on the coat rack by the door. "Had the mix sitting in the cabinet. Finally got some eggs. Little tricky working with an improvised oven and a wood fire, but I got it to work."

"Fair enough. Might as well have at it. Gonna brew a pot. Welcome to it if you want some."

"Sure." Carrie smiled at him and set the cake carrier down on the table.

Lorelei scrambled up from Harper's lap, climbed up onto the table, and walked across it to hug Carrie. "Hi!"

"Well, hello to you, too." Carrie scooped her up, gave her a squeeze, and set her down—on the floor.

"I'll get plates and stuff." Harper stood and headed into the kitchen.

Cliff set a pot of water on the oven rack wedged into the fireplace, then proceeded to 'grind' some of the coffee they found at that place by putting the beans in a plastic baggie and walloping it over and over with another pot.

When Harper returned with plates, a knife, and forks, Carrie opened the cake and cut pieces for everyone. The scent of vanilla icing made Harper misty-eyed. She sank into her chair and stared at the slice of cake in front of her. Her friend Darci had always been a bit of a goof, even before the girl discovered marijuana. At her fourteenth birthday party, she'd somehow wound up with a dab of white icing on her nose and hadn't noticed. It took her almost half an hour to figure out why no one could look at her without giggling.

"What's wrong?" asked Madison.

"Nothing. I'm just being an emo." Harper forced a smile and picked up her fork. "A generation from now, kids won't know what cake even is. The icing reminded me of one of my friends. Haven't seen her since... yeah."

"That's so sad," said Jonathan, sounding serious. "Cruel even. I mean that they won't know what cake is."

Harper glanced at him.

"It's sad about your friend, too." Jonathan put a hand over his heart and shook his head. "But not knowing cake is *tragic*."

She smirked, but couldn't resist smiling at the silly face he made. The kids tore into their cake, Lorelei making all sorts of thrilled sounds as though she really never had seen it before. Madison ate hers in slow, surgical pieces, stretching it out as long as possible. Jonathan appeared to be fighting the urge to pick it up and bite it without using the fork.

Harper set her elbow on the table, chin on her hand, and stared at her cake, thinking about Darci's party. She remembered some stupid old song playing constantly in the background, but couldn't remember the title or even if it had been Rolling Stones or Grateful Dead. Her friend mostly listened to her dad's favorite music. She'd gotten a guitar for her birthday and tortured them by 'playing' it most of the afternoon. The more she thought about her friends flopped all over the living room making cat wails in protest of the off-key assault, the more she wanted to run to her bedroom and cry herself to sleep.

So, she forced herself to stop remembering for now, faked a reasonably believable smile at Carrie to thank her for bringing the cake, and dug in. Cliff muttered something about not being able to eat cake without coffee, and didn't touch his piece until he had a mug in hand. Carrie, too, sipped coffee with her cake.

Cliff finished his round at the game, but sat out the next one. He and Carrie talked while the kids switched to Uno. Harper caught a few snippets, mostly rumors that people had seen someone or something sneaking around town at night. Some saw a giant furry monster, some a person in dark clothes. So far, nothing had been stolen or damaged as far as anyone had noticed. All the sightings had been to the north around the former golf course, exactly the area Harper had been assigned for patrol. It didn't worry her *too* much since they hadn't made her patrol in the dark.

Though, it did make her think about creepy little Mila Cline and her talk of the Shadow Man.

*That kid's got so many issues, her nightmares have nightmares. There's no such thing as ghosts or shadow monsters.* Harper scraped up the last bits of cake crumbs and icing on her plate. *Possible she had someone in dark clothes try to grab her. She's nine. Everything scary is a monster.*

Harper shuddered at a brief memory of her father's death, and the horrible, howling cheers coming from the 'blue gang.'

*People are the worst monsters of all.*

# 5

## ATTACHED

The morning brought clear skies and a stiff breeze.

Harper wanted to take Lorelei to the med center first thing after breakfast, but lost about forty minutes chasing a little squirrel around the house. She gave up any hope of catching it under a pot, instead focusing on attempting to herd the critter toward the front or back door so it could escape outside. The whole time she ran after it, climbing over the sofa, circling the living room, going back and forth down the hallway, Cliff teasingly suggested shooting it. Madison wailed "No!" every time he brought that up.

"Harp! Don't let it die!" would echo in her head all day.

Finally, she lunged just right, and the squirrel zipped out the front door that Jonathan held open while hiding behind it. After a breakfast of Lucky Charms and boxed almond milk, Harper walked with Lorelei down Hilltop Drive to the frontage road that paralleled Route 74, and up to the improvised medical center.

When they entered the waiting room, Lorelei darted away from her, running over and hugging four men, two women, two kids, and Ruby, the woman who served as an assistant to the doctors, mostly for record keeping.

Once everyone had been duly greeted, Lorelei returned to Harper's side.

"Well, good morning to you," said Ruby. "I don't have you on the sheet for anything today."

"Just a checkup. She's got a bit of a cough going." Harper patted the girl on the head. "Mostly want to make sure it's nothing to be concerned about."

"All right, go on and sit down."

Harper took a seat, but Lorelei didn't stay idle long. She and the other two kids there proceeded to play tag around the waiting room. Eventually, Doctor Khan summoned one of the boys and his mother into the back. Lorelei and the other girl flopped on the floor and chattered away about random things.

Time dragged by. One by one, people went into the back and returned anywhere from ten to forty minutes later. Fortunately, none appeared in bad spirits on the way out. A little less than two hours after walking in, Tegan emerged from the hall and called Harper.

She stood, collected Lorelei, and followed the doctor to an exam room.

"Good morning," said Tegan. "Are you here for anything specific?"

"Yeah. She's picked up a bit of a cough, still seems kinda skinny, and, umm…" Harper pulled Tegan a step or two away and whispered, explaining about the girl's statement that she never took baths before, didn't know what cake was, and how she became visibly distressed if Madison or Jonathan left the room even for a few minutes.

"All right. Let's have a look." Tegan approached the girl, who'd been sitting patiently on the exam table.

"Hi!" chirped Lorelei, before hugging her.

"Hey there, cutie." Tegan grinned. "You're such a little ball of happiness."

The girl beamed.

Harper sat in a chair, quietly observing a physical exam while trying not to fidget with the shotgun. It still felt odd to bring it into a doctor's office, but she'd gotten used to taking it with her everywhere when she left the house. Tegan didn't appear overly concerned while using a stethoscope, listening to the girl breathe and also appeared pleased when weighing her. Not until the twenty-minute exam ended did Harper notice the lights in the ceiling were on.

"Oh, holy shit," whispered Harper. "There's power!"

Tegan glanced over at her. "Yes, been online for about four days. It's only the medical center at the moment as a test. Jeanette's trying to work out some kinks with the relay or fuses... something like that. Prone to overloading and we've been browning out a couple times a day."

"Cool. Any idea if they'll be able to get it to the rest of the town?"

"No idea. Much of the wiring here is underground, which let it survive. But... some of the component boxes above ground had issues. I think she said all the transformers fried."

She stared up at a working light bulb and felt far too much like a primitive tribal girl worshipping a magic object for her liking. It had only been six months since she lived in the modern world. A working light shouldn't be so earth-shattering.

Tegan proceeded to talk to Lorelei for a while, having a conversation with her that included questions about how she felt about people she loved, people she didn't like, strangers, and so on, all of whom she thought deserved hugs. The doctor tried to ask about her parents, but the girl didn't say much beyond 'Mommy was always mad at me' or seeming confused when asked about things her parents would say or do with her. Lorelei's smile went away whenever she talked of her mother. She also didn't appear overly affected by losing her. The child didn't appear to know what happened to Mommy other than 'she went away,' offering shrugs and 'I dunnos' when asked if her mother had been hurt. Regarding her time between the 'sky burning' and Tyler finding her, she said, "I was alone and didn't have food." From what little the doctor coaxed out of her, it sounded as though she roamed the empty neighborhood where she'd lived, unsure where all the people went. She'd foraged food from bags of chips or cookies she found in houses, but eventually couldn't find any more when she got to a scarier part of town.

Once out of questions, Tegan made a 'wait here a sec' gesture at Harper, and brought Lorelei out of the room. Her distant voice asked Ruby to watch the child for a moment, then she returned, easing the door shut.

Harper looked up with dread radiating from her eyes. "How bad is it?"

"First of all, relax. She's probably come down with a mild cold. I didn't hear anything alarming in there, though she's got a bit of mucous buildup. Has her coughing been severe or has she complained of a sore throat?"

"No... but I'm not sure she would even if she had one."

"All right. I think there's some children's cough syrup left. It's a gentle expectorant, so it should help break that stuff up."

Harper nodded.

"Physically, she's doing well. Lorelei's still a few pounds shy of where a girl her age should be, but she's also under-sized, short for her age."

"Yeah, first I saw her, I thought she was like four."

"What concerns me more, though... I believe she's suffering from attachment disorder. She's excessively friendly with total strangers. My guess is that she experienced moderate to severe neglect early in life."

"Early?" Harper sat up straight, eyebrow raised. "She's only six."

"Yes, early. Our attachment processes develop between the ages of one and three. You saw her mood flatten when talking of her mother, and she's never said anything about a father. I bet she was underweight even before the war, probably had a distant single mother who provided only the bare minimum of care. Whether the woman died or simply abandoned her after the attack, I can't say."

Harper choked up.

"Of course, I'm a medical doctor, not a psychiatrist. This is my educated guess. It's also possible her mood shift when discussing her mother came from watching her die and nearly starving to death after being orphaned or abandoned. Not wanting to talk about her mother could be repressed memory as easily as there not being any real memories *to* talk about if the woman had been neglectful."

"Is it bad? What should we do?"

Tegan folded her arms. "Usually, from what I can remember, the best treatment option for it is simply changing caregivers to someone who is attentive to the child's needs. That's already happened for her. She needs stability, and you're giving her that. So, what you need to do is basically continue as you are."

"Okay."

"The worst risk is her failing to recognize a threatening adult as a danger. She loves everyone and may lack the capacity to differentiate the level of threat most children are able to pick up on."

"Okay, so... keep an eye on her."

"Yeah, basically. Health wise, she's improved considerably from when I first saw her. So, you and Cliff are doing a great job so far."

Harper slouched in relief. "Cool."

"Oh, I've been trying to talk Ned into making a trip to Denver to raid hospital stores for meds. I'd like to gather as much as we can before it goes bad or other people get to it. He's been hesitant about the idea since you mentioned that gang. I'm hoping those idiots won't go ransacking a hospital's pharmacy, as the average person doesn't even really think about there being a large store of drugs at a hospital. You say drugs, they think 'pharmacy.'"

"Umm. Denver's gone bad. I dunno if that's a good idea. We'd *definitely* have to shoot our way in. I don't know how many of those jackasses are there." She fidgeted. "But it's been a couple months."

"Ned keeps giving me the 'I'll think about it' answer, which is more or less a 'not now.' It's important to Evergreen that we maintain a stock of medical supplies. I realize the medicine won't last forever since all the producers are gone, but the more we can stockpile, the better. Think you could put in a sympathetic word with him for me?"

She shivered, figuring asking him about it would all but guarantee she'd wind up having to go on the scavenging trip. But, medicine could make the difference between any of her siblings—or herself—living or dying at some point. "Okay."

"Don't sound so confident." Tegan winked and patted her on the back. "It's fine if you don't want to."

Harper steeled herself. "No, you're right. We need meds. It's something we have to do. I'll mention it next time I see him."

"Wonderful. Thank you." Tegan hugged her.

"Thanks for checking on Lori."

"My pleasure. Everything okay with you?"

She shrugged. "Yeah, basically. How long am I going to randomly think about my parents or friends and get sad?"

"Oh, probably for a while. That's normal. Gets me too."

"Thanks, Doc."

"Anytime."

Harper left the exam room, collected Lorelei from Ruby, and followed the giggling child on the run back home.

# 6

## THAT GIRL

The remainder of the day struck Harper as eerily normal—other than the lack of electricity.

After lunch, the kids went out to explore the area with Becca, one of Madison's friends from before everything went crazy. The little blonde girl no longer looked like she'd crawled out of a warzone and seemed pretty much the same as Harper remembered her. Although both of Becca's parents remained alive, well, and here in Evergreen with her, it didn't seem right that she would be so… unaffected. Hell, at seventeen, Harper *still* randomly cried over having to abandon her childhood home. She hoped Becca really had coped with everything and didn't simply bury it all and it would crush her later.

Maybe being reunited with Madison had helped her, too.

Becca had turned ten on February 4th. Her parents threw a small birthday party for her with a box of Devil Dogs scavenged from Walmart standing in for the cake. Madison's tenth birthday had come and gone October 9th while they'd been hiding with their parents in the basement, not quite a month after the nuclear strike. No one had even seemed to notice, not even Madison.

Whenever Harper had nothing to think about, she sometimes debated giving her sister a late birthday party… but always chickened out. It might remind her of losing Mom and Dad and send her off to cling to that damn phone again. When she turned eleven next October, then she'd see about doing something special.

*She'll be eleven... she should be going to the mall and dance class and Starbucks, having people in line behind her ask each other why that little kid is drinking coffee.* Harper let out a long sigh to keep herself from crying. *On the positive side, she won't have any student loans chasing her into her forties... and neither will I.*

Being home with nothing specific to do on a Saturday felt strange. Harper had been working after school since junior year, so the weekend hadn't truly been a day off in a while. Even without a crummy minimum-wage summer job, she often struggled with so much homework that the whole weekend passed in a blur, leaving little time to do anything fun. Even her mother had started complaining about how much the teachers piled on her, and that had been without any AP classes.

Another part of the odd sense came from still having a job after society collapsed. At least for the time being, she had no official responsibilities with the militia on weekends—besides responding to emergency calls via air horn. So, even after the end of everything, somehow, her weekend still felt like a weekend.

Cliff, thus far, went out to do militia stuff every day of the week without any days off. Sometimes he patrolled, sometimes he'd coach other militia people on hand-to-hand combat techniques. But then again, he couldn't exactly sit around the house and relax watching television. Not to mention, most of what they did with the militia involved wandering around or standing ready, not actual work.

It bugged her that the kids had gone off out of sight, though their not-too-distant voices echoed among the trees, the kids yelling back and forth to each other, pretending to be superheroes or something to that effect. Harper flopped on the couch and stared at the dead light on the living room ceiling, daydreaming of the working one she'd seen at the medical center. At the realization she wanted electricity back more desperately than she'd wanted a car of her own when the world had been fine, she curled up and wept over her parents.

She hadn't gotten to spend nearly enough time with Mom during the past two years. It seemed like the woman had been in a perpetual state of driving Madison somewhere: dance class, school events, a brief stint doing gymnastics, soccer games, Starbucks, and so on. Whenever Mom had time, Harper had been buried under homework, stuck at actual work, or sleeping. Her memories of life at home all took on a sense of powerful sadness no matter how happy they had been. Everything reminded her of what she'd lost. She'd always joked that she'd be forty, married with three kids, and *still* calling Mom four times a week to ask her what to do.

*I'd give anything to be able to hear her voice again.*

She couldn't even remember what the last thing her mother had said was, vaguely recalling a not-quite-argument with Madison about laundry two hours before the blue gang came to loot the house.

Up until the war, Harper hadn't enjoyed a Saturday with nothing to do since she'd been fourteen. She rolled flat on the couch, staring up at the ceiling while her mind replayed old memories of hanging out with her friends when they'd all been too young for summer jobs. Life had snuck up on them. None of her crew realized the 'summer of fourteen' would be the last time in their lives that fun would be their only responsibility. The summer after sophomore year, they'd all gotten part time jobs. Of course, they still hung out, but not as often.

Now, she'd probably never see them again.

Harper closed her eyes and sighed. *Same thing would've happened next year anyway when college started... Dad hasn't seen his high school friends in forever.* She tried to reframe her memories of having so much free time with her friends in a 'that part of my life was over anyway' happy/nostalgic way, but only wound up crying more—as though her whole crew had died.

She drifted into a nap, waking to the kids' voices close by the front of the house. From the sound of it, they'd found a rope or cable and used it as a jump rope. Jonathan, ever the sport, joined in. Harper somewhat pitied him for being stuck around three girls, but the kid had chosen dance class, so maybe he didn't mind. He adored spending time with Cliff doing survivalist stuff, too.

Becca's voice filtered into her awareness from the general din of loud children outside. "... she said someone was following her home from school..."

Harper stood and hurried over to the front window, peering out at the kids.

"Emmy still thinks the sky fire's gonna come back." Jonathan's pants slipped down when he landed, causing him to grab them and stumble over the jump rope. "She's scared of everything." He tightened his belt and took the end of the rope from Becca.

*They're all getting thinner.* Harper scratched at her stomach, which grumbled in response. She *really* wanted a burger... or something. Pizza.

Chinese take-out, Indian, hell, even the sorry excuse for chicken parmesan her school cafeteria served would've been like filet mignon.

"If *you* saw people evaporate, you would be scared of everything, too," said Madison barely over a whisper.

Jonathan and Madison spun the clothesline for Becca to jump while Lorelei cheered them on.

"How did"—Becca jumped—"she see people"—she jumped again—"evap'rate?"

"Out a window, I think," said Madison. "Like, the bomb light came from behind or to the side of her building so she didn't look straight at it, but someone outside stood right in it."

"Eww," said Lorelei.

"That would'a still blinded her. I think she's making it up." Jonathan scratched his head with his free hand.

Harper opened the door. "Guys? What did Emmy say about being followed?"

"Just that she thought someone was behind her, but when she looked, she didn't see anyone." Madison shrugged. "Mila said it was the Shadow Man."

"Everything's the Shadow Man." Jonathan shook his head.

Madison made a 'yeah, no kidding' face at him.

"Shadow Man's just lonely. He needs a hug." Lorelei wrapped her arms around herself.

Harper bit her lip.

"It's not real. Mila's loopy," said Becca.

"Like I was." Madison looked down.

Jonathan grimaced. "You weren't loopy. You were so sad you didn't know how to deal with it."

"Maybe Mila's the same way. I had a phone; she has the Shadow Man." Silent tears ran down Madison's face, but her expression remained neutral.

Lorelei zipped over and hugged her.

Madison giggled, already seeming over her sad moment.

Harper sat on a flimsy white plastic chair at the edge of the small concrete slab serving as their house's front porch. A wooden split rail fence surrounded a front yard two feet lower than Hilltop Drive, making it feel a bit like a bunker. It unsettled her that she thought of the fence as getting in the way of using the dirt wall beneath the road as a covered position to shoot from. Still, if trouble came home, the kids could dive flat to the ground and have a decent amount of protection from stray bullets… at least until the world ran out of ammunition.

She spent the rest of the afternoon watching over the kids while worrying if Emmy had actually seen someone or jumped at ghosts. The war may have destroyed many things, but it wouldn't have eliminated creeps. A possibility existed that one or more of the new people to arrive in Evergreen over the past few months presented a threat to kids. Even the blue gang, bastards they were, would have let Madison get old enough before doing anything like *that* to her. One of them even said it outright. Granted, she didn't exactly trust idiots who ran around abducting people and looting. She certainly didn't trust anyone affiliated with the group responsible for her parents' death.

"From now on, I see a blue sash, I kill the bastard wearing it," muttered Harper.

"*Tombstone?*" asked Jonathan.

"She's not quoting a movie. She's serious," deadpanned Madison.

A little color faded from Jonathan's face.

"I was thinking about that movie, though. Pretty sure the sashes were red in the film." Harper stood. "Gonna get started on dinner."

The kids made happy noises in response to that announcement.

Harper went inside to the kitchen and looked over the cabinets, taking stock of what she had to work with. "Looks like soup surprise… again."

She opened a few cans of soup, mixing chicken rice with chicken noodle, adding one can of plain chicken broth, another can of sliced mushrooms, one box of dried macaroni, and a can of green beans. They still had some of the healthy bread left. Cliff's explanation that people 'way back when' routinely cut mold off bread and ate the clean parts didn't make it any less gruesome to think about. However, she would much rather eat the untainted parts of a moldy bread loaf than bugs or grubs. And, as hungry as she'd been for the past few weeks, slicing the green bits off didn't bother her anymore. Fresh, unspoiled bread felt like a long lost luxury item.

After adding some firewood to the cinder block grill, she built a little stack of kindling, then scraped some shavings off a hunk of fatwood, making a neat pile of basically sawdust. That done, she took the ferrocerium rod and scratched the knife down its length. Each pass spat sparks onto the kindling, which eventually developed a flame that she nursed into a fire. Despite understanding the chemistry of the rod, it still felt like magic to scratch metal with metal and make a shower of white-hot sparks.

Soon after setting the pot on the grill, a distant woman's voice called Becca home. The kids pretended not to hear her for a few minutes until the girls' mother started to sound worried.

"Coming!" shouted Becca.

The kids' earlier talk of someone watching them made Harper want to escort the girl home. *Better paranoid than wrong.* She grabbed the shotgun and dashed out front. "Jon, would you keep an eye on the grill for a bit?"

"Where are you going?" asked Madison.

Harper trotted after the little blonde girl. "Going to walk Becca home. She's almost half a mile away on Thunderbird Lane."

"Wow, your mom yells loud." Jonathan laughed.

"It's not far," said Lorelei. "We pass her house coming home from school."

"I know. Just wanna make sure she gets there."

Becca stopped and looked back, likely having heard the conversation.

"Sorry," said Harper. "You just got me worrying with what Emmy said."

"It's okay." Becca smiled. "It's nicer to walk with someone than be alone. It's almost dark. Don't tell Maddie, but I'm kinda scared of the dark now."

Harper nodded. "I won't. Umm, did something happen?"

"Not really. Just the lights went out and we sat in the dark listening to scary stuff. Whenever it's dark, I think about people screaming. A lot of people screamed outside, but we stayed in the basement." Becca looked up at her. "I'm really sorry about your parents. They were cool."

"Thanks."

The girl lived up at the north end in the fringes of the golf-course-turned-farm, where most of the families with school age kids had been assigned. Harper walked with her past Carrie's house and took a left onto a dirt trail somewhere between huge driveway and road. It led between that house and the next, allowing car access to two more houses well removed from the street. She headed across the grass at the end to a strip of gravel that connected to a street she knew as Sun Creek. It curved back and forth in a repeating S bend until ending at a crossing street.

They continued straight north over dirt and grass to Lewis Road, went past it, and marched up a grassy hill covered in thick trees to save time. A direct path felt more like she hiked a forested wilderness than walked across a town, but that route would make the trip much quicker.

"Have you seen anyone scary following or watching you?" asked Harper.

"Nope. Except when I visit you guys, I don't walk alone. Mila's always alone 'cause no one really likes her."

Harper sighed.

"I mean, she says scary stuff that's weird, always about dead people. Some of the kids talk about her behind her back. Do you think she does it on purpose to make people stay away from her?"

"Not sure. Has anyone tried talking to her?" Harper scaled a steep spot and paused to look around for anyone watching them.

"Yeah." Becca grabbed a tree for balance while following up the hill. "Phew. Why are we climbing? The roads are easier."

"Got food on. Don't want it to burn so I'm taking a shortcut." She smiled.

"Yeah, I tried talking to her, but she kept saying weird stuff like the Shadow Man's gonna get me. Do you think there's really a Shadow Man? Or someone watching Emmy? Is that why you wanted to walk me home?"

Harper decided to follow Medinah Drive once they reached it. After they passed the house with the pale driveway, she'd cut to the right across the hills and go straight to Thunderbird, where Becca lived. "I don't know. Wanted to be extra cautious."

"Cool."

"Hey, if you hear any of the other kids talking about being watched, please let me know? Or tell someone else on the militia?"

Becca nodded. "Okay."

Mr. Perry emerged from the house when they approached. Becca thanked Harper for escorting her home and darted inside. Her father also thanked Harper for keeping his daughter safe, and made pleasant conversation for a little while. She almost mentioned that a girl said she'd been followed, but didn't want to ignite a panic so she kept that to herself and hurried toward home once the man went back inside.

She didn't mention it because she'd only heard second hand information, and from kids overhearing another kid at that, not even an adult. Also, anything she said would be taken as the word of the militia, which still made her feel awkward as hell. If she elevated something one kid said and another kid took the wrong way to a town-wide state of alarm, it would not go over well with Walter Holman.

She'd have to find more concrete evidence first.

THE FRANKENSOUP SHE'D THROWN TOGETHER CAME OUT GOOD.
However, in all fairness, her standard for 'good' food had fallen quite a bit in recent months. Any food that met three conditions: not bugs, sorta-hot, and didn't make her gag, amounted to a good meal. On the rare occasion they ate something approaching pre-war normal, it amounted to a feast. She'd never admit it to Madison, but she loved it whenever Cliff brought home chicken or venison. Some militia teams had been out hunting lately, but didn't have much luck.

She gathered up the cans and the box the pasta had been in, then carried them out to the yard behind the house. The box went into the burn barrel with other food scraps, the cans into a big plastic trash bin since they wouldn't burn. Mayor Ned wanted everyone to save the cans in case the town ever needed to melt them down and make stuff out of the metal.

"Not even nuclear war can stop us from recycling." She shut the lid and chuckled.

Harper started back to the house, but paused at a sniffle from behind. It sounded like someone on Butternut Lane, a short loop road that ran past the front of the house behind hers where Dennis Prosser—another militia member—lived. She grumbled to herself for again leaving the shotgun inside, having only intended to walk into the backyard for as long as it took to put out the trash. Fast as she could, she dashed inside to grab it, threw it over her shoulder on its strap, and ran around the back neighbor's fence.

A pretty, blonde teen in a plain yellow dress with white ballet flats meandered down the street in no great hurry to be anywhere, crying quietly to herself. Harper had seen the girl briefly around town, one of the kids who showed up on the bus the same night Tyler flaked out. They'd all come from a high school in Colorado Springs, or rather from Denver while on a trip to play hockey as the visiting team. Had they been *in* Colorado Springs that morning, they wouldn't be around anymore.

This girl looked like a sophomore and moped along with her head down in a manner that suggested she'd just broken up with her boyfriend, or suffered an attack of the sads like Harper so often did whenever she thought of her parents. While that concerned her on a human level, it relieved her from a militia standpoint. Still, since she lacked psychic powers, she couldn't merely assume the cause of the tears. If someone had hit her or did worse, she'd need to deal with it as part of her job.

Harper trotted up behind her. "Umm, hi."

The girl stopped and turned, looking up with an almost-embarrassed expression. Red ringed her bright blue eyes. Within seconds of them staring at each other, Harper felt her defenses going up, old instincts kicking in. This girl had perfect movie star looks, which made sense considering she'd been a cheerleader for the hockey team. Though some boys, especially Colt Parrish who she'd had a mild crush on freshman year, told Harper she was pretty, she never really felt like it. Not since Freddie Brown used her as an example to explain the difference between 'cute' and 'hot' to one of his friends right out in the cafeteria where everyone could hear him.

"Umm... That's a gun." The girl stared at the shotgun and took a step back. "Are you allowed to have that?"

"Yeah. I'm Harper Cody. I'm on the militia."

"Oh, cool. Oh wow. Really?"

"Yeah, really. I know I'm only seventeen but—"

"Ooh." The girl's face took on an almost psychotic mixture of broad smile and crying. "You're like a minor celebrity."

"Uhh, no I'm not."

"You're on YouTube."

Harper groaned mentally. Of course, Dad posted videos of her shooting competitions. Teen prodigy and so on. "Oh, that..."

"You don't like it?" The girl wiped at her eyes. "My father made me watch some of them, trying to get me to the range. I'm terrified of guns."

"Oh. Ehh, they're okay. My dad just bragged a lot about me. It got kinda old. I wasn't exactly the sort of person who liked all that attention."

"Why'd you come running over? I'm not in trouble, am I?"

"No. Just... well, are you?" Harper smiled the way she did when comforting Madison. "Kinda looked like you were upset and wanted to make sure no one had like attacked you or something." Talking to this girl only a year, maybe two, younger than her like a police officer talking to a kid gave her a strange little spike of confidence. She shrugged off the sense of being the introverted sweet girl everyone overlooked facing off against a popular princess.

"Nah, no one did anything. I'm just freaking out about missing so much school. They're gonna make me repeat a year and it'll screw up my pre-admission to Berkeley. Everything's gonna fall apart. I worked so hard for it."

Harper blinked. "Are you serious?"

"No, I'm Grace. Grace Hughes." She offered a hand.

"Right…" Harper shook hands with her. "I mean, are you serious about that school thing or messing with me?"

Grace flailed her arms. "My parents are on me twenty-four-seven about school and everything. If I get held back a whole year and blow my chances at Berkley, they're gonna kick me out of the house. I get grounded and screamed at if I get Bs. A-minuses only get me screamed at."

"Umm."

"What?" Grace fixed her with a brittle stare. "It's really upsetting. I have a right to be upset. My whole future is at risk, even if it's a future my dad set up for me. I… umm… I don't even know where I am right now. Kinda got lost."

*Oh, this girl's checked out.* "Grace," she said in as soothing a tone as she could manage. "There's been a nuclear war. I'm not sure exactly how to say this gently, but there is no more school. Neither one of us is going to college."

The slightly younger girl jumped as if startled, then looked around at the trees and houses. "You ever fall asleep in the afternoon and wake up when it's almost dark and forget what day it is?"

"Couple times, yeah."

"I, umm… wow. Okay." Grace let out a long, sad sigh. "Guess it wasn't a dream. I guess I was maybe kinda half sleepwalking."

"That's a thing?"

Grace brushed her hands at her hair. "Apparently. I woke up thinking the bus made a weird wrong turn and we'd been lost out here for months. Hey, you're on the militia? Can I complain? They're not letting me go to school. They said I'm too old at sixteen. I don't want to waste all the time I spent studying. And please tell me there's coffee somewhere? Need some bad."

"There's no point for us to go to school anymore. We're old enough to do necessary stuff. Everything's broken. Someone has to put it back together. It's not 2019 anymore. Welcome to *1819*."

"No… no… that can't be right." Grace whirled about in a circle, gesturing wildly. "Everything can't be gone. I need to go home! My parents are in Colorado Springs."

Harper suppressed a cringe and grasped her by the shoulders, giving her a little shake. "I'm sorry. The only thing we can do is keep on surviving."

"It's not fair! I got into Berkeley as a junior. Do you know how hard that is? What am I going to do now?" Grace broke into sniffles again.

"There's no sugar-coated way to say this. We're no longer living in a world of diet mocha lattes or vegan smoothies where soccer moms scramble to shuttle their daughters from school to dance class to gymnastics, making sure the kid's never late for anything and still has time to plow through a mountain of homework every night while scarfing down microwaved Hot Pockets because cooking real food takes too long." Harper looked down, kicking her sneaker at the road. "Used to be, no one had time to even talk to their family... now, family is all we have left."

Grace shuddered. "But I don't have any left. They're all dead. My parents, my brother... even my cat."

"I'm sorry. I didn't mean it that way. My parents are dead, too." Harper reached toward her. "I meant the family we make. I'm not related to anyone in my house except my sister Madison, but Cliff's basically my dad, Jonathan and Lorelei are siblings."

"Oh. I guess. I don't even have that. They put us in the house with Anne-Marie and this girl Summer because they had extra room. Feels more like a dorm than home. I know what you mean about the racing around. My life was like that, too. I used to have *so* much to do I spent the past two years constantly busy. Cheer, drama club, homework... I used to joke with my father that I couldn't wait to get out of school and start my career so I had time to act like a kid again."

Harper laughed. "Wait, actual drama club or do you mean your friends."

"Actual drama club." Grace rolled her eyes. "But my friends wrote way more drama than the theater teacher."

"I'll bet."

Grace brushed at her dress. "They're probably all gone. Everyone keeps saying Colorado Springs was flattened, nothing left."

"Sorry."

"I didn't really like any of my friends. I'm sad they're dead, but I'm not like devastated. Does that make me shallow?"

"If they weren't really friends, I guess not." Harper fidgeted. "How can you hang out with people and they're not your friends?"

"My mom thought it would be good for me to spend time with particular kids my age. She picked them all for me. But every one of us had schedules. Outside of school, we didn't really hang out that much. It felt like we skipped straight to our thirties and sometimes bumped into each other and did brunch."

Harper chuckled.

"So it really happened?" asked Grace.

"Yeah. I'm sorry."

The girl drew in a deep breath, gazing around at the greenery. "It's so hard to believe it all went away so fast. I don't know if I should hope my parents survived. It's not like I've seen home and know it's gone. Just hearing people tell me. They could be wrong, right?"

"Guess it's possible. But a lot of people who never met each other all saying the same thing makes it probably true. And I'm sorry for saying that."

"I know. They're probably dead. Do you think it's better to know for sure that someone you care about is dead or not know?"

Harper cringed. She studied the road while her brain chewed on the idea of being separated from Mom and Dad and not knowing what happened to them. "Umm. I dunno. That's a hard question. *Knowing* they're dead makes them definitely dead. Not knowing, either way, there is still some hope that they might not be gone, but I can understand how not knowing is really hard."

"You know, don't you?"

"Yeah." Harper looked off to the side.

"I'm sorry." Grace regarded her with an odd expression. "Can I hug you?"

"Sure."

The instant they embraced, Grace burst into tears. Harper caught the contagious sadness and wept as well. They stood there holding each other for a while, awash in the shared grief of lost parents.

Eventually, the girl let go and struggled to compose herself. "Thanks for talking. No one ever really talked to me for real before."

"No problem," said Harper. "Umm... why wouldn't anyone talk to you?"

"They talked *to* me, but not for real. I was *that* girl. My dad was a federal judge, I was popular, had money. Other kids wanted to be around me because it made them feel important, not because they cared about being my friend. To my mother, I was like some younger version of her that she showed off to her friends. Dad wanted me to be a lawyer like him, eventually become a judge. My whole life was planned out for me... except for a husband. They didn't quite go that far and arrange a marriage."

Harper whistled. "That's... wow. Sorry. Sounds so lonely."

"It was."

"The popular girls at my school weren't like you. So snobby and fake. Like the machine that makes Barbies got stuck and kept printing out the same stuck-up priss over and over."

Grace laughed.

"This one girl, Tabitha, even threw a fit because the school wouldn't let her bring her dog to class. She tried to say it was a service animal, but she had one of those little ones you can put inside a purse."

"Ugh. I really hate it when people do that. Service dogs are no joke."

"Yeah."

"So what were you studying for?"

"No idea." Harper shrugged.

"Really?"

"Yeah. I couldn't make up my mind what I wanted to do."

"Wow, that's so out there I can't even picture what it would be like not to know."

"Did you *want* to become a lawyer?"

Grace made a 'what can you do?' face. "Not really. I would've preferred going into particle physics and working with the collider or maybe helping develop usable ion propulsion for spacecraft."

"Wow." Harper stared.

"Yeah, I know... I look like an airhead, but I'm not." Grace lowered her voice to an almost whisper. "Don't tell anyone, but I really hate being the center of attention."

"So, naturally, you became a cheerleader."

Grace frowned. "Mom. There's no saying no to that woman. Apparently, any woman who became anyone had been the head cheerleader in high school. Inside, I'm screaming, but I can fake it outside. Hated those stupid games. So cold. So loud. So many people looking at me. All I wanted to do was go home, hide in my room and read or study."

"I feel that. I'm like the biggest introvert. And yeah, I know... shy ginger, go figure."

"So, naturally, you became a cop."

Harper made a noise like a goose hit by a car as the weight of losing

Dad strangled her attempt at a laugh to silence. Without even thinking about it, she told Grace about why she couldn't give up the shotgun, then rambled over the whole thing with Madison and the phone. By the time she finished, Grace had teared up again.

They got into a conversation about the stuff they missed about the world while Harper auto-piloted home, Grace following.

"Wanna come in for a bit?" asked Harper.

"Sure."

Cliff sat in his usual recliner, reading. All three kids sprawled on the living room floor around the board game. Harper considered it a 'win' that Cliff didn't give this girl the same kind of stink eye he'd given Tyler.

"We waited for you a bit, but you were taking too long so we started," said Madison. "We can start over if you want."

"Hi!" Lorelei jumped up and ran over to hug the new arrival. "I'm Lorelei. What's your name?"

"Grace."

"That's pretty." Lorelei faced Harper. "Is she gonna live with us?"

Harper laughed, as did Grace. "No, kiddo, she's just a friend. Hanging out for a bit."

They flopped on the couch and kept talking about random stuff. The former popular girl's old life reminded Harper somewhat of her present situation, an introvert who'd rather be left to her own devices forced into people's faces. Thankfully, Grace didn't ask her if she'd killed anyone.

The last hour and a half before dusk shot by in a blink. When Jonathan remarked that it had become difficult to see the game board, a reality check smacked Harper upside the head. Sitting there chattering away with Grace had been so much like being with Renee or Christina, she'd almost forgotten that society crumbled. Before she grew too maudlin over her old friends, a surge of elation at making a new one hit her, and she wound up slightly on the happy side of neutral.

"Yeah, it's getting dark." Madison set her cards down. "We can finish this tomorrow. Can we leave it set up?"

"Umm, sure," said Harper, eyeing Cliff as if to ask him if it was okay.

"Knock yourselves out." He squinted at his book. "Yeah… getting about that time."

Lorelei scrambled to her feet and ran around hugging everyone, including Grace, before zooming down the hall to get ready for bed. Jonathan stretched and let off a fart.

"Eww!" yelled Madison, before crawling away into a run.

"On that note..." Harper got up and grabbed the Mossberg. "Might as well walk you home."

"You don't have to go back outside. I'm just down Hilltop a bit. Anne-Marie's place is right next to the city hall or whatever they call it."

*Drat. I didn't get a chance to tell Cliff about what Emmy said.* "Nah, it's cool."

"You seem worried. Is there something I should be concerned about?" asked Grace.

Cliff looked up.

"Well... I don't know if it's anything yet. One of the kids at school, Emmy, supposedly said that someone had followed or watched her. It could be nothing."

"Cameron reported seeing something moving the other night. He'd been at the buses on sniper duty, thought he saw something cross the road behind him near the old kennels. Could've been anything from a raccoon to a bear to someone who had too much of Earl's moonshine." Cliff stood and set his book on the cushion. "If it makes you feel better, go on and walk her home. Just don't stand there talking for hours. I'm the one stuck paying the phone bills."

Both girls laughed.

Harper led the way out the front door. After a short walk down Hilltop and up an overly long driveway shared among three houses, they stopped at the porch to Anne-Marie's rather large dwelling, possibly a five- or six-bedroom house.

"It was cool meeting you. Sorry for being a basket case." Grace blushed. "I'm not handling this well."

"Don't think anyone really is. We're all stuck in varying degrees of OMG."

"That's one way to put it." Grace sighed. "See you around."

"Yeah. Definitely." Harper smiled, excited and—for the first time in a while—hopeful.

Grace wasn't a child she needed to take care of, nor a person who would take care of her, but another teen at the same level. Having a friend again soothed a wound inside Harper she hadn't fully even realized existed, or at least consciously acknowledged beyond a persistent sense of grief over her old friends. It made sense how reuniting Madison with Becca had helped her kid sister so much.

It would be much cooler if she had all her friends back, but she couldn't change the world, undo the nuclear war, or resurrect the dead.

She felt fairly certain her friends would've survived the strike, since none lived all that far from her old home. What happened to them after that, she had no idea.

She closed her eyes and wished that they were all okay, even if she never saw them again.

# 7

# CRASH AND BURN

Wednesday evening, approximately five hundred residents of Evergreen gathered in the rolling fields to the northwest of the quartermaster's building for a 'town dinner.'

More or less everyone who lived in the north part of town showed up. The residents in the southern end where Janice Holt ran the militia would have a separate simultaneous gathering, mostly so no one had to travel two miles or more to dinner.

Anne-Marie Kirby, Summer Vasquez, and the staff from the quartermaster's set up all the folding tables they could scavenge from the middle school, and the former senior-care facility that had become the quartermaster's. Janice's group raided the old high school down in the southwest part of the city for tables. That building probably wouldn't serve as a school again any time soon. Not like any kids would need to prepare for college or have to obtain a high school diploma to get a job.

The schools also provided an army of cheap metal folding chairs.

Harper sat across the table from Cliff, Madison on her right with Grace beside her on the left. Lorelei sat on Cliff's right, Jonathan on his left. People who worked with Liz Trujillo, the quartermaster, went by with pushcarts doling out food to everyone. Evidently, a mountain lion had gotten into town and mauled one of the cows. This initially prompted the somewhat-rushed 'feast,' so as not to waste the leftover meat. Along with that beef, they tapped industrial-sized cans as well as giant plastic bags intended for restaurants. Those provisions hadn't been allocated out to individual people or families due to their size, as without working refrigerators, the contents would spoil before any individual person or small family could've finished it.

The farm hadn't yet produced anything edible as the planting process only started a week ago. Still, between the farmers' reasonable attempt at making cheese, bagged beef stew, canned mashed potatoes—that according to Cliff came from the Army—and piles of canned corn, it appeared they had plenty to feed everyone for at least one meal. No doubt the entire population of Evergreen had the same constant gnawing hunger that had plagued Harper since early February. Stretching scavenged canned goods over a whole town made things lean. The unexpectedly dead cow provided a much needed bit of relief. Prior to the animal attack, the farm manager hadn't wanted to slaughter any of the cows until they bred up to a more stable population.

She took her time with the portion of fresh, grilled beef, savoring every bite. This 'town meal' reminded her of a cookout from the civilized world.

"It's wrong that we're eating a whole cow," said Madison, though she didn't hesitate at attacking her portion. "She wanted to live, just like we do. How much does it suck that the poor cow survived a nuclear war only to wind up on our plate? We're humans. We can eat anything we want. There's no reason we have to make animals suffer."

A few people close enough to hear glanced over with varying degrees of 'is she for real' in their expressions.

"No one killed that cow for food. A, umm, mountain lion got it." Harper winced. "Don't worry, they cut away the parts the cat touched. But they didn't want to waste anything since we're kinda low on food. The poor cow was dead anyway. Why throw away food people need?"

"Eww, really?" Grace stared at her portion. "That's unsanitary."

Jonathan grinned. "They got rid of the parts the cat chewed on. Besides, it's been cooked. All the germs would be dead."

"Oh." Madison frowned. "That's not so bad, but I still feel guilty."

"Be guilty and well nourished," said Cliff. "There's starving children in... oh, North Dakota who'd sell their souls for that food."

"That's not funny," muttered Harper.

"Wasn't trying to be. I respect how she feels about animals, all life being sacred and that, but... as long as she's a kid, and I'm looking out for her, I'd much rather she be a depressed idealist than a dead one."

"This is so weird," whispered Jonathan. "Having everyone all together for dinner."

"In medieval times," said Cliff, "people used to do this sort of thing all the time. Though… not quite with the whole town. People would cook big dinners and share it with any neighbors nearby. Makes more efficient use of resources and food."

"They said it's to help people be friends." Jonathan stabbed a hunk of steak with his fork.

Harper looked out at the crowd, still feeling conspicuous for having the shotgun over her shoulder. "Mayor Ned is trying to build a sense of unity among everyone. Like going back to the forties or fifties when everyone in town knew everyone else in town."

"Yeah, like when kids could just roam around safe because the whole community would look out for them, or Maude at the diner knew which guys cheated," said Grace with a hint of a chuckle. "Or I've watched too much old TV."

"Right. Back before people who lived next door for thirty years didn't even know each other's name." Cliff scooped mashed potatoes into his mouth.

"Kids at school are saying we're running out of food 'cause the farm isn't growing fast enough. This big dinner is to make stuff last longer." Madison stared at the hunk of meat on her fork. "Are we gonna starve?"

"No." Harper put an arm around her sister. "You will probably have to cheat a bit on the vegetarian thing, but I won't let you starve. If it gets to that point, you can have some of my food, too."

"So *you* starve?" Madison shook her head. "That's not good either."

"There's gotta be more cans out there." Cliff reached across the table, gingerly grasped Madison's wrist, and made airplane noises while nudging the hunk of steak toward her mouth.

She shot him highly unamused side eye, but bit the meat off the fork.

Conversation over dinner started off about school, which had changed somewhat with the arrival of adults who'd come in with the hockey team. Violet had help, three people who had been legit teachers before the war. Due to the small number of kids, and that they'd gotten used to being all together, the teachers hadn't yet separated the students into different classrooms. However, each age group now had a dedicated instructor who worked with them all day instead of Violet trying to scramble around and cover everyone at the same time.

Lorelei loved school. No surprise, the girl seemed to love everything, though she had no reaction to everyone being together—almost as if she'd never been to school before the war. Jonathan thought it 'cool' to have everyone from six to fourteen in the same room. Sometimes, projects crossed grade levels and they got to work with kids older or younger. Madison didn't seem thrilled about having to go to school *after* the end of civilization, but she didn't complain *too* much. Mostly, she dragged her feet or groaned here and there, but kept up with the work. At least none of them had homework. Lack of textbooks to give out, lack of electric lights after dark, learning on the farm, and just trying to survive made the mere idea of homework impractical.

Harper and Grace drifted off into a separate conversation about 'stuff to do around here' as well as what sort of job Grace should ask for. Since the girl had been interested in advanced science, Harper nudged her toward working with the doctors as it seemed the most scientific thing around. Grace appeared open to the thought, but laughed because she hadn't wanted a career that forced her to deal with people, preferring to sit in a lab somewhere… and the girls found their situations ironically similar. Both Harper and Grace felt awkward in social situations and took 'jobs' that forced them to deal with people.

Cliff, Jonathan, and Lorelei discussed what they'd been learning on the farm as well as their plans to go 'house exploring' again soon.

Madison bounced back and forth between the two conversations for a little while until she silenced the girls with one line: "That boy keeps staring at you."

Harper glanced where her sister looked, at the hockey team sitting one table over and a little to the left. Twenty-one players, two little brothers, and five cheerleaders had been on that bus, along with four adults. The teens more or less stuck together with a few outliers drifting off to sit elsewhere. The boy Madison referred to appeared to be a senior, still wearing his varsity jacket. His dark blond hair no longer had the perfect 'sculpted' appearance it did when they'd first arrived, and he'd sprouted a rough beard—as had most of the men in town. The whole team had evolved from yearbook-perfect preppies into rejects from a lame grunge-country fusion band. Three of the cheerleaders sat with the team, the girls also looking in her direction.

That boy made eye contact and smiled.

Heat rushed to Harper's face. She averted her gaze back to her plate. "They're probably just wondering why Grace is over here instead of sitting with them."

"Doubt it. I never really got along with the others. They all thought I got squad leader because of who my father is. Brittany wanted to be head cheerleader, so she's been like my nemesis for the past year."

Harper laughed. "Brittany? Seriously?"

"What?" asked Grace, eyebrows furrowed.

She shrugged. "You know, it's just like… in every movie with a stuck up clique, there's *always* a Brittany."

"Or a Claire," said Madison. "Or a Brooke, or Heather."

Grace and Harper giggled.

"Madison's a snooty name, too," said Grace, booping her on the nose.

Madison raspberried her. "I'm not snooty."

"Buffy?" asked Jonathan.

"Think that one's *too* stereotypical. No one actually names their kid that." Cliff scraped the last bit of food off his plate onto his fork.

"So who is the boy checking my sister out?" Madison peered over at Grace.

"Zach Alexander, team captain. Not a bad guy really, if you don't mind an ego that barely fit in a school bus. His dad was on like the board of directors for some giant chemical company. Bought him a new Mercedes for his eighteenth birthday."

"Eww." Madison scrunched up her nose. "Why would *he* be interested in Harp?"

Lorelei blinked, confused. Jonathan started to laugh but covered his mouth.

"Be nice," mumbled Cliff past a mouthful of food.

"No, he's like popular and rich. He's supposed to date the head cheerleader." Madison reluctantly stabbed another piece of steak with her fork, and grinned. "I didn't mean Harp's face looks like a butt."

"Hey!" Harper attacked her with a playful fake choke hold.

"He tried, but we only dated twice." Grace nibbled on a bit of bread. "I got tired of his attitude that since he made captain and *some* people considered him the most popular guy in school that I *had* to be with him. I really hate that superficial crap."

Madison stopped pretend-struggling and stared at her. "Wow, really?"

"Yeah. Trust me, I didn't ask to look like this. Or even to be on the cheer squad. Or to be anything. The only thing I ever did that I liked was drama club. Makes sense as my entire life is basically me playing a role… spoiled princess." She paused a moment, sighed, then muttered, "Was."

Harper looked at the hockey team again. Sure enough, Zach continued making eyes at her, but that didn't strike her as new. Boys at her old school often assumed the pale blue-eyed redhead would be the wild girl. Hopefully, if he bothered to approach her, he'd get the hint real quick she had no interest in a casual hook up. At this point, she couldn't really see herself becoming involved in a real relationship either. Too much could go wrong and she didn't want to deal with another emotional wound. The ones from losing her parents still hadn't stopped bleeding.

In some strange way, she almost felt grateful that Tyler had attacked Madison. That let her hate him enough to blank out whatever feelings she might have had toward him before that. She'd gone from 'that kid is weird' to wanting to kiss him too fast to make any sense. Carrie called it a mixture of teenage hormones, fear, and grief. Or, as she put it, 'people do dumb things when they're scared and lonely.'

Harper forced herself to keep her head up and observe the people around her, despite wanting to crawl into a secluded spot. Every time she looked in Zach's direction, she caught him staring at her. Once, he elbowed the kid next to him and grinned. Probably wrongly assumed Harper checked him out, too.

Most people went over to the row of carts for seconds, which no one minded as the goal of this feast had been to get good use out of this food before it went bad—and everyone could use the extra food. Anne-Marie and Summer had done a good job estimating how much to prepare, and eventually, only a few scrapings remained in the aluminum serving trays.

For the first time in weeks, Harper actually ate until full.

As people finished, adults got up from the tables and gravitated into clusters to talk, some popping open beers from Earl's place. Younger kids ran around playing tag. At the sudden appearance of a soccer ball, the tweens and up organized themselves into teams—except for Mila Cline, who hovered off at the edge of everything, sitting in the grass and observing. She seemed neither interested in being social nor distressed at being left alone. At least Madison joined the soccer game, though demanded she be on the same side as Becca.

If she had a choice, Harper would've been happy to go home and curl up with a book and avoid the massive crowd. Technically, she was 'working' at the moment, so had to stay. However, that didn't mean she couldn't go check on Mila. She felt sorry for her, even if the kid made Wednesday Addams seem bubbly.

Grace followed, still chatting about her choice of job. The most sciency thing likely to exist in Evergreen would be either learning medicine from the doctors, working with the farm administrator like a botanist, or trying to learn solar panel stuff and electrician skills. However, the electrical stuff required a certain amount of 'getting dirty' hands on that she didn't seem too keen on.

*Heh. Still a bit of princess in there after all.*

"Hey," said Harper, upon reaching Mila.

The nine-year-old looked up, her long, stark black hair draped over half her face. She elevated paleness to an art form, having even less color than Madison. Not that Harper could criticize anyone for being pale. Someone at the quartermaster's had a dark sense of humor as they'd given Mila a cute black jumper dress with a pleated skirt and a little white cartoon skull on the chest. Then again, knowing this kid, she probably chose it herself.

"I'm glad the Shadow Man didn't take your sister," said Mila in a toneless voice.

"Thanks. I am, too."

Mila stared blankly at her for a few seconds. "You don't really believe me. You're just saying that to make me feel better. I suppose I should thank you. But, the Shadow Man is real. You'll believe me when he takes someone, then it will be too late to be sorry."

"Whoa, umm…" Grace gave Harper side eye. "What happened to this poor kid?"

"Where'd you get the talking Barbie doll?" asked Mila.

"Mila," said Harper. "There's no need to be nasty."

"I'll apologize when she says she's sorry for calling me nuts. And before you say she didn't, she implied it."

Grace lowered herself to sit on the grass. "Sorry. I didn't mean to call you nuts, just… you saw some bad stuff. You're hurt."

"Sorry for calling you Barbie. It doesn't bother me to be alone. You don't need to sit with me out of pity. You're in danger if you stay close anyway."

"From what?" Harper remained on her feet, thinking she'd probably get in trouble for appearing too relaxed while on duty.

"The Shadow Man," said Mila matter-of-factly. "He's coming."

"What's a shadow man?" asked Grace.

"A man. But he's made out of shadows." Mila's stare said 'duh, what else would he be.'

Jonathan jogged over. "Hey, Mila."

"Hi."

He sat close to her, observed her for a moment, then traced a finger across her forehead, gathering her hair off her face.

She furrowed her brows. "What did you do that for?"

"It was over your eye."

"So?" asked Mila.

"It looked annoying." Jonathan's hair had gotten a bit long, almost to his shoulders. "I hate it when it's in my eyes."

Mila picked at a small hole in her black leggings that exposed a spot of pale skin the size of a thumbnail. "I won't see the Shadow Man when he comes for me anyway, so it doesn't matter."

*This poor kid. Maybe I should talk to her parents.* Harper couldn't remember if the girl still had parents or if she'd come in as an orphan. She'd have to check with Anne-Marie to figure out where the kid lived. Even though she most likely stayed in the area around the old golf course, Harper hadn't seen her much while patrolling.

"Carry a light then." Jonathan gestured as if turning a flashlight on. "Light kills shadows."

Mila didn't appear impressed. Something in the distance drew her attention. "Ugh. Why are *more* people coming? This is the exact opposite of being alone."

Everyone—except Mila who already faced toward the crowd—turned to look. Zach the hockey captain and one other boy, also in a varsity jacket, walked toward them. Harper shrugged the Mossberg off her shoulder and held it sideways in a ready posture, hoping to appear unapproachable. Undeterred, the boys walked up to them. Both ignored the kids, mostly focusing on Harper.

"Hi, I'm Zach. Don't think we've met, but I couldn't help but notice you checking me out."

She forced herself to make eye contact, something Cliff had been trying to coach her with. If she kept looking down all the time, people would walk all over her. "We haven't, and I wasn't. I have to watch everyone."

"Ouch." The unknown player smiled at Grace. "Hey. Where ya been?"

"Around. Dealing with stuff."

Sensing the disinterested tone in her voice, he leaned back and regarded her. "Nice dress. Which designer is that? Walmart Dior?"

"Go to hell, Kirk." Grace rolled her eyes.

"We did that already." He frowned.

"It won't matter. We're all going to be dead soon anyway," said Mila.

"Whoa. What's her damage?" asked Kirk.

Mila stared at him. "When the Shadow Man comes for me, no one will hear me die. But, when it's your turn, you're going to scream and wet your pants."

"Aww," whispered Harper. She crouched beside Mila. "I'm not going to let him get you."

"Evergreen's nice," said Jonathan. "It's not hell."

"I meant in general, not this town specifically." Kirk stuffed his hands in his pockets. "The whole world went to hell."

"The heck is *he* doing here?" Zach gestured at the boy. "You come to check out what your country did to us?"

Harper lunged to her feet and got in Zach's face. "What did you say?"

Jonathan scrambled around to hide behind her.

"Oh. My. God. Zach," blurted Grace. "I knew you were a douche, but had no idea you're a racist, too."

Harper peeled her glare off Zach to look at her. "Is everyone on that team a jackass?"

"No just the inner circle." Grace sighed.

"I'm not racist." Zach held up his hands. "Just saying, the damn Koreans attacked us."

Furious, Harper leaned toward him, despite being eye-level with his chin. "Did *he* attack us? He's ten, he's not Korean, and I've had enough of people being shitty to him. He's my brother!"

Zach grimaced. "Sorry. Didn't know."

She glared at him a moment longer, grabbed Jonathan's hand, and stormed off, pulling him after her. He hadn't quite started shaking, but the fear in his eyes couldn't have been more obvious. His parents had been killed by rioters for 'looking Korean.' Worse even than his being Chinese—not Korean—no one really knew which country had been responsible for the nukes that fell on the US. The news had been complaining about North Korea all the time in the months before the strike, but it had sounded like more of the same… some unstable dictator running off at the mouth. Not even Harper's father had believed he'd do anything significant. Dad didn't even believe North Korea even *had* operational nukes.

*Ugh. What is wrong with people? The world's been burnt to a cinder.*

"Assholes," she muttered.

"Damn," said Kirk, some distance behind her. "Crash and burn, dude."

"Hey!" said Mila.

Worried the idiots might be messing with the girl, Harper stopped and looked back—but relaxed at the sight of Grace carrying Mila over to where she stood. The small gloom queen folded her arms and scowled, looking way too much like a grumpy housecat carried against her will, but offered no real protest to being relocated.

"Sorry about those guys," said Grace upon reaching Harper and Jonathan. "I know I'm not really one to say this, but they're not used to living in the real world."

"They ruined my perfectly quiet Sanctuary of Isolation," said Mila. "Now I have to find a new one."

"You don't have to be alone," said Jonathan, offering a hopeful smile.

Grace set Mila down. "Well, that was about the most disastrous attempt to ask someone out I've ever seen. I don't think he's going to bother you again."

"The Shadow Man is going to come for me, and he'll kill everyone nearby." Mila gazed off into nowhere.

Harper bit her lip. *I really need to bring this poor kid to see Tegan.*

"I've got a flashlight." Jonathan stood tall. "I'm not scared of shadows. I won't let him get you."

"Kid…" Grace crouched, face to face with Mila. "If the next words out of your mouth are 'you should be,' I'm going to legit conduct an exorcism on you."

Mila stuck out her tongue.

# 8

# ONE MORE TIME

Once the sun started to weaken in the sky, Anne-Marie Kirby announced the communal dinner event over.

She and her small staff, plus a few militia including Cliff, got to work breaking down the tables and folding chairs up. Children ran to their parents or caretakers with varying degrees of reluctance at having to go home. Madison and Becca stood about twenty yards away from Harper, Grace, and Mila, talking.

Harper looked around for Lorelei, but couldn't find the tiny platinum-haired sprite. Her heart raced with worry. All the talk of shadow men, mountain lions, and possibly someone watching children filled her head with tragic thoughts.

"Oh, shit."

"Huh?" asked Grace. "Something wrong?"

"Lori!" shouted Harper.

A brunette girl of around fifteen who'd arrived with the hockey players looked over at her. "What?"

"Sorry. Not you." Harper let the shotgun hang on its strap and cupped her hands around her mouth. "Lorelei!?"

"Lore!" yelled Jonathan. "Where are you?"

The din of collapsing tables and conversation faded as everyone in the area started looking around.

"Lorelei!" bellowed Cliff from across the field. "Where'd you get off to?"

Harper's hands shook. She advanced into the crowd, looking left and right. Seconds before total panic set in, a tiny, "Here!" rang out from the north.

Lorelei emerged from behind a tree about 200 feet away, adjacent to the dirt road separating the 'farm proper' from the still-open field of Elk Meadow Park. Grinning and laughing, she raced over to Cliff, hugged him, then continued the rest of the way to Harper.

"There's rabbits over there! They're *so* little and fuzzy!"

Harper about melted into a puddle. *Am I paranoid, over-cautious, or should I be wound this tight?*

"We found a big cat carrier in one of the houses." Jonathan looked up. "We could put Lorelei in it so she stops wandering off."

Madison giggled.

"No," said Harper. "Don't put your sister in a cage."

"She'd probably think it's hilarious." Madison smirked.

Harper sighed. *Yeah, she would.*

Becca walked off, heading for her parents. Madison followed. The two girls stood together, talking for a few minutes, neither in any hurry to go anywhere.

"C'mon, Maddie. Time to go home," said Cliff.

Madison looked back with a desperate expression, but kept on talking until Becca's parents called their daughter away. When the girl reluctantly walked off after them, Madison trudged over to Harper, head down and crying.

"Hey, Termite." Harper put an arm around her. "It's okay. Just bedtime. You'll see her again tomorrow."

"I know." Madison sniffled.

"You had fun playing soccer though, right?"

"Yeah. The older kids aren't that good. They couldn't catch us. We won seven to two."

"Ouch," said Jonathan. "You owned them."

Harper whistled. "Wow, seven points in one game?"

"Yeah, seriously." Madison nodded. "They didn't even *try* to pass. And every time the ball got anywhere close to Christopher, he tripped over it and ate grass."

Talking soccer on the walk back home appeared to improve Madison's spirits. Harper couldn't quite shake the worry that something might be out there posing a threat, so she kept her attention mostly on their surroundings until they arrived at the house and went inside.

No house in the 'officially re-settled' areas of Evergreen had working locks—at least the ones that had been abandoned by former residents during the evacuation—as they'd all been removed to allow new people to claim them. The majority had deadbolts at least, so once someone had gone inside, they had a little security. Another relic from days gone by had returned, a town where almost no one locked their doors.

However, tonight, Harper wanted to flip the deadbolt... as soon as Cliff got back.

Being sent home with the kids, ostensibly as their guardian, bothered her as much as it relieved her. Whether or not anyone on the militia from her fellow 'soldiers' to Walter the boss *intended* to go easy on her for being young, they certainly seemed to. On one hand, she liked being able to personally watch over Madison and the other two, and didn't mind the safety of it. Of course, if anyone would ever take her seriously as a member of the militia, she shouldn't appear too happy to be coddled. Though, actual complaining could wait a few years until Madison had more of a chance to defend herself should something happen.

All three kids piled into the bathroom to brush their teeth. Harper paced around the living room, still holding the shotgun. Lorelei vanishing for those few minutes had her on edge and seriously contemplating giving the kid a bracelet with bells on it. Not for a minute did she believe in Mila's shadow person, but a mountain lion had gotten in and killed a cow. Or at least, everyone believed a mountain lion had done it.

Jonathan and Lorelei exited the bathroom together. He went to his bedroom, the smallest of the three, which the prior owner of this place had used for a little computer room. Lorelei, trying to pull her dress off and run at the same time, crashed into the wall and bounced to a seat on the floor, laughing. A few minutes later, the girls emerged having changed into their night clothes, and flopped on the living room floor to pass the almost-hour they had left until it became too dark to see.

At first, Harper figured Madison had to use the toilet, but after a few more minutes and no sign of her, she grew worried. She slung the Mossberg over her shoulder—since leaving it in the room with kids still didn't feel right—and went down the hall, knocking lightly when she reached the bathroom door.

"Maddie? You okay?"

Quiet crying from inside made her open the door and peer in.

Madison did sit on the toilet, though fully dressed and with the lid closed, a foamy toothbrush still hanging out of her mouth. From the look of her, she'd been crying fairly hard since her siblings left the room, trying like hell to stay quiet.

"What's wrong?" Harper went in, pulling the door closed behind her. "Maddie? C'mon, Termite. Talk to me."

She looked up with a 'leave me alone' glare, but it melted away into an expression like an abandoned kitten. Harper took the washcloth off the tub edge and dabbed toothpaste from her sister's face.

"Did something happen?"

"Nmm." Madison plucked the toothbrush from her mouth. "No."

"What's wrong?"

Madison stared at her, open-mouthed for a few seconds. "What's wrong? What *isn't* wrong? Mom and Dad are dead. People stole our house, all our stuff. I miss Eva and Melissa, and Mrs. Lopez' dance class. I don't even know if any of them are still alive. Our whole lives are gone, and everyone's just pretending it's all fine and we're okay. But we're not okay." Her voice blurred with tears. "I'm not okay."

"Oh, Termite…" Harper sank to kneel beside the toilet and pulled her sister into a hug.

"I'm not okay," whispered Madison, before bursting into silent sobs.

Overwhelmed with a sudden spike of loss for her parents and friends, Harper cried, too.

After a moment, the Mossberg wobbled from Madison tugging at it. "You're carrying a gun around all the time, and it's like totally normal. No one's even yelled at you. I hate that you had to shoot people. You can't even kill bugs, and you've shot *people.*"

Harper squeezed her, shuddering with guilt and grief. "Those weren't really people, Termite. Just bad guys from a horrible video game who wanted to hurt you."

"Becca is just ignoring it all happened. She won't even talk about Eva or Melissa. Whenever I say anything about them, she just says 'I dunno' and talks about something else. I hate not knowing what happened to my friends."

Harper leaned back from the hug to look into her eyes. "We stayed home for two months. Almost everyone evacuated, thinking more bombs could fall. No one wanted to be in a big city. They probably left with everyone else."

"I miss Mom *so* much." Madison's face warped with grief as she struggled to keep talking past her tears. "I just want her to take me to Starbucks *one* more time. Or yell at me for having music on too loud just once more. I want her to yell at me that I'm gonna be late for gymnastics just one more time. I want..." She buried her face in Harper's shoulder and bawled. "Mom and Dad aren't gonna call me. I'm never gonna talk to them again."

Everything Harper thought to say sounded lame, so she just rocked her and rubbed her back, muttering 'I miss them too' or 'yeah' or 'it's okay to cry' randomly. A creak near the door suggested either Jonathan or Lorelei came to see what all the crying was about, but crept back to the living room without intruding.

*Probably Jonathan. Lorelei would've run in and tried to cheer us up.*

Eventually, Madison cried herself out to silence, but kept clinging.

A few minutes later, the *whump* of the front door closing announced Cliff's return.

Madison finally released her hug, head down as if ashamed of herself. "I'm just so *bored.* There's nothing to do here."

That seemed a rather superficial thing to complain about, but her sister's tone of voice gave away some unspoken meaning, so Harper said, "I miss video games, too," hoping to pull more information out of her.

"It's not just that." Madison wiped her eyes. "We were always rushing around, trying not to be late for soccer or dance class or whatever. This place is *so* slow. It's weird not always feeling like Mom's gonna be mad at me for not moving fast enough. And..." Fresh tears ran down her cheeks. "I was always busy or in the car going somewhere. Now, I'm just here with nothing to do and it makes me think about Mom."

"The whole world slowed down. I think I've got the shakes from internet withdrawal."

Madison almost smiled, but didn't quite manage it. I wanna pretend everything is still okay. Like we're on vacation. Maybe I can make myself believe it and not be sad."

Harper brushed her sister's hair off her face and kissed her forehead. "It's not good to lie to yourself. I wish none of it happened, too. I want Mom and Dad back more than anything, but... the best thing we can do for them now is survive. They'd want us to survive. It's not really that bad here. Sure it's primitive and boring, but we're safe."

"Yeah, but you were gonna wind up with some stupid office job." Madison flicked her hair off her shoulders. "I was gonna be a rich and famous dancer." For a few seconds, she appeared serious, but a flimsy smile broke the act.

Harper stuck out her tongue. Madison's smile advanced from weak to somber but genuine.

"C'mon. It's almost bedtime. Finish up in here and get your nightgown on. My turn to use the bathroom."

"Okay." Madison started for the door, but stopped to peer back at her. "I'm giving you fair warning. There might be more crying tonight."

Harper sat back on her heels and exhaled hard. "That's fine. I think we both need to let it out. This crap isn't easy to deal with."

"Do you think I was nuts?"

"Huh?"

Madison shifted her weight. "The phone."

"Did you really expect them to call?"

"I dunno. I don't really remember it. Every time I think about it, I see Mom and Dad when those men attacked us, and then we're in that place with the huge chocolate muffins. Maybe I was legit nuts for a while there, but I'm trying not to be crazy anymore. Not like Mila. She's a little scary."

"Shock," said Harper. "We were both in shock. And... something happened to that girl. She probably watched someone hurt her parents."

"Oh." Madison looked down. "Just like us. I'll try to be nice to her, but she doesn't really like anyone." She spun and whisked off to the bedroom.

Harper got up, leaned on the sink, and stared at herself in the mirror. The reflection gazing back at her looked dusty, exhausted, and had this strange faraway look in her eyes. Whether it had come from killing thugs, the trauma of witnessing her parents' murder, or being on high alert for so long, she couldn't tell. But, the young woman gazing back at her didn't seem much like Harper Cody anymore.

*I'm worrying Maddie. That's what's freaking her out. She knows I'm fried.* Harper closed her eyes, let all the air out of her nose, and took a deep breath. *I'm still me. I'm still who I used to be... mostly.*

The voice of Ryan Prentice, king of the junior prom, echoed in her mind over the auditorium's PA system. *And for sweetest person... Harper Cody!* That spotlight moment embarrassed her so much she had still been blushing when senior year started... all two weeks of it before the nukes ruined everything.

When the cheering of students died down, she imagined him pulling another card, reading it, and announcing, *Most likely to kill someone... Harper Cody!*

"Ugh. I should be staying up 'til midnight studying, complaining about the stupid people who shop at the mall. A lot of stuff *should* be, but isn't." She threw a few handfuls of water on her face, then toweled it off before grabbing toothpaste. "This is the new normal. If I can't get a grip, Maddie never will."

After brushing her teeth, she used the toilet, then crossed the hall to change into her nightgown. Since Cliff was home, she decided to give Madison a little sense of normal by leaving the shotgun on the floor by the bed and going out to the living room as just Harper instead of 'militia girl.' The four of them played Uno while Cliff sat in his recliner, reading. Right around the time it became too dark to do anything other than go to sleep, a knock came from the door.

"Hey, it's me," said Fred Mitchell.

Cliff got up, set his book down, and got ready to go out on night patrol.

"Be careful." Harper grabbed a blanket from the sofa, wrapping it around herself before Fred could see her in the gossamer nightie.

"That goes for you, too." He pointed at her, winked, and headed out.

She followed him to the door.

Fred waved at her with a warm smile, then walked off with Cliff down the road.

She shut the door, pondering the deadbolt, but didn't lock it since 'dad' would be back in a few hours. Soon, it became too dark for the kids to play the game, so she shooed them all to bed. Everyone took a turn in the bathroom, then crawled in under the blankets. Harper lay flat on her back with Madison clinging on one side and Lorelei curled up on the other.

Until sleep took her, she stared at the ceiling, faintly visible in the moonlight, trying to figure out how she could possibly cope with what happened and be more like her old self. For all her positive talking, she still *looked* like she'd given up and merely coasted along on an empty tank. She convinced herself to be brave, to fight, to do whatever it took to protect her little sister, but had those experiences changed her *too* much? Had she become another person entirely? Madison must have sensed something in her that set off her meltdown tonight.

Or had she? Maybe a person carrying too much pain inside could fake normal for a while, until they ran out of energy and crashed. Either way, that girl she saw in the mirror didn't help. She had to find a way to accept their parents' deaths, accept what happened to the world, and move on from it. Harper had to stop feeling like someone who'd gotten a fatal dose of radiation and merely stumbled along waiting for the end.

*That's the problem...*

As much as she'd been telling everyone to cheer up, to keep fighting, that life remained worth living, she hadn't really convinced herself of it yet.

*If I keep thinking about everything we've lost, it's gonna devour me. Who would I have been in the 1800s? No video games, no Starbucks, living in the Frontier... People all carried guns back then, not a big deal. Okay, that's a bad comparison... I wouldn't have been allowed to be anything but a nice little lady back then. I need to think positive stuff. Maddie's still alive. Everyone here in Evergreen is still alive.*

*I am, too.*

# 9

# WATCHING

The next morning, everyone sat around the table to enjoy a magnificent breakfast—of Cocoa Puffs with almond milk from a box.

"This is kinda weird," said Jonathan. "There are actual cows here, and we're eating nut milk."

Cliff almost choked on his cereal laughing.

Lorelei and Madison looked up from their bowls, confused.

Harper's face burned with blush. She hadn't taken what the boy said in *that* way until Cliff laughed at it.

"What's so funny?" asked Madison.

Cliff waved about in a 'need a moment' gesture until he stopped coughing. After clearing his throat, he chuckled. "Oh, just what he said about there being cows and we're using fake milk. It's funny."

"People aren't supposed to drink milk. It's for baby cows," said Madison. "Besides, if it's not, umm… those two big words I don't know, we're gonna get sick from it. I'm okay having nut milk."

Cliff covered his mouth, his cheeks reddening.

"Can we please call it *almond* milk?" asked Harper. "And you didn't mind normal milk before."

"They don't have to kill the cows for it, but the dairy farms are really cruel to them sometimes. The cows here aren't being mistreated. But they aren't doing the thing to it. Untreated raw milk is like really dangerous. It makes a lot of people go to the hospital."

"Pasteurization," said Cliff. "And it's not out of reach. Just gotta bring milk to near-boiling for like twenty seconds and let it cool. I'm sure the doctors are aware of the risks of raw milk and have warned Ned about it."

"That's probably why we're having *almond* milk," said Jonathan.

Lorelei looked up from her cereal. "How they milk ommonds? Do ommonds have udders?"

Harper snickered, which set Cliff off laughing again.

The six-year-old looked at them, confused. "What?"

Jonathan snickered. "No, Lore. Almonds don't have udders. They like grind them up or something to make this."

"Aww. Poor ommonds," said Lorelei in an adorably sad tone.

Madison stirred her cereal, making a 'bleh' face at it. "Can we have something hot for breakfast? Like pancakes or oatmeal or—"

"Eggies!" cheered Lorelei.

Madison flinched, but didn't protest beyond an 'eggs are cruel' expression.

"If it's a day where we need to heat the house, sure." Cliff pointed over his shoulder with a thumb. "We don't want to use firewood too fast."

"At least it's not super cold anymore," said Jonathan.

Lorelei stretched one leg up and rested her pink-sock-covered foot on the table. "I love my socks! They are warm and fuzzy."

"Feet don't belong on tables." Madison gently pushed the girl's leg down.

Harper smiled. *The world is truly broken when a six-year-old is thrilled about getting socks for Christmas.* For the rest of breakfast, conversation focused on the theoretical mountain lion after Madison begged Cliff to make sure no one kills 'the poor kitty.'

Lorelei jumped on the 'no kill' side because 'kitties are cute and fuzzy.' Jonathan seemed to prefer the cat be left alive, but didn't have a problem with shooting it if it attacked a person. Harper agreed with him while Madison claimed it a lie that mountain lions attack people, stating they would rather run away than fight a person.

*They're probably as hungry as we are.* Harper decided not to say that, and tried to act as normal as she could. *We're just having breakfast at home. Not like a nuclear war happened or anything.*

Eventually, the empty cereal bowls wound up in the sink. Jonathan and Lorelei headed back to their bedrooms to change out of their sleeping clothes. Madison dawdled by the sofa.

"Go get dressed. It's almost time for school."

"The apocalypse ate my homework," deadpanned Madison.

Cliff snickered.

"Do I *have* to go?"

"Is something happening at school that's making you feel unsafe?" Harper walked over to her.

"No, just... it sucks that the world blew up and I *still* have to go to school." She flapped her arms at her side. "We used to get three days off when it snowed, but they don't call school on account of nuclear fishing."

"I think you meant fission." Cliff paused in washing the bowls to smile back at them.

"See? You need school, Termite." Harper patted her on the head.

"I'm—was—in fifth grade. We didn't learn about nuclears yet." Madison looked down, raised and lowered her toes, then sighed. "Going to school feels too normal. I hate that everyone's just trying to pretend like all those people didn't die, and everything's the same."

"Going to school makes you angry that everyone's not as sad outside as you feel inside?" asked Harper in a gentle tone.

"I guess, yeah."

"Everyone's sad, but they're dealing with it in their own way. It's important not to give up. You want the world to go back the way it was right?"

Madison nodded.

"Then we can't let people grow up uneducated." Harper booped her on the nose. "If we give up, we can never fix things."

"I guess." Madison ground her toes into the rug. "Mila's really sad. She just shows it weird. I'll try to stop being mad at school."

Harper patted her shoulder. "If you're ever feeling too sad to deal with school, and just need some time to be alone and decompress, you can skip a day or two. But don't abuse it, okay?"

"'Kay." Madison nodded. "You sound like Mom now... 'decompress.'" She sorta-smiled and hurried off to get dressed.

"You okay?" asked Cliff.

"No not really, but I'm okay enough." Harper raked her fingers through her hair. "Do I look like I haven't slept in a month?"

"Nah. Your hair is far too neat."

She rolled her eyes, chuckling. "It looks the same no matter what I do... unless it's humid, then *poof!* Hey, did you see anything last night?"

Jonathan and Lorelei walked in and stood by the front door, waiting to walk to school.

"No sign of a mountain lion if that's what you're asking."

"I was thinking more of someone possibly stalking kids."

He walked over, still drying his hands on a towel. "Could have been a resident keeping tabs on them. Might also have been a kid's imagination." He wagged his eyebrows. "Or a shadow man."

"Stop." She poked him. "There's no Shadow Man. But I don't think Emmy would've said what she did unless she really had seen something that put her on edge."

"Almost everyone in this town has been through some serious shit. Except for those who lived here before... all they lost was power. "

"Yeah, but—"

Madison screamed.

"Crap!" Harper sprinted down the hall to the bathroom, catching herself on the doorjamb to avoid falling over from stopping so fast. She stared in at her little sister standing on the sink.

"Harp! It's huge!" Madison bounced, whined, and pointed at the floor.

"What's huge? There's nothing."

"A massive bug!"

*Oh...* Harper relaxed. "Can you please do me a little favor?"

"What?" asked Madison, squirming.

"Save screaming like that for serious emergencies?"

"But it *is* an emergency! It's bigger than my hand! It might be radioactive or something an' bite my face off."

Something black moved behind the toilet.

The sudden, unexpected motion made Harper jump.

*Whoa, okay that is big.*

Once the initial shock wore off, she crouched for a closer look and spotted a black beetle about three inches long with serrated antennae. "Oh, it's just a beetle." She herded it out from behind the toilet, then scooped it up in the little plastic wastebasket so she could carry it outside. "You can come down now. Hurry up and get dressed, you're going to be late."

"Eww! It's huge!"

"It's not that big."

Madison cringed away. "It is!"

"No it isn't." Harper winked, then carried the house invader outside.

She tossed it in the grass by the back fence, returned the little trash can where it belonged, and once again picked up her shotgun. Ever since she'd been caught in the middle of a gunfight without it, she'd been overly diligent about keeping it close. At times, she envied the militia guys who only had handguns, since wearing a smaller weapon on her belt wouldn't be nearly as cumbersome as lugging the huge Mossberg everywhere. If she had a pistol, she could get away with leaving the shotgun home for short trips—basically whenever she didn't officially go on patrol.

Madison emerged from the bedroom in a long-sleeved pink-and-white-striped dress over red leggings. "Feels weird not carrying a backpack."

"This school has no homework!" said Jonathan with a note of triumph.

"Only because there aren't enough books." Madison folded her arms.

Lorelei looked back and forth between them for a moment, then blurted, "My socks are toasty."

"What?" asked Madison. "Are you feeling okay?"

The tiny one's smile became cheesy. "I dunno what homework is."

"It's a particular form of cruelty invented by teachers to make sure kids don't have too much fun after school," muttered Madison.

"Oh." Lorelei nodded as if that made total sense. "Mommy used to do that."

Everyone fidgeted, staring at her.

*Ugh. That woman.* Harper picked Lorelei up and swung her around, grinning. "Well, don't worry about her anymore. I say you should have as much fun as you want after school... just be safe."

Lorelei giggled.

Harper led the kids outside and down Hilltop Drive, alert for danger while Madison and Jonathan explained homework. According to Jonathan, they used to have to do more school stuff in a day than they had time for, so some of the learning had to go home with them. According to Madison, teachers lived in the constant, desperate fear that children might think about having fun, so they had this horrible weapon called 'homework' they used to ensure that didn't happen.

This, of course, left poor Lorelei utterly confused.

While she couldn't claim to have liked school as much as Jonathan seemed to, Harper hadn't minded it. In her opinion, it just 'had to be done' to avoid winding up poor later in life. At least, that's what Dad said. She enjoyed her science classes, even math, but she didn't know if she could make a career out of it. Mom thought she should consider being a veterinarian. Had the war not happened, she might actually have tried.

Neither one of her parents would have ever imagined she'd pursue a career in law enforcement.

She scoffed to herself, having the ten-thousandth moment of 'what the hell am I doing'. As she'd done 9,999 times before, she brushed her doubt aside and kept going. Though, after looking at herself in the mirror last night, she wondered if Mayor Ned had seen the same thing in her eyes when she objected to surrendering the Mossberg. He hadn't offered much protest at all to a skinny seventeen-year-old wanting to join the militia, clearly doing so only to keep her father's shotgun and not out of any true desire to defend the town. Could he have noticed the 'I've killed people' distant stare and figured he'd let her on the militia since she'd already been broken?

Cliff had once confided in her that a normal person could never get used to killing. He described it as this thing that always followed him around, watching him all the time ever since he returned from the Middle East. Wherever he went, he'd never quite felt like he belonged there anymore. He'd left civilized society behind in Iraq the instant he'd taken a life. Working as a mall cop, he would observe people every day going about their ordinary, civilian lives, feeling apart from it. Every day, he'd see someone and think, 'they've never had to kill anyone' 'they don't know what it's like' and so on. Fortunately, he'd dealt with it, but he'd known a lot of guys who couldn't. Four of the men he'd served with had taken their own lives.

In the past three months, Harper hadn't fired a single shot. The gang thugs she'd killed, she tried to file away as something from a video game. Not people, merely generic 'bad guys.' Cliff's fate hardly awaited her— civilization didn't exist for her to feel apart from, but she still didn't want to end up with his mindset, constantly consumed by what she'd had to do. Of course, she hadn't actively gone into an enemy location and shot people offensively. Every single time she'd killed, that person had been a direct threat to her, or her family, through no fault of her own.

She clung to that semantic point, trying not to feel like a killer.

Life here had been relatively peaceful, and not needing to pull the trigger for a while gave her hope. However, she had been involved in a few physical altercations: two cases where someone started a fight at Earl's while drunk, and one time an outsider who'd slipped into town decided he wanted the Mossberg and ambushed her, trying to grab it and run. The first bar fight, she hadn't accomplished much but getting picked up and thrown into a wall, a nuisance the men dismissed with barely any effort. Since then, Cliff had been working with her on jiu-jitsu. Luckily for her, she learned fast or that guy would've stolen Dad's gun.

To avoid having to climb hills or fences and weave twisty roads each morning, she'd gotten into the habit of walking straight down Hilltop Drive to Route 74 and taking it north in a straight line until nearer the former Evergreen Middle School. Soon after leaving the road and going up the tree-covered hill into the residential area around the old golf course, a rustle came from the right. Harper pulled her mind back from thoughts of hand-to-hand training and swiveled to aim at a blur of motion.

Mila Cline jumped out from behind a tree only a few feet away from them.

Madison, Jonathan, and Lorelei all screamed—though Lorelei's shriek of alarm mutated into giggling.

"Gah!" Harper jerked the shotgun away from being pointed at a child. "Don't do that!"

"If you shot me, at least the Shadow Man wouldn't get me."

Harper blinked.

"You *want* to die?" asked Madison, stunned.

Mila shook her head. "No. Not really. I just know it's going to happen and I would rather it not hurt."

"Why are you hiding next to the road?" stammered Harper, her brain tripping over the concept of a nihilistic nine-year-old.

"Someone was following me and watching me. I think it's the Shadow Man."

"Did you see them?" Harper turned about, scanning their surroundings.

"No. That's why I think it's him. You can't see him until he"—Mila pounced on Jonathan from behind, covering his mouth with one hand —"*takes* you."

Madison shivered, looking terrified. Jonathan didn't seem to mind Mila grabbing him.

"Maybe the Shadow Man just wants a hug?" asked Lorelei.

Harper mentally rolled her eyes at the idea of a supernatural shadow person. However, something about Mila's pleading stare made her fear come off as genuine. A ghost man didn't seem possible, but that didn't mean no living threat existed. Whatever had gone wrong in Mila's head could easily reframe any and all dangers into the Shadow Man. Assuming, of course, she didn't have legit schizophrenia and see hallucinations.

Now she had two kids claiming someone followed them. Alas, she still didn't think she could get anywhere taking it to Walter yet. One kid, she hadn't even spoken to in person, and the other... well, the entire town knew Mila had issues. If Harper had only the word of a child everyone thought of as the 'creepy girl,' people would blame it on mental trauma.

*At least she tried to hide from it. That's good. Means she doesn't want to die.*

"You always feel like that," said Jonathan, taking Mila's hand. "The Shadow Man isn't real."

Mila's expression gave off resigned pity, as if to say 'you poor boy, you don't know the danger you're in.' It also seemed far too... serious for a girl her age. Though, she didn't appear to object to holding hands with him.

Since Harper didn't see anything out of place or anyone hiding nearby, she resumed ushering the kids along. They exited the trees onto a small loop road and followed it around to the left onto South Hiwan Drive, which went straight to the school. Harper looked around at the houses they passed, a trash can here or there that would never again be collected by guys driving a big truck. A few cars sat in driveways, not one of them having moved in six months. If she ever wound up patrolling this area after school let out, she'd probably see kids riding bikes or playing stickball, street hockey, or whatever in the road.

*This is Schrodinger's reality. The world has simultaneously ended and keeps existing.*

They arrived at class a little late, though the teachers didn't appear to mind. Not like people had working clocks. The school building did, since it sort-of had power. Solar panels had been installed there prior to the war, and Jeanette had gotten them working. Unfortunately, the EMP surge had fried just about every transformer in the area and done quite a number on the battery at the school since it had been hooked up to the town's electrical grid as part of some power-sharing type arrangement. Any excess energy the school's panels made used to feed back into the town, and the school could run off municipal power on gloomy days.

The sight of working ceiling lights again mesmerized her. For seventeen years, she'd never thought electric lighting to be at all impressive, merely something that existed everywhere. For the second time in a week, she felt like someone from the 1800s seeing a light bulb for the first time.

Lorelei zoomed over to the youngest group and half climbed onto the desks to see what Mrs. Stevens showed the others. The woman had been the only female adult with the hockey team, mother of one of the cheerleaders who'd gone along as the chaperone for the girls. Prior to the war, she worked as an elementary teacher handling first grade, so she'd fallen right back into her element.

Violet continued working with the largest segment, the nine-to-twelve group. The handful of kids between thirteen and sixteen had Mr. Simon for a primary teacher. Before the war, he'd taught chemistry at the high school.

Madison, Jonathan, and Mila took their seats.

A few of the kids waved at Harper. She waved back, and gave Violet a beckoning look.

Violet approached, eyebrow raised. "What's up, hon?"

"I don't want to start a panic, but I gotta say something." She lowered her voice so the kids wouldn't eavesdrop. "I heard some of them talking, saying that Emmy told them someone had been watching her. This morning, I found Mila hiding from someone she said had been following her."

Violet pursed her lips.

"Yeah, I know... but I don't think it's all in her head. Again, I'm not saying we need to panic, but if you could keep your ears open and let me know if you hear any of them talking about being watched, followed or whatever? It could be nothing, but I dunno... something just doesn't feel right."

"All right. I'll let you know if any of them say something like that. Now, let me get back to it."

"Thanks." Harper smiled, waved again to her siblings, and left.

Worry hounded her as she plodded out the doors and crossed the parking lot in front of the school. Rather than resume a meandering patrol as usual, she headed south along the road they'd walked in on back to the spot of woods where Mila had been hiding.

Once off the paving, she slowed to make herself quiet and held the shotgun up as if stalking a bad guy. *If someone was spying on Mila, they saw us leave. They wouldn't still be around here... unless they're maybe waiting for her. That girl's always alone. Maybe I can find a footprint or something?*

She tried not to think about what the person would do to Mila, but couldn't stop hearing that cop years ago saying that while rare, abduction by a stranger tended to be the most dangerous. *Why am I assuming the worst? What if it's Mila's mom or dad? No, that's stupid. Her parents wouldn't spy on her like that if they were still alive... unless they're like Tyler and know they're too dangerous to be with her.*

*Argh.*

A few minutes into her search, the scuff of a shoe on dirt came from beyond the corner of the northernmost house at the end of the loop behind her. Harper whirled, pointing the shotgun in that direction, but no one was there. She froze, listening. The rustle of fabric accompanied a few rapid, soft footsteps.

Harper rushed to the corner of the house, pressed herself flat against the wall, and peered around. Nothing but trees and a field of open grass stood between her and the road back to the school. A few houses further north all appeared calm. No sign of any people appeared anywhere in sight, either normal or malign. She watched the area for a few minutes before feeling confident enough to step around the corner. Clusters of trees offered ample hiding places, thick enough to shadow the ground even in broad daylight. Motionless as a spooked deer, Harper stared at every spot someone might have been able to run to in the few seconds it had taken her to reach the house and peer around it.

*Okay, I definitely heard someone. They didn't just turn into shadows. No. There's no such thing as ghosts or monsters. I'm just not looking hard enough. Someone really is spying on kids.*

Despite seeing nothing, she couldn't shake the feeling that someone watched her... someone who wanted to harm her.

That thought made her clench her grip on the Mossberg tight.

She crept around the field between the houses, poking into tree clusters, examining windows or doors, but still nothing offered definitive proof someone had been there. It took her almost an hour, but she eventually admitted to herself that she wouldn't find anything. Whoever had been there had evaded her and gone away.

Of course, she might've pulled a Mila and hallucinated it.

*No. I know what I heard. But... it could've been an animal. Or... no. Animals don't wear clothes. That definitely sounded like the swish of pants.*

Frustrated, Harper stormed back onto the road heading south. Other than the near total silence and lack of moving cars or airplanes going overhead, Evergreen looked much like it must have before the war. Most of the parents who lived here would be away at this hour, helping out on the farm or doing whatever jobs they agreed to take on. Her experience with work hadn't amounted to much more than four months at Wendy's, a summer working at Starbucks, and a few months at the mall, working as a retail clerk at a teen clothing store. None of the jobs in town came close to any of those things, but it still felt odd to think about people doing work without a paycheck.

In the midst of her trying to imagine what the world had been like living as villagers before the concept of a 'day job' happened, Leigh Preston walked into view off Hearth Drive, approaching from the east, her fluffy curls bouncing. The woman had to be ten years older than her, but probably still got carded all the time if she tried to buy beer. She carried her AK47 rather than wore it on its strap, but didn't appear to be expecting combat.

Harper stopped in the middle of the road to wait for her.

"Hey." Leigh nodded at the shotgun. "Something up? You look on edge."

"A bit. One of the kids came up to me and said she thought someone had been hiding and watching her. Came back to check the spot and I thought I heard someone run off, but didn't see anything. And it really did feel like someone wanted to hurt me, but I couldn't find anyone."

"Ack." Leigh looked around. "That's not cool. No idea who?"

"Nope. It could've just been one of the residents, but why would they hide from me?"

"Sounds like someone's up to no good." Leigh hardened her gaze. "I was just about to head back to the field, but if you want me to stick around with you I can."

Harper gestured with the shotgun at the AK. "Are you expecting trouble, too?"

"Thought I saw an animal track. Tried to follow it, but I didn't see anything."

"That lion killed a cow. Do you think it might try to grab a kid? And, I'm sure what I heard was a person. Lions don't wear clothes."

"You heard clothes?" Leigh blinked.

"Yeah." Harper shifted her weight onto her left leg and swung her right one back and forth to make her jeans 'swoosh.' "Like that."

"Oh. Duh. Okay, yeah, that's scary. I'll go let Walter know about it."

"Are you sure? I don't have any proof and Mila was the kid who told me someone followed her."

"Oh. Well, that poor girl *is* in her own little nightmare world, but I don't think she'd lie about something like that. I'll let Walter know it came from her. What exactly happened again?"

Harper explained everything she'd heard or been told so far. Leigh shouldered her AK and hurried off to the southwest, heading for the militia HQ.

"Being a cop had to be so much easier when radios worked." She sighed at the air horn can hanging on her belt, then resumed walking, more vigilant than she'd been in weeks.

If someone truly did prowl around looking for a child to attack, Mila made about as perfect a target as a creep could ask for: usually alone, always staring down at the ground, quiet. No one would even notice anything had happened to her for hours.

That thought led to an equally frightening one—Lorelei. Small for her age, overly friendly, and super trusting. A creep wouldn't even have to sneak up on her. That girl would run right over and hug him, not even knowing he carried her away to do horrible things.

Worry and anger grew with each step she took down the street. It had been three months since she used up a shotgun shell, but if some guy prowled the town with the intent to harm a child, she'd happily pull the trigger. Her only regret would be if any kid had to witness it. She held the Mossberg tight, more grateful than ever that she'd made the decision to keep it. Sitting around helpless to do anything to protect her siblings as a 'civilian' would have totally sucked.

Remembering the proud smile on her father's face the first time she showed interest in shooting put a lump in her throat. What had once been a piece of sports equipment had become a lifeline, Dad's last ability to protect his kids—even if she had to use it herself. In some way, it made her feel as though he walked right beside her.

*I'm not going to just execute anyone for staring. But so help me, if they do anything more than watching...*

# 10

# SQUATTERS

A new worry joined the unease that orbited Harper's mind after Leigh walked off.

Would Walter or the rest of the militia start thinking of her as too ready to jump to alarm over every little thing? Two kids had reported someone following them, and Harper, too, had a strong sense that a hidden person had been close by, watching her with malicious intentions. She didn't exactly hear one little rumor and flip out. No, she'd much rather risk being thought of as a skittish 'child' than stay quiet and potentially allow a child to be hurt.

*It's not like I'm taking Mila's shadow man seriously. I don't think it's a real ghost. First Emmy, now Mila.* Talking to Lorelei and telling her to be wary of people she didn't know probably wouldn't work. Tegan might not have been a psychiatrist, but her suggestion of 'attachment disorder' fit the girl's behavior enough to where Harper accepted her adopted sister had some legit mental problems. One couldn't simply tell a depressed person to cheer up. That worked about as well as telling an amputee to 'just grow a new hand.' Likewise, she couldn't simply tell the princess of cling to distrust people.

As soon as they got home that afternoon, Harper would pull Jonathan and Madison aside and warn them to help keep tabs on Lorelei. Having three people on high alert, even if two hadn't yet turned eleven, beat one shell-shocked teen who didn't trust herself not to screw up.

*Yeah. We all have mental damage.* She half chuckled. *Guess that was true even before.*

Mom and Dad pushed them both to succeed, though nowhere near as hard as Grace's parents. Hearing that they'd screamed at her for getting even an A- in a class sounded psychotic. It almost seemed kinder for her new friend to be orphaned. As soon as that thought crossed her mind, she cringed with guilt.

Today, Harper hoped to find evidence of the mysterious 'watcher.' Rather than wander the roads in her usual patrol path, she cut across backyards, fields, and the mini-forests interspersed among the houses. Leigh had been reassigned to the secondary farm on the old golf course, mostly in an attempt to mitigate people tromping around in search of vegetables to swipe before Liz Trujillo could assign food out. Nothing had matured enough to produce food yet, and they didn't want anyone destroying the plants.

Roughly two hours after she'd dropped the kids at school, a man's angry shouting came from the woods ahead. The distance blurred most of what he said other than F-bombs and threats of shooting someone. All the yelling came from a large, beige house near the eastern edge of the residential area surrounding the old golf course.

Harper pulled the air horn can out of its holder, cringed, and sounded a long '911' blast, then grabbed the Mossberg in a two-handed grip, charging toward the house from the back, following the path of a huge wooden privacy fence around the right side.

"The hell on earth was that?" shouted the same, angry man.

"Easy, man. Relax," said another guy.

"You're in my goddamned house. I have every right to shoot you where you stand."

"Dude, calm down!" yelled the younger man. "Please don't shoot. There's a child in here. We'll ask for a different place."

The wailing of a toddler started up inside.

Harper crept to end of the fence and took cover, aiming around the corner at a fiftyish man in a button-down shirt and jeans on the porch with a huge handgun pointed at the doorway. Disheveled wavy black hair and a beard with hints of silver in it gave him a wild look, but then again, most guys sported that style now.

She moved her finger onto the trigger and yelled, "Drop the gun!"

The man jumped, then turned his head toward her and went wide-eyed... but continued holding his weapon up.

Answering pips from air horns came from the distance at varying degrees of loudness.

"Stop pointing a goddamned gun into a house with a two-year-old," yelled Harper. "Now!"

"Who the hell are you? Damn looters should be shot." The man glared at her.

"Drop the goddamned gun now or I'm going to drop you. There's a little kid in there." Harper focused all her attention on his gun hand. *Please put it down. Please don't make me shoot you.*

He stared at her for a long moment. Eventually, he seemed to get the feeling she really would fire, and tossed the handgun into the bushes to the right of a path connecting the porch to a driveway—which held a silver BMW sedan she didn't remember seeing before.

"All right." The man kept staring at her. "The hell is going on here, kid?"

Marcie Chapman shouted, "You see anything?" a short ways off to the left.

"Here!" yelled Harper, stepping out from behind the corner, keeping her weapon trained on the guy. "Evergreen militia. Kevin and Diane aren't looters. They're survivors. We all are."

"They're in my damn house," said the guy.

"We can get a different one." Kevin stepped out onto the porch. The scrawny twenty-ish guy only had boxers on, his hair wild, one eye not quite open... like he'd gone from deep sleep to panic in a matter of seconds.

"Militia? What the hell is that nonsense?" The guy took a step toward Harper. "What the devil are those people doing in my house?"

Marcie ran out into view from the opposite corner, holding her Sig 9mm in a two-handed grip, but not quite sure who to point it at. "Harp, what's going on?"

"This guy was threatening the Parkers. Gun's in the bushes."

The man held his arms out, gesturing at the building. "I'm Al Gonzalez, and this is *my* damn house. I came home and found the lock broken and looters inside."

Harper lowered the shotgun a little. "Most of the houses here were abandoned. Homes are assigned by the town manager. The Parkers can go live in a different empty house. There's no reason for anyone to get pissed off enough to start shooting. In case you missed it, we had a nuclear war."

"There's no looters around here," added Marcie while retrieving the dropped gun. She eyed the car. "Damn… that thing still run?"

"Yeah." Al sighed. "I just about had enough gas to make it back here, but it doesn't have much left."

"How?" Harper relaxed a bit more since the guy didn't appear likely to become violent. "I mean, how is it still working? All the cars are dead… and that's a nice one with a lot of electronics."

Al shrugged. "Lucky I guess. Underground parking garage must've shielded it. One hell of a ride getting back here from L.A."

"Los Angeles? Are you serious?" Marcie gawked. "It's still standing?"

"Not really. LA is one giant pile of debris. I was out there on a business trip, attending a conference. West Coast had a little more warning than New York, but not much. Bunch of us made it to the hotel basement before the shit hit the fan."

Ken Zhang jogged into view, hurrying over to stand beside Harper. "What's the emergency?"

She re-explained the situation to him.

Diane Parker walked out, carrying her son, Kendall. The two-year-old had stopped scream-crying and gazed around at everyone. "We don't have much stuff, but we'll get our things out."

"What happened to the woman who was here?" asked Al. "My wife."

"Probably went with the evacuation when the Army came through." Ken took the handgun Marcie offered, examining it. "Hmm, a .45 extended barrel. You don't look like a long-slide sort of guy."

"Ehh." Al shrugged. "Some, uhh, *things* happened between here and L.A. Took it from a gentleman who attempted to steal my car. Like that little sweetie said, there's been a nuclear war."

Harper's eyebrows drifted closer. *Little sweetie? Seriously?*

"The Army? Christ…" Al shook his head. "Where the heck would they have taken her?"

"Somewhere up north as far as we've heard from a couple people who've returned." Marcie holstered her 9mm. "Mayor Ned's policy is to let anyone who lived here before keep their houses. We're using the school up the road still, so anyone with children gets assigned to this area first."

"Ehh. Place has room. I don't mind. What's an old man like me gonna do with all this house alone?" Al scratched his head.

"I'm not sure I feel comfortable sharing a house with a man who almost shot me," said Diane.

"It's a new world." Kevin chuckled, then yawned. "You don't really know a guy 'til they've pointed a gun in your face."

Diane glared at her husband with 'are you serious' practically written across her forehead.

Al hooked his thumbs in his pants pockets and gazed off at the north. "Besides, I might go try to find the old woman. No need shooing them out if I'm just gonna go off and chase my own tail."

The Parkers got into a murmured conversation. Kevin figured he would have reacted pretty much the same as this guy had the war not happened and they came home to find strange people in their house. After a brief back-and-forth, Diane relented, mostly out of not wanting to go through the labor of relocation.

"Call it a misunderstanding then." Kevin offered a hand.

Al shook it. "Yeah. Sorry about that. Been a rough couple of months." He glanced at Ken. "You folks gonna keep that, or mind if I take it back?"

"I don't think it'll be a problem," said Harper, "But you should come with us first. All new arrivals need to go through a medical check and talk to the mayor."

"To get back to my own house?" asked Al.

"I don't make the rules; I'm just a cop." Harper gestured to the left. "It doesn't take long. Only a routine check."

He chuckled, shaking his head. "You're a little young to be a cop."

"I got a nuclear exemption to the four-year degree requirement."

"All right, fine." Al rubbed the bridge of his nose. "Whatever. Where is it?"

"By 74 in an office building that used to have a doctor's place," said Harper. "They've expanded the clinic into the entire building."

"We moved some stuff over from the Evergreen Medical Center behind the big R." Ken tucked Al's .45 in his belt and started walking. "C'mon."

Al grumbled, following them. "Why not just use the medical center?"

"None of the machines do anything without power. The building they set up in had some kinda medical stuff in it before, but the rest of it was offices. They've kinda taken over the whole building now for the town's clinic. It's close to the tennis courts they're using for solar panels, which makes it easier to run power there." Harper considered shouldering the shotgun, but kept holding it since she didn't quite trust letting her guard all the way down yet.

"If they ever get the power grid back online, they might relocate to the old place since it's bigger," said Ken.

While they walked across town, Al answered Ken's questions, telling them that LA had been hit hard. He'd seen dozens of people sick with radiation burns, futilely trying to cling to life despite there being no real medical care left. He'd been a corpsman in the Navy back in the early Nineties, and spent the past twenty some years working as a sales consultant for a company that made medical implants. It had been a long time since he actively tried to provide any sort of direct care, but he did what he could in the hotel basement until the rads decayed as low as they'd be likely to get any time soon, at least enough for him to risk going home. Surprisingly, he hadn't seen any trace of military personnel trying to organize any sort of evacuation and figured LA 'glowed' too much for them to bother even trying.

"Eh, I probably soaked up enough radiation to chop fifteen years off my life. At least it's the adult diaper nursing home years I'm gonna lose." Al chuckled.

*This guy should adopt Mila. They're both way morbid.*

Harper spent the rest of the walk to the doctor's office sick to her stomach with worry that she or Madison might develop cancer. No nuke had gone off close enough to Lakewood to flatten any of the houses there, though most had scorching on their south faces. Some had structural damage from a blast wave as well as falling debris. She didn't know much about nuclear bombs, but that did seem a little too intense for a detonation as far away as Colorado Springs. She accepted the rumors had been wrong, and other smaller warheads really did come down much closer than she'd previously believed.

When they reached Route 74, escorting a newcomer to the med center made her think back to Darnell walking with them their first day here. She'd been so full of hope at finally reaching the 'safe haven' of Evergreen she'd been dreaming about, it hadn't even occurred to her to feel like a suspect in custody. Perhaps she hadn't been, but at that moment, she sure felt like a cop escorting someone who'd done something bad.

She waited in the med center lobby making small talk with Ruby while Doctor Khan took Al into an exam room for the standard checkup. Her anxiety spiked when the woman mentioned Jax Davis had come in three days ago for treatment of a nasty scrape on his shin. The seven-year-old told Dr. Hale that he'd fallen while running away from 'a monster in the woods' that tried to sneak up on him.

"What?" blurted Harper. "Someone tried to grab him and no one thought to tell anyone?"

Ruby blinked in surprise. "We thought the boy was playing. Monsters aren't real, you know. Are you doing all right, dear? You seem stressed."

"Harper?" Ken got up and walked over. "What's up?"

She told him about what Emmy and Mila said, and that she'd heard someone sneaking around but didn't see anything. Both Ruby and Ken appeared concerned.

"What did he say the monster looked like?" asked Harper.

"Oh, I'm not sure exactly. Some kind of shadow with eyes. He explained it to Dr. Hale and she mentioned it to me in passing. Thought he had a vivid imagination."

"Is Tegan here?" Harper peered down the hall to the back.

"Yes. Where else would she be? We live in this building, you know." Ruby pointed up at the working lights. "Never thought I'd love sleeping at the office, but it's wonderful to have such a short commute."

Ken laughed.

"Someone calling me?" asked Tegan, poking her head out from a doorway a short distance deeper into the building.

"Yeah. Quick question." Harper waved at her to come closer, and repeated her worries about what the boy saw once the doctor joined them at the front desk.

"Hmm." Tegan tapped her fingers on her arm for a moment in thought. "Well, Jax said he saw a ninja monster. A big, black figure with a metal claw."

"A claw? Singular?" asked Harper.

"That's what he said. I thought they were playing a game with imaginary monsters and he hurt himself tripping over a root. Suppose it could have been a black bear. They sometimes stand up on their hind legs. A boy could've mistaken a bear for a giant person."

Ken rubbed his chin with a playful smile. "Hmm. All black person? Could be a *shadow man.*"

"Stop." Harper poked him. "I don't for a minute think that's real. And we shouldn't pick on Mila. She's... not well." Harper looked at Tegan. "Any chance that poor kid might be schizophrenic?"

"Again, I'm no psychiatrist, but if I had to offer as professional an opinion as I could, I'd say that's unlikely. She doesn't have any of the associated behaviors. Many children have imaginary friends, hers just happens to be more of a frenemy."

"Why would a kid imagine that there's someone out there trying to hunt them down and kill them?" Ken whistled. "That's really kinda weird."

"That poor girl." Ruby clucked her tongue. "I was talking with Michelle Butler the other day, the woman who's looking after her. Says Mila wakes up most nights with bad dreams, but won't make a sound. Apparently, the child is afraid the Shadow Man will punish her if she's loud."

"If I had to offer a guess," said Tegan, "I'd say someone may have attempted to kidnap her before and it left a mark."

Harper fidgeted at the Mossberg's strap. "Those idiots tried to kidnap me a couple times and I'm not jumping at shadows." She managed a weak smile. "Much."

"You're also basically an adult. Though, I suppose it's possible she *had* been abducted and managed to escape. That could explain the fear of making any noise at night. She... well, I didn't find any evidence of assault. When she first arrived, the poor girl had numerous cuts, bruises, and abrasions, but I attributed them to climbing around ruins. I suppose it's possible some of those bruises might have come from physical abuse."

"Maybe she just watched someone get taken and never saw them again?" asked Ken.

"Possible." Tegan furrowed her brow. "But, Harper, you're saying you think there really is someone out there who might be a threat to kids?"

"I don't know." She paced, breathing into her hands. "Sounds creepy, but sneaking around spying on people doesn't necessarily prove they're going to hurt anyone."

"No, but it damn sure implies it." Ken eyed the door. "It's worth at least some extra eyes on the area for a while."

"Yeah," said Harper. She stood a little taller, relieved that they didn't think her 'crying wolf.' The sense of vindication bolstered her confidence.

An exam room door opened, admitting Al Gonzalez into the hallway along with Dr. Khan. The men shook hands, seeming in good spirits. The doctor went left into the back of the building.

Al walked up to the group, waving a scrap of paper around. "Okay, I got my permission slip. Now what?"

Harper felt too awkward to give orders to a man older than her father. "I'll show you where the mayor's office is. You can talk to Anne-Marie about the house situation."

"Bit of a runaround, but I suppose it's a small price to pay for not having to deal with property taxes anymore."

"Heh, yeah." Ken laughed. "People don't seem to care much about money these days at all."

"Can't eat it. Can't drink it. Won't keep you warm," said Ruby. "Saw some kids tossing credit cards like them ninja star things. Least they still got some use."

Everyone chuckled.

Harper led Mr. Gonzalez out to the highway and down to the next cluster of buildings, a former office plaza that had become the town seat. She introduced him to Anne-Marie, and he re-explained his entire story about being in LA. Harper cringed at the end when he had a minor meltdown about 'little girls running around with cannons' and people just taking houses willy nilly. He didn't come off as barking at Anne-Marie personally, more at the situation, but the former airline executive didn't bat an eyelash at his histrionics.

"I'd say welcome to Evergreen, but you're already a resident." Anne-Marie gave him an iron smile. "However, I must ask that you respect our militia the way you would formerly have treated the sheriff's department deputies. Most of the militia we have now used to work for them. I understand you lived here before the war, but times have changed. If you can't handle that, you're free to settle elsewhere."

"Yeah, yeah." Al waved her off. "Not used to having kids wave shotguns in my face."

"You were pointing a gun at the Parkers and shouting," said Harper. "Would 'umm, excuse me sir' really have worked?"

He chuckled at her. "Maybe coming from you, it would have. Look. I'd just driven through hell to get back here and I found people in my house. Not like you've got signs up explaining everything. How would you have reacted?"

"Perhaps considering that civilization is somewhere between gone and knocked back a few centuries, with a little more restraint." Anne-Marie cocked an eyebrow. "Or did the Parkers threaten you with a loaded toddler?"

"Hey, can't be too careful with them little buggers. They're prone to randomly exploding," said Al. "Okay. Fair point. Used to get all sorts of worked up at slow drivers, but idiots in Civics don't have anything on frickin' airplanes crashed into the damn highway. Damn interstate was one giant mess. If I never see another FedEx plane again, it'll be too soon."

"You won't," said Harper. "They're all gone."

Al's irritated expression gave way to a mixture of shock and regret.' "Yeah, well... umm..."

At a nod from Anne-Marie, Ken handed him his .45. "Careful with this thing, huh?"

"Thanks. Sorry." He tucked it into an improvised holster on his belt.

Mayor Ned walked out of his office. "Oh, Al... hey. How goes it?"

"Who died and made *you* mayor of this place?" asked Al, grinning.

"Uhh, the last mayor." Ned chuckled. "Actually, I think she left town when the Army evacuated."

Harper stood there like a fifth wheel while the men got into a familiar conversation, suggesting they'd known each other for a while. She finally relaxed enough to sling the shotgun over her shoulder since Ned appeared to trust him. Al agreed to return to his Navy corpsman days and help out at the clinic. Anne-Marie told him to let the Parkers know she'll reassign them to another house if they wanted to move, but had no issues with them sharing the five-bedroom place.

*Wow, that must've been expensive.* Harper's mind wandered, reducing the men's conversation to a constant murmur of meaningless sound at the edge of her awareness. All the buildings and houses in Evergreen, heck the entire country even, represented tons of money people had once spent, never mind all the super-expensive skyscrapers, malls, bridges, and so on vaporized by the bombardment. They wouldn't last forever though, and with the total lack of infrastructure, no one could call contractors to come fix things or build new houses. If one of the kids put a soccer ball through a window, that window would stay broken forever. If a house burned to the ground, it wouldn't be replaced by anything resembling a real house.

Would dwellings start to look like heaps of patchwork scrap in a few decades? Would people end up in tent cities like refugee camps or maybe grass huts like some Amazon tribe? Sure, some houses from the 1900s still stood, some even older than that—but how long would any of them last now without professionals to repair things? Society might recover at some point. After all, they had 'real' houses in the Wild West, but people would need to re-learn how to build things without giant machines or power tools.

*Right now, I'd be so happy if we could get the lights to turn on. Or even like an oil lamp so we can see in the dark and don't have to go to bed at like eight. Where did the oil for those things even come from? Does anyone even remember how to make it?*

Though she felt safe in Evergreen, thinking about the future made her uneasy.

And the immediate future bothered her even more. She looked at the window, desperately wanting to be out there trying to find the bastard stalking children. The light struck her as telling.

*Oh, crap. School's let out already.*

"I, umm... need to go. Kids are out of school and they're too young to be home alone. You got this?" She looked up at Ken.

"Yeah. No problem." He patted her shoulder.

"Thanks!" She offered a quick nod to Mayor Ned, Anne-Marie, and Al, then rushed out the door.

Worry that something happened to her siblings on their way home pushed her jog up to a run.

# WINGING IT

A brief period of running around in panic gave way to elated relief when Harper found Madison, Jonathan, Lorelei, and Becca exploring still-empty houses on Pinecone Lane, a short distance south from home.

She remained calm, not even demanding they stop, staying with them as they played. Somewhat farther south, they found an indoor basketball gym next to an abandoned dentist's office. Miraculously, no one had looted the place… but then again, what use would anyone really have for mass quantities of basketballs? They played for a little while before she gathered the kids and brought them home for dinner.

Several big white towels from the shower area went with them.

Cliff cooked a whole chicken on the cinder block grill in the backyard. He cut the spine out, flattening the bird so it cooked faster. Predictably, Madison wept over the poor dead creature as if it had been a pet. Under the guise of consoling, Harper pulled her off out of earshot of Lorelei and explained about the need to keep an eye on the little one.

"Okay," said Madison in a hushed voice. "Is something wrong with her?"

"Lori is… umm. Well, you know how sometimes when you look at someone, you get that feeling like you should stay away from them?"

"Yeah." Madison nodded.

"Lori can't do that. She doesn't have the ability to pick up on whatever sense that warns us about someone."

Madison's eyes widened. "Do you really think there's a bad guy?"

"I'm sure there's someone sneaking around, but I don't really know what they're up to. Better to be careful."

"Okay."

"Thanks, Termite." Harper hugged her. "Are you doing okay?"

"I dunno. Still sad, but I can deal. Mom and Dad would want us to keep going, right?"

"Absolutely."

Lorelei had apparently decided to attach herself to Jonathan that evening, so a chance for speaking to him didn't present itself until well after dinner when everyone went to bed. Harper poked her head into his room. While the boy had it all to himself, his room barely had enough space to hold a twin box spring and mattress without a frame. A strip of carpet roughly two feet wide between the bed and the wall held his modest pile of clothing as well as a few toys.

"Hey, got a sec?" asked Harper.

"Yeah." He lifted his head to look at her.

She sat on the edge of the mattress, facing the door, and explained the issue with Lorelei. "So, it's really important that you help me keep her safe, okay?"

"I will."

Squealing giggles came from across the hall.

"It stinks we have to go to bed so early all the time," said Jonathan. "I used to stay up until ten."

"Wow, that's pretty late for a kid your age. My parents didn't let me go to bed at ten until I was like thirteen. Maddie got to stay up 'til nine before I did though, but she had way more homework than I did at the same age."

He grinned. "Maybe if teachers hadn't given so much homework, people wouldn't have been mad enough to nuke everyone."

Harper laughed. "I think the problem was a little more complicated than excessive homework."

He stuck out his tongue.

"Night, kiddo."

"Night, Harp."

She stepped out into the hall—and came face to face with Cliff, practically colliding with him.

Harper gasped and jumped back, light-headed and near to fainting.

"Christ on a crutch," muttered Cliff, appearing equally startled. He caught her by the arms to keep her from falling over backward. "What's got you so jumpy?"

Once she remembered how to breathe again, she coughed and fell against him, holding on until the trembling stopped. She told him about the possible creep, but mostly, she'd just freaked out because he'd snuck up on her in the dark, even if by accident.

"Sorry. So damn used to covert ops, I just exude quiet. It becomes a lifestyle. They even trained us how to fart without a sound."

She laughed. "That's so wrong."

"Possible it's the same person who's been swiping food from the quartermaster."

"Someone's stealing food?" Harper blinked.

"Not tons. But there have been multiple break-ins at the storage area. No one's sure how they're getting in, since there's no damage and the door's still locked. I'm thinking it might be an inside job. Someone's probably sneaking food out rather than 'breaking in.' But, we're watching the place."

"Why would a food thief spy on kids?"

"Might have just been hiding and waiting for 'em to go by."

Harper folded her arms. "Mila said she was followed."

"Mila." He quirked an eyebrow.

"She's not insane. Just... creepy."

"Curtains with spider decorations are creepy. That girl's going to slit someone's throat before she's fifteen."

"Please tell me you're making a sick joke and not getting a feel off her like you did with Tyler."

He patted her arm. "Mostly sick joke. She's young enough she might grow out of it. What's your gut say about this guy sneaking around?"

"Danger." She pressed both hands into her stomach. "I'm scared he's going to hurt someone. Pretty sure he was watching me and I couldn't see him, but I just had this feeling like he wanted to hurt me."

"All right. I'll see if Roy's up for checking around the north tonight."

"Cool."

"Heard you had some excitement today."

"Yeah." She filled him in on Al Gonzalez. "What if whoever lived here before comes back?"

"What else would we do but let them have their house?"

Harper stared down at her sneakers. "Yeah, you're right. Guess I'm starting to get used to it here."

"Go to bed, kiddo."

She raspberried him. "Night, *Dad.*"

Two days came and went with little excitement.

Al settled into his old house with the Parkers. Despite the initial hostility between them, he wound up reminding Diane of her father. None of the kids had come forward with any more stories of being watched, though several militia members had received reports of someone or something creeping around the west part of town after dark. One person described an unusually round bear.

It frustrated Harper that no one had been able to find who or whatever skulked around Evergreen, but only a handful of militia patrolled at night due to the limited number of lanterns available, and those wouldn't last forever. Even though the school and the clinic kinda had electricity back, neither one had any exterior illumination. No street lights worked, no houses had power, leaving only the moon and stars to see by after dark. Cliff had been used to night watch without a light source, and he'd been working on training a few people. She'd gotten the thirty-second version: stay as quiet as possible and move slow. If she thought someone approached, sit still and look for motion. Also, peripheral vision worked better in the dark than direct sight.

Despite it being late morning, Harper still thought about those techniques while patrolling. Every time she heard a sound that might have come from a person, she'd freeze in her tracks and listen, hearing Cliff say 'the human eye is attracted to motion' in her head. It felt ridiculous to be standing there out in the open instead of diving for cover, but at night, that wouldn't matter. Without the sunlight, the darkness would conceal her more than the sudden, rapid motion of a dive.

Also, since she didn't wear anything even close to camo, standing still in the daytime wouldn't help much. However, she considered it decent practice since Walter would eventually add her to the night rotation. She kept her fingers crossed that wouldn't happen for a few years at least, until all the kids she had to watch reached an age where they could be alone. Adding Lorelei to the family bought her more time.

Rustling to her left drew nearer, fast enough that she scrambled to get the shotgun off her shoulder. She pivoted toward the motion, but stopped short of aiming at a Mom-aged woman with chestnut brown hair and a frightened expression. It took her a few seconds to remember the woman's name, Katherine Bowden. Her son Noah turned thirteen back in January.

"Harper," whispered Katherine. "Someone's broken into the house."

"Are they still there?"

Katherine looked back over her shoulder at the tree-studded hill she'd come down. "I don't think so. Some food and my gun are missing."

Harper nodded, then hurried up the incline, cutting across properties to the east, heading for a house that faced the next street over. As with most houses no longer occupied by their pre-war owners, the locks had been removed from the front door with the exception of the deadbolt. She entered with the Mossberg raised, aiming around while searching upstairs and down.

A scattering of granola bar wrappers littered the kitchen floor near the door to the yard, along with a muddy sneaker print. It looked larger than her shoe, and wider, so she didn't think a child had done this—though she had seen some freshman boys with big feet. After clearing the basement, she felt certain no one remained hiding in the house, and returned outside to Mrs. Bowden.

"There's no one in there anymore. It's safe."

"You saw the wrappers on the floor? The thief ate three of them right there, and took the whole rest of the box."

"Yeah. I saw. Someone's been stealing food from the quartermaster's."

Katherine frowned. "Can't say I'm surprised. She's not giving us enough."

"Liz is doing her best to make sure everyone gets a fair amount to survive on. Things will improve once the farm is at full capacity."

"It's hard telling Noah we have to make the food last." Katherine shot a worried stare at the cabinets. "Boys his age need to eat."

"I know. I know. We're doing the best we can with what's here. When did this happen?"

"Late last night. Whoever it was came in while we slept. Didn't notice until morning."

"Where was the gun?" asked Harper. "Did they go into your bedroom and not wake you up?"

"Umm…" Katherine looked at the floor, seeming like an older version of Madison caught doing something wrong.

*So weird. She's old enough to be my mother and she's like afraid of getting in trouble.* "Mrs. Bowden?"

"It's... it was on the coffee table. I know, stupid of me to leave it there. But I didn't want it going off in the middle of the night right next to me."

"Guns don't just randomly shoot by themselves, but I know they can be scary if people aren't used to them." She bit her tongue before saying something like maybe she's better off not having it. "So the thief didn't go upstairs to the bedrooms?"

"If they did, we didn't notice."

Harper examined the back door, discovering a faint muddy smear on the inside knob. Not like fingerprints would be of any use. *Grr. What would real cops do to investigate this?* She took the little notepad Walter gave her out of her back pocket and scribbled down the particulars of the event with a stubby pencil.

"I'll file a report. I'm guessing you don't know the serial number of the stolen gun?"

Mrs. Bowden stared at her, clueless.

"Figured. What kind of gun was it?"

"A little black one."

"Handgun... do you know what size bullets it used?"

"The ones that are round on one end and flat on the other."

Harper's eye twitched. "Did it have a part in the middle that spins around or did the bullets go in a box that went in the handle?"

"The box thing. It's pretty small, only took seven bullets at a time. Noah said it's a Sig. Does that help?"

"Yes." She smiled. "Probably a 9mm. Okay, that helps a lot. Black you said?"

Katherine nodded.

"Got it. If we find it, I'll see it's returned to you."

"You don't sound like you expect to find the thief."

Harper stashed the notepad back in her pocket, then slid the pencil into her front pocket. "It's not like police technology is what it used to be. We're pretty much stuck looking for someone with a box of Nutri-Grain bars and a handgun. Though, I doubt anyone would walk for miles specifically to target your house. Someone must have randomly come this way. I'll check other houses in the area. Might be someone snuck into town without going through the admission process."

"Okay. Thank you."

*Maybe Roy will know what to do. He used to be a city cop. Or Walter. He worked for the sheriff.*

Harper exited the Bowden house via the back door, but couldn't find any noticeable trail of footprints. She knew the two nearest houses contained official residents, both with children and both likely away working on the farm at this hour. It didn't seem likely that they would be willing to steal, but then again, they had children to feed, too. People could do desperate things for their kids.

She went to the left house and knocked. When no one answered, she entered, shotgun out, and conducted a similar search as she'd done in Katherine's place. She mostly looked for signs of burglary or someone in there who shouldn't be, but kept an eye out for a box of granola bars. Finding nothing there after about a half hour, she went to the next nearest house on the right side and repeated the process. The normality of the homes got under her skin, triggering an upwelling of sorrow. Except for the lack of power, they looked like ordinary houses where people had gotten up and left for no reason. She could almost pretend the war hadn't happened.

*Heh. I'm basically playing Skyrim for real... just walking into people's houses and looking at their stuff. All these things people bought. Televisions, stereos, video game systems... Who used to live here? Are they still alive? I bet they miss their home.* She missed hers too, but had already tried her best to let go of it. She couldn't return to the house she'd grown up in. Mostly because it held the bodies of her parents. That, and wanting to avoid abduction and assault. Also, starving kinda sucked, too.

The third most distant house from Katherine's had no official occupant, so she didn't bother knocking. After searching the kitchen and finding nothing, she went down the hall on the ground floor, performing a cursory room-to-room sweep, including closets.

At a *thump* on the ceiling, she froze, gazing up.

*Someone's in here.*

She fast-crept back to the living room and aimed up the stairs, listening for a moment, but hearing nothing. Step by step, she advanced to the second floor. The eerie feeling of not being alone and not knowing who she might encounter made the hairs on her arms stand on end. With each room she peered into and found empty, anxiety grew that some giant, hairy wild man who'd been living rough since the bombs fell would leap out at her with a knife. What if the cow hadn't fallen to a mountain lion? Could a person have done that, the same person who'd been sneaking around town? Maybe she had gotten worried over nothing and he hadn't been eyeing the kids with bad intentions but simply didn't want to be discovered?

How would he react to being caught?

... and he had a gun.

Harper held her breath and nudged the last door in the upstairs hall open with the shotgun. A queen-sized bed appeared to have been used recently by the world's most restless sleeper, the fitted sheet peeled away from one corner, the spread on the floor.

The sense that someone to her right breathed reached her consciousness.

Expecting attack, Harper spun and aimed at a figure hiding in the corner, shouting, "Don't move!" before her brain processed the information coming from her eyes: she had her shotgun trained on a slender girl around the same age as her with long, straight brown hair, wearing only a delicate gold chain necklace and several hickeys.

The naked cheerleader screamed, thrusting her hands up as if being robbed.

"Oh, shit..." Harper started to relax, but strong arms closed around her from behind in a bear hug.

"Beth, run!" yelled a teen boy.

Harper rammed her head backward into his face. He emitted a muffled *oof* and his grip slackened. Cliff's training kicked in, and without even thinking about it, she hammered the butt end of the shotgun into the guy's crotch as hard as she could.

He emitted a pitiful moan and collapsed to the rug in a fetal pose, cradling himself.

"Holy shit!" said Beth. "Why did you do that? Jaden, are you okay? Oh, God, you like totally crushed his balls."

Harper instinctively backed off to the side, keeping both of them in front of her. When she noticed the boy also had nothing on, she cringed. A few empty beer cans lay on the rug, along with a pile of clothing.

The boy made a *meep* noise.

"Sorry. But you shouldn't have grabbed me like that. Are you bleeding?"

He emitted a moan that mostly sounded like a no.

"What the hell is wrong with you?" yelled Beth. "Just walking into a house?"

Harper frowned at her. "Seriously? You two sneak in here to have sex and you're bitching at me? I'm on the militia, investigating a break-in. This isn't your house. No one is supposed to be in this one."

At the word 'militia,' Beth lost her antagonistic attitude and resumed cowering in the corner. "Are we in trouble?"

Jaden moaned again.

"No. There may be an unidentified person sneaking around town, so I was checking everywhere around the break-in." Since neither teen struck her as likely to be a threat, she averted her gaze. "Like I said, this isn't anyone's house yet, so if you guys want to borrow it, go for it."

Beth darted over to the bedspread, wrapped herself in it, and took a knee beside Jaden. "Let me see. Oh, gawd… it's bruised."

Jaden emitted a pained grunt.

Harper cringed. "Do you need help getting him to the clinic?"

"You've done enough already," muttered Beth.

"He ambushed me from behind. He's lucky all I did was hit him. And, seriously? What kind of dumbass are you, grabbing me like that? If you pounced on me just a little bit harder, I could have clenched up on the trigger and killed Beth."

"Thought," rasped Jaden, "you were gonna kill her."

"Umm. Do killers usually yell 'don't move?' You damn near *made* me shoot her by jumping on me."

He took a few deep breaths, then coughed. "What the hell was I supposed to do? I walk outta the bathroom and see someone pointing a gun at my girl."

"You could have thrown something off to the side to distract. Don't jump on a person with a rifle until it's not pointed at anyone you don't want to see dead." Harper slung it over her shoulder. "Look, I'm sorry for hurting you. Bad situation all around. You grabbed me and I just… training took over."

Jaden sat up and examined his nether regions.

Harper turned away, blushing.

"Think I'm okay. Gonna be sore for a bit. So, wow, they really made you a cop?"

"Basically," said Harper, without looking.

"Right on. Ow. Yeah, this is gonna be sore for a while."

Harper looked down at the carpet in front of her sneakers. Sudden worry that she'd get in trouble and kicked off the militia turned her back into the fidgety, shy version of herself from before the war. But, he had grabbed her. True, she probably should have tried yelling get off me and saying militia or something, but a real bad guy wouldn't have cared. Confidence returned. No, she did exactly as Cliff would have wanted her to do when grabbed by an unknown party. Fortunately, her attacker turned out to be a horny high school kid and not a crazed recluse. At the sudden realization she'd been in the arms of a naked man, she blushed scarlet.

"Seriously, we're not in like trouble or anything?" asked Beth.

"Who would we get in trouble with?" asked Jaden in a lifeless tone. "Our parents?"

Beth stared at him for a few seconds, her lip quivering, then burst into tears.

"Hey… hey… sorry." He put an arm around her. "I meant things are different now. No one's gonna care that we're together. It's just you and me, Beth."

"Until you're gone, too," said Beth past sniffles.

Harper edged to the door, whispering, "I'll just give you guys some privacy."

"Look, I know we're young, but it's like we went back in time. People used to get married at our age. I love you, Beth, and I'll always be here for you."

*Okay, nothing more for me to do here…* She slipped out into the hall and made her way downstairs. *Well, could've been worse I suppose… I could've walked in on them right in the middle of it.*

Her cheeks aflame, Harper hurried off down the street with zero interest in exploring other houses. She'd talk to Walter or Roy about the break in as soon as possible, but it could probably wait until her patrol shift ended.

*If someone's watching the kids, they might be at the school, waiting to see who walks away alone.* She changed course, heading at a fast walk to the school building.

# ROACHES

Harper roamed around the school building four times, searching all the places she figured someone might hide.

That she didn't find anyone offered relief and worry in equal measure. Class let out sooner than she expected. Based on the position of the sun, it couldn't be much past noon. Confused, she headed to the front of the building to walk her siblings home, but upon noticing the kids all remained lined up as if about to go on an organized field trip, she remembered today—Tuesday—was a farm day. She decided to join them, walking along beside Madison and Jonathan as the teachers herded the class past the building, across the sports fields behind it, and up a forested hill to Route 74. Upon noticing Harper there, Lorelei broke away from the smaller kids' up front and ran over.

Madison didn't seem too thrilled with being marched around in a line like the world hadn't been broken and she still had to obey teachers, but offered only a few grumbles on the way to the farm on the opposite side of the highway.

*Wow, they're going to walk the class across the highway? That's like as wrong as me going into the school with a loaded shotgun.*

Still, not like any cars would hit anyone. Except for having to cross a chain link fence and four lanes of empty pavement, the farm sat conveniently close to the school. The ground had a noticeable incline, but they didn't exactly have to worry about big farm machines being able to drive around. Harper coughed at the overly earthy scent in the air, like she'd gone into the garden section at Home Depot and a giant dog had an accident. Of course, the poo smell came from the animal pens farther north where a handful of cows, chickens, and even alpacas milled around.

Approximately 200 people pitched in on the farm, give or take based on what work needed to be done on any given day. Planting and harvesting would require the most bodies. In between, a smaller group took care of irrigation, constructing new planting beds and building pens for a gradually growing stock of animals. Only four people in town really understood farming as they'd worked on or owned farms before the war. The most knowledgeable, Jim Rollins, had been named 'farm coordinator' by the mayor. They had at least three actual plumbers, who'd been focusing their efforts mostly on building an irrigation system to draw from a small creek west of the farm.

For the next three or so hours, the kids broke up into groups that helped out here and there with various tasks or simply followed one of the experienced farmers while they went about their work, describing every step of the process and fielding questions from the kids. Harper didn't want to interfere, so she didn't hover too close to her siblings, instead 'patrolling' the area while the children attended to their duties. Madison wound up with a team learning how to take care of chickens. Predictably, she cried the entire time they discussed how to properly kill them when their time came to be dinner. Though her little sister had begrudgingly accepted eating meat, she doubted Madison would ever be able to kill an animal. Jonathan went with a group to check out the potato fields. Harper noted that he seemed to be sticking close to Mila.

*Does he have a crush on her or is he just being protective?*

The smallest kids, including Lorelei, went seed planting in a newly-tilled area.

Except for Madison's reaction to the killing discussion, the kids all seemed to be enjoying the time outside. Mila did try to lurk at the edges and be unnoticed, but Jonathan kept encouraging her to participate. She thought it cute, but the girl's reaction worried her. She kept looking around with a fearful, intense stare, not making faces like a surly introvert forced to be with people.

*It's almost like she's expecting to be attacked at any minute.*

Harper hadn't exactly been around a farm before, but this one felt massive. Seeing all the plants growing, the animal pens fuller than last time she'd come by, and everyone working to keep it going made it seem possible they'd actually survive. She kicked a few dirt clods while meandering along, daydreaming about the mall, watching movies, video games, hanging out with her friends, or sitting in history class trying to stay awake.

*Mr. Collins said it's easier to destroy than create. It only took hours to undo like 200 years of advancement. So much for flying cars and space ships in 2219. We'll be lucky if 2219 feels like 2019. Wait, no. I hope it's not that bad. People were too shitty to each other.*

Laughter came from a group near the edge of the farm. Harper glanced over at a cluster of hockey players, Zach at their center. She recognized Kirk beside him, but not the freakishly tall boy on the right, Paul according to the name stitched on his jacket. The fourth kid had the size of a junior but a babyish face more like a twelve-year-old's. Of the four, only he lacked any facial hair. His jacket bore the name Mike.

Zach gestured at another boy around the same age who had a light brown complexion. That boy didn't have a varsity jacket on, only a plain white T-shirt liberally soaked with sweat and dirt. Long, straight black hair hung a little past his shoulders, draped forward as he worked taking green leafy plants out of a wheelbarrow and stuffing them into a neat row along a plowed field. She couldn't remember his name, but knew he'd also come in with the team. He had to be sixteen or seventeen, too old for school, and had likely been at the farm all day.

She scowled at the jocks, wondering how long Ned would allow them to just stand there without working. They'd been hovering around the Hispanic kid for at least half an hour. If they'd been assigned to the farm, they ignored their jobs.

"Hey Ruiz," said Zach, "not even a nuclear war gets your people out of doing farm work, huh?"

The other three laughed.

"You guys are working on the farm, too *amigo*," said Ruiz. "Guess your Dad had no one to, uhh, *donate* to so you got a better job, right?"

Two of the boys laughed. Zach and Kirk glared.

"Eat a dick, Logan," said Zach.

"He already has," muttered Kirk.

The boys laughed until Logan calmly said, "Aww, Kirk... that was supposed to be our little secret. Now everyone knows."

Kirk rushed forward, raising his fists. Logan dropped a small hand shovel and took a step back, falling into an odd combat stance with his arms slack at his sides.

"Watch out for that Mexican kung fu," said Zach. "He hits you once, you'll spend all day sleeping."

"Wait, for real?" asked Mike.

"No, he's trying to make a siesta joke." Logan scratched at his eyebrow. "You're forgetting your audience, Zach. If there's any thinking required, they won't get it."

Kirk took a swipe at Logan, but he evaded with a fluid lean.

"Ooh, Lo's got moves," said Zach.

Harper hurried over. "Hey! Knock it off."

"Uh oh," said Kirk. "We're in trouble now. Here comes the poh-leece."

Three of the varsity boys laughed, though Zach didn't.

Mike pointed at her. "Maybe you should start with the redhead first, Kirk. But be careful. She looks like she could take you. Can't fight the taco boss until you get past the miniboss."

Harper shook her head. "Seriously? Is that kid actually twelve or does he only look and talk like it?"

The boys—except for Mike—laughed.

She gestured at Logan. "Don't you guys have something better to do than stand around being jackasses? You've been hanging out here for at least a half hour. Haven't you taken work assignments by now?"

"Oh, yeah, we might not get paid if they catch us goofing off," muttered Zach.

The other three chuckled.

"It's okay, they don't bother me," said Logan.

"That's not the point." She sighed at him, then stared at Kirk. "One letter on a schedule is the only reason you guys are still even alive. If that had been a home game, you would've all been in Colorado Springs when a giant damn nuke went off, and you'd be dust. Do I really need to spell it out to you that there's no such thing as paychecks anymore? No food magically showing up in grocery stores. You're not working to earn a couple bucks so you can go drinking. This is us trying to stay alive. And if you're planning on sitting around doing nothing, letting everyone else risk their lives or bust their butts, you should find a new town."

Zach approached Harper, patting Kirk's shoulder on the way, which caused him to back off from Logan. "So, hey, girl. How about you and me go do something fun?"

"I can't. I'm working. Please, just leave him alone."

"Working?" Paul laughed. "You?"

"What, you like into Mexicans or something?" Zach glanced at Logan.

She briefly considered telling him 'what would happen' if he didn't leave Logan alone like some character out of a movie, but couldn't find it in her to make threats. "Look, if you guys want to remain here in Evergreen, you will need to stop causing trouble."

Zach laughed. "Forget him, baby. Neither one of us needs to be here right now. Let's go somewhere quiet."

"Who is this chick?" asked Paul, his voice way deep for an eighteen-year-old. "You've been standing around for hours and you're giving us attitude about not working?"

She looked up at him, his chin higher than the top of her head. "I'm on the militia. Basically a cop. I'm here to make sure everyone stays safe."

Zach appeared to be fighting the urge to smile, while Kirk, Paul, and Mike all openly laughed at her.

"*You* are going to protect *me*?" Paul laughed again. "Look at this tiny chick with a giant shotgun. Bet you couldn't even fire that thing. It would put you straight on your ass."

"Probably jump straight out of her hands," said Mike.

Harper folded her arms. "I didn't realize 'jerk' was an actual occupation."

The boys snickered.

"Oh, no. We're 'jerks,'" whispered Kirk. "Better watch the language, there kid."

"How'd they wind up giving you that damn thing?" asked Paul.

"Maybe she likes holding the big rods?" asked Mike.

Zach whacked him on the shoulder with a backhand. "Dude. Don't talk to her like that."

She considered saying the gun belonged to her dead father, but these four would only mock that, too. "I had it when I got here. Didn't want to surrender it, so I joined the militia. And yes, I have fired it."

"Ever shoot anyone?" Zach leaned grinned while making finger pistols.

"Yes," said Harper, deadpan. "I've lost count."

All five of the boys fell quiet, looking at her. Zach swallowed, unnerved by the distance in her eyes. He glanced away after a moment, muttered, "C'mon, guys, let's finish that damn plow shit," and walked off.

Paul, Mike, and Kirk regarded Logan with disdain, her with a mixture of annoyance and curiosity, then followed Zach, whispering amongst themselves, mocking her calling them 'jerks.'

She shook her head. "Sorry about those jackasses."

"It's okay. They've been like that for years. Used to get the 'Mexican on ice' jokes."

"Ugh. Some people."

"They always said cockroaches would survive the nuclear war." He chuckled. "Guess they were right."

"Hah."

He offered a hand. "Hi. I'm Logan. I used to play hockey and go to school. Now I plant"—he swiped the bundle he dropped and held it up —"whatever the hell these are."

"Turnips?" asked Harper, trying not to look into his rich brown eyes... or picture him dressed like a teenage Captain Jack Sparrow, which his long hair and wispy beard would totally work for. She almost blurted something stupid like 'gotta get back to work' and hurried away from him, but he didn't give off vibes like he planned to suggest they go make out somewhere... so she stayed put.

"Could be turnips, yeah." Logan held the bundle up to study. "Hmm, probably are."

She bit her lip, worrying that if she got to know him, he'd wind up being bonkers, too. Or something else would happen. Or maybe that uneasy feeling swimming around in her gut meant she should run like hell while she still could. He might be crazy. But... meds would've run out a long time ago. *Oh, what are the odds...? I can at least be friendly.* "Hi. I'm Harper. I, uhh, used to be the quiet girl no one noticed. Now I'm a deputy... or something."

He smiled. "Sounds like you've got quite a story. Maybe you'll tell me sometime?"

She shrugged one shoulder. "Maybe. You probably got a story, too."

"Not really. Just a kid from the suburbs who liked hockey, got on the right bus at the right time. Trying to stay alive like everyone else."

"I'm sorry about your parents or family."

"Thank you." He raised his brows slightly, an inquisitive look in his eye.

She bowed her head. "Yeah."

"Sorry about your parents."

"Thanks."

"Guess we're both war orphans then."

She closed her eyes as the last few minutes of Mom and Dad's life replayed in her thoughts. Except for one cheerleader, every teen on that bus lost their whole families. The two she'd caught having—rather after—

sex had lost their parents, too. 'Orphan,' though technically true, didn't feel right. The word made her think of a lost, helpless child unable to fend for themselves—like Lorelei had been, or Jonathan. Some part of her still felt like a lost little kid not ready to be on her own. Hell, she hadn't wanted to go to any college too far away to keep living at home. But, she didn't feel helpless anymore. Sixteen, seventeen, eighteen in this new world had become adults, not orphans.

*I've killed at least five, no maybe ten people, but I've never...* She blushed. *Am I still innocent? I'm not an orphan. Orphan sounds like it should be someone innocent.*

That girl, Beth, hadn't ever killed anyone, but she and Jaden had sex. Did that make her more or less innocent than her, a virgin with multiple people's blood on her hands?

Madison had neither killed anyone nor had sex. She didn't even fathom the concept of it yet. But she'd watched their parents die. Did she still count as innocent? And what about Lorelei? That girl appeared to lack any understanding of evil—or maybe she understood it too well and had chosen to simply ignore it.

What defined innocence?

Did any of it matter anymore?

Why did she care how she 'ranked' on some scorecard of innocence?

No one seemed to care that Harper had shot people. Of course, she only defended herself. She figured the townspeople wouldn't approve of her running around randomly blowing people's heads off.

"Umm?" Harper kicked at the ground.

"Yeah?"

She looked up at him. "What do you think it means to be innocent?"

Logan leaned back, squinting at the sky, lost in thought for a while. "I think we stop being innocent the moment we understand that we're going to die someday."

"Wow..." She exhaled. "That's... deep. Going to have to think about that for a while to process it."

"Not the answer you were expecting?" He crouched and set the possibly-turnip bundle in the ground. "My dad used to say stuff like that all the time. Drove my little sister nuts. She used to call him 'fortune cookie.'"

She cringed. "Sorry."

"It's okay. He's somewhere better off now. Always said he hoped when his time came it was fast and he didn't feel anything. He pretty much got his wish."

"I'm really sorry…" Harper shivered, thinking about losing her sister. "I know everyone says Springs got leveled, but maybe they could've made it somehow?"

Logan looked up at her with a doubtful expression. "Yeah, I suppose."

"Harp!" shouted Madison in the distance.

She glanced over at her little sister, leading a charge of kids heading her way: Jonathan, Lorelei, Becca, and Mila—though she didn't run as much as tolerate being pulled along.

"Guess they're free for the day." Harper looked at him, bit her lip, and glanced away. "Gotta get them home. Nice meeting you."

Logan picked up his trowel and dug a hole for the next plant. "Great meeting you, too. Maybe we can share our stories sometime."

"Yeah, I think I'd like that."

Madison skidded to a stop next to her. "You have a boyfriend?"

"Uhh, no," stammered Harper. "He's just a friend."

"Hi!" chimed Lorelei, before leaping to hug him, almost knocking him over.

He laughed, springing to his feet and spinning her around a few times before setting her down. "Hello there."

"He's going to die," deadpanned Mila.

Everyone except Lorelei stared at her, aghast.

Mila teased her foot at the turnip leaves. "Eventually."

"Why do you say stuff like that?" whispered Jonathan.

"I dunno," mumbled Mila.

"If he isn't your boyfriend, why are you blushing?" asked Madison.

"Because you're assuming too much." Harper couldn't look anywhere near Logan. "Uhh, see ya around."

"Later." Logan smiled at them, picked up another bundle of greens, and stuffed them in the hole he'd dug.

Harper set off across the field toward the highway. As soon as she reached the road, she swung the Mossberg off her shoulder and held it at the ready. She hated that walking home felt like navigating a dangerous environment. Evergreen wasn't supposed to come with constant worry, but until she had an answer for who or what lurked around spying on kids and breaking into houses, she couldn't let her guard down.

Not even for a moment.

# SO MUCH FOR SAFE

The next afternoon, Harper headed over to the quartermaster's building.

Based on where people lived in town, everyone had specific days, once a week, to request food. This controlled traffic at the center and prevented chaos. Harper's house on Hilltop Drive fell in the Wednesday band.

A small sign on the grass next to the road leading up to it read Life Care Center. The place had been some kind of senior citizen facility before the war, but no one mentioned anything about it, and no elderly people still lived there.

*Guess the Army took them somewhere.*

The map on the wall in Mayor Ned's office showed the huge Y-shaped building as the largest in the vicinity, probably why the town chose it to house the food. That, and it had an industrial kitchen. If ever they managed to get power working again, 'town meals' would become more common. Far easier to electrify one big kitchen than provide juice to every house.

As no recent scavenging runs had come in with an entire tractor-trailer load of provisions, the place didn't look outwardly special. That meant the food thief somehow knew where to go without simply seeing a pile of stuff outside. Then again, they might have observed the townspeople going in and out of the place like a supermarket.

After a brief glance around in search of someone hiding nearby, she entered and headed down the hall to the large room set up for distribution. Numerous tables bearing pre-assembled bundles of foodstuffs based on family size filled the space behind an improvised 'counter' made of more folding tables placed end-to-end across the room as a barrier. Three men, two women, and Beth worked there. The instant the girl saw her walk in, she turned scarlet in the face and hurried to the back of the room, avoiding eye contact.

Harper almost called out 'how's Jaden,' but kept quiet despite her being sincerely concerned about him; she worried the girl would take it as a taunt.

Liz Trujillo, the official quartermaster, sat at a desk all the way to the right, going over entries in a logbook. Harper waved at her in greeting and approached the counter blocking off the rear two-thirds of the room. A group of about fifteen people, some with toddlers in tow, waited their turn in front of it. The six clerks lined up on one side of the counter, checking people off on the food tracking sheets, then running into the maze behind them to fetch an appropriate bundle.

*Ugh. I'm going to be stuck here past when school lets out.* She considered bailing and coming back later for the food, but couldn't risk missing the day. Not like they'd deny her food if she showed up on Thursday instead of Wednesday, but she didn't want to make a scene or be yelled at— thanks to a trace of old, timid Harper poking out from beneath the new outer shell she'd been growing.

More people filled in behind her as the ones in front approached the table and left carrying their allotments. *Crap. If I leave, I'll be here all damn night.* She closed her eyes and asked the universe to watch over the kids for the few minutes they'd be alone. They knew that if she didn't show up at the school to walk them home, they should go straight there and stay inside. Being on the militia, she might have to deal with an issue that wouldn't simply let her 'clock out' because kids had to go home from school.

Finally, after almost an hour, her turn came. By then, some sixty other people had joined the queue behind her.

Patricia Rivera, the clerk she approached, looked up with a smile.

"Hi," said Harper. "Here to pick up."

"Oh, hey." Patricia traced her finger down a sheet of handwritten notes. "Four, right?"

"Five. We took Lorelei in… months ago."

"Oh. Duh. Sorry. That's right. There it is. Under Cliff Barton?"

"Yeah."

"Be right back." Patricia walked back from the 'counter' in search of a bundle appropriate for a family of five with three kids.

Liz approached. "Hey, Harper?"

"Yeah?"

"Has anyone over there made any progress figuring out who the hell is stealing? Stuff has been disappearing, but no one is admitting to taking anything. Can't find any sign of a break in, and none of the locks or windows on the place are broken."

"They didn't bust out the locks?"

"Apparently not."

"No I mean the town," said Harper. "Like they did to most of the houses."

"Oh... no. The sheriff's office had a full set of keys for this place, so did the fire department. You know, in case anything happened and they had to evacuate the elders who used to be here. Thought they'd tell you that. Anyway, between its size and security, they figured we'd use it to keep the food. Either that or the high school, but no one wanted to walk all the damn way south to eat."

Harper laughed, thinking about the day she spent getting a 'tour' of the south part of Evergreen and meeting Janice Holt, the militia's second in command. Evergreen High School sat way the hell south from here, basically at the southernmost end of the town, beyond Evergreen Lake. With a few exceptions, pretty much the whole area south of the Safeway on Route 74 consisted of individual homes. Janice operated out of the old sheriff's department building, managing the forty or so militia volunteers who patrolled down there. She cringed at the thought of having to cover such a wide area, but on the other hand, one air horn bleep would attract like a dozen people for backup, whereas up here, she'd be lucky to have three show up.

"Yeah, that's a haul," said Harper. "Too far to walk carrying a box of food. But the people who live down there have to come all the way up here... so, yeah. I guess since this is right next to the farm, it makes more sense."

"That's true. Could be we end up splitting into two distribution centers eventually. Assuming we don't get cleaned out by thieves."

"Sorry. I haven't heard anything yet."

Liz sighed in a 'figures, you're just a kid, didn't expect you to know much' way. "At first, I thought it might've been one of the clerks helping themselves as there's no damage. That doesn't fit with me though. I trust my people. But, someone's gotta do something since shit's gettin' real."

"Getting real?"

Patricia returned with a pair of cloth shopping bags. "You know the drill, hon. Gonna need the bags back."

"We're already rationing tight," said Liz. "People keep stealing, we're gonna be finding ourselves short. I give it another week at most before we're at calorie levels where no one is eating enough. Think people are complainin' now, you ain't seen a damn thing yet."

Harper winced. "I'll let Mr. Holman know it's getting bad."

"Oh, I already did that. Twice today in fact. Keep your eyes and ears open huh?"

"Sure. I will."

She collected the two bags of food—mostly canned goods, some boxed pasta, and a loaf of Bobby's handmade bread. Scavenging runs had brought back a good amount of flour in addition to cans. Thinking about all the frozen food, produce, and meat that spoiled in the aftermath of no electricity made her sad. So much food wasted. Of course, as Madison so often pointed out when things had been normal, restaurants and cafeterias—especially the military—used to throw out enough edible food to feed every homeless person ten times over every day.

*At least no one's homeless anymore. A place might not have power or heat, but there's plenty of empty houses for the taking.* A person didn't own a house or land anymore because some bank somewhere said so—they owned it because their firearms did the talking. Or, like Evergreen, some combination of a small government *and* firearms.

Harper trudged at a rapid walk down Route 74 to Hilltop Drive. The allotment bags didn't feel as heavy as they had even last week. Clear evidence that the town ran low on food worsened her worries. As much as it would horrify Madison, she hoped the guys would be successful while hunting soon. A deer or five would go a long way to helping everyone not starve.

The second she entered the house, Madison, Jonathan, and Becca jumped up from the couch and proceeded to all talk at the same time, in the middle of a freak-out. Lorelei sat on the recliner where Cliff usually read, playing with two dolls, a perfect picture of calm.

"Guys, guys, guys," said Harper, holding the food bags up. "Give me a second."

She waded among the kids and headed to the kitchen.

"Harp!" Madison pulled at her. "You're not listening."

"I can't listen to all three of you screaming at once." She set the bags on the counter. "What?"

"We saw someone watching us walk home from school," yelled Madison, her hazel eyes huge with fear.

Jonathan nodded. "Yeah, he started following us, too. So we ran as fast as we could."

"It was so scary," said Becca.

*Shit! There really is someone... Lori's going to run right over and hug him.* She looked around the kitchen, as if an answer sat in one of the cabinets. Part of her wanted to race out there with her shotgun and hunt the guy down. *Son of a bitch, I should've kept looking the other day. I know I heard someone.* Leaving the kids here while she went hunting didn't sound like a good idea. Bringing them with her while she went hunting sounded like a worse one. She had to take it to Walter. But didn't want to leave the children alone even to do that. Dragging them with her to the militia HQ shouldn't be *too* risky. Since the HQ was close to the quartermaster building, she hastily unpacked the shopping bags, figuring she'd save a trip and return them now.

"What did he look like?"

"Umm. He was black," said Madison.

"A black guy? How old?"

"No." Madison shook her head rapidly. "Not a black guy, he *was* black. Like... umm, a shadow man."

Harper fumbled and almost dropped a can of Spaghetti-Os. "What? Are you serious?"

Madison huffed. "I don't think he's a ghost. He just looked like one. Like *totally* black."

"Could be a ninja," said Jonathan.

"That's less believable than a ghost. There aren't any ninjas in Colorado." Becca flailed her arms.

Jonathan grabbed at the second bag, helping unpack it. "Some guy wearing all black clothes doesn't mean he's a real ninja."

*Mila's been talking about the Shadow Man for as long as I've been here. She's probably seen this guy. She's also nine, so black suit equals ghost. Okay, that makes more sense.*

"I don't think he wanted us to see him. He jumped when Maddie pointed at him." Jonathan grinned. "He maybe chased us because he was mad."

Harper looked out the windows at the back yard. "Did he follow you all the way back here?"

The kids all shook their heads.

"Dunno," said Madison. "We ran like hell, screaming. Didn't look back."

"They were screaming, I wasn't." Jonathan climbed up onto the counter to pack away ravioli cans.

"You did too scream." Becca poked him. "Louder than me."

He pointed a can at her. "I was *shouting*, not screaming."

Harper rushed the process, jamming food here and there in cabinets without much care for organization. She could spend an hour tomorrow or later rearranging stuff. As soon as the bags emptied, she bundled them into a wad and handed them to Jonathan.

"Follow me, stay close."

"Where are we going?" asked Madison.

"I need to let Mr. Holman know about what you saw. And I'm not leaving you guys alone until we catch this guy."

All three nodded.

She went into the living room. "C'mon, Lore. Gonna go for a walk."

"Okay!" She set one doll down, keeping her favorite in hand, and scampered over.

Harper went out the front door with the Mossberg in a two-handed grip. Madison grasped her belt, holding on like she'd done the day they went into the mall months ago, gripping Becca's hand in her left. Jonathan kept a death grip on Lorelei's wrist, scanning the area for signs of danger.

That her little sister had become frightened enough to cling again made Harper furious. Evergreen should've been a safe haven, a place the kids could've been kids again, not worry if someone would try to kill or abduct them at any moment. Fortunately, the path to the militia HQ couldn't have been easier or more open. She followed Hilltop west to Route 74, and a little more than a hundred feet north to the building with the weird little 'castle tower' thing on the end.

A row of telephone poles crossed in front of the place. Unlike the poles she'd seen in Lakewood, these didn't show obvious signs of scorching, which offered some hope that Jeanette the electrician could get at least some power back. Solar panels probably wouldn't last forever, but it would be nice to enjoy electricity for a little while before the world fell totally into the past.

They followed the curving road around the side of the building to the doors. Harper went straight into Walter's office, tapping the door with the most cursory of knocks on the way past it. Walter, a grey-haired fifty-year-old former sheriff's lieutenant, looked up from whatever he'd been reading, and offered an almost paternal smile. When he noticed the four children in tow, he tilted his head like a bewildered German shepherd.

"Harper? What's wrong?" He leaned back, favoring his left shoulder, still sore from where Tommy had shot him three months ago.

Lorelei put her right foot up on his desk. "I have pink socks!"

"You sure do." Walter smiled at her. "They look nice and warm."

The child nodded, grinning. "Daddy got me them for Christmas."

Harper tugged her back from the desk. "Shoulder still bothering you?"

Lorelei stretched her leg, trying to pull her abandoned shoe close enough with her toes to step back into it.

"A bit. Doc Khan says it should eventually stop, but I think he means I'll just get used to the pain." He chuckled. "Something more than my shoulder is bothering you."

"Yes." She hesitated a few seconds, afraid he'd think her an easily-frightened child, but decided to let it out. Despite her urgency, she spoke in a calm and detailed manner, explaining what she knew about the 'stalker'.

Walter listened, occasionally nodding. Growing concern in his expression added to her confidence and calmed her enough to keep speaking in a controlled manner, though she couldn't keep her worry out of her voice entirely. Once she finished, he asked the kids to tell him again what they saw.

"We were going home from school. I just kinda looked into the trees and saw this guy watching us," said Madison. "I pointed at him and he started coming after us, so we ran."

Her description of him as being 'all black like a ghost' did make Walter smirk a little, since he'd also heard of Mila's story. However, as Harper had already mentioned thinking it's a normal person in all-black clothing, he didn't laugh them out of his office.

"All right. It does sound like this is a matter of concern. We'll put it out there to the town that no kid should go anywhere alone for the time being. Not until we find an answer to this."

"Thanks." *He doesn't think I'm crazy at least.* "Oh, Liz asked if anyone found anything about the food thefts?"

"Not yet, I'm afraid. It's being looked into. She's got every reason to be persistent, but asking us five times a day isn't helping."

"Yeah." Harper nodded. "Just passing on a message. Thanks, Mr. Holman. Gonna take the kids home and try to keep them safe."

"Okay. Drat. I wish phones still worked. Gotta send someone down to Janice." He tapped a finger on the dead desk phone.

"I miss phones, too," said Madison. "Maybe too much."

Jonathan stuck his hands in his pockets. "It's strange not having video games with me everywhere I go. Is that what it was like when you were a kid, Mr. Holman?"

He laughed. "I'm not *that* old. Video games just started up back then. We had an Atari 2600 in the living room."

"What's that?" asked Jonathan.

"A dinosaur." Walter smiled. "Kind of like me."

The kids laughed.

"Thanks for taking it seriously, Mr. Holman." Harper gathered her siblings close. "I know it sounds a bit out there and there's no real evidence, but…"

"Well, you made a good argument that something might be going on. And a little while of extra vigilance is hardly worth the risk that something might happen."

Harper stood tall, relieved that he'd taken her seriously. "Gonna take these guys home now, unless you want me to run that note down to Janice."

"I still have to write it. No sense making you sit around here. There aren't that many kids down the south half anyway. If this guy is targeting children, he won't have much reason to be down that way."

"Okay."

She stood there awkwardly for a moment, not sure if she should wait for him to tell her she could leave.

"Is there something else?" asked Walter.

"No. Just the break-in I told you about yesterday, and Katherine's missing handgun." Warmth rushed to her cheeks. "Sorry. Just thinking." After giving Walter a feeble smile, she ushered the kids out of the room and headed outside.

Except for Lorelei saying hello to random passing birds or squirrels, no one spoke as they walked down Route 74. Harper's thoughts swam around in a torrent of emotion. One moment, she hated the universe for everything that happened, wanting to go home to the world she remembered so badly it brought tears to her eyes. The next, she slipped into wondering why she bothered trying to survive at all. Whoever hit 'the button' made the decision that humans didn't deserve to exist anymore. Maybe they'd been right.

"Hi, Mr. Squirrel," chirped Lorelei.

"I think that's a possum." Jonathan made a clicking noise, which startled said unknown critter into a streak of grey fur.

"Hi, Mr. Bird!" called Lorelei, waving at the sky.

The girl's bright, cheerful tone pulled Harper back from the precipice of apathy. As Hilltop Drive came into view, she found herself on Panic Island, dreading ambush from every shadow. That lasted only a few seconds before anger took over. Evergreen should've been a haven, not a dangerous environment. She scowled at trees and the corners of houses, daring whoever had the nerve to poison her new home to show themselves.

Upon reaching the house, the kids headed to the backyard to play, going around the outside. Harper went in, startled to find Grace sitting on the couch.

"Hey. Sorry for just walking in."

"It's cool." Harper exhaled, trying to still her nerves. "On edge."

"About?" Grace followed her into the kitchen.

After resting the shotgun on the counter, Harper leaned on it while explaining about the supposed Shadow Man.

"He's not just watching kids. I'm pretty sure someone or something followed me last night." Grace smoothed her dress over her legs in a repetitive, nervous motion. "I thought it might have been a mountain lion. Think it's the same thing?"

"I'm sure it's a person." Harper proceeded to organize the food she'd put away so hastily earlier.

"Maybe there's more than one thing out there?" Grace got up and helped sort cans.

"Could be. Oh, how'd it go with the job?"

Grace offered a nervous smile. "They've agreed to let me apprentice with them to see how it goes. Guess I'm smart enough." She laughed. "It was kinda funny. Dr. Khan took one look at me and I could tell he was like, 'yeah right this ditz wants to be a doctor?' You should've seen the shock on his face once I started answering questions. He figured blondes are stupid."

Harper laughed. "That's cool."

"Mommy said I'm stupid, too." Lorelei grinned and tugged at her platinum blonde hair.

"Gah!" Harper nearly jumped out of her jeans. "Where'd you come from?"

"Outside. Can I have water?"

Harper hugged her. "You're not stupid, Lore. Don't let anyone say that again."

The girl blinked, bewildered. After a few seconds, it seemed to register with her that 'stupid' meant something bad. She briefly appeared heartbroken, but brushed it aside in seconds and hugged Harper.

Grace crouched behind her, fussing at the girl's hair and tickling her. "You aren't stupid, sweetie. You're like the happiest, cutest person I know. Us blondes gotta stick together."

Lorelei hugged her.

The girl chugged her glass of water, chirped a thank you, and ran back outside to play. Harper sighed at the door, wanting to find that girl's mother and smack her. Unable to do that, she sighed and resumed sorting food while chatting with her new friend. Their conversation started off on the unexpectedness of a girl with Grace's looks also being smart enough to apply to schools like MIT. She thought Harper intelligent as well, though probably said that mostly to be nice. She didn't consider herself abnormally smart, despite Madison often calling her 'brainy.' Sure, she got good grades and enjoyed learning, but the real 'genius kids' took AP classes and went to college at fourteen, came up with world-changing inventions by fifteen, that sort of thing. Perhaps she might have had the potential, but she lacked the drive. Grace, on the other hand, could have been halfway through college already if her parents hadn't been so married to their plan for her.

Grace drifted off on a tangent about how frustrating it had been to feel like a spectator watching her own life, and that steered them into reminiscing about their existence before the war. Surprisingly, talking about her old friends, summer jobs, school, movies, and so on didn't make Harper want to break down and sob again... but it did leave a weight pressing on her insides. Talk of past boyfriends eventually led to her mentioning the confrontation between Logan and Zach.

"I dunno," said Grace. "I don't think he *tries* to be a jerk, but it's like he can't help it. His father was *such* an..."

"What?"

Grace's cheeks reddened. She looked worried for an instant, then defiant. "Asshole!"

Harper laughed. "Umm, okay."

"I said it, and I'm not ashamed of myself." She took a deep breath, grinned, and spent a moment saying random swear words.

Harper looked at her with a raised eyebrow.

"My parents used to freak the heck out if I used bad words. They acted like if I said 'shit' once, I'd wind up homeless and hooked on heroin with nineteen babies, and all their friends would shun them. It just hit me that I'm free. Is that sick to think that my parents are both dead and it's almost… a relief."

"Umm. Maybe a little, but it sounds like they were a bit over the top."

"Oh, I miss them; they were my parents after all. And I cried a lot when I realized they were almost certainly killed, but mostly I think I was upset at the idea of not having them there to make all the decisions and take care of everything. Being on my own, having to think for myself scared me to death. I'm like a bird thrown out of her nest too early. Doctor Hale said I was too freaked out to be asked to work. But, I think I'm pulling it together. Anyway, Zach's a lot like his father. Thinks the world is his and he can do whatever he wants. Only, he's basically a giant little boy who's never been told 'no.'"

"Got that feeling already from him."

Harper decided on bread with jam for dinner since the bread wouldn't last like the canned food and they had to stretch their limited supplies. Hanging out with a girl her age and talking like she used to do with her friends got her thinking of home before the war. It melted time away in a blur of false normality that allowed her to pretend to be an ordinary high school senior with life ahead of her.

In what felt like mere minutes, Cliff walked in filthy and exhausted.

"Gah. What happened?" asked Harper.

"Went way off to the west. Rounded up a couple stray cows, and they had some objections." He chuckled. "Gonna clean up a bit."

"Okay."

He headed down the hall. Harper shivered at the idea of a cold shower. The reminder of her freezing bath on the way to the mall made her look out the window to check on Madison. Her kid sister hid behind a tree, pretending with the others to have a shootout with invisible bad guys.

Grace stood. "I really should get back to the house for dinner since we have food allotted for us. Don't want to steal yours."

"It's okay."

"I know you don't mind, but it's cool. I'll come back after. Still getting used to *not* having my whole day pre-scheduled."

"'Kay."

Eventually, Cliff emerged from the back in fresh clothes, hair wet, and wide awake from the frigid shower. Harper called the kids in for dinner. Once they filed in and took their seats at the table, she spread raspberry jam on two pieces of bread for Lorelei.

"We're having *bread* for dinner?" asked Madison with a note of disbelief.

"Nobody had to kill it at least." Cliff smiled.

Madison stuck her tongue out at him, then laughed.

"Yeah. Gotta make stuff last." Harper waited for the jam to make its way around the table back to her. "Bread will go stale if we don't eat it."

"Wow, it's not even moldy." Jonathan grinned.

Madison gagged.

"The green parts taste funny. Don't eat them." Lorelei scrunched up her face. "You'll get sick and then you'll get in trouble for wasting food."

*Oh, no...* Harper cringed at the thought that the girl's mother had given her bad food, then punished her for throwing up. She and Madison had never wanted for food, never even imagined the possibility of not having enough. Sure, she knew plenty of people around the world and even in the United States used to struggle to feed their kids. Some children got a slice of bologna on one piece of bread for dinner. More and more, her old life felt far away like a dream.

While Cliff terrified the kids with stories of eating bugs if things got too bad, her thoughts wandered. The plate with a slice of jellied bread in front of her morphed into a plate with a PB&J on her bedroom desk. She'd spent most of the last year or two eating 'dinner' while doing homework. Except for weekends, Madison ate almost exclusively microwave meals since their parents had been too busy to cook between their jobs or driving her around to all her activities.

Dad worked for Qwest, having made junior VP only eight months before the war. He'd spent six years as a director, busting his butt for the promotion—so had little time to be home. Mom, a former nurse, had an administrative job with HealthONE. Though she didn't put in the ridiculous hours her father used to, she'd encouraged Madison into ludicrous amounts of after-school activities, which entailed lots of running around.

Harper had spent more time with her family in the two months after the blast than the two years before it. She wanted a chance to go back in time, even if she couldn't stop the war, just to re-do the past four years so she could have more time with her family when things were good.

She lifted her stare off the plate, returning to the here and now. Wrinkles formed at Cliff's eyes; he laughed at something Jonathan said. His smile transferred to Harper's lips. She liked having him around, even if he would never replace Dad. It seemed so strange—in a nice way—to sit there at the table with her new family, having a father there with them who didn't stagger in the door at almost ten at night all the time or disappear for half a month on business trips.

Madison's nose scrunched in reaction to talk of foraging natural food from the woods. She'd mostly come out of her shell and appeared to be adjusting to the new normal. Though, she hadn't gone back to the goofy, bubbly kid she'd been, she didn't drift around like a zombie anymore. Jonathan laughed along with Cliff, disgustingly okay with the idea of eating bugs, even suggesting they try it so they knew what to expect if they *had* to. The boy had accepted this family of circumstance without hesitation. Harper smiled at him, then looked at Lorelei's big grin.

Desperate to stop talking about eating bugs, Madison hurriedly rambled on about what they'd been doing on the farm.

Lorelei perplexed Harper in a way she couldn't really define. A twelve-year age gap changed the girl into more of a daughter than a kid sister, which made her eerily detached happiness annoying. Harper caught herself feeling jealous, wanting the girl to love her and her new family more than total strangers. She pushed that aside, no more able to blame Lorelei for how she was than Mila for being creepy. Other people had done bad things to both of them.

Sitting there looking at the faces of the man she'd adopted as a stand-in dad and her siblings left her torn midway between guarded happiness for her new family and sorrow at the future that had been stolen from them. Only Cliff appeared better off. He'd gone from a lonely single veteran who felt apart from society working a dead-end job at the mall to having a purpose in life again, both in protecting 'his' kids and defending the town as part of the militia.

After a moment of contemplation, she decided to cling to hope and took a bite out of her second piece of bread.

*I can't fix the world back to the way it was, but I'm gonna make this work.*

# 14

# LEGAL

**M**arcie stopped by the next morning with word that they had to attend a militia meeting.

Cliff accompanied them on the walk to school after a breakfast of oatmeal. The hot meal had thrilled Madison, even if the March weather hadn't been particularly cold. No sign of anything threatening showed itself on the trip to school, or when she walked back down Route 74 to the militia HQ with Cliff after dropping the kids off.

A conference room in the former office building served as the primary briefing room, with a whiteboard and desk in front of a fleet of wheeled office chairs. Cliff and Harper joined the other twenty or so militia personnel responsible for northern Evergreen, after helping themselves to coffee from a big thermal container with a spigot like from a gas station convenience store.

*More efficient use of firewood to make a lot at once.* She sniffed the black, unsweetened coffee, not even wincing. Six months ago, if anyone had told her she'd drink it without enough sugar to knock out a moose, she'd have laughed. Now, she thought about the resource cost of preparing it. *How much coffee did places used to dump down the drain for going stale? Ugh. I really need to stop thinking about stuff like that.*

She fell into a springy office chair with blue cushions next to Cliff.

Walter took a position at the front of the room, got everyone's attention, then provided an update. The town had gained twelve new residents in the past month, lost two—an improvement over the five deaths that occurred in January due to cold. The January deaths had been older people who tried to save firewood by relying too heavily on blankets. One death last month resulted from a resident having run out of vital medication, another, a broken neck due to a slip-and-fall on ice.

After the population update, he moved on to the solar power issue. Evidently, most of the panels Jeanette and her team had salvaged and assembled on the tennis courts operated well, but they ran into problems with the distribution system. Transformers and relays had suffered burnout from the EMP surge that rode the wires in from areas closer to the bombardment. Fixing them required parts and components they didn't have. Walter announced possible future trips into the city, targeting municipal storage facilities or electrical contractors' shops.

"Also, as I'm sure you're all aware, there have been several break-ins at the quartermaster building. We will be posting a rotating night watch to keep eyes on the place twenty-four-seven until the thief or thieves are caught. Speaking of rotations, the schedule for scavenging trips is posted on the whiteboard out in the hall. Given the situation with food, we'll be casting a wider net in search of resources until the farm gets its legs under it."

Murmurs of agreement swept among the militia.

"Getting a couple complaints about kids drinking beer. How should we handle that?"

Harper glanced over at the source of the question, a late-forties guy with longish grey hair, a cowboy hat, and a mustache. She vaguely recalled his name as Randy or Roddy or Robert or something with an R. He'd made his way to Evergreen from Denver as well, joining the militia to keep ownership of an M4 carbine and SWAT Kevlar vest.

"Well..." Walter shrugged. "We've gone back a hundred years."

"More like two," muttered Harper.

"Anything could happen to any of us at any time," said Walter. "If they're being safe about it and aren't *too* young, no point quibbling a number. I figure we should draw the line at about fifteen or so. If they're past that age and aren't causing trouble, don't bother giving them any grief about a few beers. We have bigger issues to deal with. Besides, we're not exactly swimming in booze anyway."

"Earl's fixin' to change that right soon," said Fred Mitchell, chuckling. "He's almost got that brewery running."

Most people in the room laughed.

Walter cleared his throat. "Of course, if they're causing trouble when drunk, deal with the situation accordingly."

*What's that supposed to mean... accordingly? Do we yell at them? Arrest them? Not like they've issued us handcuffs.* So far, any 'arrest' she'd witnessed had involved escorting the problem to the militia HQ at gunpoint. The southern HQ had jail cells, having been the former sheriff's office, but the militia tended to punish offenses in one of three ways: yelling at people not to do it again, exiling them from Evergreen, or shooting them.

Fortunately, the third option had thus far only happened as a response to being fired on. No one had been 'officially' executed. That, she would refuse to take part in. She couldn't kill a defenseless person. Well, not unless that person had done something unforgivable to Madison, Jonathan, or Lorelei.

Dennis Prosser patted Harper on the shoulder. "Hey, guess that means you're legal to drink now."

"Yeah, great." She offered a fake smile and laugh. "Can't drink on duty. Gotta stay sharp, right?"

Cliff smiled.

"Ahh, more for me then." Dennis winked.

Introvert Prime hadn't been too interested in drinking. It cost a lot, not to mention that with her luck, she'd get caught and in heaps of trouble, plus everyone she knew who drank always complained about waking up the next morning feeling like death warmed over. Everyone except Darci. Her friend spent the majority of junior year high on pot, or drunk whenever opportunity knocked. It defied her ability to understand how no one busted that girl for using weed underage, but she'd been high so damn often maybe people just considered that to be her normal personality.

*Wonder if Darci even realized there's been a war.*

"Also, we've been hearing of an unknown individual or possibly a wild animal creeping around town. Several children have reported someone or something watching them." Walter beckoned Harper up to the front of the room. "We do not, as yet, know what we're dealing with or what motivations may be in play here. It's as likely to be a person in dark clothing as it is a bear. Harper, would you mind sharing what you've learned so far?"

She froze statue still, platter-eyed.

*Come on. Get up. Speaking in front of a group isn't half as scary as being shot at.* She swallowed dry. *No, it's scarier.*

Cliff patted her on the back. "You good?"

Again, she swallowed dry. Pressure like a bowling ball settled in her stomach. Neither her arms nor her legs wanted to move. Her hands shook, defying her ability to control them. She'd barely managed to handle presentations in school, having to grip the podium and keep her eyes on the paper to get through it. Any eye contact with the class would've stolen her voice, and those had been kids she'd spent years around. With a few exceptions, she barely knew anyone in the room with her here.

But, she hadn't been asked to discuss the inner meaning of some 150-year-old piece of poetry... what she had to say could potentially stop a nut-job from hurting someone, especially a kid like Lorelei who had no defense against a creep. That girl would probably run over to hug Jason Voorhees.

Then again, she was so lovable and cute even an undead killer would probably pat her on the head and keep going.

Harper gritted her teeth, stood, and nodded. "Yeah. I'm good."

She moved to the front of the room and, careful to look people straight in the chest, started to describe everything she knew about the situation. At first, she spoke in a wavering voice that some strained to hear, but a few minutes in and no one seeming to tune her out, her nerves settled. She risked eye contact with Cliff. He nodded. Gradually, her voice gained confidence, her posture straightened, and she went from feeling like a kid talking to the police after witnessing a crime to a member of a group explaining a situation to her equals.

"... and that's as much as I know. Does anyone have any questions?"

"All the sightings have been up near the school?" asked Ken Zhang.

"So far." Harper nodded.

Walter tapped a paper on the desk. "Janice hasn't had any reports like this from her area."

"Could the cow attack, animal tracks, and unknown party seen by children all be the same thing?" Sadie clicked her fingernails on the M-16 balanced across her lap. "We don't know for sure that a lion killed the cow, and the only ones who've seen something are little kids. Could be anything."

"Grace Hughes also saw what she thought was a man watching her," said Harper. "Most wild animals wouldn't hide, right? They'd either run away or come charging."

Mixed murmuring sounded mostly like agreement.

Harper glanced at Walter. "As I'm sure Walter's already told everyone, the unknown person is possibly armed. A compact 9mm handgun was stolen from Katherine Bowden."

"Yeah, we figure *everyone* is armed until proven otherwise," said Fred. "Safer that way."

Most everyone chuckled.

"All right." Walter scratched at his forehead. "For the time being, get it out there that we don't want any children traveling alone. Harper, would you mind letting Violet know to keep students at the school until further notice until an adult is there to pick them up?"

"Sure." She nodded. Sensing her 'speech' done, she eagerly returned to her chair, practically melting into a puddle of social anxiety as soon as her butt hit the cushion.

"Ya did good," whispered Cliff.

She let out a weak chuckle. "Maybe I *should* have a beer."

# 15

# POWER

The militia briefing over, Harper returned to the school to inform Violet and the other teachers about the situation. They decided to tell the children that a possible mountain lion roamed the area rather than stoke nightmares about a kidnapper.

She left the classroom after only a brief visit and resumed her patrol route. While possible that the kids had seen a mountain lion or bear, she *knew* she'd heard cloth. Calling a person who hid among trees and spied on kids a possible kidnapper might be jumping to a conclusion, but normal people didn't do that. What possible reason could anyone have for doing something like that? Crazy parent afraid to make contact with their kid? Crazy person in general merely trying to avoid being seen?

*I should be grateful they haven't tried to grab anyone. Wait, that boy Jax... the kid said the ninja tried to grab him.*

The oddity of it bothered her. Worse, her gut told her to be afraid. She'd ignored it with Tyler and it almost cost Madison her life. She had no intention of brushing aside her worries this time. And so, she roamed the area around the houses with the mindset of a soldier hunting the enemy, not simply following the roads like a small-town cop.

A group of men passed on the road, pulling a wagon made from the back end of a pickup truck, loaded high with huge chunks of cut timber. Liz Trujillo had suggested gathering firewood in the warmer months and stockpiling it. By the time it grew cold and people needed it, the wood will have dried and become ripe for burning. None of the men noticed her watching from the trees, which surprised her.

*Guess that standing still thing really works.*

Harper checked around every area she thought offered a hiding place from which someone might ambush a solitary person on the road. Figuring it would be difficult to drag a struggling child or teen far without being noticed, she focused on areas near unoccupied houses. If the guy intended to kidnap someone, they would likely want to get the victim out of sight as fast as possible, drag them into a house where they could do whatever horrible things they had in mind without anyone catching them. Disgusted with herself for even thinking that, she decided to search unoccupied houses for any signs that someone had prepared for such a crime, stashing rope or whatever.

She did find some muddy footprints in one place that made her think of the house with the stolen granola bars and handgun, but other than learning that someone with dirty shoes had been exploring the place, didn't spot anything else suspicious.

Eventually, she reached the south edge of her assigned area, where Lewis Ridge Road ran east-west. The sight of the town's lone operational tractor-trailer parked next to a building beyond a multicolored stone wall attracted her curiosity. She walked down a strip of gravel-paving into a parking lot, which also held a fleet of non-working dump trucks, plows, and some excavators. Someone mentioned the building here had been a county asset, a base of operations for the road maintenance crews.

Jeanette and her team unloaded solar panels from the back of the trailer, arranging them in rows. It seemed the wide-open parking lot would serve as another staging area for a solar farm since the nearby tennis courts had been filled. Wires as thick as a child's arm spanned the grass between the courts farther down the hill to the south and the maintenance garage.

"Careful," said Jeanette, trotting over to Harper. "Kids shouldn't—oh, wait, you're... right. Sorry. Didn't recognize you at first."

"It's okay. Just saw the truck and got curious."

"Collected a bunch of panels from the last run to Littleton." Jeanette grinned. "It's starting to look like we'll have the production capacity to power up the north part of town, if we can get the distribution worked out."

"Awesome." Her eyes widened at the prospect of working heat and hot water again. "Any idea when it'll be done?"

"Like I said, based on the number of panels we've collected, we can produce sufficient juice. Even set up a decent battery unit." She gestured at the road works building. "Of course, Ned's already talking about limiting power use to absolute needs like heat, hot water, cooking."

"What else would anyone use it for? Not like there's internet or TV now."

"Computer games and such, if any of them still work. Not sure how he plans to enforce something like that without sending you folks snooping into everyone's houses. Figure by this time next year, Evergreen might feel sorta normal again. Once we get the solar up and running, gonna start looking into the possibility of some wind-powered generators. Those should last longer than solar panels."

"That's…" She bounced. "Amazing news. You rock."

"Aww, I'm only an electrician. Never really worked solar before, just kinda winging it." Jeanette leaned side to side in a stretching motion. "Well, I oughta get back to it. And please stop looking at me like I'm Jesus… I just plug wires in."

Harper laughed. "Sorry. Just… you know, electricity is one of those things that I never really thought about before. You think it'll stay up? Or should I get used to living like the 1800s?"

"No telling how long my franken-circuitry will keep going. Haven't heard anything from the outside world. Depends on how much of the grid is smashed. Lots of places had a real crap show of infrastructure. Some substation yards I've seen were still using gear from like 1930. It's unbelievable how little electric companies cared about modernization. The US power grid was so unstable it's damn amazing it worked at all. I can almost guarantee you it's all junk now. That EMP wave would've fried damn near everything. Though, some of those old-ass copper loop houses might have survived it. Kinda ironic that the ancient crap took it better than cutting edge. Maybe humanity has like a technology ceiling that we shouldn't go past. Horse-drawn carriages and electric light bulbs might be the ideal."

"Hah. Yeah…" Harper let out a somber chuckle, and squinted at the small ocean of glimmering silver panels set up in the distant tennis courts.

Jeanette waved and headed back to help her crew arrange the panels and bolt them to the framework they'd been building.

*We might have power sometime soon.* Giddy, Harper walked up the driveway and back to her patrol, daydreaming of working lights and trying to remember what it felt like to take a hot shower. Not having to wait an hour or so for water to boil in a pail whenever she wanted a hot bath would totally rock. Being able to take a hot bath more than once a week would be awesome. What Jeanette said about the power grid eventually got her wondering about the state of the country as a whole. What happened to power plants? Some places used nuclear reactors for electricity. How long would they operate without human intervention? Did their computers have the ability to realize all the people went away or would they go haywire until melting down?

She didn't think they would explode like a nuclear bomb. That plant in Japan had a meltdown and didn't create a mushroom cloud. The idea of a nuclear plant left unattended for weeks terrified her. Even if the systems had been programmed to handle the sudden absence of a crew, what if some random idiot got inside one and started pushing buttons?

*Those places are tough, right? Maybe the people working there when the war happened survived. They could've been alive long enough to shut everything down.* Not like she could flip on the news or check the internet to hear about nuke plants across the country. More than likely, little remained of power stations, nuclear or otherwise. Most of the ashes that had fallen like snow over Lakewood, even two months after the bombs fell, had come from fires. Ordinary power lines caught fire under the EMP surge, transformers had exploded. The breaker box at home had burst into flames. Fortunately, Dad kept a couple fire extinguishers around and put it out.

Harper sighed out her nose. Evergreen might have power again, if only for a few years… but it seemed like it would take a lot more than a few electricians and some solar panels to fix the rest of the country.

# 16

# EVAPORATED

C hildren's laughter filled the backyard.

Harper stared into the cabinet, surveying the canned food she had to work with. She peered out the window at her siblings plus Becca standing in a cluster by the large tree behind the house. Despite wearing a pale pink sweatshirt and jeans, Madison decided it warm enough to run around barefoot, even though Harper thought it still a touch chilly. Lorelei also took her shoes off, putting her prized pink socks in a safe place on the dresser. She didn't want to get them dirty or ruin them by going outside sock-footed.

She smiled at the kids, then turned her attention back to the question of dinner. Last night's bread and jam had been a touch lean, so she wanted to give everyone a bigger meal tonight, but worried that doing so would result in a problem by Tuesday before she could go back for another ration.

*I should ask Cliff to try fishing at the lake.*

Amazingly, no one had complained of having canned ravioli so often. They'd recovered several pallets of it from the Walmart run. Harper bit her lip, debating back and forth between intelligence and emotion. With a sigh, she decided to be cautious and not use up too much food too fast. She could short herself three raviolis to give one extra to each of the kids.

"Rawr!" yelled Jonathan, out in the yard. "Time's up! I'm coming!"

*Where is Cliff? He should have been back by now.*

She started to reach for her belt, where she'd worn her iPhone for the past three years... and grabbed empty denim. "Duh. How the heck did people survive without cell phones?"

Shaking her head, she opened two large cans and dumped them into a pot, then scraped as much of the sauce out as she could with a wooden spoon—nearly dropping both when Madison screamed.

"Gotcha!" shouted Jonathan.

Harper braced herself against the counter, taking a few breaths to recover from the spike of adrenaline her little sister's scream triggered. She peered out the window. Jonathan dragged Madison out from under the trampoline that had been in the back left part of the yard. *Hide and Seek...* Annoyed, Madison folded her arms and pouted, standing there with a scowl while Jonathan resumed searching around for Becca and Lorelei.

*Oh, screw it.* She grabbed a small can of ravioli and opened it, too. *Rice is super filling. I'll save that for Tuesday.* After dumping more ravioli into the pot, she scraped the can clear of sauce. *That should be plenty.* Harper went to the front door and wandered out onto Hilltop, looking left and right in hopes of seeing Cliff on his way home.

"Hmm. He's late. Something happened."

That didn't necessarily mean he'd gotten in trouble. Most likely, he responded to a crisis and couldn't leave until it had been settled. At least, she hoped he hadn't been hurt. Not hearing gunshots went a long way to reassuring her he'd get home eventually.

*Sound carries out here. There's nothing to drown it out. He'll be back.*

She returned to the kitchen, grabbed the pot, and carried it outside to the cinder block grill.

"You win, Lore," called Jonathan. "I can't find you."

Harper looked over at him. He stood at the far left end of the yard where the angled fence abutting the rear neighbor's property formed something of an alcove by trees.

"C'mon, Lore," yelled Madison on the other side of the yard. "The round's over, you won."

Becca waved while running by on her way into the house while saying, "Gotta pee!"

Harper set the pot on the grill. "Jon, go grab the fire thing."

He hurried over. "Umm, okay. Will you tell Lorelei to stop hiding? I can't find her and I'm getting scared."

"Where was she last?"

"In the yard." He flailed his arms. "We told her not to leave the yard. Just supposed to play hide and seek here."

"She's not around front," yelled Madison.

*No...* Harper put a hand on her chest; her heart turned into a lead weight, barely beating. "Lorelei! Stop playing. Come out right now."

Jonathan cupped his hands over his mouth. "Come on, Lore! I give up. You win."

Madison ran around shouting for her.

"No... no... no..." Harper spun in place, totally blank, her brain doing a spot-on impression of a bowl of scrambled eggs.

"Harp?" Jonathan tugged on her arm.

She looked down at him. The worry in his expression slapped her out of her fog. "Did anyone see where she went?"

"No. I was covering my eyes," said Jonathan.

"She just evaporated," whispered Madison.

"Maybe she's inside?" asked Jonathan.

"You two, check inside." Harper ran around the yard, looking wherever a little kid might have tucked themselves. Maybe she got stuck somewhere tight and passed out. She alternated between furious that the girl did it on purpose to mess with everyone and ready to break down in sobs. *I swear I won't be mad. Please be nothing.*

In her mind, she pictured the Shadow Man creeping out of the trees to grab Lorelei, the girl merrily running over to him to say hi... and being carried away, never to be seen again. The girl wouldn't have even screamed, mistaking it for an extended hug.

"Lorelei!" shouted Harper, her voice tinged with tears. "Come out. Please. It's not funny anymore."

A tiny dirt footprint on the fence behind the trampoline caught her eye. She sprinted over and leapt the fence. Dennis' yard didn't have much in the way of hiding spots except for climbing one of three large trees. To the right, fencing enclosed an area of mostly open grass with no way out other than a door to the house. Harper went left around the house to the dirt driveway that connected to Butternut Lane.

She crouched and examined the ground, nearly shouting when she spotted little footprints heading toward the street. The trail led to the fence end on the left side. There, she found a small black-haired doll in a princess gown. The same doll Madison gave Lorelei for Christmas, the doll she'd been carrying around near constantly since.

Someone had posed it seated on the ground with its back to the fencepost.

Both directions down Butternut Lane looked deserted.

*Someone grabbed her.*

"Lorelei!" shouted Harper, her voice frayed with desperation. "Lore!" she shouted even louder, tears rolling down her face. She pivoted to the left, shouting again.

"Harp!" yelled Madison.

She and Jonathan ran up behind her, the boy carrying the Mossberg, which he held up for her to take.

Madison offered her the air horn, sniffling. "I'm sorry. You wanted us to watch her but…"

"It's not your fault." Harper took the shotgun, slung it over her shoulder, and pulled both of them into a hug. "Neither of you guys' fault."

"She's gonna be okay, right?" asked Jonathan in a teary voice.

Harper took the horn from Madison. "Go back to the house and stay inside. Don't let Becca go anywhere unless her parents show up to get her."

Both kids nodded, then ran back through Dennis' yard to the fence, which they climbed.

*How could she disappear so damn fast? She's too trusting. Too friendly. I knew this was going to happen.*

She blared a single long 911 tone, clipped the horn to her belt, and spun in place. No footprints existed on the road to suggest which way the guy went, but a right turn offered the fastest way to tree cover. All the houses close by had been assigned to militia, so she doubted a kidnapper would've gone inside one.

*He's been watching us for a long time. He knows which houses are empty.*

Her hands shook with rage and panic. Right now, some bastard could have Lorelei in a house somewhere, doing… horrible things. She sprinted to the right as answering air horn chirps came from all around.

Darnell Buck emerged from the house at the curve where the road turned north. "Harper? What's going on?"

"Have you seen Lorelei? She's missing."

"Aww, shit. No. Give me a sec to grab shoes, be right there."

She nodded, but kept going, shouting, "Lorelei!" over and over.

The fence at the end of the curve gave her a flashback of Tyler running off with Madison, but her sister had fought like hell. Lorelei couldn't process that someone would want to hurt her. Would the man kill her afterward? What if he didn't? An already-traumatized child enduring further abuse... Harper's brain ran away, picturing her littlest sister turning into a junkie or ending up pregnant at thirteen or—. *Wait. She can't become a junkie. No one is making drugs anymore.*

Marcie and Leigh ran into view to the southeast and north. Upon seeing her, they both stopped and shouted over, asking if she'd sent the signal or knew where it came from.

"Lorelei's missing," yelled Harper.

The women started going door to door, assisting in the search.

Darnell ran up to Harper. "What happened? Where'd you see her last?"

She raced an explanation of hide and seek. She'd been getting dinner ready and the girl just evaporated. Something made her climb the fence and go into the next yard, maybe to hide. "He left her doll on the ground, like a giant middle finger. Ha ha, I got your kid." Harper clenched the shotgun tight, itching to find the son of a bitch.

"We'll find her. Stay focused. The whole damn militia will stay out there until we've got her."

"Thanks." Harper fought back tears.

Darnell ran off to the west, heading for Route 74 in case the kidnapper used it to cover a lot of ground fast.

She jogged across a large dirt lot behind a house, jumping its fence to the next street, Sun Creek. A woman stood at the end of a sidewalk that ran along the left side of a giant house split into three apartments, waving at her.

Harper ran up to the woman. "Did you see her?"

"See who?"

"Lorelei."

"Not sure who that is."

"Six, platinum blonde hair, tiny. White dress?"

"No, sorry. I thought I saw someone skulking around last night though."

"Where? When?"

The woman pointed west. "Over by the old dog kennels, near the quartermaster's. Maybe an hour or two after midnight. Looked pretty big and round. Could've been a bear."

*What the hell was she doing out there at that hour? Uhh, probably the food thief. Maybe it's the same guy...* "Thanks. We'll check on it."

"Okay. Hope you find that kid."

Harper nodded and ran down the street, calling for her sister. Shouts from other militia came at random from every direction, along with air horn signals. It sounded as if the entire town searched for her, but no one had any luck.

Tears blurred her vision, defying her best attempt to be too angry to cry. Somehow, losing Lorelei was her fault. She'd messed up, done something wrong. Not watched her well enough. Harper hated the universe in that moment for its bastardly irony. *She* had been the one to make everyone aware of the creep, so naturally, he targeted her family.

She stumbled to a stop almost a half hour later, back on Butternut Lane, too hopeless and lost to even choose a direction to go next. Her throat burned from shouting so much, and a heavy, aching hollow had formed where her heart should be. It felt like her littlest sister had been gone for days already. How much time did they have left to find her before the worst happened? Harper shivered, dreading the sight of a tiny body left abandoned in the woods somewhere. She couldn't even begin to imagine how she'd handle that... if she could handle it at all.

Harper kept turning in place, staring into the deepening shadows cast by a sun racing to tuck itself behind the mountains in the west. What would be going through Lorelei's mind as the man did whatever to her? Would she fight at all or just sit still thinking it a game, or that she needed to be nice and let him?

*Stop thinking such horrible things. Maybe it's just some crazy lonely person who wanted a child to take care of.* She looked down at her stomach, bubbling with anxiety. Her instinct told her the person sneaking around was dangerous. *I can't just stand here. Every second could mean the difference...*

"Harper?" called a male voice she should've recognized but couldn't put a name to in her present state.

She spun around, squinting at an imposing two-headed silhouette striding up the road toward her. For a second, all Mila's talk of shadow men came back to her. Her muscles locked up, and only the nagging sense that she knew this guy's voice kept her from running like hell or raising the shotgun—so she stood there like a deer in the headlights, staring mutely at him.

"Heard you misplaced this."

Harper blinked.

Roy Ellis, former Denver police officer, appeared out of the gloom, carrying Lorelei, who perched on his left arm.

"Lori!" shouted Harper.

"Hi," chirped Lorelei.

Harper ran over and tried to hug him before realizing she carried a shotgun. As soon as she slung it over her shoulder, he handed the girl over. Harper grabbed her in a tight embrace. A moment later, a small finger tapped her on the side of the head.

"Air please," wheezed Lorelei.

"Where were you? What happened?" Harper shook with emotion, barely managing not to break down in tears.

Roy gestured back up the road. "Apparently, ol' Sam went by with his food ration and had a bit of trouble carrying everything. This one saw him struggling and helped carry a box for him. Found her up on Aspen Lane."

"The old man tried to carry too much," said Lorelei.

Harper sighed at the clouds. "I was so scared. When I saw your doll on the road, I thought…"

"I had to put her down to carry the box. It was as big as me!" Lorelei held her arms out to the sides. "But it wasn't heavy."

Harper leaned into Roy, melting into a puddle of relief. "Thank you…"

"All good. Guard your ears, gonna send the all clear." He plucked an air horn off his Kevlar vest.

Harper nodded at him and hurried a few steps away, cringing. Lorelei clamped her hands over her ears. Roy sounded three short pips, waved, and headed off to resume his night patrol. Answering air horn chirps came from the distance. Roy shouted, "We found her, all clear," a few times.

"Oh, Roy?"

"Yo?" He swung back to face her.

"Where's Cliff?"

"Uh, last I heard, they had a minor incident to clean up. Someone assaulted Dave O'Brien in his house over on Elk View Drive, south of the quartermaster on the west side of 74. Dave heard someone moving around inside, went to check on it. Got a whack over the head from behind. By the time he came around, they'd gone. Cliff's investigating."

"Oh, okay. Damn. Any idea why someone would break into that guy's house?"

"Best guess is looking for food. Getting lean for a bunch of folks."

Harper nodded. "Right, so deadbolts on." She squeezed Lorelei. "Speaking of food… I totally forgot about dinner."

"I'm hungry," said Lorelei.

*I'm not.* She hugged the girl again, fading adrenaline manifesting as a full-body shake she couldn't stop. "Okay, let's go fix that."

Roy waved and walked off.

Harper carried Lorelei a touch faster than walking in case the unknown 'ninja' might be watching them. She paused at the fence to pick up the doll. "Lori, please don't ever run off like that again. It's good that you want to help people, but you have to tell me or Cliff that you're going to do it, okay?"

"But you were all the way inside, and Mr. Sam needed help."

"I understand that, but you still have to tell me first. Someone might hurt you. People sometimes hurt each other."

Lorelei nodded, still smiling. "Okay."

Since Harper didn't want to put her down even long enough to climb a fence, she headed one driveway farther left, cut across that yard, and slipped past the next-door house onto Hilltop. Lorelei quietly groomed her doll's hair on the way.

When they reached the front door, the girl looked up at her. "You said sometimes people hurt each other?"

"Yeah. I only want you to be safe, okay? So please... don't run off without telling us."

Lorelei fixed her with a curious, innocent stare. "Do you think the man watching me was gonna do something bad?"

# 17

# UNWANTED

Harper almost fainted. "What?"

"Another man was watching me when I talked to Mr. Sam. Do you think he wanted to hurt me?"

She stared into the little girl's bright blue eyes, too stunned to think of anything to say.

Madison and Jonathan ran outside. The boy cheered while Madison burst into tears and leapt into a hug.

"What man?" asked Harper, struggling under the weight of both girls.

"He was black." Lorelei pointed at the shotgun. "Like that."

"Like a shadow," said Jonathan.

"Yeah." Lorelei nodded.

*Shit.* "C'mon. Let's get inside. It's almost dark."

Madison stopped hanging on Harper and grasped Lorelei's hand in both of hers, holding it while they entered the house. "You scared me, too."

"Becca's dad came for her. She didn't leave alone." Jonathan jogged ahead to the kitchen. "I got the fire going. The ravioli is probably hot enough now."

Cliff hadn't returned yet, but Harper flicked on the deadbolt as soon as she went inside, intent on staying awake until he came home so she could let him in. While she hovered at the back door to watch, Jonathan went out to the grill, grabbed the pot, and carried it inside. A few minutes later, they sat around the table with dinner in front of them and two candles burning for light since they had their meal much later than usual.

Harper kept Lorelei in her lap and forced herself to eat, explaining between bites to Madison and Jonathan that their little sister had simply wandered off to help old Mr. Sam carry his food boxes. Her head filled with imaginary monsters in the shape of ninjas, everything from skinny men wearing black to inhumanly large ebon-skinned mutants. It bothered her that kids had been able to spot this guy, but she hadn't seen him.

*Is this some kind of folklore gone nuts? Are the kids at school talking about 'the shadow man' and making up sightings to scare each other?* She wanted to dismiss it as that for a little while, until she remembered Grace seeing him, too. Her sixteen-year-old friend had no reason to make up stories like that.

Banging came from the front door before they finished eating. Jonathan jumped up and ran to check.

"Who is it?"

"Me," said Cliff.

Jonathan undid the deadbolt. Cliff stormed into the kitchen, scowling like he itched to rip someone's head off, but didn't look upset with anyone there. After falling heavily into a chair, he pinched the bridge of his nose and groaned.

"Bad?" asked Harper.

"Frustrating. I picked up on a trail, but whoever it was used roads too much to follow them back to where they came from. I can't tell if they did it on purpose or got lucky. One area looked like someone deliberately obscured their tracks with a branch, and regularly jumped sideways to interrupt the trail."

"Someone who knows how not to be followed?" asked Harper.

"More like someone who watched too many bad ninja movies." Cliff chuckled.

Madison fetched a clean bowl from the cabinet, poured the last of the ravioli into it, and pushed it in front of Cliff.

"Thanks."

Harper hugged Lorelei like an overgrown child clinging to a teddy bear.

"Something wrong?" asked Cliff, peering into her eyes. "You seem... upset."

"Uhh… just had the crap scared out of me." She explained what happened with Lorelei.

"Where'd you see the guy?" asked Cliff.

"In the trees." Lorelei pointed at the wall.

"One street up, Butternut," added Harper.

"Don't be scared. I won't be kidnapped." Lorelei smiled. "My mommy isn't that lucky."

Harper gawked at her.

"Jesus F"—Cliff muffled himself with a napkin. "She said that?"

Lorelei nodded. "Uh huh."

"Umm." Madison made a face that said 'uhh, getting kidnapped *isn't* lucky.' A moment later, her eyes widened with pity as realization dawned. "That's so sad."

"I know." Lorelei's permanent smile weakened. "Mommy was always mad at me. Alla time, she said she'd be happy if she got a bortion. I saved up three dollars and fifty cents so I could get her one for Christmas so she could be happy, but the store didn't have any bortions. They gotta be awesome 'cause the store lady cried when I asked."

*Oh, my God.* Harper squeezed her, too choked up to speak.

Cliff glared at nothing in particular. "Some people shouldn't be allowed to have kids."

Jonathan and Madison exchanged confused glances.

"Umm. Don't worry about that anymore, okay? You're home now." Harper kissed her atop the head.

Lorelei giggled. "Okay."

"Gonna go look around. You lot should get to bed." Cliff stood and gathered the bowls. "I'll wash these when I get back."

"I got it." Harper stood, carrying Lorelei over to the sink. "It'll dry out and get hard to clean before you get back."

"Are you going to carry her around all night?" asked Cliff, grinning.

"Yeah. Pretty much."

Lorelei giggled again. "I gotta go to the bathroom."

Jonathan stood. "I'll do the dishes. You can't do 'em one handed."

"Are you going to hold her over the toilet, too?" asked Madison, then stuck her tongue out.

"No." Harper finally let herself smile.

She did carry the girl *to* the bathroom, but set her down at the door.

A short while later, with the dishes done, everyone's teeth brushed, and the Mossberg close by, she lay in bed with Madison on her right,

Lorelei on her left against the wall, and a cloud of toothpaste fumes hanging over them. She and Jonathan had rigged empty cans on every window as well as the front and back doors. Hopefully, they would be loud enough to wake her up if anyone tried to sneak into the house.

Harper stared at the ceiling, furious and heartbroken at Lorelei's birth mother. She assumed the woman had told the girl multiple times that she 'should have gotten an abortion' and/or she wished someone would kidnap her. Whether Lorelei didn't understand or chose to ignore the meaning, she couldn't tell. Though, the girl talking about trying to buy an abortion at a store—as if it were some object—gave her hope the child truly had no idea how her bio mom felt about her.

Worry kept her wide awake. Though the time couldn't have been *that* late, probably not even eleven yet, she dreaded the approaching morning like she stayed awake until 2:00 a.m. Her body had gotten used to sleeping soon after sunset and waking soon after sunrise, like people did before alarm clocks.

She closed her eyes and listened to the sound of her sisters' breaths until finally, sleep snuck up on her.

# 18

# INTUITION

A few days later, Harper walked the kids to school like she led a bunch of small soldiers on a sneak attack raid deep into enemy territory.

Once at the classroom, the kids zipped over to their desks. Harper hovered at the door, tempted to spend the whole day there, not wanting to let her siblings out of her sight. However, she did trust the teachers to keep them safe. With three of them in the room, it didn't seem likely that a moody child could up and walk away without being noticed. Also, the 'Shadow Man' would probably avoid such a large group.

Before she could leave, Violet hurried over. "Harper... one sec."

"Hmm?"

"Mila Cline didn't show up today. Would you mind checking on her? I'd just like to make sure her mother kept her home sick and it's nothing to worry about."

An ill feeling writhed in Harper's gut. "Uhh... sure."

Violet picked up on the alarm in her eyes and clenched her jaw. "Trying not to jump to conclusions. The other kids have been avoiding her, so I'm thinking she might've not wanted to show up anymore to avoid being teased."

"Hope so. I'll go right now."

"Thanks." Violet smiled, then hurried back to the nine-to-twelve-year-old students.

Harper fast-walked down the corridor to the main entrance, heading along the road to the right. Mila and her adoptive mother lived in a house off Pinehurst Drive, reasonably close to the school. Pinehurst paralleled Route 74 at the westernmost edge of the development. In fact, Mila could probably see the farm from her bedroom window. Before the war, whoever lived in that house got to enjoy all the noise of traffic on the highway.

Her nerves still hadn't fully recovered from the false alarm with Lorelei. Anxiety drove her to a light jog, sweating hands made holding the shotgun a challenge. She had no explanation for why her fear had ramped up so much, but an inexplicable sense told her something bad had happened.

She followed the road south from the school until she took a right onto Canyon Circle. At the loop, she cut between houses and went into the forest, knowing that if she kept going generally south, she'd reach Brookline Road, to which Pinehurst connected. Days of walking around memorizing street signs finally paid off. She really felt like she knew the area backward and forward. Violet said 'Mila's house' and she knew exactly how to get there as fast as possible. Only a horse would speed things up. The militia did have some mountain bikes, but they wouldn't work too well in the patches of forest between houses.

By her estimation, she'd made it about halfway to Brookline when a soft *thump* broke the silence up ahead. It sounded like a rock landing in the dirt. Harper slowed, raising the shotgun just in case, and changed course a bit to the left where the noise came from. Another, similar, thump happened a few seconds later. Harper advanced in that direction, half expecting to find a mountain lion pawing at something.

Mila strolled into view among the trees about fifty feet away, head down. She wore her usual black jumper dress with the pleated skirt and ballet flats. The girl kicked a pinecone, sniffled, and kicked at another one. "Everyone hates me, but I don't care. I gotta stay away."

*Aww.* Harper exhaled relief out her nose. *That poor kid. How do I explain to her that the creepy act is making the other kids avoid her?* She lowered the shotgun, stood out off her tactical crouch, and walked after her.

Mila sniffled and wiped her nose on the back of her arm, which appeared to be trembling. "No one's gonna care when I'm gone."

*She's terrified... That girl really thinks someone's after her.*

Harper stepped up her walk to a jog. She resisted the urge to call out, not wanting to spend the next ten minutes chasing her. That girl had been hiding how scared she'd really been for weeks. If she got caught shaking and crying, she'd run away.

When she caught up to within about thirty feet of the girl, a dark form leapt out from the trees at Mila's right, pouncing on her and lifting the child off her feet. Mila emitted a yelp of surprise, muffled by a hand over her mouth. She didn't struggle or kick, hanging limp in his grasp almost as if she knew it pointless and had simply given up.

Harper whipped the shotgun up to aim at a man wearing a black hoodie, gloves, and baggy, black pants. A quite physical—non shadowy—live person. "Hey!" she shouted. "Get off her!"

The man spun toward her. A featureless, rounded black mask like a fencer's covered his entire face, except for two cut eye holes, some substance smeared around his eyes underneath to darken the skin. His left arm encircled Mila's body. His right hand covered most of her face.

"I said, get off her." Harper took five rapid steps, closing to within twenty feet. "Do it now!"

He released his left arm, supporting the girl entirely by the hand over her mouth, clutching her head against his chest.

*Always watch their hands,* said Cliff in her memory. He'd shot that guy when they found Summer. Harper hadn't even noticed him going for a weapon until he lay dead on the road.

She lowered her gaze to his left hand, which crept toward his belt. In an instant, she made the decision, trusting years of training at the target range with way more faith than she ever expected to need.

Harper snapped her aim point up to his face and fired.

His skull jerked backward. Something flew from his left hand and whistled past her ear. Mila slipped out of his grasp, tumbling to the ground at the same time the man collapsed over. The girl grabbed her forehead and curled up in a ball. Harper advanced, closing to within two paces of him, still aiming at his chest. True, his face appeared about the same size as the pie plate targets she'd pumped full of buckshot for years, but not one of those targets had a nine-year-old's head a mere six inches below it.

"Nice shot," said Mila, calm as anything.

The man still appeared to be breathing. She leaned closer, examining his face where she'd shot him. A few pellets had embedded in the mask, not penetrating it. Three had made holes, surrounded by fibrous frays, suggesting at least some of the buckshot had gone into his cheeks. *That's armor... I think I just knocked him out.*

"Wow…" Mila picked herself up and crept over to hide behind her. "You got the Shadow Man! You really got him! He… he's…" She burst into tears.

"Shh… It's okay." Harper's heart raced. All the emotion of nearly losing Lorelei a few days ago came crashing back down on her, almost making her pull the trigger again—but she stopped herself.

"Gunshot," shouted Marcie in the distance.

"He's not a monster," whispered Mila. "You got him. I thought he was gonna take me and nothing could stop him, but you stopped him." She clung to Harper from behind, trembling.

"Yeah…"

"Who's firing?" yelled Darnell.

"Over here! Need backup!" called Harper. "Got the son of a bitch!"

Two small wounds oozed blood into the black fabric of his shirt at the base of his neck. Harper almost threw up at the sight, but not because of the blood. Those pellets had to have passed mere inches from Mila's head.

Darnell jogged into view from the southwest, probably coming from Route 74. Marcie approached from the east. Both sped up to sprinting once they spotted her.

"What the hell?" asked Darnell, eyeing the guy on the ground.

"That's the bastard who's been sneaking around spying on kids. Mila missed school today. Violet asked me to go check on her. Found her wandering around the woods and this guy just jumped out and grabbed her. Tossed something at me, so I shot him."

"Knives. The Shadow Man has lots of knives. Special knives. He throws them and they stick in people and they die," said Mila.

Marcie sounded two short blasts, a 'need help' tone.

Darnell stooped over the guy, patting him down. "Damn, this guy's suit is full of hardware. All sorts of knives and shit."

The man stirred. Mila ducked completely behind Harper, shaking. Darnell jumped up, pointing his hunting rifle at the guy, who moved a little, but appeared to lose consciousness again.

Ryan Herman and Ken Zhang came jogging over within two minutes. While Marcie filled them in on what happened, Harper turned to check on Mila. She almost passed out at the sight of blood running in a trickle down the child's face, but before total panic set in, she realized a crescent shaped welt and small cut marked her forehead… probably from the plastic wad swerving down and hitting her. *Not* a lead pellet. Red ringed Mila's eyes from crying.

Harper cringed, barely able to believe she'd taken the shot. Gingerly, she traced a finger over the mark. "I'm sorry…"

"If you didn't shoot him, you'd be dead. Then I'd be dead, too. It hurt, but it's okay." She smiled despite still crying.

"Wait here a bit, okay? I'll walk you home as soon as I can."

Mila nodded.

Harper took a deep breath and approached the other militia.

"Crazy shot," said Ken.

"He went for a knife. I… like ten feet away. Not much spread. Just instinct. Knife went flying off to the left."

Ryan knocked on the facemask. "Wow, is this Kevlar?"

"Walmart Kevlar." Darnell laughed. "Probably fiberglass or maybe someone got a hold of Kevlar weave and made it themselves. Definitely not military grade."

"Bah." Marcie rolled her eyes. "Military grade only means it costs ten times what it should."

The guys laughed.

Ryan and Ken removed multiple belts and bandoliers containing strange leaf-shaped knives with tiny handles as well as four larger combat knives. Harper and Marcie roamed around in search of the knife he'd thrown, but couldn't find it. Mila stood a short distance away, staring at the man as though she expected him to spring back to life at any second and kill everyone there. The sight of 'creepy girl' looking like a frightened normal child struck Harper as beyond weird.

"Well, let's haul this guy to the doc." Darnell grabbed the man's left arm.

Ryan took the other one. The two men proceeded to drag him off with Ken keeping a gun trained at him.

"Why don't you go on and bring her back to her mama," said Marcie. "Head over to the HQ and explain what happened to Walter once you got her settled in."

"Okay. I will." Harper approached Mila. "C'mon. Think this is worth a day off school."

The girl emitted a feeble chuckle.

Marcie followed the men to the highway, also keeping her weapon trained on the unconscious man.

"Are you hurt… umm except for your forehead??" Harper cringed. "Sorry."

"No. I'm okay." Mila bit her lip. "Please don't tell anyone I was crying, okay?"

"Sure." Harper took the girl's hand. "So, that's the Shadow Man?"

"Yeah."

*Did she see him before? How long could this guy have been around here?*

"Did you know he was going to attack you today?"

Mila walked along at her side, staring down.

"Hon?"

"No. Not today specifically, but I knew he would get me. I can't believe shooting him worked."

"Do you want to talk about why you didn't go to school?"

Mila shrugged. "No one likes me. And, umm, I didn't want the Shadow Man to hurt them when he came for me. Guess I don't have to be so weird now."

"Nothing wrong with being weird. Maybe turn the dial down from eleven though. Weird is fine, but you could ease back on the morbid stuff."

"I'll do that tomorrow. Gonna be too busy having nightmares today."

They passed a house surrounded by trees and continued to the road, following it around a leftward curve before taking the right onto Pinehurst. Mila lived in the first house on the right. As they approached the door, Harper noticed the girl had a leaf-shaped throwing knife concealed in her right hand.

*No wonder I couldn't find the darn thing...* She bit her lip, debated for a moment, and grasped the girl's wrist.

Mila gave her a pleading stare.

"What are you going to do with it?"

"Keep it in case the shadow man escapes and tries to get me."

"You're not gonna cut yourself, are you?"

Mila shook her head. "No. It's for him."

"Okay." Harper let go of her arm. "Just be careful with it."

Mila looked up at her, then with barely a second's glance to her right, threw the knife. It stuck with a soft *thok* in the 0 of the house number, 2401. "I just gotta hit him in the eye."

She glanced at the knife, back at Mila, at the knife again, and blinked. *What the hell did I just witness?*

The girl walked over to the porch, stood on tiptoe, and plucked the little weapon out of the wood. "Mom isn't home right now. She's at the farm. I think I want to go to school so I'm not alone."

"Umm... Someone just tried to kidnap you. Are you sure you don't need time to deal with that?" She glanced again at the house number. "We could go to the farm and find your mother if you want."

"You're right. I'm probably going to have a meltdown once the shock wears off and I process what almost happened."

"Mila?"

"Yeah?"

"You're too good at that creepy act."

"Thanks."

"Come on then. Let's go find your mom."

Mila took her hand.

HARPER WALKED INTO THE MILITIA HQ, NOT SURPRISED TO FIND MARCIE and Ken already there.

"How is she?" asked Walter.

"Held it together until we got to the farm and she watched her mother's reaction as I explained what happened. As soon as Michelle grabbed her and started crying, Mila fell to bits. I think there's probably a normal little girl in there somewhere." *Normal nine-year-olds don't whip a throwing knife at a two-inch target without even aiming. Something's not right with her.*

"That's good to hear. Excellent work by the way." Walter smiled.

"Yeah, no shit. Damn nice shot." Ken whistled. "I'd have choked. Too afraid of hitting the kid, even with a rifle—and you did it with freakin' 12-gauge."

She almost said she figured if she didn't shoot, both she and the girl would die anyway, but in truth, no *thought* had been involved. The shot *felt* possible at that range, buckshot wouldn't spread out *that* far in the short distance, but the risk of an aberrant pellet spinning downward hadn't fully registered until after.

"Well, that's one way to combat a food shortage." Harper fidgeted. "I'm so sick to my stomach I don't think I'm going to eat anything today."

"As I'm sure you're assuming, this is as official an inquiry as it gets. Happens most times a militia person discharges a weapon inside the town. Don't panic, I just need to hear what happened." Walter gestured at a chair facing his desk, then sat behind it. "Already got an idea from these two, so you're in the clear."

"He didn't die, did he?" Harper sat, resting the shotgun across her lap.

"No. His nose is broken," said Darnell. "And he's in surgery to remove a few pellets from his face. Janice is sending some guys up to bring the dude to the holding cells once the doctors clear him."

"Okay." She relaxed. She probably wouldn't have felt *much* guilt at killing a guy trying to abduct Mila, but she also didn't mind not having to deal with it. "Violet asked me to check on her..."

Walter listened to her retelling of everything that happened, nodding, seeming pleased with what she said. "How are you holding up?"

"Good. Nervous... mostly about firing so close to Mila, but I'm okay. That attack in the Walmart rattled me way more than this."

Marcie rubbed her throat, smiling gratefully at her. "Yeah, no kidding. That was rough. I still owe you one for getting that crazy bitch off me."

"All right." Walter closed his notebook. "Your choice. Feel free to head home and wind down or go on back out there as usual."

She stood. "It'll be worse just sitting around the house alone staring at the walls."

"Kid's got spirit," said Darnell.

Marcie patted her back. "Damn straight she does. Good work today."

"Ehh, more luck than anything. Right place, right time. If I hadn't been going *to* her house, I never would've been there in time." That thought made her feel worse than shooting the guy. One little decision made the difference between life or death.

Assuming, of course, the man intended to kill Mila once he finished. Why else would he have wanted her? Then again, organized law enforcement went up in smoke with most of the rest of the world. Would a creep really care if his victim told anyone someone touched them? Though, something didn't sit right in her gut with that thought. Mila had been expecting to die, not be molested. Who wants to assassinate a nine-year-old? Something went on here that didn't make any sense. Harper picked at the shotgun with her thumbnail. Maybe she wouldn't have been that upset if she'd killed him.

"Umm." Harper looked up. "Is anyone going to question this guy? Why was he trying to grab her?"

Walter emitted an uncomfortable sigh, suggesting he also assumed the same thing as she did about what the guy wanted to do. "Probably exactly what everyone's thinking he wanted her for, but yeah, I'll ask Janice to grill him."

She stood there.

"You keep doing that. Are you waiting for me to say 'dismissed' or something?" Walter smiled. "This isn't the Army."

Harper laughed at herself. "Yeah, I guess I am." She flashed a weak smile, sighed out the last of her racing adrenaline, and walked out.

# 19

# WHOLESOME

Another break-in at a house near the south end of Harper's patrol territory kept her a little more than an hour beyond when the kids would've gotten out of class.

Someone had cleared the pantry out of the place where Anna Dominguez lived with her eleven-year-old son, Christopher. In this case, she didn't spot any muddy footprints. She couldn't even rule out that the man she'd shot in the face hadn't done it, since the theft had occurred last night. Anna didn't notice anything had happened until afternoon when she'd popped home for lunch.

Of course, the man she shot did not have a small 9mm handgun on his person... so either he'd tossed it or they had *two* people sneaking around.

When Harper finished at the house, taking as many notes as she could and assuring Anna the militia did everything possible to find the thief, she headed up to the school to pick up the kids. The teachers wouldn't have let them leave without an adult yet, as word the Shadow Man had been caught didn't have a chance to spread. A few kids remained, but none of the ones supposed to go home with her.

Violet looked up from her desk. "Marcie stopped by. She took them home already."

"Okay."

Not *quite* calm, Harper rushed home. Children's voices in the backyard relaxed her enough to slow to a walk. Her three siblings, plus

Becca, ran around tossing a Frisbee back and forth. Relieved, she took a seat on the porch and watched them play.

The sky turned ominous not quite an hour later. As soon as a raindrop hit the concrete slab beside her, Harper called the kids inside, including Becca. Her parents would hopefully understand the rule about rain and expect she'd stay here until it stopped.

Everyone relocated to the living room, where the kids flopped on the floor around a board game. Harper reclined on the couch and resumed reading *The Secret Garden*.

Cliff arrived home about fifteen minutes after the rain began in earnest. He shut the door and stood there dripping for a moment, smiling at her. "Heard what happened. Ballsy shot, but it paid off."

The kids looked up.

"What happened?" asked Madison.

*I'm never going to finish this book.* She closed it, set it on the cushion, and told the kids about the Shadow Man. All four listened with rapt attention. Madison, who'd been to the gun range with Dad once a week for at least the past three years, gawked at her.

"Wow," said Jonathan.

"Glad you listened." Cliff pointed at his eyes with two fingers. "Watch the hands, always."

"Yeah." She exhaled hard. "I remembered."

He headed down the hall to change into dry clothes.

"Why did he grab Mila?" asked Madison.

"Not sure yet."

"He wanted to hurt her?" Lorelei tilted her head.

"Yes, I'm pretty sure he did. But, he's not going to be hurting anyone now."

The kids resumed the game. Lorelei still struggled to understand the fairly complicated rules, but tried her best to participate. Jonathan and Madison patiently helped her. Watching them brought a smile to Harper's lips, and she found their game more entertaining than reading. Or perhaps it merely required less mental focus from a brain that felt like a wrung out sponge. Four happy children felt like a soothing balm for her soul.

Cliff exited the hallway and lit some candles, set them on the dining room table, and entered the kitchen. He started humming while sifting among the canned food. "Feels like a good day for soup."

*It's a good day for any food we can find.* "Yeah."

Michelle had a mild freak-out when Harper had brought Mila to her at the farm. Evidently, hearing that the Shadow Man the girl had been going on and on about for months actually existed hit her hard with guilt for not having believed. The woman never even entertained the idea that it might've been a normal guy in black, dismissing it entirely as a ghost story. She and Mila hadn't even known each other up until last November, Mila having arrived in Evergreen only a week before Harper. Yet, the woman reacted like any true mother at being told she'd almost lost her daughter.

Overcome with grief for her parents, Harper slipped off the couch and padded into the kitchen, hugging Cliff from behind.

They stood in silence for a moment, the rattle of dice and murmurs of children in the background.

"You okay?" asked Cliff in a quiet voice.

"Mostly." She let go and leaned on the counter, explaining how Mila's adoptive mother had taken the news and admitting it made her feel like being 'with her dad.'

He smiled past a frizz of facial hair. "Yeah, well, you buggers have kinda grown on me, too."

"Speaking of growing on, you might want to trim that beard or Fred might mistake you for a bear."

"Ehh, my breath ain't that bad." He lined up several cans of various soups: two beef noodle, a minestrone, and two vegetable. "Those should mix decently enough."

"Yeah. Maybe add some pasta to stretch it or should we save?"

"Love to, but we should probably save it."

"Is it weird that living like we're in the 1800s is starting not to feel weird?"

He snickered. "Do a thing long enough you can get used to almost anything. Except tofu."

"Lies!" called Madison from the living room. "Tofu is awesome. And we should totally get some oil lamps like in that movie."

"If we can find them." Harper folded her arms and let her head loll back. "I'm either going to sleep like a rock tonight or have nightmares."

"That sounds about right," muttered Cliff. "Used to know a lot of guys in that situation."

She cringed. "Sorry."

"Nah, it is what it is. You're just a kid but you've been through shit. Some of those guys weren't much older than you are when they hit the shitstorm in Fallujah." He popped the lid on the minestrone can, sniffed it, and smiled. "Ahh, that brings back memories."

"Getting nostalgic over soup?"

"Used to have this stuff at the mall. Late shift, only two of us in the entire building. Microwave up a giant bowl of this, sit back, and watch movies."

"Two of you?"

"Yeah, one other guard worked with me on night shift. Most of 'em only lasted two weeks, maybe two months before they transferred to days, went to a different site, or figured out that working as a security guard is incredibly effing boring."

"What happened to the guy with you the night, umm… yeah."

"Roberts… he always left early. Our shift didn't end until six, but he had a habit of skating ten minutes to and leavin' me to do all the end of shift logs. Probably on the road going home when the strike hit. I'd say serves him right for stiffing me with extra work for a year, but death via nuclear evaporation is a bit extreme for being a douchebag."

"Ouch."

"Nah. He didn't feel a damn thing."

"Do you think we're gonna be stuck in the 1800s or are there enough people left to recover?"

"No idea. Haven't been watching the news lately." Cliff poured the last soup can in the pot.

She smirked. "What was it really like back then?"

He gave her side eye. "You calling me old?"

Harper twirled some hair around her finger. "No, just asking. Every show or movie I've ever seen set in that time period was like wholesome and stuff. They never had stories where like men grabbed kids, or anything dark like that. Were people actually like that?"

"Hate to say it, but of course. People don't change that much. The same crap went on back then that happened nowadays, but they didn't have the internet or cable news to tell everyone about it. People still did sick shit to kids, murdered their wives, sliced up prostitutes, did unseemly things to their neighbor's donkey…"

She almost laughed.

"The real difference is back when they made those movies about the Old West, people didn't put that sorta awful stuff in film. But, it happened in the real Old West. In those days, people simply didn't talk about things like that in polite company. Small towns dealt with stuff like that in their own way. Guy does something he shouldn't with a girl a little too young, guy disappears, no one knows what happened to him."

"Is that what's going to happen here?"

"Doubt it. Far as I know, Walter, Anne-Marie, and Ned were discussing what to do with him. They don't want to execute him outright, but they're afraid he would be a threat, especially to kids, if they let him out of jail. He's not talking. We still don't know for sure what he wanted to do to Mila, we're all just assuming the worst. Guy won't say who he is, where he came from, or why he attacked her." Cliff shook his head, chuckling. "That mask was pretty freaky though. Homemade Kevlar."

"Shouldn't that have stopped buckshot?" asked Harper.

Cliff picked up the soup pot and carried it into the living room to the fireplace. "Professionally made armor would have stopped it, yeah. But at the range you fired, plus it being a hand-made piece of crap, not so much. He must've gotten Kevlar weave off eBay or something and epoxied it to a hockey mask. And it wouldn't have done a damn thing against a high-powered rifle. Standard Kevlar brain buckets, an AK will punch a hole right through them. Maybe deflect a glancing shot, but a direct hit... only thing the helmet's good for is keeping all the pieces in the same place."

She cringed. "Eww."

Jonathan scrambled over to help Cliff get a fire going.

"The man with the mask was watching me," said Lorelei, sprawled on her chest by the game board, scissoring her feet back and forth. "He looked like he needed a hug."

Harper stared at her, a shiver of dread rattling her bones. The man she shot could've carried the tiny girl off with one arm. "You remember what I asked you, right?"

"Uh huh!" Lorelei nodded. "Gotta ask you or Daddy if it's okay to hug someone first."

"That's right. Please don't forget." She sat on the floor near the kids, too tired to do anything more than stare at the soup pot over the fire.

Lorelei scooted over and leaned against her, showing her the cards in her hand for the game. "Which one do I use next?"

"No fair," said Becca in a joking tone.

"She's better off picking herself right now." Harper yawned. "My brain's done."

# 20

# A LITTLE CREEPY

Dreams of hanging out in the mall with Christina, Renee, and Darci took a turn for the weird.

Faceless men dressed all in black appeared in the crowd and began chasing them around. Harper ran down a back hallway, tripped over a pile of trash bags, and slid on her chest... but didn't stop. The floor became a slide, plunging down into a tube. Water came out of nowhere. Dark became bright light, and her clothes morphed into a neon green swimsuit.

She flew face-first out the end of an epic waterslide tube into a small kiddie pool set up on the front yard of her old home.

Mom and Dad stood on either side of the new Ford Explorer, both of them holding AR15s. Behind them, a perfect glowing mushroom cloud bloomed in the sky.

"Come on, Harper, it's time to go," said Dad.

"You're going to be late." Mom waved at her to hurry up, opening the Explorer's back door. "Get in, sweetie. It's time to go."

Two-year-old Madison, secure in a car seat, waved a pair of 9mm handguns around.

Harper pushed herself up out of the pool, shocked to find that she'd gone back to being a rail-thin nine-year-old version of her former self. The sight of toddler Madison with weapons should have been the most glaringly wrong thing here, but for some reason, her brain seized upon the notion that she hadn't been allowed to wear a two-piece swimsuit until fourteen. She didn't own that particular green one until last year.

Toddler-Madison appeared in front of her, pulling at her hair as if to drag her out of the pool by it. "'Mon, Harp. Get up."

The too-weird scene faded to black, though the sensation of tugging at her head remained.

"'Mon, Harp. It's morning," said Madison.

Her head felt like stone, and she had no interest in moving even if she got detention for cutting school. Didn't she have a test today? Why couldn't she remember studying last night? *Ugh, I did it again. Up until two in the morning.* "Tell Mom I'm staying home today."

"Harper," whispered Madison. "Mom's dead. Why would you say that?"

Dread seeped in beneath the heavy malaise making her want to go back to sleep. She forced her eyes open to the sight of a wan caricature of her younger sister hovering over her in a thin nightie. The girl had always been skinny, but her ribs looked too prominent, her eyes too full of grief.

It took a moment for the strange, foreign quality of the bedroom to wear off and the memory of the past six months to flood back, crushing the momentary reprieve of her dream. She hadn't quite overslept yet, thanks to Madison shaking her.

"I'm awake." She yawned, then reached up and brushed her fingers at Madison's side.

The girl squirmed, grabbing her hand, grinning. "Stop tickling me."

*She's losing weight.* Harper slid her left hand up under the covers, feeling around her stomach and side. *So am I.*

"Hey, I'm peeing!" yelled Jonathan from the hall.

"Okay," said Lorelei.

The boy emitted a frustrated sigh. "That means you're supposed to wait."

*I need to talk to her about personal space.*

"Why'd you say that about Mom?" asked Madison.

"I wasn't all the way awake. Still dreaming about being home. Thought you were Mom trying to wake me up for school."

"Oh."

Harper sat up and swung her legs off the side of the bed. Surprisingly chilly air blasted away the remainder of her sleepiness. A house with only a fireplace for heat got darn cold at night. She sighed at the electric baseboard heaters. *Please let Jeanette fix things.*

Madison traded her nightgown for a pink-and-white striped shirt and a denim skirt. "Why did they give us so much pink stuff?"

"You didn't hate pink before."

"I don't hate pink." Madison frowned. "I hate them thinking I *have* to wear pink because I'm a girl."

"I'm sure they didn't mean it that way. We can't exactly go shopping whenever we want."

"Yeah, I know." Madison sighed.

Lorelei walked in wearing her pink socks—but carrying her nightgown.

Harper laughed, taking some comfort in that the formerly-starved child looked much less skeletal. Ironic that she gained some weight while everyone else lost it. Lorelei had a ways to go yet to reach 'normal,' but she didn't look frighteningly thin anymore.

*Maddie and Jon are still giving her extra food.*

Humming happily to herself, Lorelei rooted around in the dresser until she found a basic child's dress, more spoils from the Walmart run. She carried it over and held her arms up. Harper took the garment and pulled it over the girl's head. *She's six. She should be able to get dressed on her own by now. Does she not know how or is this just her wanting me to take care of her? How do I give her a reward for getting herself dressed when we're thrilled to find an extra box of crackers?*

"Thank you!" Lorelei hugged her.

*Maybe she just wants the affectionate contact.* Harper patted her on the back, let go, and stood. "Okay, come on. Time to eat. I'll be right there."

She headed to the kitchen by way of the bathroom, the icy seat destroying any lingering temptation of going back to sleep. The kids took their spots at the table while Cliff portioned out cereal. Harper sat, gasping at another jolt of cold to her backside.

"Forget something?" asked Cliff.

Harper looked down at her nightie. "I'll change after I eat. I'm already here."

He set a bowl of cereal in front of her, some bland-as-hell flakes the store they'd scavenged from had tons of because only people who lost their ability to taste ever bought them.

None of the kids whined at the lack of sugar, which felt beyond wrong. *They shouldn't eat old folks' cereal without complaining.* Jonathan's cheeks had lost some of the roundness they used to have. She couldn't see his ribs under his shirt, but figured they probably looked as prominent as

Madison's. They all needed more food than they'd been eating, but she couldn't exactly do much about it yet.

Everyone munched in relative silence.

After breakfast, Harper returned to the bedroom to change. She grabbed her least filthy pair of underpants, which she'd already worn at least six times since it had last been washed, frowning at herself for putting off doing laundry so long. She'd attend to it that afternoon. At least the house had come with a few bottles of Tide, even if she had to wash everything with cold water in the bathtub and hang it outside to dry.

*Now I know the world is screwed. I'd be happier having a working washing machine than a new car.*

Flannel shirt, jeans, sneakers, and shotgun later, Harper headed out to the living room and collected the kids for the walk to school. The sunny morning matched her lighter mood. Now that she'd dealt with the Shadow Man, it didn't feel like she had to guide the children across a warzone.

They chattered back and forth about school, the farm, maybe going house-exploring once class ended, generally sounding happy. Harper's good mood dipped a little when they arrived at school and she noticed the other kids also appeared in dire need of a good meal. Violet, too, had lost enough weight that it showed in her face.

*No wonder someone's stealing food. I'm not sure I could even be angry with whoever it is.* She waved at the teachers, then made her way outside. *But, we can't let them keep stealing. Gotta be fair with the food.*

She paused at the edge of the sidewalk in front of the school. *Not worrying about some creep being a threat to the kids felt wonderful.* The absence of a driving sense of urgency pushing her to go out there and find him before he did something horrible to a kid made a day of patrolling feel like a vacation.

"Hi," said a child behind her.

Harper damn near fainted. She jumped and spun, clutching her chest and staring at Mila, who stood only three feet away in a white dress with tiny daisy patterns. The garment looked entirely odd on her since the girl had thus far worn black every time she'd seen her.

"Crap, don't do that…" wheezed Harper.

"The Shadow Man isn't gonna stay in jail. I'm sorry for bringing him here. It's my fault. I wanted to thank you for saving me, and say goodbye before I leave."

"What?" Harper blinked. "Leave? What do you mean leave?"

Mila clasped her hands in front of herself, looking down. "I have to go away. The Shadow Man will keep following me and I don't want him to hurt anyone else. That's why I said creepy stuff. It's okay if the other kids tease me. If they stay away from me, he won't hurt them. My mom doesn't know I'm leaving 'cause she'll make me stay, and then she'll die, too. I don't want her to die."

"Listen to me..." Harper crouched and grasped the girl by the shoulders. "You're nine, Mila. You're not going to run away. There's far more dangerous people out there than some random creep in a ninja costume."

"He's not." She shook her head. "He can split apart into like five copies with magic. The Shadow Man did that when he chased me around Boulder before I came here. He even caught me for a little while and put me in jail."

"What?" Harper sank to sit on the curb. "Put you in jail? What did he do to you?"

"He said he would make me a shadow, too. Forced me do stuff, throwing knives, running, hiding, and climbing, but I had to sleep in the jail 'cause he knew I wanted to escape. I hadda shoot someone dead to become a real shadow, but I didn't wanna. The magic would have gotten into me and made me evil if I did that. I escaped, and he's mad 'cause shadows can't leave or they die. But I'm *not* a shadow 'cause I didn't kill that man. The boy did, and the shadow gave him food. He only gave me a little food as punishment 'til I'd prove killing." Mila held her hands up, pantomiming chewing tied wrists. "But I got away. I can move quiet, and he didn't hear me 'til the door squeaked. I ran and hid. The Shadow Man used his magic to turn himself into copies, but he didn't find me."

"Mila..." Harper stared up at her, not knowing how to process any of that. "He's not a ghost. Maybe you were just so scared you thought you saw him everywhere." *Or she's got a wild imagination. This is kinda dark and weird for a little girl to make up... but what kid her age could throw a knife like that, right into the zero.* "You were kidnapped."

She nodded. "But I got away, and now he's mad and gonna kill me for knowing secrets. He's gonna turn into darkness and float out of jail. I don't want him to hurt my mom either, so I gotta go away."

"No, Mila. You don't have to go away. He's just a man. I know he's big and scary to you, but he's not magic. There are bad people out there, so you need to stay here where it's safe. Maddie and I almost got kidnapped by a gang in Lakewood."

"That's different. They weren't gonna make you shadows. They were just mean."

Harper nodded. "Those men wanted to take us and force us to join their gang. They would've hit us and made us do bad things. Steal, hurt people... But, they're only humans. *Bad* humans. Not shadow spirits or whatever. The man who tried to grab you is only a man."

"Crazy people were all over after the sky lit on fire." Mila sat next to her on the curb and leaned against her. "I don't think my parents are alive. Everyone ran around screaming and hitting each other. Threw stuff at windows, lit fires. Soldiers shot at people. After I escaped the Shadow Man, I was alone for a long time. At night, I'd go in a dumpster or trash can or car so he wouldn't see me. He can't go outside when it's sunny or he'll melt away. Some people found me. I was afraid of them at first, but they didn't yell at me or throw bricks or try to shoot me. They brought me here and Anne-Marie took me to stay with my new mom. I think she really loves me, but she thinks I'm creepy."

"Well, you do kinda act a little odd." Harper put an arm around her. "But it makes sense after what happened to you."

Mila reached down between her feet to fuss with a tuft of grass poking up from a seam in the concrete. "I watched people die. Everyone went crazy, and I couldn't find my parents. I didn't cry. Only wimps cry."

"Where'd you hear that?"

"An Army man yelled it at another Army man when everyone was going nuts. Then they shot people. They didn't see me under the car, or they'd have shot me, too. They're both dead now. I cried when you saved me from the Shadow Man, and Mom cried when you told her what happened. That made me cry more, too. Guess I am a wimp."

"He's wrong. It's absolutely okay to cry... especially after nuclear war. And no, Mila, you're not a wimp. You're a kid."

Mila looked up at her and narrowed her eyes. "For now."

"Heh."

Her expression fell back to neutral. "Assuming I live long enough to grow up."

"Aww." Harper squeezed her. "There you go again with the creepy stuff."

"It's not creepy. It's realistic. People think it's safe here, but it isn't. Evergreen isn't *dangerous*, but nowhere is safe anymore."

Harper imagined that guy in black handing Mila a gun and demanding she kill some dude tied up on the floor. *Sick son of a bitch. This poor kid.* "It is a little creepy for a girl your age to be so blasé about death."

"What's blasé?"

"Umm. Talking about it like it's no big deal." *Logan said we stop being innocent when we know we're going to die someday. Mila's too young.*

"Why, 'cause little girls are supposed to be sweet and nice and never say anything bad?"

"No. It's not that… Umm. Like, sometimes when you talk about death, it almost sounds like you're happy about it."

"I'm not. I'm telling lies, trying to not be scared." She took a quivering breath, seeming at the verge of tears, but held it in. "I don't really want to die. Just scared of the Shadow Man."

"He's not magic. Just crazy. A different kind of crazy than the people you saw rioting, but still crazy. Normal people don't try to turn children into killers."

"I thought he was a demon."

"Nope. Just a guy in a stupid costume."

Mila stretched her legs out, examining her flip-flops. "You're right. I shouldn't run away in these. My other shoes are too thin for hiking, too. Okay, I'll stay."

*I hope she's just being cute and crappy shoes aren't the real reason she's changed her mind.* Harper hugged her. "C'mon. You should go back to class."

"Okay." Mila looked up at her with sudden vulnerability in her eyes. "When he escapes jail, will you protect me?"

Harper brushed a hand over the girl's head. "You bet."

"Thank you." Mila fought back the sniffles, then sat there staring into space.

"You should really go back to class."

Mila nodded. "I know. Just waiting for my eyes not to be red anymore so no one laughs at me for crying."

Harper sat there with her, sick with dread that she might not be able to find Mila in time if that guy ever did manage to escape. It didn't seem all that likely, but she couldn't help but consider that a man capable of training a nine-year-old to throw knives with deadly accuracy in only a few weeks' time could probably get out of a little town jail.

# 21

# SILVER BULLET

Not sure what else to do once Mila went back to class, Harper headed from the school to the militia HQ and told Walter Holman what she'd learned.

She had the feeling the man had kept the girl in a literal jail, probably having taken over a small police station somewhere in Boulder. She didn't want to risk traumatizing her more by dredging up bad memories, so had left the questioning light.

The revelation that this guy actually *had* come here specifically targeting Mila and not hunting random children surprised Walter. Though, she had mentioned some boy who'd also been abducted. Once he'd done what he meant to do to Mila, either killed or captured her, he very well might have tried to abduct other kids to join his 'shadow' group. Walter suggested he might have been spying on her siblings because Madison somewhat resembled Mila from behind, both having straight, black hair.

Harper hadn't thought to ask for more details about the boy. 'Boy' could've meant anything from child to teen. She worried that a mentally traumatized child might be stuck in a jail cell somewhere without food, trapped while this idiot tracked Mila all the way to Evergreen. However, she couldn't justify trekking cross-country on a search for a boy who may or may not be real and might not even be locked up. Or, sad as it was to think about, even still alive. Mila had told her the boy *did* shoot a man as ordered, so possibly, the creep trusted him enough as an 'official shadow' not to keep him prisoner.

"The guy still hasn't said anything." Walter exhaled hard, fluttering his lips. "We're still trying to figure out what to do here. Letting this man go would surely present a direct threat to little Mila, or other children. Or you... anyone here really. Someone who'd track that kid halfway across Colorado because she refused to murder a helpless man and join him..."

"Might want to kill everyone here out of revenge," said Harper.

"Seems like it would be best to put a bullet in him, but I don't feel right making that call. And I don't think we have too many people here who'd be willing to play executioner."

Harper nodded, certainly not wanting to do that. One thing shooting a man about to hurt her or someone else, but murdering him when he isn't a threat didn't sound much different from what he tried to force Mila to do. "Why not have a trial? We have a lawyer."

"Hah! I'm sure Arturo would adore that. But... what if we do and a jury trial comes back with a death sentence?"

"He didn't kill anyone.... That we know of."

"So we keep him locked up, draining our food for how long?"

She cringed. "I dunno."

"Thanks for bringing this information to our attention. That poor girl. How's she doing?"

"Shocked, I think. She had this guy built up in her head as some kind of demonic supernatural creature. She even thinks he can split into multiple copies of himself. When I knocked him out with a load of buckshot to the face, it kinda shattered her world... in a good way. She'd been stuck in a bad world. It needed shattering."

Walter chuckled.

"That's it, really. If there's nothing else..." She started to turn toward the door.

"Dismissed," said Walter.

Harper stuck her tongue out at him.

He laughed.

SCHOOL LET OUT EARLY FOR FARM DAY.

Harper went with the class across the highway again, figuring it couldn't hurt to watch the lessons and maybe pick up a thing or two about how the farms worked. Madison's group spent their two hours learning about caring for cows. Lorelei and the smaller kids got to feed chickens, and Jonathan's cluster walked with Jim Rollins, the farm manager, as he gave them an overview of how the irrigation system they'd hand-built worked.

She decided to follow that group roaming back and forth around rows of potatoes, carrots, turnips, tomatoes, and whatnot. Seeing all the plants made her stomach growl, but none of them had yet matured enough to produce anything edible. The size of the farm did give her hope, though. They had only to weather a few lean months and maybe everything would work out.

Daydreams of a time when she complained about food she didn't care for and never once imagined still being hungry after dinner distracted her from Jim's lecture. She mentally drifted off, craving pizza, French fries, or that surprisingly decent chicken ranch salad her high school cafeteria made.

*Does Madison really* like *tofu or does she just feel so sad about animals she accepts eating it as punishment for being human?*

"Hey," said a boy. "Everything okay?"

Harper looked up at Logan Ruiz. He still had on the same clothes she'd seen him in before, standing a few feet away with his hands in his pockets, head tilted a bit to the side, hair fluttering in the wind.

"Yeah, just thinking."

He wandered closer. "What about?"

"You know, pizza. Usually what comes to mind when standing by rows of… whatever this is."

"Potatoes." He nodded toward Jim's group, which had progressed a decent distance away during her mental check out. "Tour group left you behind."

"Heh. I kinda left them behind. It's okay. I'm not really a student anymore. Just pretending." A mild gust threw her hair over her face. She puffed at it, blushing. *Can I be any more awkward?*

Logan chuckled. "Hey, you want to hang out later?"

"I dunno. I got my siblings to keep an eye on."

"What about your dad? Can you slip away for a bit after dinner? There's a spot south of the dirt road. You know, where we had that barbecue like a week ago."

Harper wouldn't have thought twice about going out to spend time with her friends before. Now, it felt like doing something wrong. She needed to be with her family. Though, Madison's clinginess had fallen back to almost pre-war levels, especially when Becca came over. The idea of taking a little time for herself to have some fun did appeal to her. With the supposed Shadow Man contained, the pervasive sense of dread that had been hanging over Evergreen had faded.

*Maybe I should. I've been wound so tight lately.* She fidgeted. Hanging out with a group of random teens at night had never been her scene. That usually meant underage drinking, possibly weed, possibly stronger drugs. Definitely breaking rules. The few times Christina had dragged her to parties, she'd mostly spent the whole time standing in the corner desperately waiting for it to be time to leave. The 'good' parties, people left her alone. The not so good ones, someone invariably couldn't believe that a 'girl like her' felt uncomfortable around crowds. Some called her 'too pretty' to be shy. Others couldn't grok that a ginger lacked a wild streak. The bad parties, she'd get grabbed or pawed, or someone would try giving her a drink with something in it. Harper had no idea how often people *tried* to roofie her, since she'd never once accepted a drink anyone tried to hand her. If she hadn't been ashamed to tell Veronica and Darci how she really felt about going to parties, they probably would have stopped encouraging her to go.

But the world changed. Spending time with a small group of survivors didn't have the same vibe as a house crammed full of a hundred teens racing each other to see who could pass out first.

"Umm. Maybe. I'll try."

"Cool." Logan's smile melted off with a sigh. "I gotta get back to work, but I'll see you tonight?"

"If I can get away. My sister is kinda brittle." *Oh, yeah. Blame Maddie. Way to big sis properly.* "But she's getting better."

He nodded, looking off to the side. "All right. Don't feel guilty if you can't make it."

"'Kay." She cringed at reminding him of his sister, who probably died. "I should be able to make it."

Logan smiled. "Cool. See you there."

Harper watched him walk back to a plot of some short bushy green plants. He picked up a white bucket and scooped something from it onto the ground as he made his way along the row.

Her father's imagined voice told her not to give up on life just because the world changed.

*Okay. Okay. If Maddie can handle me disappearing for an hour or two, I'll go.*

Moonlight provided a surprising amount of illumination when no electric lights worked anywhere nearby.

Harper stayed home until after dinner, chickening out and not mentioning anything about going to spend time with kids her age until it started to get dark. Madison surprised her with a casual 'okay' that made her wonder if her little sister also thought she needed to relax for a change.

Of course, Cliff had been mortifying. He assumed she ran off to pull a Beth-Jaden. She'd been too embarrassed at the implication to even tell him that she'd never done more than kiss a boy, and had no intention whatsoever of going all the way with a boy she'd spent less than two hours talking to. Hell, she had no intention of even kissing him. 'Just hanging out with friends' got an 'uh huh' from him, plus a knowing smile.

Evidently, the man underestimated the powers of Introvert Prime.

She followed the road to Route 74 and hooked a left onto the dirt path that ran north of the open field where the 'town meal' had been held. She didn't see a gathering of teens anywhere, and spent a minute turning in place, searching around.

*Guess I missed it.* She slouched with the same relief that always came over her when she found an excuse to avoid going to a party. *Oh, well. Guess I'll go home.*

Footsteps scuffed the dirt to the south.

She turned, spotting Logan walking toward her from a tree. As soon as she faced him, he waved her over.

*Oh, crap. It's not like a party... it's just him.*

Fortunately, no one could tell she blushed in the dark. Nothing about him struck her as threatening, intimidating, or even offbeat like Tyler had been at his most approachable. Besides, she had a shotgun.

*He's just trying to be friendly. Talking won't hurt anyone.*

One seventeen-year-old boy she kinda spoke to already shouldn't scare her more than a crowd of teens she didn't even know, but Harper had to force herself to walk closer to him. Even though it seemed unlikely he'd do anything inappropriate, she suspected he liked her a little more than as a simple friend. Why else ask her to a place where they had time alone?

"Hey," she said when finally getting close enough not to shout.

"Hey yourself." Logan smiled. "Is your sister okay?"

"Yeah. She, umm, didn't even seem to mind. I didn't see you at first. I'm sorry for making you think of yours."

"It's okay. I know you didn't mean to do that. Luisa was fifteen. Maybe she still is. Like you said, we haven't actually *seen* Colorado Springs... just heard like everyone say it's completely gone."

"They could've been in the basement?" asked Harper. "Sorry. I'm just saying stupid crap now."

He nodded back toward the tree. "Never a bad thing to hold on to hope, even if it's unlikely. Sorry for startling you. I was stargazing. Want to join me?"

"Sure." She couldn't quite look at him.

He walked back to the tree and stretched out flat in the grass, staring up at the sky.

Harper sat next to him, laying the Mossberg on her right. A vast sky of stars above felt like a beckoning depth she could fall into.

"The stars are so much more intense without the light pollution of cities," said Logan. "I mean, it totally sucks they nuked us... but sometimes I think that maybe technology hurt us more than helped."

"Maybe. But I wish it didn't happen."

"Yeah. I know. Me too. But, it did, and we can't undo it... so why not find things to be happy about?"

She leaned her weight back on her hands, not quite comfortable enough to lie down. A cool night breeze teased at her hair as she tried to remember anything about constellations. He had a point, the stars *did* seem much brighter than she remembered. "I think I forgot how to be happy."

"My grandmother died a few years ago. Grandpa kept telling jokes about her."

"That's awful."

Logan chuckled. "No, I mean, he loved her *so* much, but he knew she wouldn't want him to give up on life just because she'd gone away. They'd be together again at some point, so why stay sad all the time?"

"Not sure I believe in that stuff. Afterlife and all."

"Even if there isn't, do you think your parents would want you to be happy, even now?"

"Yeah, probably. Parents are supposed to die before us, right? But… not quite so early. I wish I had more time with them. Dad spent so much time at the office, and Mom was always either working or out with Maddie. Maybe that's why I'm not completely crazy now, sitting in a ball in the corner of some room crying myself to sleep every night. I basically spent the last like two years living alone. We saw each other a little in the morning and a little at night."

"That's sad. Come on, something's got to have made you happy recently." He regarded her with a roguish grin. "Tell me something that made you smile in like the past month."

"Umm…" Harper thought, tilting her head side to side. "The first time Madison ran outside to play with her friend Becca and didn't take her dead phone. That made me happy, but I kinda cried more than smiled."

"Just one thing?"

"When I found Lorelei okay a couple days ago. Thought she'd been abducted." Harper eased herself down, lying flat on her back, and laced her fingers over her stomach. "And yeah, I cried there, too. I'm such a cliché."

"How so?"

"I am The Girl Who Cries At Everything. Used to cry when my father killed spiders."

"Seriously? A girl who likes spiders?"

She glanced over at him. "I don't *like* spiders, but that doesn't mean I want them to die. What about you? What's made you smile lately?"

"The look Zach gave you when he walked away."

"Ugh. What's that guy's problem, anyway? Has he always been a racist idiot?"

Logan shrugged. "Probably. He didn't show it that much before. I mean, yeah, when I joined the hockey team they made the 'Mexican on ice' cracks, but it never felt mean-spirited until now. Maybe he's stressed out over losing his parents. That boy's not used to the real world."

"We're not in the 'real world' anymore. We're in some meth-addicted strung out cousin of the real world."

He laughed. "Seeing the plants come up… those first bits of green showing in the dirt made me smile, too. Like if hope existed as something physical, it would be those leaves."

"Yeah. That is something to smile about."

She swished her feet back and forth, her thoughts swirling among her worries about her siblings not having enough food or fearing that they'd get sick. Someone could invade the town, go crazy, start shooting randomly. While true that people she loved could've died at any moment even before the war to a car accident or any of a dozen different things, the reality of it hadn't ever settled in her brain. No one really ever considered that every time they got in a car they might die. No one ever spared a second's thought that a trip to the mall to go shopping might end with them being shot during an armed robbery. It *could* happen, but the odds were so remote as to be out of mind.

Now, Harper couldn't stop thinking about every way a situation might go wrong.

Too many worries plagued her already without adding a boy to the mix. Logan seemed like a nice kid. Thinking of a boy as 'nice' could lead to thinking of him as more than that, to wanting to spend time with him, maybe even do the holding hands thing. How could she even think about dating a boy with the world in its present state? She had to protect her siblings, help protect the town, not spend her time running around with some boy. Maybe if her biggest fears remained getting into college and Starbucks not running out of sugar-free mocha syrup, she'd have the mental capacity for a relationship, but…

Her time to goof off with friends, not caring about anything but having fun, had evaporated in a nuclear fireball. Did she owe it to the millions of dead to remain somber, living in what amounted to an enormous graveyard named the United States of America? Did she owe it to Madison to set everything aside and focus only on keeping her safe? Or, might she owe it to herself not to let the war kill her inside as it had killed her parents?

"What are you thinking? You've been quiet a while." Logan stretched, then clasped his hands together behind his head.

"Just stuff. Mostly bad stuff. Feels selfish to think about trying to have fun or be happy after so many people died. I have to keep Maddie safe."

He sat up. "I think you should keep her safe *and* happy. What's the point of existing if we're consumed by guilt and never allow ourselves to experience joy?"

"Don't they call that Catholicism?"

He chuckled. "I'm serious, Harper. We're all trying so hard to survive, we can't lose sight of being human, too."

"I guess. Maybe I'm traumatized, too. It still doesn't seem real that I've had to kill people. Been thinking about it like I've gone inside a video game. Just nameless, generic bad guys, not people with names, families, friends... Before the war, they'd have been like anyone else. How do people go from working a nine-to-five to looting, murder, and kidnapping? Some things those creeps said to me *still* makes my skin crawl. Like two months ago, some guy who used to, I dunno, check groceries or something grabbed me from behind and whispered in my ear what he would do to me. How does that happen?"

"Who knows? Maybe they lost their families and went crazy. Maybe they'd already been criminals and just didn't get caught. Some people would have done crazy shit if they knew they could've gotten away with it. The only thing holding them back had been the police, fear of going to jail. Now, that's gone."

"That kinda makes sense. And now that I think about it, I bet everyone who'd been in jail got out... at least if they survived the blasts. Maybe that's where the blue gang came from. They'd all been criminals before the war."

"Possible."

They stared up into the vastness of the stars, talking about life before the war. She spoke of her parents, her worries about school, her friends, all the while feeling a deep weight in her gut over everything she'd lost. Though, the more she shared of her memories, the more she found herself coming to terms with what happened.

Logan told her a little about his younger sister Luisa. She'd turned fifteen in July, loved music, wanted to become a singer. She'd done a bunch of YouTube videos, even auditioned for *The Voice*, but hadn't been selected for airtime. The two of them had been close, and the way he described her reminded Harper of the protectiveness Jonathan showed toward Madison. He didn't dwell on his family for long, soon shifting the topic to his joining the hockey team mostly because his parents wanted him to do 'something physical' and he didn't feel like taking karate classes. He also had two older siblings, a brother and sister who'd both already moved out. The elder sister had been attending college in Florida. His brother went into the Navy three years ago. He didn't know if either one of them survived the war. Head down, he admitted assuming his parents and little sister had all died in the blast.

"What sucks the most is Luis and Ana probably think I died, since Colorado Springs got erased off the map."

"Wait, you have a brother Luis and a sister Luisa?"

Logan smiled. "Yeah. Dad had a weird sense of humor."

She sat up, crossing her legs... and almost took his hand. "Your brother and sister might not know. How would they? There's no internet or TV anymore."

"True. Think they nuked Orlando?"

"Who would be cruel enough to blow up Disney World?"

With a bad Russian accent Logan said, "The mouse must be destroyed as symbol of capitalist society."

Harper giggled.

He smiled at her, though it came off forced.

"Oh..." Her mood crashed. "Sorry. Your sister was there, right?"

"Yeah. She went to the University of Central Florida. Orlando was a major city, so it probably got hit."

"Hey." She poked him. "We're trying to think of stuff to be happy about, right?"

"Yeah. Sorry. It's kinda nice here. Never thought I'd quit school and work a manual labor job, but..."

She smirked. "Not quite the same. We're not working *jobs*. Everyone's doing what they can to keep it going. I mean, we're desperate. They even let *me* be a cop. I've got like the exact wrong personality for that."

"Bet you're good at it."

"Ehh. Not really. I can't investigate for crap. Not much of a fighter. But hey, I can hit a flying clay at thirty yards."

"Heard you tagged that guy right in the face while he was holdin' some little girl hostage."

"Y... yeah. I had to." She hurried an explanation. "Stupid wadding swerved low and hit her right in the forehead. I feel awful."

"Was she hurt?"

"Just a welt, a small cut, and a bruise. It's only plastic. Still. I shouldn't have taken such a reckless shot. Like some William Tell crap with a shotgun. Sometimes pellets have burrs and they can spin wild out of the cluster. I could've killed her." Harper stared at the dirt, thinking back to the guy who'd grabbed Madison. That guy had been even closer. She felt guilty as hell for a moment over possibly valuing Mila's life less than her sister's, risking a shot with her that she couldn't bring herself to take when it had been Madison's life in the balance. But, that had been a *long* three months ago. Harper had changed. The 'sweetest girl in class' had developed a hard candy shell. When that guy hid behind Mila and went for a weapon, she'd trusted her instincts, reacting without deep thought. And, as much as she hated to admit it, she had become desensitized to killing people.

Not that she could randomly end total strangers, but if someone threatened her or an innocent kid, she wouldn't hesitate anymore. In a way, the blue gang *had* killed Harper Cody. Or at least the girl she had once been.

"You wouldn't have taken the shot if you didn't trust yourself. No time to think, right? You saved her life. Bet that made you smile."

"Yeah... once I got done freaking the hell out."

"I bet."

Clattering drew her attention to the side.

A headless, blue glowing apparition crossed the field toward them. For a brief instant, Harper had a mental freak-out at a legit ghost coming right toward her... until she realized she stared at Grace wearing a dress so white it glowed in the moonlight. The metallic noise came from her left hand, a six-pack of silvery cans dangling from her fingers. Harper pursed her lips, caught between relief at not being alone with a boy and unexpected annoyance at not being alone with *this* boy.

That second part confused her enough to keep quiet.

"Hey." Grace plopped down in front of them, forming a circle. "Heard there was supposed to be a party out here."

"Umm." Harper blushed. "I was expecting there to be more people."

"My fault. I didn't exactly make it clear," said Logan.

"Oh... Sorry. Am I interrupting your date?"

"No!" blurted Harper and Logan at the same time.

She glanced at him.

Logan sat up, resting his elbows on his knees. "We're just hanging out, yanno? Talking."

"It's kinda weird seeing you with a girl," said Grace.

"As weird as seeing you wearing something that came from Walmart."

She laughed.

"Why is it weird seeing him with a girl?" asked Harper.

"Just haven't before. He didn't even stare at the cheerleaders."

Logan grinned. "You just didn't see me."

"Oh, that's only a *little* bit creepy." Harper whistled.

"Kidding. I used to be real busy with AP classes, hockey, and stuff. Never worked out that I met anyone."

"So, you like girls?" Harper tilted her head at him.

"Yeah. Kirk's just an idiot."

Grace held up the Coors. "You guys want one?"

"Where'd you get that from?" asked Harper.

"Umm, the bar. That guy Earl. Don't even have to hide it. So weird. They're letting us drink if we're sixteen or older now. Thought there'd be more people here... I didn't like want to get hammered or anything. Figured I'd only drink one and share the rest."

Logan took one. "Thanks."

Harper waved her off. "Nah. I don't really like the taste of beer."

Grace and Logan popped a can each, sipping it while the three of them talked about true world tragedies like the lack of any new movies coming out for the summer. After a while, Harper came down with a case of the screwits and grabbed a beer.

"It's weird to think that most of the people involved in producing this beer are probably dead now, and the company is gone." Harper examined the can, half tempted to leave it sealed as some kind of memento of the world that came before.

Logan nudged her. "Harper, you really need to cheer up."

"No pressure," said Grace. "Don't feel like you have to."

"I'm thirsty, it's here, and one beer won't do much."

"Do you drink often?" asked Logan.

"No, not really. I think I was the only kid in my entire high school who had no interest in alcohol."

He grinned. "Well, don't drink it too fast then."

She popped the tab and took a sip, cringing. "Bleh. This stuff is nasty."

Grace and Logan laughed.

"It's not *that* bad." Grace took another sip. "Beer, in general, takes a little getting used to."

Harper coughed. "Something that 'requires getting used to' is probably not good for people to have."

"Does that include broccoli?" asked Logan.

"I'd *adore* some broccoli right about now." Harper sighed. "I'd eat almost anything if I could have enough to feel full."

"Anything?" asked Grace, wide eyed.

Logan coughed.

Harper gawked at her, blushed like hell, and couldn't look at either one of them.

"What? Oh... no!" Grace cackled. "I meant like... oh, liver and onions or something horrible. Escargot?"

"Cliff might teach us which bugs we can eat," said Harper, still too embarrassed to look at either one of them. "Last December, I almost threw up at the thought. Now... I think I'd eat grubs if I had them."

"Wow, that's hungry," said Logan.

"As long as someone else cooked them and they weren't still moving when I tried to eat them."

"Ugh," said Grace.

"Maddie's even stopped complaining about meat. She's a vegetarian. She still cries a little whenever Cliff comes home with chicken or venison, but she eats it. Her ribs are showing. Mine, too."

Logan glanced over at her. "Really? That bad? Let me see?"

Heat settled in her cheeks. "I haven't had enough beer."

"No worries." He drained the last of his can.

Harper felt awkward as hell for the next minute or three while the other two tried to decide what movie they'd seen ranked as the 'best of their lives.' Feeling random, she pulled her shirt up to expose her ribs.

Grace and Logan paused, staring at her. She giggled, but he looked concerned.

He reached over and placed his hand on her side, his skin so warm it almost burned her. She shivered as he traced his fingers over her ribs and the grooves between them. It occurred to her that she'd never had a boy touch her like that before. Not that showing her stomach crossed any line. She had no problem with a two-piece bathing suit. Strange boys had *seen* her before, but never up close, never making contact with her beyond holding hands or kissing.

A glint of moonlight shone in his eyes, radiating concern. Time seemed to stop.

Harper couldn't move, her left hand clutching a bundle of flannel, her right, the lukewarm beer. Cool night air brushed across her face and bare stomach, a few errant strands of red tickling her cheek.

"I can help a bit if you want, bring over some of my rations." Logan lowered his hand, leaving a warm spot behind. "You maybe should eat a little more."

She let her shirt drop, not bothering to tuck it in, and gazed at the Coors can, unable to even remember what to do with it.

"You guys are so cute," said Grace.

Harper gasped. "We are not."

Logan tried to drink from his empty can, then attempted a casual 'I meant to do that' smile.

When the awkwardness grew too strong to remain still, Harper took a big sip and nearly choked on the unpleasant flavor. "Gah. Is this stuff stale or is it supposed to taste like this?"

"No idea." Grace shrugged and took a sip. "I wasn't allowed to drink before."

"Like that stopped you," muttered Logan.

She stuck her tongue out at him. "I had wine or mixed drinks. Not beer."

A distant canine howl broke the silence in the west.

"Eep." Grace sat up tall, looking around. "What was that?"

"Wolves or coyotes probably," said Logan.

Harper smacked her lips, cringing at the flavor, but took another sip only to avoid wasting it. Beer had calories, after all. "Do you think nuclear radiation might've made like mutant werewolves?"

"It doesn't work that way," said Grace. "Any genetic aberrations caused by exposure to gamma radiation would take multiple generations to appear... and they'd probably be detrimental, like birth defects."

Harper gave her side eye. "Right..."

"If we're about to be attacked by werewolves, at least we have the silver bullet." Logan held up his can.

Grace shook her head. "Wow."

"A werewolf would take one whiff of this stuff and run." Harper held the can out, estimating she'd consumed about half of it. Her head did feel a little funny—probably why she'd pulled her shirt up. "Here..." She handed it to Logan. "I shouldn't get tipsy while carrying a gun around."

He took it. "Yeah, that's probably not a good idea."

"Oh, darn. There goes my nefarious plan of getting both of you drunk." Grace whistled innocently.

They all laughed.

"Hey is it true you caught Beth and Jaden screwing?" asked Grace, giggling.

"No." Harper shook her head. "That isn't true."

She leaned forward with a teasing grin. "Then why is your face as red as your hair?"

"I didn't catch them doing it. They'd already finished when I found them."

"Technicalities." Grace tilted her head back, emptying the last of her beer. "Umm, yeah. I think this stuff might be stale."

Harper rubbed her stomach, already disliking what the beer did down there. "I shouldn't really say anything. It's bad to gossip."

"Not like you're gonna get sued for talking about it. You weren't like investigating *them*, just some kid who stumbled on other kids." Grace smiled. "No different than if you'd walked into the wrong room at a house party."

A flash off to the right caught Harper's attention. She forgot what she'd been about to say in response to that, and stared at... headlights. Seconds later, the growl of an operational engine grew loud enough to hear.

"Oh, whoa," said Logan. "Someone's coming."

Harper grabbed her shotgun and sprang to her feet. "Stay down. Gonna check it out."

When she started running toward Route 74, they both followed.

"Guys," whisper-yelled Harper. "Get down."

"You aren't older than us," said Grace.

"Just... be careful." Harper swung the Mossberg up into a ready grip and jogged for the road.

A large SUV type vehicle with wide-spaced headlights approached Evergreen along the same route she'd walked in on, heading straight for the bus barricade. Two militia on night duty hunkered down, aiming at the approaching driver.

"Aww, hell," said Cameron. "That's a machine gun. I got the gunner, you watch the rest."

"Okay," replied Sadie. "But don't shoot unless they're going to fire on us first."

Harper ran to the left end of the buses, taking cover at the corner and peering around. The vehicle rolled to a stop about twenty feet away, but she couldn't make out anything past the glare of the lights. For a moment, the world seemed to pause, the oscillating rumble of a diesel engine sounding almost foreign.

*That's not the greatest way for a first date to end... with machine guns.* She bit her lip. *That wasn't a date.*

# 22

# BRIGHTER

"**E**asy," said a man from the direction of the vehicle. "Just here to talk."

"How about you let go of that .50 cal and then we can talk?" asked Cameron.

"Fair enough. Hooper, at ease."

Harper squinted at a trace of motion above the headlights.

"Relax, kid," said the same man from the shadows. "We're the good guys. Damn, what are you, fourteen?"

"Who are you?" called Harper.

A man wearing green Army pixel-camo walked into the glare of the headlights. An M-16 hung over his shoulder on a strap, and he also wore a pistol on his hip. Numerous pouches and pockets lined his belt as well as a harness over his chest. He looked thirtyish, pale, and not particularly threatening.

Her eyes adjusted somewhat to the glare, enough to make out the front shape of a Humvee in olive drab.

"Oh, crap. The Army? Are you guys legit? Or did you just find a Hummer and uniforms somewhere?" Harper stood, but kept half hidden behind the bus.

"We're the real deal, kid. I'm Sergeant Clarke. Private Hooper and PFC Sanchez with me."

"What are you guys doing out here?" asked Sadie from above.

"Standard recon, assessing damage, that sort of thing. Wasn't expecting an armed barricade in the middle of the road." Clarke chuckled. "We had a couple of people at Eldorado Camp saying people had holed up in Evergreen."

"That's true. Hang on a sec." Cameron climbed down the ladder to the road. "Hey kid, go get Ned."

Harper whispered, "If this is a trick, I should stay."

"I got it." Logan pointed back over his shoulder. "Same place we met him on the way in?"

"Yeah, he sleeps in there," said Harper.

"Whatever. Just someone should go get him." Cameron walked around the bus and approached Sergeant Clarke, offering a handshake. "You heard right. We're re-establishing a town here. Hope you boys aren't looking to uproot us again."

Logan ran off down the road.

"Nah." Clarke shook his head. "Any fallout that's gonna come down has come down by now, and it's not likely we'll see a straggler warhead six months later."

Harper crept out onto the road in front of the bus wall, eyeing the Humvee. A twentyish woman with dark brown skin sat behind the wheel. Another pale guy, younger than Clarke, stuck half out a hole in the roof behind a big machine gun. He shifted toward her but didn't lift the barrel up.

"Relax, kid," said Clarke.

"I am relaxed."

"Private Hooper would feel much better if you slung that cannon." Sergeant Clarke smiled.

"That's not really fair, is it?" She eyed Hooper. "We put our rifles down, but he keeps pointing a machine gun at us?"

"Sarge?" asked Hooper.

"It's okay. They're civvies."

"Copy." Hooper rested the .50 cal's barrel in a holder, then sank back into the Humvee.

Harper hung the Mossberg over her shoulder on its strap. "So you guys are real Army? Did you collect people from Lakewood? I haven't seen any of my friends since the bombs fell."

"The Army has been relocating survivors to Eldorado Camp, but I don't know names. It's possible people you know are there."

"Eldorado Camp?" asked Sadie, still atop the barrier. "What is that?"

"We've established a tent city near Eldorado Springs. It's gotten pretty damn big at this point, absorbing citizens from Boulder, Denver, smaller places. Initially, Command wanted to use it as a temporary settlement until we could assess levels of radiation and damage in the surrounding communities, but logistics have gotten interesting. Seems like it's easier to just keep everyone in one place so there's enough water and food to go around."

Harper pictured a cramped, overcrowded mess surrounded in chain link fence... a cross between refugee camps she'd seen on the news and a poor district in some Third World country. "Christina Menendez, Renee Nichols, Andrea Orton, Veronica Jackson, Darci Sutherland? Do you know if any of them are in the camp?"

Sergeant Clarke shook his head. "Sorry, kid. They might be. I don't know names. You'd have to check with the commandant's office, but people can come and go as they please. So, no guarantee anyone on the list is actually there."

"Oh." She looked down.

Mayor Ned and Logan jogged up the road. Harper faded into the background of the ensuing conversation between the men. Ned appeared to accept the soldiers as genuine and gave them a general overview of Evergreen's status while the soldiers filled him in on the situation in the area. The soldiers confirmed that the damage in Lakewood everyone blamed on one big nuke landing on Colorado Springs had, in fact, been the result of numerous smaller warheads peppering the area, much closer to Denver. A big one *did* land on Colorado Springs, reducing it to a wide expanse of essentially blank ground. Due to the radiation, the Army hadn't gone near the place, and no survivors he knew of made it out from anywhere within twelve miles of the city center.

Logan stared at the ground while Sergeant Clarke described the destruction of Colorado Springs. Harper reached over and held his hand. He managed a weak, grateful smile, but didn't—or couldn't—say anything.

"Unfortunately, we're pretty much on our own at the moment," said Sergeant Clarke. "We haven't had communication with any sort of centralized command structure since the bombardment, so I figured the US got kicked pretty damn hard in the nuts. But... we hit them harder. General Ayala is running things like the Pentagon is okay, just having a communication breakdown, but most of the guys think we're isolated.

*Some* form of contact would've happened by now if anything still operated back east."

*We hit them harder? Seriously? Is he actually happy we killed millions of civilians?* Harper gawked at them. *Like, burning down some entire other country worse than they hit us somehow constitutes 'winning'? All they did was mess up the planet even more.*

"Do you know who 'they' are?" asked Ned. "Who actually hit us?"

"Uhh." Sergeant Clarke scratched the back of his head. "No one out here knows for sure. CENTCOM might have had that information, but no one bothered wasting time trying to pass it on. I don't *think* we fired first. Fair bet we took inbound fire from Russia and China. Maybe even North Korea, who knows? Heard some guys talking about a North Korean submarine possibly firing the first shot. They'd have had to get close since they don't have anything land-based that could reach the US."

"Kinda useless worrying about who did it at this point, isn't it?" asked Harper.

"I suppose." Sergeant Clarke sighed. "Sounds like things here are reasonably safe. You mind if we run around with the testing equipment, checking for radiation?"

Mayor Ned perked up. "That would be wonderful. I do hope you intend to share if you find any problems."

"Of course."

"Umm," said Harper. "I have a question."

Everyone looked at her.

"When I was on my way here, back in Lakewood, I saw a couple guys in camo like arrest three people, cuff them, and drag them off against their will. Were they real Army? You said you're not keeping people prisoner at the Eldorado place, right?"

"No. We intended it as a temporary shelter until radiation levels fell off, but people are staying there because it's large, organized, and well-protected. Without seeing them, I can't say for sure if you observed Army personnel detaining looters or just random people who wore camo. If they were troops, the people being detained had probably raided supplies from a forward camp. As far as I know, any prisoners taken would've been moved to Eldorado. General Ayala doesn't come down hard on people who are just trying to survive."

"Oh. Okay. If I gave you a list of my friends' names, could you maybe let them know I'm okay and here in Evergreen? Or if you're going to come back here, let me know if they're okay?"

Sergeant Clarke offered a 'why not?' shrug. "Can't say when or if we'll come back, but I can drop off a note with the commandant's office. No guarantee of anything, but I'll see what I can do."

"Awesome. Thanks."

Harper pulled out her little notepad and pencil, scribbling down the names and ages of her friends, as well as Madison's two as-yet-unaccounted-for friends, Eva and Melissa. While she wrote, Mayor Ned asked about any possibility of food assistance as the farm hadn't started producing. The soldiers apologized, saying they could only feed people who relocated to Eldorado Camp, since they also struggled to budget supplies, but between military rations and still-working refrigeration units, had enough to keep everyone going until their farm project matured.

The quartermaster building in Evergreen did have quite a few huge refrigerators in the kitchen, but no power. She briefly wondered if Eldorado Camp might be better than staying here, but three things kept that thought from becoming more than an idle musing: overcrowding, figuring their power came from generators which would eventually run out of fuel, and she'd already come to feel at home here. Even if Evergreen lacked modern comforts, she'd rather live in a town where people knew each other than be another faceless, desperate body crammed into a tent with ten other shell-shocked people, merely sitting around waiting for something to change.

Harper handed Sergeant Clarke her list. "Thanks."

"No problem."

She stared at the little scrap of paper he tucked into his shirt pocket, hopeful that he wouldn't just toss it aside after leaving town. Maybe, just maybe, word might reach her friends that she'd survived. Assuming, of course, any of them had. Lakewood had turned into a dangerous area, but it had taken two months to decay to that point. With any luck, her friends had gotten out by that point. If Eldorado Camp was real, if these soldiers actually did belong to the legit Army, a chance existed her friends would have been brought there.

"Umm, can I ask one more question?"

Mayor Ned and Sergeant Clarke both chuckled, pausing their discussion about the radiation testing. Evidently, the soldiers would be driving around in the Humvee looking at instruments while Clarke walked alongside with a detector.

"Shoot," said Clarke. "Not with that Mossberg, though."

She forced a fake laugh. "How is that Hummer working? All the cars are dead."

"Most military vehicles are shielded from EMP surge. Our problem is that we're running out of diesel. Another year or so and we'll all be hoofing it."

"Gonna wind up putting the cavalry back in cavalry," said Ned.

Clarke laughed. "Something like that."

Though fascinated by the working truck, Harper hadn't stayed up this late in months. She'd told everyone she would be home around bedtime, and had gone pretty well past that. Guilty at making her family worry, she turned to face her new friends.

"I really should get home. It's late."

"Yeah, same here," said Grace.

"Right. Sun comes up early." Logan yawned. "Still pretty cool to see not everything's gone."

"Did you hear him?" asked Grace as they walked down the road into town. "They lost contact with their commanders in six months. That's not a good sign."

Logan kicked a small rock off the road. "Yeah. They hit the big red reset button."

Harper couldn't find the urge to speak, the need to get home to her family too heavy in her chest.

"Night. Thanks for hanging out." Logan waved and kept going south down 74 when the girls turned left onto Hilltop.

Grace swung the three remaining beers back and forth. "Sorry for getting in the way."

"You didn't. I really thought there'd be a big group hanging out. You didn't mess up our date because we didn't have a date. Just hanging out like friends."

"Okay," said Grace, too innocently.

Harper glanced sideways at her.

"Awful lot of blushing for friends."

"Your house is here." Harper pointed.

Grace flashed a cheesy smile. "Just playing. Trying to not think about all the bad stuff. Sorry if it bothers you."

"It's cool. Night."

"Night." Grace waved and ran off to Anne-Marie's house.

Harper walked on down Hilltop Drive, gazing up at the stars.

*He's right. They really are brighter now.*

# 23

# RATIONAL THOUGHTS

S aturday morning came late for Harper.

She would have slept even longer, if not for the excruciating fullness of her bladder. Voices from the distant living room announced everyone else had already convened for breakfast. Groaning at the discomfort of moving, Harper dragged herself out of bed and stiff-legged it to the bathroom. Never in her life could she remember having to go that badly. Once she finished, she just sat there for a few minutes enjoying the lack of pain.

By the time she got dressed and went to the kitchen, the kids had already vanished out the door to play outside. Cliff's AR15 sat in pieces on the end of the table closer to the living room. He scrubbed at the bolt carrier with a toothbrush. Her portion of cereal waited for her in a bowl next to the box of almond milk.

"Sorry."

"For?" asked Cliff, not looking up.

"Being so late last night."

"How'd the date go?"

"Wasn't a date." She fell into her chair and dumped milk over her Oat Bland flakes.

"Okay."

"Really." Harper ate a spoonful. "We just talked. Grace showed up. Then the Army rolled in."

Cliff shifted his gaze to her. "When I was seventeen, I had a girl over. The next door neighbors came over to complain about the noises coming out of my bedroom, but I never made a girl howl so loud the damn Army showed up."

Her cheeks burned. *"Dad!"*

He tilted his head.

She nearly dropped the spoon, then stared down at her cereal. "I mean... uhh... Cliff."

"I'm sure your old man won't mind the occasional slip. So, I guess nothing happened. Well, except for the Army showing up."

"We just talked." She told him what happened, flinching a little when mentioning Grace bringing beer, but he didn't react.

"Hmm. Not sure how long they'll keep trying to hold it together if the chain of command collapsed, but nice of them to check for radiation around here."

After rinsing out her bowl, she unloaded the Mossberg and cleaned it. Cliff glanced over every so often, giving her tips or pointing at a spot she missed. They chatted about the bombardment, and he admitted thinking weapons had landed much closer than Colorado Springs.

"Yeah, I had a feeling something came down nearby, but you didn't look like you could handle any more bad news at the time. You were pretty checked out."

"Not *that* checked out. I still remember everything. Guess I was just running on autopilot or something."

Cliff reached over and squeezed her hand. "You're a lot more alive now. Good to see."

"Thanks. Still not sure what I'm doing, but I'm trying."

"No one *knows* what they're doing. We're all faking it in varying degrees. Anyone who tells you with perfect confidence they know what they're doing is full of shit. Probably trying to scam you."

She laughed. "Yeah."

Eventually, she reassembled the Mossberg, reloaded it, and set it back on the table.

That done, she went out back and practiced with the compound bow for a little while until Cliff joined her in the yard for more jiu-jitsu. They threw each other around working on takedown techniques for about two hours before the kids returned in search of lunch.

After a meal of peanut butter smeared on graham crackers, the kids again raced off to go exploring houses and generally run around. Harper didn't exactly adore the thought of them being out of sight, but Cliff assured her the Shadow Man had not melted into a cloud of darkness and seeped between the bars of his holding cell, nor had he cloned himself.

The town council—Ned, Anne-Marie, and Walter—still hadn't decided what to do with him, and the man continued refusing to say anything.

Much to Harper's delight, Cliff set out after lunch on a hunting expedition with Roy and Dennis. Though she thought deer cute and would have been horrified at the idea of shooting them six months ago, watching everyone gradually become thinner reorganized her priorities. *Needing* deer meat to survive felt entirely different from shooting animals for the thrill of it—or even hunting when they could go to the supermarket and get food easily.

She daydreamed about being able to eat until she felt full again.

*We'll get there. The farm's growing.*

With Cliff off hunting and the kids somewhere in town having fun, Harper decided to go for a walk. Despite it being her official 'day off,' the Mossberg still went along. She fussed at her jeans, which quite needed a wash, remembering she hadn't gotten around to doing laundry. *Soon as I get home. I only have two pairs. Maybe Liz will let me grab another one if they have any in my size. Will she let me grab a dress too? Be nice to have one for when it gets hot and I'm not on duty.*

Harper headed down the road toward the quartermaster's.

When she reached Route 74, a din of shouting from up the road rose in the distance. Harper sped up to a jog, encountering an angry crowd gathered at the quartermaster's building, shouting about the rationing and demanding more food be given out. A few people brandished handguns or baseball bats. Sadie Walker, Ken Zhang, and Leigh Preston stood between the crowd and the main entrance, their rifles trained on the ground by the group's feet. Liz Trujillo hovered in the doorway, one hand on her .44 revolver.

Harper circled left around the angry group to stand with the other militia between the upset gathering and the building. She left her shotgun on its strap over her shoulder, refusing to point her weapon anywhere near the townspeople. Facing down a huge, angry crowd kicked her square in her terror of public speaking and stole her voice. Still, she tried to stand tall and fake confidence.

"Someone is stealing from the stores," yelled Sadie. "That didn't cause the shortage, but it's not helping. If the person doing that can hear me, maybe if you stopped, the rationing would improve."

A barrage of angrier shouts came back.

Hearing the woman blame the people for their own misfortune made Harper cringe. Something bubbled up inside her and she shouted, "Everyone please hang on a sec!"

The crowd's rumbling lessened to a tentative silence, everyone looking at her.

"Guys..." Harper looked at Sadie, Leigh, and Ken. "These are our neighbors, the people we're supposed to be protecting. Put your guns down." She looked at the crowd. "That goes for you guys, too. No one needs a gun out right now. Please, we're all just trying to survive here."

After a tense moment of staring, handguns went into pockets, baseball bats became walking sticks, and the militia slung their rifles.

Harper's hands shook from her being the center of attention, but she stuck one in her pocket and clutched the shotgun's strap in the other. "Yes, I know the food situation is... not great. I'm like always hungry, too. I see my kid sisters and brother getting thinner. We're all eating lean. It's not like there's a handful of people in charge hoarding all the food while the rest of us are chasing rats. That farm is our best chance at survival, but it doesn't just spit out food overnight."

"The land wasn't previously farmed," said Ken. "It's taking a little longer than expected, but we are making progress."

"Getting angry isn't going to help anything." Harper looked back and forth over the crowd. "If we blow through the food we have before the farm is ready, then we'll have nothing at all for however long it takes. Eating small portions sucks, but eating nothing for days sucks a lot more."

"We'd hunt if they didn't take all the damn guns," yelled Mr. Rhodes, a late-fifties man in an Air Force jacket.

"They're out hunting right now." Harper gestured in a random direction. "There's no working refrigerators, so if they get something we'll probably have another community dinner."

Anne-Marie Kirby walked up the drive with the poise of a teacher finally showing up to quiet down an out-of-control homeroom. "All right, everyone. Let me say a few things and if anyone has questions or concerns, I'll be happy to hear you all out. First, we are not being stingy with the food just to be stingy. There is math involved. We've tried to assign out calories to people based on what we have in stock to maximize the length of time we have before it's the farm or nothing. Yes, there is food disappearing from the stores and the militia is working on figuring out who is responsible. Jim tells me that we should start seeing some useful produce in another week or two. The chickens are breeding well and it shouldn't be long before we have a good source of protein."

"There's gotta be more cans somewhere," shouted a woman near the back of the crowd.

Harper clenched her jaw. *I'm high on the list. If they send out a scavenging run, I'm going to be on it.* That scared her more than having people looking at her, and she found herself no longer shaking. A sick feeling swirled in her stomach at the idea of leaving Evergreen.

*Hopefully, Anne-Marie and Liz will find a way to make the provisions work.*

The crowd thinned, though a handful of people remained with questions. Having overdosed on people for the day, she decided not to bother requisitioning more clothes, and headed home.

HARPER STOOD IN HER BEDROOM, STARING AT HER SAD LITTLE WARDROBE.

All the clothes she had in the world consisted of three T-shirts, two pairs of jeans, one pair of yoga pants, half a drawer of undies, a dress, some socks, and two nighties. Worse, every single article of clothing had been worn for at least a week or more, including her underwear. Some of the socks had started to feel rigid in spots. The mere thought of putting any of her undies back on again without washing them made her skin crawl. Her old home back in Lakewood may or may not still have her much more impressive wardrobe... clothes she'd bought when it still mattered what they looked like or what other people would think of them. Now, she only cared about two things: not being naked and keeping warm.

Well, three things... she couldn't bring herself to wear a garment so dirty it came close to qualifying as a separate life form.

Overwhelmed with disgust, Harper stripped completely, then wrapped herself armpit to knees in a towel, which she secured in place with a few safety pins, making an improvised dress. She blushed, but at least the towel was clean, having come from the basketball place a few days ago. She'd much rather put up with it than even touch any of her filthy clothes. Besides, washing *everything* in one shot both saved detergent and would let her wardrobe last longer before she had to do another batch of laundry again.

*What are we going to do when there's no more detergent left? I don't think they had Tide in the 1800s.*

She gathered all her clothes, holding her breath while carrying them to the bathroom and dropping everything in the tub. After turning the water on, she added a capful of laundry detergent, then ran back to the bedroom to grab Madison and Lorelei's clothing, which she dropped in the tub as well.

When the water rose to the midway point, she cut the faucet, knelt beside the tub, and scrubbed things as best she could with her bare hands. Whoever had run around town taking everything useful from the various abandoned houses had fortunately left her a laundry basket. After she finished washing each garment, she rinsed it in the sink, wrung it out, and dropped it in the basket to take outside later.

Thinking about how she used to complain whenever her mother asked her to do laundry lodged a lump in her throat. Emptying hampers, sorting everything into color groups, and stuffing them in a machine took only a few minutes and little manual labor. How trivial it had been, yet she'd often complained like Mom had asked her to walk to Canada and back.

*I'm sorry, Mom.*

Her fingers went numb from the chilly water; her sinuses flooded with the smell of detergent that also left a weird slimy feeling on her hands. One by one, she washed and rinsed each item of clothing, getting the hang of a technique to scrub them by rubbing two fistfuls of fabric back and forth.

The kids still hadn't come back, but it didn't really matter. She wouldn't have asked them to wear towels so she could wash the clothes off their backs. *I could just let the water sit here until something dries for them to change into.*

Once the basket filled with wet stuff, she lugged it to the backyard. Walking outside in the towel dress made her blush, but she'd already soaked every article of clothing in the house and had little choice. The towel *did* offer more modesty than the two nightgowns the quartermaster gave her, both embarrassingly close to transparent. It also covered more than any swimsuit she'd ever owned.

*Ten years from now, we'll all be wearing towels and trash bags, blanket togas.*

The rest of the afternoon went by in a blur of laundry—and trying to figure out what the ever-loving hell happened to some of Jonathan's briefs.

*What is it with boys! Good grief, I'd burn these if I could buy new ones.*

The whole time she worked, she couldn't stop thinking about her dread of leaving Evergreen. Anxiety hung over her about the next scavenging trip as though she'd done something illegal and the cops knew about it. At any minute, one would knock on the door and arrest her.

She'd make herself go on that scavenging run, but that didn't mean she wanted to.

Eventually, the kids returned.

"Harp?" called Madison. "Are you here?"

"Yeah," she shouted.

The three of them all came to the bathroom—and laughed their butts off at the sight of her in a towel held on with safety pins.

"Why are you wearing that?" asked Madison.

"I'm trying to make the detergent last longer by washing as much as I can. The clothes I had on were filthy. I couldn't stand touching them."

Lorelei pulled her dress off and tossed it into the water too fast to intercept.

"Argh. Lori!" Harper couldn't help but laugh. "Oh well. Put a towel on. Don't run around naked."

"I'm not naked," said Lorelei, a look of genuine confusion on her face. "I have socks on!"

Madison and Jonathan laughed.

Harper grabbed a towel and wrapped it around the girl.

"I'm not gonna wear a towel," said Madison.

Lorelei looked at her. "Why I have'ta wear a towel if Maddie isn't gonna?"

"That's not what I mean!" Madison half-yelled, half-laughed. "I'm not gonna throw my only dry clothes in the tub."

"Can we bath tonight?" Lorelei held up her hands to show off dirt-ringed nails. "I's dirty."

The question made Harper itch everywhere. She *still* hadn't gotten used to only taking a bath once a week. "Yeah… sure, why not. It's been a while."

The kids went to the living room to play while Harper finished up the last of Cliff's laundry. She drained and rinsed the tub, then collected the big metal pails from the back room, filling them from the tub spigot and hauling them out to the cinder block grill. If she lit the fire now, the water would be ready for a bath by the time they finished eating.

Dinner consisted of refried bean paste from a can stuffed into stale hard taco shells. Cliff returned in the middle of the meal, smiling. They'd bagged two bucks, which currently hung out behind the school to drain. Since the school building had power from its existing solar panels, the refrigerators in the cafeteria worked... something Harper hadn't even thought of. The meat would be stored there for a day or two while the town organized another big barbecue.

And, Cliff also mentioned they planned a scavenging trip.

Harper lost her appetite. "Yeah, I figured."

"Why are you looking like that?" asked Madison. "What's wrong?"

"It's my turn to go with them again."

Her little sister stared at her, eyes huge with worry.

"I know... When I decided to join the militia, I did it to protect you." She looked at Jonathan and Lorelei. "You guys, too. And part of protecting you is making sure you have enough food."

Madison moved her chair to sit right next to Harper, but didn't say anything.

The rest of dinner passed in somber silence.

After, Jonathan and Madison ran outside to collect the laundry off the lines, sparing Harper the need to go outside in a towel again. Cliff graciously brought in the first hot water pail for the bath. Soon, the girls crowded into the bathroom to share the warm water and soap.

When Madison pulled her dress off, Harper almost gasped. The girl didn't look quite as bad as Lorelei at her starving worst, but had become frighteningly bony. Seeing the girl so scrawny cemented Harper's resolve. Instead of being terrified to leave town, she couldn't wait for morning. They needed to do something. She couldn't let Madison get any thinner. Also, more than her family needed food. Every kid in that school probably looked like her sisters... and Harper. She couldn't be afraid of the scavenging run. Madison counted on her.

"Maddie..."

The girl looked up at her, a faint blush on her face. "What?"

"You're so thin now."

"I know." She stepped into the tub and sat. "It's because there isn't enough food."

"I'm going tomorrow to find more."

"You said you were gonna stay here and protect me—us. Jonathan and Lorelei, too."

Harper looked down. "I am protecting you... from starving."

"You promised you won't die."

"I remember." Harper eased herself into the water. In seconds, a sheen of dirt appeared on the surface. At *not* being grossed out, she let off a resigned sigh. *I really miss showering every day.* "Wouldn't it be nice not to be hungry all the time?"

"Yeah. But why do you have to leave Evergreen?"

"To look for canned food or pasta or something we can eat."

"Everything's gone already," droned Madison. "There's lots of people out there looking for food. It's been months."

"Maddie, a lot of people died. Like, a serious lot. And the Army rounded up more people. There's big stretches of land with no one in them."

"You're guessing."

"I'm done with the soap!" shouted Lorelei, before dropping it in front of Madison.

Harper looked up. The six-year-old had turned herself into a foam statue. She almost yelled at her for overdoing it and wasting soap, but couldn't be angry at that giant smile.

"Okay." Madison picked up the soap and started washing herself. "I trust you. Can you get some tofu if it's on sale?"

Harper laughed. "If they have any, sure." She reached past her sister to scoop excess soap off Lorelei.

"I'm kidding. It's all gone bad now. They don't put tofu in cans." Madison stood to wash her legs.

"What's tofu?" asked Lorelei.

"The essence of absolute nothingness coalesced into solid form," said Harper.

Madison raspberried her. "It tastes like whatever you cook it with."

"Right. It has no flavor of its own, hence it's nothingness."

"It's good!" shouted Madison.

Harper tickled Madison's sides. "If you say so."

Squealing, Madison flung soap at Harper and dropped to sit, guarding her ribs with her arms. "Stop!"

Lorelei cheered and splashed them both.

"Come on. Keep the water in the tub. Don't waste it." Harper leaned forward and hugged Madison. "And you... Tomorrow night, you're going to have a real dinner."

"'Kay. Just don't die. If you do, I'm never gonna forgive you."

Harper used a big plastic bowl to pour water over her hair. "Every place isn't full of people like those guys in Lakewood. We could go somewhere and come back and not even see anyone else."

"Yeah, right," muttered Madison. "What if the truck breaks?"

"Then we walk home. But… Rafael is driving and he's the mechanic. So it won't break."

"We're gonna starve, aren't we?"

"Not if I can help it."

Madison squirmed around to face her. "I'm just scared something's going to happen. I know you have to go, and it's okay. Just come back."

"I will." Harper draped a washcloth over her sister's head. "I can't let you get any skinnier."

Madison poked her in the side. "Look who's talking."

# 24

## NOT SO SAFEWAY

The knock came during breakfast the next morning.

"It's open," called Cliff.

Marcie Chapman stuck her head in. "Morning. Harper? I know you're off on Sundays, but—"

"Caravan. Yeah, I'm ready. One sec." She hurried the last few spoonfuls of cereal.

When she stood, Madison ran over and clamped on in a hug.

"Please be careful."

"I will, Termite."

Madison stepped back, nodded, and walked stiffly down the hall to the bedroom, fighting the urge to run.

*She's going to cry the whole time I'm gone. I have to do this. She needs food. We all do.*

Harper hugged Cliff.

"You want to tag team?" he whispered.

"Nah. They'll just put me on the next one anyway. And I actually convinced myself that I want to do this."

He patted her shoulder. "Good mindset. Going into an op expecting it to be a shit show is a great way to make sure it turns into a shit show."

"Shit show!" shouted Lorelei.

Cliff sighed at the ceiling.

"Nuclear fire devoured the world. Is it really a big deal if a kid swears?" asked Harper.

"Hey, we gotta have *some* standards." He winked. "Hold off on that word until you're at least twelve, kid."

"Shit! shit!" shouted Lorelei.

"No, not that word. You can say show." He tapped her on the head with one finger. "The other one."

Lorelei giggled.

Harper hugged Jonathan and Lorelei at the same time. "Be back later. Stay out of trouble."

"Ready?"

"As ready as I can get." Harper followed Marcie outside. "Did you remember the coupons?"

"Hah."

"Any idea where we're going?"

"Idaho Springs. It's not too far off to the west. Small, but there's a downtown with a supermarket."

"People there?"

Marcie shrugged. "I don't know, but we're going to find out."

"Like last time, right? Not planning to attack people to steal, just looking for unclaimed stuff."

"Exactly."

She nodded.

The tractor-trailer waited for them on Route 74 near the quartermaster's. Harper jogged over to the passenger side and climbed up.

Deacon, the muscular former convict, grasped her hand and pulled her in. "Hey, how you doin' girl?"

"Okay." She smiled and climbed over him to the sleeper cab.

Roy Ellis sat on the mattress next to a militia soldier she hadn't spent much time around before, Josh Webb. Despite being in his early thirties, his short buzz cut and boyish face made him look like someone who'd just joined the Army straight out of high school. His being here made Harper not the palest person on the team—they tied for that spot.

She squeezed in to sit between Roy and the wall. Marcie climbed in and flopped between the guys, pushing Josh left against the other side. Roy checked his weapon, which Harper recognized—thanks to *Call of Duty*—as an H&K Mp5. Josh had a bolt-action hunting rifle with a scope, and would likely provide any needed sniper support.

Deacon pulled the door shut and Rafael started the engine.

"How long are we going to have gas for this thing?" asked Harper.

"Diesel," said Rafael.

"You know what I meant."

He grinned. "What we got in the tank now is what we got. Big tanks on this rig, though. Might be able to produce a biodiesel eventually. But, I don't think we'll really need the rig for much longer. Can only go so far out looking for crap, right? Eventually, we'll need to become self-sufficient… or move."

The others got into a conversation about the farm. Optimism at their chances allowed Harper to smile and settled her nerves about the trip. She liked that Deacon was there. One look at him would probably make most people run the other way. Unless they had a gun. And true, he'd been in prison, but for bank robbery, breaking into a vault at night when no one else had been in the building. Though she still figured most prisoners who survived the bombardment had likely formed the start of gangs like the one who killed her parents, not *everyone* in prison had violent tendencies.

Rafael drove north up Route 74.

Riding in an operational vehicle felt simultaneously weird and sad. It almost let her pretend the world hadn't changed… until she looked out the window ahead at a road with no other cars on it. She kept her head down for most of the trip, except for when the others pulled her into the conversation about crazy things they'd seen since joining the militia. Harper shared the story of catching Beth and Jaden naked in an abandoned house. Her description of hammering him in the balls with the Mossberg made Rafael cringe hard enough to swerve the semi.

"Oh, man. That ain't right," said Deacon.

"Shouldn't have grabbed her." Marcie patted her on the shoulder, then shared a story of an old man she'd run into who'd gotten blind drunk on moonshine and ran around into other people's houses with a broom, thinking it a rifle, intending to 'drive the communists' back to Russia.

Laughter ebbed when Deacon asked about the kidnapper.

Harper went over that story.

Roy paled at her description of taking the shot over Mila's head. "We need to get you some slugs."

"If we can find them, sure."

Deacon whistled. "Slug would've gone right through that mask."

"Save the town some damn food," said Rafael before continuing to mutter in Spanish, something about guys who grab little kids.

They drove down highway lined on both sides with tall hills, arriving a little over a half hour later, according to the clock on the dashboard, in the little mountain town of Idaho Springs. Rafael pulled off Interstate 70, rounded a traffic circle, and rolled to a stop in the middle of the street. A McDonalds and a gas station sat on the left, to the right, a Starbucks/Subway and a Wildfire restaurant.

Josh climbed up on top of the trailer near the cab and lay flat on his chest.

They hit the restaurant first, entering via a broken panel in the glass door. No one dared open any of the refrigerators, but they discovered a decent haul of canned vegetables, flour, and bagged sugar. Harper insisted they raid the Starbucks for coffee. No one objected. After cleaning the place out of coffee beans, and still-edible bagged snacks, they hit the McDonalds, not expecting to find much. All the buns were long stale. Deacon threw one at the wall and it bounced off like a stone. The coolers held a horror show of decaying beef, rotting potatoes, and dead pseudo-chicken. Canned goods there mostly consisted of ketchup or salad dressing, though they did grab more coffee. The Subway proved equally disappointing, except for a fair supply of canned tuna as well as some olives and fruit salad.

Rafael nudged the semi down the road a little more as the team raided a Carl's Jr. on the left. More flour, coffee, and some canned vegetables went into the trailer. They continued down the street past a Shell station, again stopping at a 'Marion's Restaurant.' The building had no windows left intact, though whether that happened as a result of a nearby nuclear explosion or rioting after the fact was anyone's guess. Considering they still found usable food in the back, Harper figured a shockwave had done the damage.

Harper grinned at the lack of blue-sash-wearing thugs here, though a totally empty, abandoned town struck a chord of eerie that would haunt her dreams for a while. The restaurant offered a fair assortment of usable food, though much of it came in giant commercial cans that would probably be held for a community dinner rather than given to a resident. If nothing else, Marion's Restaurant provided Evergreen with a two-year supply of canned peas.

Upon spotting an auto parts shop, Rafael stopped the truck again and ran in the door himself. The militia stood around by a big brown dumpster waiting and 'guarding' while he gathered several boxes from the place and stashed them in the cab.

From there, they raided a small barbecue place on the right, a pizza shack on the left—mostly collecting flour. Harper walked on the left of the semi, about halfway down its length, when they resumed creeping down the main drag of Idaho Springs. It felt so surreal, like she'd stepped into CNN footage of troops in Iraq.

*I can't believe I'm doing this. I should be playing video games and goofing off with my friends.* She closed her eyes and saw Madison's too-skinny figure. *We're almost done, kiddo. See, just like I told you, not everywhere has thugs.*

After a brief check of an Asian café, they kept going, reaching a large Safeway supermarket on the left. Right as Rafael started to turn into the lot, something moved on the roof. Glint flashed.

"Sniper!" yelled Harper and Marcie at the same time.

Josh swiveled to aim. He fired a split second after a gunshot came from the Safeway roof. Harper ducked and ran for cover across a gravel road left of the Safeway lot. She hunkered down against the building next door, pressed against beige siding with a diagonal board pattern next to a red door with a camera icon on it. Back pressed to the wall, she breathed in short, rapid puffs.

Rafael jammed on the brakes hard enough that Josh slid off the trailer, tumbled over the cab, and landed on the pavement. The truck's gears groaned as it backed away, Rafael ducking down to avoid sniper fire, blindly steering the semi onto the road. He tried to reverse behind the cover of the same building Harper leaned against, but the trailer hit a stray car on the road, forcing him to stop with the cab exposed to sniper fire.

Marcie and Deacon ran with the semi, scrambling around to the far side away from the shooter. Roy started to aim around the nose end, but ducked as a bullet ricocheted off the street beside him.

A howl of pain came from Josh.

Harper peered past the corner. Josh lay sprawled on the parking lot, the left thigh of his khaki pants soaked dark with blood. His rifle hung off the truck's side mirror, caught on the strap, lost when he went flying, probably the only reason the sniper on the Safeway roof hadn't finished him off.

"Josh is hit," shouted Roy.

"Mon' and git' him," yelled a distant man.

Harper held the Mossberg up, but didn't at all trust her odds of hitting a man roughly a hundred feet away on a roof with a shotgun from her position. Of all the weapons the team had brought with them, only the dangling rifle had a real chance of being accurate on a target that far away, but anyone going for it would eat a bullet. Roy's Mp5 had the next best chance. Marcie only had a 9mm Beretta handgun, putting the sniper way out of range. No one tried to grab the dangling bolt action rifle. Rafael stayed down low in the cab to avoid taking a bullet through the windshield.

"C'mon. Yer boy's bleedin' out," yelled the guy atop the Safeway.

Roy stuck his Mp5 over the truck's hood, but a loud *crack* from the roof made him duck back. "Fuck this guy."

"No thanks," said Marcie. "He's not my type."

Harper couldn't see any of her friends through the truck. If she tried to run to Josh, she'd take a bullet before she got anywhere near him. The lot had no cover, not even a single car. She flattened her back against the wall and glanced to her right past the camera door. Josh howling in pain kicked her in the ass. She bolted down the street away from the supermarket. At the end of the beige building, she hooked right into an enclosed parking area, but a narrow gap between two buildings on the back side let her slip through to the next street. She dashed out onto the road, which lined up with the Safeway building, and ran past houses and a row of skinny birch trees lining the sidewalk.

The bright, sunny day made the gunfight all the more surreal.

She slipped across the street to the left sidewalk, dodging a utility pole where the road came to an abrupt stop against the Safeway property. Straight ahead stood the white-painted cinder block wall of the supermarket. This spot brought her close enough to the building to be concealed from the sniper overhead. It also offered a painful view of Josh writhing on the ground in the lot to her right. A little blue house stood to her left next to the supermarket, its yard raised several feet up from the ground behind a retaining wall.

A bed of decorative stones abutting the road slowed her to a creep so she didn't make any crunching sounds. If the man up there heard her coming, she'd be as good as dead. She advanced into an alley between the house and the supermarket, hurrying left to the back end of the building. A vent unit sticking out of the wall plus a dumpster offered a risky way to the top. She slung the Mossberg over her shoulder and climbed as quietly as she could to stand on the dumpster before shimmying to the end and stretching up on tiptoe to reach the vent.

The sniper fired again, making her jump. He cackled. "Come on, what ya waitin' for? Don't want a bullet in yer theivin' heads?"

She pulled herself up by arm power alone until she braced a foot in the bricks and got a knee on top of the vent housing. From there, she stretched to hook her fingers on the roof edge and eased herself up to stand on the fan cabinet, crouching to keep her head from poking above the wall.

The next time the man cackled, she felt confident that he still sat near the front side of the building. Hoping he wouldn't see her, or at least that she'd have time to duck, she decided to look. She rose to her full height, peering over the wall—at a giant HVAC unit. To the left, the vast roof remained empty. To the right of the equipment, a narrower space also appeared empty.

*Awesome. I've got two tons of steel between me and a crazy man.*

Slow and quiet, she pulled herself up, slithering over the wall onto the roof, flat on her stomach. She eased her way to her feet, pulled the shotgun off her shoulder, and stood there for a few seconds to catch her breath.

"Guys," shouted Josh. "Either get me the hell out of here or finish me off. Damn, this hurts."

"We're—" shouted Roy before the sniper in front of her fired again.

Harper crept to her left, moving to the end of the long HVAC machine. She went down on one knee and leaned around it, aiming toward the front of the building. Twenty-ish feet ahead, a man in an olive-drab poncho lay flat on his stomach behind a pile of cat litter bags set up like sandbags from a war movie.

*This is just like the stupid snipers in Call of Duty. They really don't ever see people sneaking up behind them.*

It bothered her to just shoot a guy in the back, even if he had shot Josh.

Harper rose to her feet and stepped out from behind the HVAC unit, keeping her shotgun trained on the guy as she snuck up on him. When she came within ten feet of him, she had a clear view of the truck—and Roy staring at her. A few 5.56 brass lay on the roof near the guy.

"Don't move," said Harper.

The man jumped. "Gah!" He lay still, but turned his head to glance back at her. Wispy white-grey hair hung down from his hood like the work of a crazed spider. He appeared to be in his sixties, his cheeks covered in silvery-black beard. Sunken eyes above thin, wrinkled cheeks regarded her. Up close, he didn't feel threatening at all.

"Damn. Must be slippin' in my old age not ta hear ya comin'."

"Let go of the rifle," said Harper. "Please don't make me shoot you."

"Aww, shit. You're just a little kid. What are you doin' with a gun, sweetie?"

"No one's just a kid anymore." She kept aiming at his face.

The man shifted his weight to the right in a slow roll away from the rifle that left him on his back with his hands raised. His cheap poncho concealed most of his body, as well as any other weapons he might have on him.

"Why did you shoot at us?" Harper sidestepped left toward the edge and yelled, "Clear to get Josh!"

"Aww, hell," said the man. "Everyone's always tryin' ta steal my shit. I foun' this place. 'Tis mine. And yer boy there pointed his rifle my way. Should I have waited for him to fire first?"

"We're not looters. We wouldn't have attacked you to take your things. You ever hear of talking first?"

"Talkin's how ya get dead real easy. People lie a lot these days."

Roy and Marcie sprinted to Josh and dragged him behind the truck cab.

"Well, I'm not lying to you. If this Safeway is yours, we're not going to attack you to take anything. We're from Evergreen, just looking for food to survive." Her entire body trembled from vast amounts of adrenaline in her system. She stared at his hands, begging the universe that he wouldn't go for a weapon. The instant he reached under that poncho, she'd fire. "Since this is your place, we'll leave in peace, okay? You don't fire at us anymore, we don't shoot you."

"Not sure if I believe ya. Ya seem seven shades o' terrified, sweetie."

"I'm not scared. I'm shaking because I'm expecting you go for a handgun or something and forcing me to shoot you in the face. I really don't want to."

The man smiled, revealing a brutal row of yellow-brown teeth. "Can't say I fancy being shot in the face either, so we got that in common."

"Harp? What's going on?" yelled Marcie.

"Having a chat with..." she shouted, then lowered her voice back to normal. "What's your name?"

"Lonnie Blanchard."

"Lonnie," shouted Harper.

"Shoot the son of a bitch," rasped Josh.

"We don't kill people to take their stuff. This guy claimed the Safeway already." A tremor started in Harper's left arm from squeezing the shotgun too tight. She relaxed the grip a little. "Right?"

"He attacked us!" shouted Josh.

"He says he only fired because you aimed at him," yelled Harper.

"Son of a…" Josh gasped. "He'd already pointed his rifle at me!"

"All right, who attacked who is a bit of a grey area," said Deacon.

"Are you the only one in Idaho Springs?" Harper kept her attention on the old guy's hands, twitching when he rubbed a finger under his nose.

"Reckon I am. Or was. You all are here now."

*This guy has the entire supermarket to himself.* Though that didn't seem at all fair while people in Evergreen struggled, she couldn't murder a guy for food when they still had options to search other places. He could probably last a good long time on the canned goods, being alone. Assuming he lived long enough to eat all of it.

"It's probably lonely. That's an awful lot of food for just one person. Why don't you come with us back to Evergreen instead of staying here alone?"

"Why should I leave? Got plenty of food here. Everything I need."

"Do you? Cans will run out eventually. What about water? Even someone to talk to? What if a group of thugs finds you when you're sleeping? We've got a farm. Going to have food that lasts a long time."

"Then what do ya need mine for if'n ya got a fancy ol' farm?"

"I'm not hearing any gunshots!" rasped Josh.

"Because I'm not gonna murder an old man," yelled Harper before saying, "Our farm is too new to produce food yet. It's a couple months short. We need something to keep us going until then."

"He freakin' shot me! Ow!"

"Stop squirming until I get this bandage set up," said Roy. "It's a through-and-through. Missed the bone at least."

Harper's arms grew tired. "Lift up the poncho a sec? You got any guns under there?"

"Aye." He peeled the plastic garment up, revealing a large revolver on his hip.

"Can we call a truce here? Will you promise not to shoot me?"

Lonnie ran a hand over his head, pushing his hood back and scratching his greasy hair. "I ain't wanna shoot no kid. Why don't you relax?"

For the first time in her life after turning sixteen, Harper *didn't* mind someone calling her a kid. "If I believe you won't shoot me, I'll relax."

"You've killed already, haven't ya. Can see it in your eyes."

"I don't like kidnappers."

Lonnie laughed into a cough. "You're an interesting mix, sweetie. Cute and deadly."

"I'm only deadly when cornered. I hate having to shoot people. Even people who laugh at hurting others."

"I figured you was thieves."

"So you just shot Josh? Before we even said one word?"

"He pointed a high-power rifle at me. Only real threat. Had to neutralize him first. Gave him a nice little wound to disable, not hittin' the femoral or smashin' the bone. Two handguns, submachine gun, and a kid with a shotgun can't get me up here."

Harper fidgeted. "Kid with a shotgun *did* get you up here."

"You ain't shot me, right?" He grinned the ruin of his teeth at her again. "I was right. Y'aint a threat. And, I believe you ain't thieves. Thieves would'a shot me already, even a kid. You really gonna leave my shit alone if I ask ya to?"

"Yeah. My little sisters… all the kids in town are wasting away slowly. Lori's like forty pounds."

Lonnie glanced off to the side, grumbling. "Tryin' the guilt now, eh?"

"There could be enough food in this place to keep us from getting sick. But we're not going to steal it." She lowered the shotgun. "I probably should tell you to toss your weapons aside so you don't shoot me while I leave, but I believe you really don't want to shoot a kid."

"I don't, but yer too trusting. Someone not like me would pop you in the back as soon as you looked away." Lonnie gestured at the wall. "Tell ya what. You convince yer friends what we had was a misunderstandin', and you're welcome to the store. Maybe I'll take ya up on that offer o' movin. Does git kinda lonely here."

Harper's heart swelled with hope. "Oh, thank you! Hang on." She approached the roof edge, still keeping half an eye on Lonnie. "Guys… he says we're welcome to the food if he can come back with us and live in Evergreen."

Josh cursed up a storm.

"The boy sounds upset," said Lonnie.

She raised an eyebrow at him. "You did shoot him. That would upset most people."

"You make a fine point." He emitted a wheezy chuckle.

"He willing to come down here and talk?" called Roy.

Lonnie nodded.

"Yeah. He is." Harper picked up the rifle he'd been using, a bolt action 5.56 with a battleship-grey housing made of plastic. She stared into his eyes for a moment. Trusting her gut, she handed the weapon back to him. "Is there an easier way down than climbing the wall?"

"Heh. Yeah. Stairs, right over here." Lonnie ambled off toward a small structure beside the HVAC machine, carrying the rifle at his side.

*Kooky old man. One minute he's laughing and shooting at us, now he's like the weird old friendly grandpa.*

She followed him down the stairs to a deserted supermarket with an eye-wateringly horrendous stench in the air. The mixture of rotting seafood and meat forced her to breathe in tiny sips. *That's one way to fix starving. I won't be able to think about food again without throwing up. Gah.*

Lonnie shoved a barricade of magazine racks out of the way of the front door, revealing Roy, Marcie, and Deacon right outside the sliding glass door, which Lonnie unlocked. The old guy struggled to pull it open, so Deacon put one hand on it and pushed, moving it aside.

"Whoa, dear. You's a big'un." Lonnie blinked up at him.

"Damn, it's ripe in there." Deacon waved back and forth past his face. "I can see why the guy wants to leave."

"Roy Ellis, former Denver PD." He offered a handshake.

"Lonnie Blanchard, former just about everything except doctor, lawyer, and dentist. Course, now I s'pose all that matters is USMC sniper, '78 to '88."

"Semper Fi." Roy fist-bumped him. "2009 to 2015."

"So, the little lady here tells me ya got a bunch of starvin' kids."

"Well, *starving* is maybe a little strong, but it's not too far off the mark." Roy nodded. "Things are lookin' real lean at the moment."

"Heck is that damn smell?" asked Marcie.

"Seafood aisle's a bit past the expiration date," said Lonnie. "I tried tossin' it, but the fish has become liquid."

Everyone made discomfited noises.

Harper stepped outside for fresh air. Roy and Lonnie got into an easy conversation about their respective time in the Marines. Eventually, he got the nod. Harper figured Roy wanted to feel the guy out to measure the crazy before agreeing with her suggestion to invite him back to Evergreen, and he passed.

They spent the next hour rapidly wheeling shopping carts of canned goods out to the trailer. Josh lay in the sleeper cab, his leg wrapped in a field dressing. Roy checked on him every few minutes, but seemed satisfied with his condition that he didn't demand they cut things short and rush him back to the doctor's.

Once every bit of usable space in the trailer and cab had been packed full of cans, boxed pasta, flour, crackers, usable dry goods, soap, toothpaste, and coffee, Rafael pulled back onto the road. No one mentioned 'looter's privilege,' content to let all the food go into the pool for the town. The Safeway had more than could fit in one trailer load. Being that only a half hour ride separated the spot from Evergreen, everyone planned to return for more after they unloaded. Everyone except Josh of course.

Harper leaned back against the wall in the sleeper cab, eyes closed, and tried to decompress from the OMG factor of rushing at a sniper's nest. The carefree life she'd never really appreciated had been pulled out from under her like a tablecloth magic trick... only all the dishes had smashed on the floor.

But... things could be far worse. Her present situation didn't seem all that bad. She could make Evergreen work. She had to. For Madison, for Jonathan and Lorelei... and for herself.

She bowed her head. *I'm doing it, Dad. Whatever it takes to keep Maddie safe.*

# 25

# DINNER GUEST

**H**arper accompanied them on two more runs to the Safeway in Idaho Springs, clearing the place out of everything remotely useful—even the paperback novels on endcaps.

That night, she and her family ate a big spaghetti dinner complete with jar sauce, enough that everyone moaned and grabbed their bellies afterward. By Monday afternoon, Liz and her team had finished cataloguing the haul and upped the food distribution back to 'normal' levels. While eating to stuffed every night wouldn't happen, they'd have enough food not to be constantly hungry, at least until the farm kicked in.

Josh would limp for a while, and required a blood transfusion, which the doctors had to do live from a donor once they found someone compatible. Lonnie donated his rifle as well as a box containing 538 rounds of 5.56 ammo to the militia as a show of trust, declining to join due to his age.

Monday, Harper had an uneventful patrol until the school let out, then walked her siblings plus Becca and Mila back to the house. The 'creepy girl' continued to maintain her weird attitude, but stopped saying overly morbid things and appeared to be gradually opening up, allowing others close.

The kids spent most of the afternoon playing in the yard. Between the children laughing and the peace of mind that came with knowing her name had gone back to the bottom of the list for scavenging, Harper felt genuinely happy for the first time since the skies burned. A note of sorrow still tainted everything about life, as she'd never forget losing her parents, friends, and the security that modern society offered. But no amount of being angry or glum about it would undo the effects of idiots pushing 'the button.'

Harper left the kids playing in the yard and headed to the quartermaster's to collect the supplemental ration assignment they'd been giving out. Upon returning home, she packed away the cans and boxes, as well as another loaf of bread. Bobby had put together a big wood-burning oven in his backyard, and had become the town's primary source of baked goods. Considering they'd brought in roughly half a tractor-trailer of flour, people would have bread for a while.

Within the next few months, there would also be vegetables from the farm. Naturally, Madison didn't much like the idea of cows and chickens being raised for food. Milk and cheese didn't bug her, just meat that required killing the animal. However, when informed about the venison community meal tonight, she'd only offered a glum 'that sucks but okay' stare.

Harper hadn't quite decided if she should feel guilty for encouraging her to eat meat or grateful she'd accepted it a harsh necessity of the world they'd found themselves in. She considered talking about how these animals weren't being raised on cruel mass-production farms that kept chickens in tiny cages or whatever, but her sister mostly objected to the killing. The cruelty merely iced the cake.

*She really would rather choke down that horrible oat flake cereal than have a hamburger. Well, the farm should let her stay vegetarian if she wants to.*

All the children's giggling turned to screaming in an instant.

The back door blasted open; Becca sprinted inside, shrieking. She ran up to Harper, babbling and pointing at the back door, too freaked out to form words.

Harper started to run outside, but stopped short with one foot on the little concrete porch.

A black bear meandered around the middle of the yard, about six feet away from Madison, who struggled at the base of a tree, trying to climb but unable to pull herself up. Jonathan clung to the branches about twenty feet off the ground. Mila had vanished entirely.

Lorelei stood next to Madison, smiling, no trace of fear in her at all. "Hi, Mr. Bear."

Madison grunted and hurled herself at the tree trunk, but kept sliding down.

"Don't run! It'll chase you," yelled Jonathan.

The bear shifted to the right, disregarding the two girls at the bottom of the tree, sniffing toward the burn barrel that held the scrapings from lunch, breakfast, and last night's dinner.

"Shoo," whispered Harper. "Bear. Shoo." *What the hell am I doing?* She dashed into the house, grabbed the Mossberg from the dining room table, and ran back to the yard.

Lorelei walked *toward* the bear, raising her hand as if to pet it. "Mr. Bear, you're so fuzzy!"

The bear's attention went from the barrel to Lorelei.

Madison gave up on climbing and spun to put her back to the tree, hyperventilating in panic.

"Lori! Get back!" shouted Harper.

The bear flinched, jumping to the side before swiveling to face Harper.

"Aww... bear?" asked Lorelei with a sad expression. "He's fuzzy and cute. I wanna hug him."

"He'll eat your face," yelled Jonathan.

"Back!" shouted Harper. She didn't bother pointing the shotgun at it, since a bear wouldn't understand the threat. But if it moved toward either child, she'd empty the weapon into it as fast as she could pull the trigger.

The bear edged away from her, appearing startled at her yelling.

Harper yelled, "Back!" again.

The bear flinched. She yelled random nonsense at it, merely attempting to be loud. A moment later, the bear bounded off to the rear corner of the yard.

"C'mon into the house," whispered Harper. "Move slow."

Madison stared at the bear, her whole body shaking.

"Bye, Mr. Bear." Lorelei waved at it and walked to the back door.

Harper pulled the child behind her. "Where'd Mila go?"

"Up here," said Mila from directly above her. "On the roof. Bears don't climb houses, but they can climb trees."

"*Now* you say that?" asked Jonathan.

The bear turned back, briefly sniffing at the air, but lost interest in the burn barrel and climbed over the fence out of sight.

"Aww... bear." Lorelei waved at the fence. "Bye."

Madison sank to sit on the ground at the base of the tree, shaking. Jonathan slid down, moving from branch to branch with ease.

"What the hell…" Harper huffed all the air out of her lungs and sank to sit on the edge of the concrete slab, head down, shotgun across her lap.

"Why didn't you climb?" asked Jonathan.

"I never climbed a tree before," replied Madison in a quivering voice.

"Never? Wow. Seriously?"

"There's no trees in Starbucks," said Harper.

The sound of a raspberry came from Madison's direction.

"I gotta teach you how to climb a tree. What kind of kid can't climb trees?"

"The kind who doesn't want to break their arms," said Mila from the roof.

"Get down from there," muttered Harper.

"Okay."

"C'mon," said Jonathan. "Hey didn't you take gymnastics? Climbing a tree ought to be easy for you."

Madison looked up at him. "There's no trees in gymnastics either."

He tugged her to her feet. "Okay, I'll show you how to do it."

"That was a bear." Madison grabbed two fistfuls of his shirt at his neck. "That was a *bear*. I wanna go inside for a while in case it comes back."

"Why did Mr. Bear leave?" Lorelei tilted her head. "He's fuzzy. I wanted to hug him."

Harper stood, ushered all the kids inside, then closed the door. "We don't hug real bears."

"Why?" Lorelei gazed up at her.

"Because bears are afraid of people, and when people get too close, they bite them." Harper set the shotgun on the kitchen counter, then picked her up. "Hug me instead."

"Okay," chirped Lorelei, clinging.

"Becca?" called Harper.

"In here," said a small voice under the sofa. "I'm okay."

"Right, so we're going to stay inside for a little while." Harper sat on the couch.

"What'll we do if the bear shows up at the barbecue?" asked Jonathan.

"Cook it, too," deadpanned Mila.

"No," said Madison and Lorelei at the same time, with nearly equal horror in their voices.

Becca slithered out from under the sofa.

"He almost ate you." Mila poked Madison.

"It's not his fault. He's a bear. We shouldn't kill him for doing bear things. He didn't hurt anyone." Madison jumped on the couch and attached herself to Harper's side. "No one said anything about there being bears in Evergreen."

"Fuzzy," whispered Lorelei, grinning.

Harper put one arm around each of her sisters, and stared up at the ceiling while trying not to have a nervous breakdown at a six-year-old wanting to hug random bears. *This kid is going to give me a heart attack before I'm nineteen.*

# 26

# BAD DREAMS

Harper awoke in the middle of the night, unsure why.

No alarm bells rang in her bladder. Both Madison and Lorelei remained asleep beside her. Subdued not-quite-snoring came from Cliff's room.

*Why am I awak—?*

A creak in the distance sounded an awful lot like the back door opening.

She slipped out from under Lorelei's arm, sat up, and grabbed the shotgun from where it leaned against the wall. After listening to silence for a few seconds, she eased herself to her feet. Without being under blankets, her gossamer nightie didn't do much for warmth. Jaw clenched, skin prickling at the cold, Harper crept to the bedroom door. A soft creak might have been the floorboards shifting or the house reacting to the wind.

A figure appeared in the bedroom doorway.

Harper jumped, barely managing not to fire in response to something jumping out in front of her. She stared over the gunsights at Mila's pale moonlit face, wide-eyed and terrified.

The instant she recognized a child, she tilted the Mossberg away. "Mila? What's—"

Distant gunfire rang out, three shots rapid, then one a few seconds later. Another shot came from a different direction, also sounding far away.

Mila emitted a faint whimper and ran in, diving to the floor and crawling under the bed before whispering, "He's here. He chased me. You said you'd help…"

Cold crept up under Harper's nightgown. Shivering, she edged past the doorjamb, aiming toward the living room. Seeing nothing unusual, she crept into the hall and padded forward, quiet as a held breath, her toes sinking into chilly carpet. At the end of the hall, she stopped, scanning left to right. The back door drifted inward, slow like the wind pushed it.

Harper shifted her aim toward the door.

A black figure all but floated into the kitchen, making so little noise he could have been a ghost. His head turned toward her, a featureless black mask over his face.

She pulled the trigger.

The Mossberg bucked into her shoulder, emitting a deafening *boom*. She lowered her aim point to his chest and fired again, two shots in two seconds. He crumpled to the ground, half on the porch, his legs sticking into the kitchen.

A heavy *thud* came from Cliff's room.

Jonathan started screaming.

Harper kept the gun trained on the man in the doorway, but he didn't move.

Cliff's door swung open. Her father of circumstance stalked out into the hall in boxers, handgun raised. He shifted his gaze to her.

She held up one finger, then pointed toward the guy. Cliff nodded, advancing past her into the living room. After aiming briefly toward the front door, he crossed to the kitchen and peered at the guy.

"Hmm. *This* mask wasn't made out of Kevlar." Cliff leaned back.

Harper cringed, then blinked. *Holy shit… what's wrong with me? I just killed some guy trying to sneak into the house and I'm not freaking.* She closed her eyes. *I will not let anyone hurt Madison or my family… or a terrified little girl who came running to me for help.*

A scattering of air horns went off outside, from multiple directions.

"Figures, crap goes down on my night off." Cliff shook his head, then ran back to his room. Fifteen seconds later, he reappeared dressed in camo with his AR15. Harper started following him to the door, but he spun and grabbed her arm, giving her a 'stay here' stare.

"What?"

"You're wearing a nightie thinner than used tissues. Stay inside."

"Oh. Yeah. Right." She backed up to the bedroom as Cliff ran out the front.

Jonathan poked his head into the hall, not a trace of sleepiness in his expression.

"Stay down," whispered Harper.

He nodded and zipped back into his room.

"What's going on?" asked Madison in a bleary voice. "What was that boom? Did you shoot?"

Harper peered back at the bed. Madison sat up, rubbing her eyes. Lorelei sprawled next to her, still zonked. "Yes. Don't leave the room."

"The Shadow Man is angry," said Mila, still hidden beneath the bed.

"Why are you hiding?" asked Madison. "I thought you said he would get you and you'd just stand there."

"I changed my mind."

"Mila, the man who followed you tonight is dead," said Harper.

Jonathan crawled over to his door, peering out. "Mila's here?"

The blanket lifted up from the floor. Mila peeked out. "What?"

"I'm not going to tell a nine-year-old to go look, but trust me."

Jonathan darted back into his room.

Mila tilted her head. "You saw him die?"

"Technically."

Jonathan ran across the hall, flashlight in hand.

"What do you mean technically?" The girl narrowed her eyes.

"It's dark. I saw him fall over. Cliff checked him and said his mask wasn't made out of Kevlar."

Madison glanced at the window and crawled into the corner by the pillow, hiding her face behind her knees.

"Eww," said Mila.

"Yeah, exactly." Harper shivered. "We're all going to stay right here for a bit."

Mila crawled out from under the bed, stood, and scrambled into a hug. "The Shadow Man got outta jail by turning into ninja bodies all over the place. He tried to grab me out of my bed, but I was awake. Bet he's sorry he made me throw the knives 'til I could do it without looking."

"What?" asked Harper.

"Put it in his eye."

Harper gawked. "They what? You... what?"

Mila made a tossing gesture. "Before I escaped, the Shadow Man made me throw the little knives over and over at a wood board 'til it would stick every time, 'til I could hit a little dot, 'til I could do it with a cloth tied over my eyes. Every time I missed, he beat me with this long stick that stung like bees."

"Oh, my god..." Harper sank to her knees and wrapped her arms around the girl. "That's horrible."

Jonathan added himself to the hug.

"I know," said Mila. "That's why I escaped. Is my mom okay?"

Harper released the hug and picked the Mossberg back up. "I'll check on her as soon as Cliff's back."

Madison shivered. "Is there really a dead guy in our house?"

"Umm." Harper bit her lip. "Technically, no."

"Technically?" asked Madison, Mila, and Jonathan at the same time.

"Just his legs are in the house."

Madison gagged.

"No," said Harper. "He's not in pieces; he's in the doorway."

"Oh." Madison pulled the blanket up over her head. "That's still bad. I'm gonna have bad dreams now."

Mila looked at the lump in the bed. "No, you won't. You're not going to be able to sleep again. You'll have bad dreams *tomorrow* night."

Madison made a noise that could've been either laughing or crying.

"I won't let the Shadow Man get you." Jonathan held the flashlight up like a weapon.

Mila poked Lorelei's foot. "Is she still alive?"

"Yes, she..." Harper couldn't help but run over to check. "Yeah, she just sleeps hard."

Gunshots went off in the distance.

"Eep!" said Madison.

"Everyone stay down." Harper sat on the floor in the corner opposite the bed. From there, she had a clear line of fire on the door as well as anyone sneaking in the window. *I'm covering my freakin' bedroom door with a gun. I don't like this world. I wanna go home.*

Mila crawled over and huddled up against her, holding on.

Jonathan sat somewhat in front of her as if to shield her from the doorway.

"If you tell anyone I got clingy," said Mila, "I will deny it."

"I won't." Harper gave her a quick squeeze, then put both hands back on the shotgun.

A few more gunshots rang out in the distance, sounding like firecrackers.

Harper stared over the gunsights at the bedroom door. *C'mon Cliff. Be okay.*

# 27

## QUARTERBACK

Astonishingly, Mila fell asleep while clinging to Harper.

Madison kept hiding under the blankets. Lorelei hadn't even woken up.

Jonathan squirmed after a while. "Is it okay if I go to the bathroom?"

"Sure. Just do *not* go to the kitchen. Once you're done, come straight back here… or go to your room if you want."

He nodded and zipped out.

The sound of the boy taking a leak filled the tomb-silent house. Harper fidgeted in discomfort. Hearing it made her want to go, too. Soon, Jonathan returned and curled up on the floor beside her.

"Are we in danger?" he whispered.

"It's been long enough, probably not," said Harper. "Just being extra careful."

A squeak came from the front door. She tensed her grip on the gun.

"It's me," said Cliff. "Assuming you're still up."

"Yeah." Harper let her head fall back against the wall, and all the strength out of her muscles. The Mossberg dipped to the floor. "Holy crap."

"Sit tight a few more minutes. I'll be back"

"Okay, Arnie." Harper couldn't quite bring herself to laugh.

Men murmured in the distance. Based on the footsteps, shuffling, and grunting, she figured they collected the guy she'd killed and dragged him off. She didn't move from her spot, resting rather than guarding.

Roughly twenty minutes later, the door clattered again.

"Back," said Cliff.

Footsteps thudded across the house and into the hallway. He appeared in the door, AR15 over his shoulder. The relief in his eyes soothed her frayed nerves. She set the Mossberg on the floor and stretched her arms to chase away the aches from sitting there so long without moving.

"We got four bodies in Walmart ninja costumes and weird masks," said Cliff. "All dead."

Harper nodded.

"What?" Mila sat up, wide-eyed. "Are you sure they're four different people? The shadow man can make himself into clones. If the one in jail is still alive, he'll just keep making more copies."

"Nah, kiddo." Cliff shook his head. "Five different dudes all wearing the same sorta getup. One black dude, one Indian, three white. Definitely *not* clones."

Mila looked confused for a moment, then scowled. "Seriously?"

"Yep." He nodded.

She blushed. "I'm an idiot. I really thought he had magic."

"You're nine." Harper patted her on the head. "I believed in magic at that age, too."

Cliff approached, lowering his voice. "Fred took a knife to the chest. Not sure if he's gonna make it."

"Oh, no…" Harper covered her mouth and cried. "Fred…"

"He's a tough bastard, so he might pull through." Cliff set his hands on his hips, shaking his head. "Something damn sure went wrong with those guys. Guess they got confused or something."

"What do you mean?" asked Harper.

"They all had these balanced throwing knives, little leaf-shaped suckers. One idiot had a knife embedded in his eye socket. Guess his buddy got jumpy and they had a little friendly fire incident."

"That was me," said Mila. "I hit the Shadow Man in the eye when he tried to grab me outta my bed."

He blinked at her. "Wait, *you* threw a knife at him? What's going on here?"

She nodded.

"Umm," said Harper. "Mila's been telling me some really scary stuff.

Sounds like they were trying to be ninja assassins or something. From what she said, they abducted and forcibly trained her."

"They told me to kill this man they had tied up. But I wouldn't do it. They said they wouldn't give me food 'til I proved myself, but I escaped. Shadows are bad. I'm sorry for bringing them here."

Cliff ruffled her hair, smiling. "Not your fault, kid. But, if those guys were ninjas, Harper's an NFL quarterback."

"I've never even touched a football. That's not a great analogy."

He laughed. "That's exactly the analogy. Those guys were about as stealthy as a cow on roller skates."

Harper furrowed her eyebrows. "They snuck up on me... but I'm not an ex-Ranger. Guess they would seem like idiots to you."

"Bunch of Dorito-munchers who watched too many ninja movies." He winked.

Harper opened her mouth to make a Dorito quip about Cliff's extra mall security guard pounds, but... he'd lost them. *Why does it annoy me so much that I couldn't find those guys and he laughed at them? I'm a kid; he's a commando.* "At least they're gone."

"Yeah. You planning to sleep here or head home?" asked Cliff.

"I'm worried about my mom." Mila stood. "Can we check on her please?"

"All right."

Harper picked up her T-shirt and jeans. "Be right out."

"I'm already dressed. Don't wanna leave the kids alone, do you?" asked Cliff.

"I..."

Mila smiled. "It's okay. They need you, too." She hugged her. "Thank you for protecting me... again."

Cliff took Mila's hand and led her out. Harper stood there a while, mind going in circles. Eventually, she dropped the clothes she didn't need to change into and hit the bathroom. When she returned to bed, Madison clamped onto her.

"I don't like having gunfights in the house. Next time, will you please take it outside?"

Her little sister sounded so much like Mom yelling whenever she and her friends messed around with a soccer ball in the house that Harper teared up. "Sorry. Won't do it again."

Madison sniffled. "Good."

Minutes passed in silence, Harper staring at the ceiling, her thoughts blank.

"Damn," whispered Madison.

"What?"

"Gotta go to the bathroom."

Harper laughed.

"Shh," said Lorelei. "You're makin' too much noise. People are tryin' ta sleep."

# VARSITY

T he next day, Harper stumbled down the street from the school after dropping the kids off, feeling like a zombie after too much Thanksgiving turkey.

Sneaking into an unclaimed house and taking a nap sounded like an awesome idea, but if anyone caught her, she'd probably get kicked off the militia. However, going into a situation half-awake could hurt someone. She hadn't fallen asleep by the time Cliff came home, bringing the good news that Mila's adoptive mother had been fine… didn't even wake up. As best Harper could figure, she'd gotten about three hours of rest before sunrise.

She crossed her fingers, hoping to take advantage of how infrequently she ran into any other militia people this far north, and slipped into a small unused house off Inverness Drive. That the place didn't look much different from before the war made it eerie, as if eighty percent of the people in the country had simply vanished into thin air one day.

Ever since she'd run off into the ashes with Madison, she'd become a light sleeper. Trusting her newfound ability to wake at slight noises, she flopped on a brown sofa in front of a big flat panel TV. Someone's PS4 still sat on the rug, probably left out by lazy kids the night before the blast. She sighed at it, hoping the family who used to live here made it to safety. Before she could feel too depressed at that thought, she passed out.

Harper woke in what felt like mere seconds, though stiffness in her muscles suggested she'd been out for much longer. With great effort, she resisted the urge to close her eyes again and got up, walking a few circles around the living room to stretch her legs before using the toilet down the hall. That the flush worked surprised her. She remembered the town still having three actual plumbers, and wondered how long they'd be able to keep running water operating. Hopefully, some of the kids would take on apprenticeships with them. With a sigh, she trudged down the hall to the front door and went outside.

Based on the sun, she estimated it to be about an hour before school let out. Her nap had been near perfect in length. Hopefully, no one noticed she disappeared for five-ish hours. She headed up the road, acting as casual as can be, as if she'd been patrolling all morning. A few minutes after taking the left onto Canterbury Circle, and a right on Interlocken Drive, the scuff of footsteps approached from behind.

She peered back over her shoulder at Zach jogging closer, wearing a Colorado Rockies sweatshirt and jeans a little too big on him, suggesting he'd finally gone to the quartermaster for additional clothes he hadn't packed for his away game.

Since he didn't give off any threatening vibes, she kept walking.

"Hey," said Zach, falling in step at her side.

"Can I help you?"

"I was kinda hoping you might be able to."

"What's the problem?" she droned.

"Need to report a case of felonious loneliness in the first degree."

*Gawd.* She fought the urge to sigh. "That's a serious accusation. You should probably go straight to HQ and inform Walter Holman."

"Thought about that, but I needed a special investigator. And you've got the qualifications."

"Sorry, Zach. You're not my type. And I'm not really looking for a boyfriend now. My head is still spinning from, you know, the whole damn world blowing up."

He continued walking at her side, making a series of strange faces, stumbling on half started words. She glanced off into the trees, at the houses, generally anywhere but at him.

Eventually, Zach blurted, "You should be with a *real* man."

In the back of her mind, Veronica snapped, *Too bad there aren't any real men around here.* Harper couldn't bring herself to say that though. Her voice wavered a bit under the memory of her lost friend. "That sort of attitude is exactly why I am never going to date you."

"So it's true? You're seeing that border jumper?"

She stopped short and whirled on him. "I'm not *seeing* Logan. We're friends. I lost my parents a couple months ago. All my friends are gone. I don't know if they're alive or dead. My whole life got taken away and replaced with… whatever this is. The *last* thing on my mind right now is finding a boyfriend. Hanging out with a boy and talking is not *throwing myself* at him. I'm not ready to even think about a relationship now. I…" She faced away. "I dunno if I ever will be."

"You just haven't met the right guy yet."

Harper glared at him. "Yeah… I still haven't." She clenched her fists, about to yell, but couldn't think of what to say and stormed off.

She'd barely had the nerve to date when the world had been normal. Too shy. Sure, she'd had boyfriends, but not like some of her friends who obsessed constantly about being with whatever boy they dated at the time, acting as if they somehow screwed up at 'girl' if they didn't have a guy. Harper's boyfriends had thus far basically been 'friends who happened to be boys,' barring the odd kiss or two, hand holding, or trite dates like going to the movies or ice skating. Christina used to tease her that she dated like a twelve-year-old. The closest she'd ever felt to love had been this kid Kyle she'd gone out with sophomore year. They'd met in a Starbucks one of the times Harper had been there with Madison and their mother.

The boy had triggered all sorts of weird feelings in her gut and she kept racing from being thrilled he noticed her to worried he wouldn't call her back to convinced the second time he saw her, he'd realize she wasn't pretty enough and leave. But all that anxiety disappeared when he did show up again. Alas, they only dated for the rest of that year. He'd moved to Washington State that summer. She'd been bummed out for a whole month, but barely thought about him after that.

But, now… every time she started to think about boys, it just made her dwell on the world being blown up. 'Ooh, I think he likes me' turned into 'we could go to the—no we can't, it's destroyed,' and that sent her down a rollercoaster of sadness at everything she'd never be able to do again, like spend time with her parents or friends.

Zach jogged to catch up. "Hey, Harper… you can't let what happened kill you inside."

She stopped walking, peering over at him, one eyebrow raised in shock. *Whoa. Did this guy actually say something sincere and thoughtful?*

"I want to help you heal. Okay, so the world's a mess, that's true. I lost my parents, too. Everyone on that bus with me did, well, except Cheryl. Her mom was with us. But, I mean... I know what you're going through. But we can't give up. People existed long before electricity or cars. There's so much potential in the world. You need a guy like me, not some Mexican."

Harper blinked. *Nope. So much for thoughtful.* "I can't believe you just said that. Wait, yes I can... Your varsity letter isn't in hockey, it's in douchebaggery. For a second, I almost thought you might have really been sincere, but you're just saying whatever you think you need to say to get into my pants." Again, she stormed off, fuming. She ranted and screamed in her mind, everything she didn't have the nerve to say to his face about being a racist moron.

It took Zach a moment to decide to try again. At the sound of him jogging up behind her, she walked faster. A weird, rapid clicking noise came from a bend in the road up ahead. Seconds after she noticed it, Walter Holman cruised into view on a mountain bike. He looked straight at her with an 'aha, there you are' sort of expression.

*Crap. What's* he *doing all the way up here? I'm so busted. Someone caught me sleeping.*

She kept fast-walking toward him, head down like she marched to the principal's office to be sentenced to expulsion.

"Harper... been looking for you." Walter rolled to a stop next to her. "Hello, Zach."

"Mr. Holman..." He nodded and kept right on going.

She slouched in relief. Getting yelled at for sleeping would be totally worth ditching that jackass. "Sorry. I'm here."

"That boy bothering you?" asked Walter.

"Not really. At least, not yet."

Walter nodded. "With Fred Mitchell injured, would you be willing to take his spot on a quick scavenging run?"

*I'm not busted!* Elation at getting away with napping stomped on any trepidation about an excursion. "Umm. Sure."

"Thanks. I realize you just went to Idaho Springs... three times, but this came together at the last minute. Jaylen's kinda new yet and, well to be blunt, she's a little jumpy. We hadn't been expecting to send anyone out this soon, next couple of people on the roster were up 'til sunrise watching the quartermaster's place."

She managed a nervous smile. *I caught up on sleep... damn karma.* "It's no problem. I understand. Why the sudden trip?"

"Doctor Hale managed to convince us that we should hurry over to St. Joseph's hospital and try to collect as many medical supplies, drugs mostly, as we can before someone else gets to them."

"Uhh…" She blinked. "That's in Denver."

"Yes. Is that a problem?"

"Near Lakewood."

"I've only seen the color drain outta someone's face that fast when they've been handed a death penalty, life sentence, or the donut place ran outta Boston crèmes. There something that bad in Lakewood?"

She sputtered. "Well, it's… I used to live in Lakewood, and it's full of… The bastards who killed my parents." Harper took in a stuttering breath, trying not to break down crying in front of him.

Walter put a hand on her shoulder. "It's all right. I can wake someone up."

"I'm okay." She closed her eyes and swallowed. "Just hard to talk about them, yanno? We ran into the same gang at the Walmart. Don't know if they're only in Lakewood or if they'd be north in downtown as well. Maybe they're not. I'll go. Someone's been up all night, they're gonna make a mistake."

"Are you sure?"

*I take back what I said about karma. I got sleep, so I need to do this.* "Yeah. How is Fred doing?"

"According to the doctors, he has a good chance of pulling through, but he's going to be in bed for a few weeks. He and Josh are keeping each other company."

She grinned at the hopeful news. "When's it going? Do I have time to tell Madison? It would really mess with her if I just disappeared."

"Looking at within the hour, but sure. Go on up to the school and let them know."

"Can you get word to Cliff?"

He chuckled. "Don't have to. He's going on the run, too."

"Umm. You're sending us *both* out? What about the kids?"

"Cliff already made arrangements with Carrie next door to look after them until you're back."

*Dr. Hale's been asking for those meds. We're going to need everything we can get to make this work. If he can't find people willing to go, they might change their mind and not do it.* "Okay. Let me run up to the school so I can tell them what's going on, then I'll meet the truck in the usual spot?"

"Sounds good. Oh, they're not taking the semi."

She stared at him.

"No, you're not walking. Rafael has a van working. We figured the city might present a challenge to navigate in a big rig, since the streets could be clogged with cars and debris. And there wouldn't be enough medicine to pack a fifty-foot trailer. That, and the truck is getting low on gas."

"Oh. Wow. *Two* working cars?"

"Progress." He smiled. "All right. Thank you, Harper. Go on and let your brother and sisters know, then meet in front of our humble little hospital."

She nodded and rushed up the street. It didn't hit her until she reached the school that she'd been so relieved at not being in trouble for sleeping that she hadn't fully processed what she'd been asked to do.

Go back into Denver.

Near Lakewood.

Near the blue gang.

She stopped by the school entrance, looking down at herself. *Here's hoping I don't fall to pieces the second I come face to face with my greatest fear... and if I can handle telling Madison I'm going to Denver, I can probably deal with those idiots.*

# 29

# INDEPENDENCE

R afael had breathed life into an old white Ford van that presently carried them down the highway.

Harper stared at the rear doors, the Mossberg across her lap, trying to settle a war between her emotions. Plenty of things bothered her about this trip now that the reality of it had time to seep into her consciousness.

Her little sister had, as expected, been upset. However, rather than scream and beg, she'd withdrawn and stopped talking entirely. The reaction could've meant she hated Harper had to go on the scavenging run but understood it necessary—or that she expected never to see her again. Since they wouldn't be loading an entire tractor-trailer, everyone thought this run would be quick.

She hoped it would be as—relatively—painless as the last run, but prepared herself for the worst. At least the 'blue gang' wore those stupid sashes. Those would spare her the worry of wondering what a stranger wanted. Anyone who belonged to that gang, she'd shoot as soon as she saw them.

Before meeting the van, she'd run home to grab ammo. For walking patrol during the day, she only carried twenty extra shells. Going back into Denver, she'd stuffed about fifty into a hip satchel. It had been three months since she'd been anywhere near her old home. Maybe the 'blue gang' had already been wiped out, or split up into smaller groups that killed each other off. Unfortunately, they could also have grown.

In addition to torturing Madison with worry and facing the dread of going into the city again, this run bothered her for another reason: Zach had come along. Apparently, he'd decided that 'farming isn't cool.' Or at least, he'd told Walter that. She figured he considered farm work 'beneath him,' or maybe he asked to join as part of some lame bid to impress her.

She did, however, find no small amount of amusement in Walter issuing him a varmint rifle chambered in .22 rimfire. Sure, in skilled hands such a bullet could kill, but she didn't think anyone who knew anything about guns would ever carry a weapon chambered for .22 long rifle into battle when other options existed. Harper didn't consider herself an authority on guns, at least nowhere near as much as someone like Cliff, but she knew enough to snicker under her breath when Zach called it an assault rifle. Someone had modded it up with a synthetic stock and pistol grip so it *looked* impressive, but it remained a .22 rimfire.

Cliff made a joke to the effect of if they got attacked by 'gang squirrels,' he'd be good to go. Zach laughed, totally missing the mockery.

*He should be relatively harmless with that thing... I just hope he keeps his damn head down and doesn't get himself killed.*

Rafael chatted with Cliff, who sat in the passenger seat, about the van, a 1982 Chevy that they'd found sitting in someone's garage. It had apparently been recently restored as a hobby project and only took a little bit of work to get it running since the engine didn't have much electronics. Rafael, the town's mechanic, considered it a tragedy that whoever spent all the time fixing this thing up never got to enjoy it due to the war.

Harper sat on the floor in the cargo area, her back against the bench seat they hadn't removed, which currently held Zach, Teagan (Dr. Hale), and Annapurna. The third and fourth row seats waited in the parking lot outside the clinic to make room for the medical supplies they hoped might still be in the hospital's storage room.

Tegan insisted on going with them because the trip had been her idea, and also because she would know what to grab, what would be useless, and what would be dangerous. Of course, she could have identified dangerous or useless meds after they'd been brought back to Evergreen, but given the smaller size of the van compared to the semi, it made sense not to waste space on transporting crap.

Walter had loaned her a 9mm Beretta for this trip, even though she had never handled a firearm before in her life. At least Zach had gone hunting a couple of times with his father and brothers. Even if he couldn't tell the difference between a varmint gun and a 7mm Remington magnum, he still knew generally how to operate a firearm. Dr. Hale got a quick course before they left town, but she hoped to stay out of a firefight if at all possible.

Madison probably lay curled up on Carrie's couch next door, crying. Harper hoped that talk of going to Denver didn't do damage and send her back to the mental state where she kept trying to get calls from their parents on a dead iPhone.

Tegan once told her that grief came in waves. It didn't seem likely her kid sister could handle another tsunami.

If anything happened to Harper out here, Mila would seem as cheerful as Lorelei by comparison to what Madison would become. For her part, Lorelei had responded with an "Okay, don't do the stupid" when told about the trip. Even Jonathan became emotional, crying a little and hanging onto her until she peeled him away.

The two of them insisted on following her to the van, and Walter had seen their reactions. He certainly looked guilty, perhaps even coming close to changing his mind and telling her to stay. She suspected she'd be at the bottom of the scavenging roster for a while as a thank you for going on this one. Maybe even until her siblings got older. Then again, once the farm matured, the need for scavenging at all might end.

Driving to St. Joseph's Hospital from Evergreen meant going straight east on Route 6—right through Lakewood. Rafael estimated it would take 'about an hour' to get there, but admitted he based that on pre-war traffic. Without speed limits, cops to enforce them, or other cars on the road, they could make it there much faster. Of course, if the debris they expected got in the way, the trip could also take significantly longer.

Harper swung back and forth between two extremes. One moment, she wanted to stay down on the floor, not even looking out the windows. The next, she came close to asking if they could stop at her old house. Part of her didn't want to see anything even remotely familiar for fear that it would trigger a waterfall of painful memories. A smaller part wanted to jump at the chance to maybe recover some of her stuff. Clothes, mementos, framed pictures of Mom and Dad, even if that meant possibly seeing their bodies. Unless the gang had moved them, her mother would still be in the kitchen, her dad in the dining room. She could go upstairs to get photos without looking at either one of them.

But how horrible would it smell there after bodies had been sitting for three months?

She closed her eyes in a futile attempt to hold back tears. Thinking of her parents as 'bodies' went past a line she couldn't handle. Harper curled up in a ball, doing her damndest to sob without making a sound. She couldn't let Zach see her that vulnerable. He'd definitely take advantage of it.

Anger at him helped her force any thought of going home or of her dead parents out of her mind. She wiped her face on her sleeves, then stared at the floor between her sneakers, mentally playing a modified version of *Call of Duty* where all the enemy soldiers looked like blue gang members.

Her weight shifted to the right from the van taking a turn. The motion pulled her away from her daydream. *I can't be a wimp. I'm going to see stuff that's gonna kick me right in the feels, but I gotta hold it in until I get home.* She lifted her head to look outside.

The van turned off 6th Ave, weaving among a handful of stalled cars before pulling two quick right turns and rolling into the lot of a Loaf 'N Jug gas station, stopping beside the wreckage of a white and red canopy that had once covered the pumps. A blast wave from the south had knocked it over forward, creating a wall between the pumps and the convenience store.

"Okay. We're gonna try and siphon some gas for this beast out of the ground tanks," said Cliff. "Rafael can handle that part on his own. Everyone else, keep your eyes open for anyone who appears hostile. You see someone wearing a blue bandanna around their neck, or something similar, and they see us, you call it out. They don't see us, mention it quietly. Got it?"

"Got it." Annapurna nodded.

"Yeah," muttered Harper.

"Copy that, chief." Zach smiled.

"I ain't no chief, son. Didn't go into the Navy." Cliff patted the roof twice. "Any questions?"

"What do you want me to do?" asked Dr. Hale.

Cliff twisted to smile at her. "Stick close to me or Harper."

Everyone except the doctor got out of the van.

Harper took up a guard position at the back right corner. Annapurna went around to the driver's side while Zach hovered by the van's side door, seeming more interested in picking his nose than keeping watch. Tegan remained in the van, sitting low, trying to stay out of sight.

Cliff stepped around the wreckage of the gas pump canopy to check the convenience store. The building mostly appeared intact, though large portions of its roof had vanished. No glass remained in any of the windows, only brown aluminum frames across gaping holes. Windblown dirt and trash had gathered inside, collecting on shelves that had been looted months ago of anything useful.

"Incoming," said Annapurna. "Left, hill."

Harper ducked around the back end of the van, taking cover at the corner and aiming to the west. Four people in dingy street clothes caked in grey dust approached, crossing a wide hill of ash-covered grass that separated the gas station from a row of tight-packed houses. A young black woman at the far left sorta-aimed an AR15 at Annapurna. Next to her, a skinny Hispanic guy held a shotgun resting back over his shoulder, the barrel pointed to the rear. The third guy had to be six and a half feet tall, muscular but thin, bald, and carrying some manner of machine gun with a huge ammunition box. At the far right stood a guy with a massive ginger beard and an AK47, which he generally pointed at Cliff. Several hatches dangled from a pair of leather belts in an X across his flannel shirt.

Fortunately, they didn't wear blue sashes, but they also didn't look too happy to see visitors.

Everyone stared at each other for a silent moment.

*They're checking us out.* Harper looked each of them in the eye one after the next. The woman gave off a 'please don't be hostile' vibe while the tall guy with the big gun felt more like he expected to fight but the idea didn't thrill him.

"Yo, Jay, that your sister?" whispered the guy with the shotgun, nodding toward Harper.

The man with the huge red beard shook his head. "Nope."

Cliff raised his left hand in a gesture of greeting.

At a scuff from behind, Harper whirled to her left. Zach rushed around the van and stopped next to her, raising his rifle while shouting, "Got left!"

"No!" shouted Harper, swinging her shotgun up into his varmint rifle, knocking it skyward a second before it went off with a sharp *snap*.

The woman dove to the ground on her side, aiming at Zach/Harper.

The other three also all trained their weapons in her direction. Annapurna and Cliff took aim at the guy with the machine gun.

"Hey!" yelled Zach, shoving his gun against hers, trying to push her out of his way.

"Don't shoot!" screamed Harper, her voice childishly high from fear and ragged from anger. She hooked Zach's leg and rammed her shoulder into his chest, knocking him over.

He landed flat on the concrete, barking like a kicked goose as the impact knocked the air out of his lungs.

She froze, her back to the four people pointing guns at her. They had her dead to rights if they wanted; her maneuver to take Zach down left her two steps away from any cover. Considering Zach had shot at them, she couldn't believe they hadn't shredded her already. As furious as she was with him, having a firing squad focused on her made her tremble.

Four seconds of silence passed.

Zach coughed and groaned. "Ow."

"What the hell's his problem?" asked a deep-voiced man.

*Thank you...* Harper exhaled, hoping that if they hadn't shot her yet, they wouldn't.

"FNG," said Cliff with a note of scorn. "Always the FNG."

Harper gradually turned her head to the right, peering over her shoulder at the people who all still pointed guns at her. Maybe they aimed at Zach on the ground at her feet, but if they fired at him, they'd tear her up, too. She almost dropped the shotgun and put her hands up, but that felt too much like surrendering, so she merely stood as still as possible. Cliff had his AR15 trained on the tall man, who continued to cover Harper with the machine gun, though his eyes had shifted to lock stares with Cliff. It seemed he knew he'd be the first one dead the instant any more bullets flew.

"The hell was that for?" wheezed Zach.

"If you sit up, I'm going to shoot you myself," said Harper. "But I probably won't be able to before the guy with the machine gun shreds us both."

"Who are you people? What are you doing here?" asked Beard.

"Scouting group from Evergreen," said Cliff. "Just stopping here for some gas. Not looking for trouble."

"They ain't wearing blue scarves," said Beard.

"Neither are you." Annapurna lowered her AR15. "That's why we're trying to talk."

"Evergreen?" asked the black woman.

"Yeah. Town up in the hills. Little rough at the moment, but we're working on it." Cliff eyed the tall man. "That's some impressive hardware. Where'd you find a '249?"

He glanced at Harper, then back to Cliff, still not lowering his weapon. "Flipped Hummer. Things got kinda rough around here month or two ago."

"Just a little," said Harper.

"Amazing the kind of respect ya get while carrying one of these." The tall man hefted his machine gun.

Harper twitched.

"No doubt," said Cliff, perhaps inadvertently doing a Clint Eastwood impression.

Zach started to sit up, but Harper put her foot on his chest to hold him down.

"Just, don't… everyone's still ready to shoot each other."

"Speaking of," said Cliff. "We're a dog fart away from some real unnecessary bloodshed. What say we all stand down?"

"It's cool, man." The Hispanic guy lowered his shotgun. "You ain't got no blue sashes on, so we can chat. You okay, Nikki?"

"Yeah." The woman glowered at Zach, ceased aiming at them, and got back up off the ground.

Harper clenched her grip on the shotgun in anger at the realization he'd targeted the black person first. Though, the woman did stand at the left end of their formation, so that didn't necessarily prove he'd decided to fire at her for her skin color despite the stuff he'd said about Logan. He might have merely thought 'kill them from left to right.' Though, Zach had achieved the impossible—he'd made her dislike him even more.

Cliff and Annapurna relaxed. When the guy stopped pointing a machine gun at Harper, they shouldered their rifles on their straps. Jay, the man sporting the big ginger beard, shifted his stance to hold his AK47 sideways, but didn't appear completely at ease.

Harper exhaled, slouching with relief. "Okay. Get up slow. Don't even think of pointing your rifle at anything."

"Whose side are you on, anyway?" snapped Zach.

"The side of not killing innocent goddamned people." She scowled, took a step back from him, and turned to face the strangers, keeping her posture as non-threatening as possible.

Cliff approached the tall man, offering a hand. "Cliff Barton." He proceeded to introduce everyone. When he referred to Harper as his daughter, a wave of warmth crashed into a wall of guilt for her real father. But, he'd died. *Dad would be happy I've got someone willing to look out for me.*

"All right," said the tall man. "I'm Will Gordon. Good to meet someone who ain't shit nuts."

"Nicole Rawlings." The woman also approached to shake Cliff's hand.

"Eddie Alvarez, but you can call me Al." The guy with the shotgun laughed as if he'd told a joke.

Cliff also chuckled. Harper furrowed her eyebrows at missing the humor.

"Jay Gibbs," said the ginger, also shaking hands.

"Excuse me one moment." Cliff turned on his heel and 'military walked' over to Zach. He grabbed him by his collar, shoving him against the side of the van, up off his heels. "One more like that, and you're gonna disappear out here. This ain't some kinda game, you got that *bro*?"

"Uhh…" Most of the color faded from Zach's face. "Yeah. Got it."

Cliff leaned close, nose to nose with him. "You pull a stunt like that again and something happens to her, I swear I'll wrap that little pop gun they gave you around your neck like a damn bow tie and hang you from a streetlamp by it."

"N-no problem. Won't shoot at anything 'til you say to."

"Zach, you do have a brain in that thick ass skull, right?"

"Yeah."

"Use the damn thing. You see someone about to get the drop on one of us and they look like they're *definitely* going to attack, fire. You see someone in a blue sash… if they're not holding their hands up and yelling don't shoot, feed them a bullet. Don't be the asshole who turns a conversation with normal people into a gunfight."

Zach nodded so fast it looked like his head might fall off.

Cliff let go of him. He glanced at Harper with an expression that said 'bringing this punk was a bad idea.' "Nice sweep."

Nicole, Eddie, Will, and Jay walked closer to the van, appearing somewhat more relaxed, the tension gone.

*Whew. That was too damn close.* Harper shouldered the Mossberg and spent a minute or three taking deep breaths until the adrenaline faded enough that she stopped shaking. Zach remained leaning against the van with an expression like a small boy who'd been torn a new one by his dad in front of his friends. He seemed incapable of making eye contact with anyone, no doubt second guessing his desire to be on the militia.

She almost felt bad for him... almost. Harper wouldn't do anything to get him killed out here, but if this trip scared him off the militia, she'd hardly complain.

While Rafael roamed around searching for the couplings used to fill the underground gasoline reservoirs, the rest of the adults got into a relatively casual conversation. Harper hung back, still too rattled by coming within inches of having four people shoot her to be interested in talking.

"I've known Eddie for years," said Will. "We used to live next door to each other. Spent a couple weeks living outta my basement, but the MREs are almost gone, so we headed out. Ran into Nicole here about a month ago when she'd been shooting it out with the Lawless."

The woman spat to the side. "Every last one of those mother—" She eyed Harper. "Bastards can die."

"There's been a nuclear war and I'm seventeen. I can handle the bad words." Harper managed a weak smile. "What's the lawless?"

"Them crazy sons of bitches with the blue sashes," said Will. "Call themselves The Lawless."

Nicole scowled off to the side. "Their recruitment policy is only slightly less aggressive than the damn Witnesses."

"Last time I checked, Witnesses don't shoot people who aren't interested in joining." Jay chuckled.

She sighed at him. "War done melted down your sense of humor."

"Join?" asked Harper. "Those guys tried to grab me and my kid sister... and I didn't get the feeling they wanted to *recruit* me. They had a different word starting with r in mind."

Nicole, who appeared to be in her early twenties, gave her a pitying look, then a brief hug. "Oh, baby girl, they would'a done me like that, too. But that ain't *all* they want. They take anyone they can get, force 'em to run with the gang."

"Especially kids, the smaller the better. Easy to mold them into little psychopaths." Eddie frowned.

Harper couldn't help but think of the 'shadow man' who'd abducted Mila. They sure as hell tried to warp her. Maybe they'd even succeeded to a point. How many nine-year-olds could nail a man in the eye with a throwing knife and be more upset that magic wasn't real?

*She's gonna be okay. That girl's mom loves her.*

"Those dudes sorta established a city in the rubble. Usin' Mile High Stadium as some kinda fortress. The guy runnin' things came from the penitentiary, supposedly multiple life sentences. Mostly a bunch of cons at first, but they've been growing." Will shook his head. "Total *Mad Max* BS if you ask me. Anyone who refuses to join and kill for them, they use for entertainment."

Harper shivered.

"Not just that." Will flicked a switch on his machine gun—probably a safety—and let it hang from a strap around his chest. "Yeah, sure they do *that* to some, but word is they force others to knife fight like some sorta MMA-to-the-death bloodsport."

Jay whistled. "I heard they got this maze of concrete road dividers and junk. They make people 'run' it while a couple snipers try to pick them off. Tripwire bombs, spike pits, fire barrels, all sorts of crap, too. Say anyone who makes it to the end, they let go, but never heard anyone made it."

Nicole pursed her lips. "And this is why my ass wasn't gonna let them sumbitches take me."

"Are you guys serious?" Harper swallowed bile at the thought of some crazy warlord in football pads sitting on a throne like something out of a Roman gladiator movie ordering Madison to 'run the maze' and laughing as guys tried to shoot her. *No, wait... girls they would've kept until they got old enough to...* "Please tell me you're just trying to freak me out?"

"Sorry, kid," said Will. "Just what we heard. No idea if it's true. Probably is though, which is why we're getting the hell out of here."

Harper nodded, smiling at these four people. *At least not everyone in Denver has gone crazy.*

"Surprised you guys are out here wandering. Army's got an encampment up at Eldorado," said Cliff.

"Yeah... been there." Jay shook his head. "Place smells like a latrine that's been lit on fire. Way overcrowded. Got people jammed twenty and thirty per tent, like zero privacy. Bunch of shit going down at night no one wants to talk about. Assault, theft, drugs, prostitution, people getting into fights over food. I guess some are keepin' themselves safe, but you can't jam that many people into such a small area without some friction."

"So yeah, we ain't going there." Will chuckled.

Rafael ran back to the van, got in, and moved it around the wrecked canopy, backing up to a cluster of round metal plates on the ground, one of which he'd opened. He hopped out, unloaded a bunch of gas cans from the back, then fed a red rubber hose into the hole. Zach wandered over to the van, brooding off away from the majority of the people. He didn't bother trying to talk to Rafael either

Harper kept an eye on him, worried he might simmer for a while before lashing out, either at her or Cliff. He didn't seem like the type of boy to take losing gracefully. More like the sort of kid who wound up on the news because he brought a gun to school and killed the girl who refused to go out with him. Though, aside from trying to shoot Nicole, he hadn't been violent. That felt more like panic when faced with a group of unknown, armed people.

Still, she didn't trust him. She also wondered if Cliff really would 'make him disappear' out here if he screwed up again, or if that had merely been an over-the-top threat to scare him straight.

"Eldorado Camp ain't *horrible*," said Nicole. "Just... desperate. We're looking for something better.

"You could head up to Evergreen." Annapurna smiled, describing the place and the farm.

Harper zoned out, not really paying attention to her explaining life in Evergreen. Her mind ran in circles picturing her friends stuck in an overcrowded refugee center, trying to survive from day to day without being groped, stabbed, or ending up prostituting themselves for food. Worse, hearing that the 'blue gang'—or Lawless as they called themselves—had gone full psycho and turned a stadium she'd been to as a child numerous times into a sadistic base camp went beyond surreal. More than simple distance separated her from the city she'd grown up in. Denver, at least the Denver she knew, truly felt as though it no longer existed. Granted, rumors had a habit of growing with every person they touched, so it remained possible that the outlandish stories weren't true.

Mile High Stadium could be as likely to hold a handful of Lawless sitting around drinking beer as a neo-Roman emperor who'd abandoned any claim to sanity. The mere chance it *might* have gone that far meant she could never let them get her. Where once she thought it a good thing that they'd hesitate at simply killing her because they'd try to kidnap her for being a girl, now, she agreed with Nicole: she'd rather go down shooting. If the Lawless wanted to take her prisoner, they would damn sure bleed for it first.

Annapurna's description of Evergreen appeared to intrigue their new friends until she mentioned they would have to surrender any firearms bigger than handguns or join the militia. That didn't go over well with Jay or Will, who preferred to remain independent. Eventually, the group said they planned to travel northeast, trying to survive on their own for now.

Once everyone felt assured no one would spontaneously decide to start shooting, the four wanderers made their way off to the east while everyone else resumed a defensive posture around the van.

With each passing minute, Harper's anxiety grew. She no longer so much cared about successfully obtaining medicine from the hospital; only getting home to her family mattered. As if it didn't scare her enough to be near the Lawless, Zach had been promoted from douchebag to *dangerous* douchebag. If the gang thugs didn't kill her, Zach's recklessness—or bruised ego—might.

She exhaled out her nose, watching him as much as she watched for approaching trouble.

Finally, Rafael gave up trying to siphon anything more from the tank and reeled the hose in.

Harper jumped in the van, sat on the floor, and tried to hold her anxiety in check. At least riding in the cargo area meant she didn't have to look at Zach.

# 30

## ST. JOSEPH'S

Rafael started the van and drove back up onto Route 6.

No one said a word.

Though she couldn't see anything but her hair hanging over her face, Harper sensed the mood behind her. Annapurna and Cliff both quite likely believed Zach nearly got them all killed. She clung to the idea that her father of circumstance would have been more upset at her death than dying himself. Whether or not true, she liked to think it. She'd only been with him for a little over three months. How long did it take for a familial connection to form?

A while back, he'd said something about combat forging brothers… or sisters in some cases. Soldiers who'd 'been through it' together wound up more like literal brothers than mere friends. Surviving the trip out of Lakewood back in November had bonded them into perhaps the closest thing to a family two people could have in the absence of genetic relation or marriage.

*Heh. It's a totally new world. Anne-Marie writing down that he's my dad probably is legal.*

"Why'd you decide to open fire?" asked Cliff, a minute or two into the ride.

After a momentary pause, Zach replied in a timid tone. "I thought they were gonna attack us."

"Why her?" asked Harper, dying to know if her suspicion proved true.

"Left end… first target I saw." Zach sighed. "Sorry. I know I panicked."

He answered fast enough and didn't stumble, so she accepted it hadn't been a racial thing.

"Which one of those four was the biggest threat?" asked Cliff.

"Uhh, they all had guns. Does it matter?"

"Harper?" asked Cliff.

"Is it really a good idea to ask me to answer a question he gave an obviously wrong—or clueless—answer to? He's already pissed at me."

"No, no…" muttered Zach. "You were right. I shouldn't have shot at them. Thanks for stopping me from screwing up even worse. Who would you have shot first if they were a threat?"

"Umm." She pictured the line of people… then added blue sashes. "Probably the guy with the giant machine gun."

"Duh," said Zach. "Yeah, that makes sense. I just saw people with guns."

"Harper's not entirely wrong, but her answer isn't totally correct either." Cliff smiled.

"Okay, now I'm confused, too." Annapurna scratched her head, looking back and forth between everyone.

Cliff chuckled. "The correct answer is that there is no single correct answer. Threat evolves. An opponent can go from being no big deal to a huge problem in a split second. What if the smiling guy with the shotgun pointed away from us whipped out a hand grenade? Maybe the dude with the M249 couldn't hit the broad side of a barn with it, but the young woman with the rifle could put bullets up your nose? That's the damn hard part about combat. You have to recognize potential threats, prioritize them, and act on them all in a second or two. And no, I don't expect either of you to be able to do that. My point is, you came charging around the van trying to shoot the first target you saw. That's a good way to get dead. Never just run out into the open. Also, make sure the person you're about to shoot at actually *is* an enemy before you fire."

Zach didn't say anything.

*Ugh.* Harper stared down at the carpeted floor, going back and forth over that group of people and trying to figure out how she could've possibly evaluated who was the most dangerous in mere seconds. Studying for the SATs didn't feel like such a horrible task anymore. Nor did having to speak in front of people. She closed her eyes, offering the universe a deal: she'd give a speech in front of her whole high school in only her underwear if the world could go back to normal. Alas, a moment later when she looked, she remained in the back of a van driving among the ruins of Denver.

Rafael followed Route 6 east past Lakewood. Harper looked out the window despite not really wanting to. Fortunately, her old home on Newton Street sat a good distance south, way too far to see. Still, the glimpses she did catch of houses close to the highway hit her like a gut punch. Roofs holed by falling debris, sometimes whole houses flattened as if a giant had stepped on them. Eight in ten buildings had burned to some degree, many to their foundations. Light poles and trees tilted to one side, and cars piled up in clusters everywhere, several even embedded in the sides of houses. The blocks around her house hadn't looked *too* bad, but this area left no doubt the apocalypse had occurred.

She cringed, imagining traffic at nearly six in the morning when the blasts happened, people rolling along at sixty, seventy miles an hour, then blinded by a sudden flash, their cars knocked out by the EM pulse or physically hurled off the road when the blast wave rolled by.

It no longer snowed ash at least, though everything still looked like the middle of a grey winter. The van kicked up a cloud in its wake, despite how slow Rafael had to drive to navigate the numerous abandoned and crashed vehicles.

The devastation everywhere made Harper want to run back to the hills more than ever. That remoteness, the lack of damage in Evergreen pushed the reality of the destruction a few steps back. As they drew closer to downtown, the damage pattern changed. North, some parts of Denver looked like never-developed open land. Buildings and homes had been so flattened by an airburst that little evidence remained anything had ever been there. East and south, the damage didn't reach the same level of totality, but still looked far worse than what had been near her old house.

After a long, depressing fifteen minutes, they weaved among smashed cars and broken high-rises in the Denver downtown. The city resembled a popsicle stick model that someone dropped on the floor and kicked a few times, then dusted with a copious layer of ash. Harper pulled her shirt up over her mouth and nose at the first whiff of burning. The toxic haze she remembered hanging over everything had abated along with the ash-fall, but fires still had to be burning somewhere for it to smell so much like char. Or perhaps that stink had permeated everything so deeply it would take another nuke to get rid of it.

Warped metal girders jutted out from the sides of skyscrapers like the ribs of wounded giants. One building had partially disintegrated to a skeleton of naked steel, the upside-down tail end of a char-blackened jet liner still sticking out from where it had been thrown into the building by the force of the nuclear explosion. Concrete chunks ranging in size from watermelons to small cars littered everywhere.

She braced herself for the sight of bodies hanging from poles or trees like some totemic warning from the Lawless, but mercifully, none of that existed. They passed plenty of bodies, though all had been left where they'd fallen, most well advanced into decay... too far gone to tell men from women.

Eventually, St. Joseph's hospital appeared on the right, a giant rectangle full of smashed windows, scorched walls, and beige bricks bearing the negative silhouettes of people who'd been vaporized. Less-burned spots where bodies had shielded the wall from the scorching flash formed a ghostly monument to their last split second of life.

"Whoa," said Zach.

Harper gazed up in awe at the six-story building. The lower two stories had once been almost entirely window. A strip of slats ran across at the level of the third floor like some giant air intake for the world's biggest central air unit. Above that, smaller, narrow windows had also blown out, along with a 'jewel' at the top of the structure where a two-story square of glass formerly stood between a pair of brick-faced towers.

"Go around to the other side," said Tegan. "Take the next right past the parking garage, then right again on Eighteenth. We should use the emergency entrance. Less walking that way."

"You got it, Doc," said Rafael.

"Actually, hang on. Keep going to Franklin. There's a Walgreens pharmacy."

He drove onward, passing the first right and pulling around the Walgreens building. That place looked as though war reenactors had used it to recreate Normandy—with live ammo.

"Someone already hit this place," said Cliff.

"We should look anyway." Tegan leaned closer to the window. "It's likely looters would have only taken the drugs they recognized... OxyContin, morphine, Xanax, that stuff. Could be antibiotics and other therapeutic drugs left behind."

"All right." Cliff nodded to Rafael. "Let's check.

Rafael swung the van around and backed it up to the pharmacy entrance.

When it stopped, Harper shuffled over to the back doors and

opened them, then jumped down. The initial breath of air stained with the reek of burned plastic and rotting meat nearly doubled her over, heaving. In both directions down the street in front of the Walgreens, decaying bits of body littered the road here and there, some near car wreckage, some jutting out from under large chunks of debris that had fallen on top of people. Much of the human remains had partially burned. The lumps still present had to have been shielded from the nuclear flash.

*Oh, God... I'm gonna throw up.* She flinched away from the carnage, beyond grateful that her old neighborhood had been far enough from a detonation site to escape such a grisly fate. Madison hadn't seen gore like this. As long as Harper lived, she'd never forget the sight of half a corpse, disintegrated where the corner of a building hadn't shielded him at the moment of detonation. Some of his head, his left arm, and left leg had been behind a wall. The rest of him no longer existed.

"Zach, you stay here with me, keep an eye on the van. Anna, Harp, you guys go in with Doc. If you see trouble, back off if possible. If it hits the fan, we'll be right behind you."

"Okay," said Annapurna, taking the lead into the pharmacy.

Harper forced herself not to vomit, eager to get inside. She rushed after Tegan and Annapurna, her sneakers crunching over the garbage left behind from looters tearing open bags of candy and chips. Various things not immediately useful to looters such as adult diapers, paper plates, dish detergent and so on lay scattered everywhere on the floor. No one appeared to be in the place at least, but despite the apparent emptiness, she still kept a tight grip on the Mossberg.

Tegan bee-lined for the back, jumped the counter into the pharmacy area, and raced around shelves. Upon encountering locked cabinets, she took a step back and aimed her Beretta.

"Wait," said Annapurna. "Shooting them open might attract trouble. Someone hears a gunshot, they're going to come running."

"So..." Tegan glanced at her. "Got a better idea?"

"Yeah. Harper, would you please go tell Rafael we need him in here to deal with locks?"

"Sure."

She jogged outside. Cliff, Rafael, and Zach all stood at the front of the van, watching the street.

"Rafael? They need you in there to open a locked cabinet."

"Aye, *chica.* One sec." He reached into the van to grab a small box from under the driver's seat, shut the door, and followed her back to the pharmacy counter.

Harper paced in circles, sick to her stomach from worry. A few minutes after Rafael jumped the counter, Tegan called out, asking someone to get a shopping cart.

"A cart's not gonna make it down these aisles," said Harper. "There's too much crap on the floor."

"Grr. Baskets then."

Over the next twenty minutes, they ferried handbaskets of fat white bottles to the van. Tegan's guess proved accurate. Most of the painkillers with recognizable names like Percocet and so on had been taken already, but the looters left behind a good amount of other medications that the average person wouldn't have the first clue what it did.

Tegan also had them grab bandages, gauze, disinfectant, and various non-pharmaceutical medical supplies that would be good to have on hand. Harper nabbed a couple more bottles of laundry detergent and dish soap just because. Once they had cleared out the Walgreens of meds, they piled back into the van for the short ride to the emergency entrance of St. Joseph's.

Rafael and Annapurna stayed with the van.

A short distance into the hospital, away from the wind that reached in the smashed windows, the strong stink of death hung in the air, watering Harper's eyes. Zach clamped a hand over his mouth, shuddered, and fell to his knees, vomiting.

Cliff scrunched up his face. "That's not a good smell."

Harper heaved a couple times. She'd been sorta handling the odor, but when Zach started puking, she lost control and painted the wall. Fortunately, it had been a while since her meager breakfast, so she didn't waste too much food.

Everyone followed Tegan without question, but it soon became obvious she didn't exactly know where to go. They walked a hallway past some offices and took the stairs to the next floor. The reek worsened, and the reason became evident after a few minutes of hunting around for the hospital's drug storage area.

Numerous beds held the rotting remains of patients. After making eye contact with a heavyset older guy who'd turned almost completely purple and swelled up with bloat, Harper refused to look through any more doors.

"Guh," she muttered, near to vomiting again. It took her a moment to gather herself enough that she didn't think she'd throw up the instant her hand left her mouth. "They just left them to die?"

Tegan pulled her shirt up over her nose and mouth. Thus far, she'd managed not to throw up. "My guess is they were critical patients on life support who probably passed away when the power failed. They were already gone before any organized evacuation effort could even start."

"Or the people running the evacuation triaged lost causes," muttered Cliff.

Tegan bowed her head. "I suppose anything is possible. People have to make desperate decisions at a time like that."

A loud *slam* echoed from the far end of the corridor.

Everyone froze. Harper sidestepped left, taking cover in a doorway. Mercifully, that room had no patient in it. Zach ran across to the opposite side, also taking cover in a doorway. Cliff brought his rifle up and advanced one door in front of Zach. Tegan darted past Harper into the room, completely out of the corridor.

Harper stared over the Mossberg down the hall at the spot from whence the noise emanated. Voices grew louder, men laughing, a woman calling out in a taunting tone, more men laughing. A stairwell door flung outward a short distance in front of where Cliff had taken up a position.

Three guys barged into the hallway, clad in a disparate mix of jeans, polo shirts, khaki's and T-shirts. Behind them, a thirtyish woman in a denim jacket and camo pants made a mocking cry gesture at someone still in the stairway. All four carried weapons—and all four wore the blue sashes of the Lawless.

The man at the front of their group stopped in mid laugh, staring at Cliff, Zach, and Harper. "Well now. Looks like we got some new friends. Recruits or corpses, you decide."

"Pass. Heard your benefits plan sucks," said Cliff. "Get lost or get dead."

Harper tried to assess them as fast as possible: talker had an Uzi hanging over his shoulder on a strap. The man to his left carried an AK47 in one hand, up, resting on his shoulder, which he started lowering into firing position. The third guy had two handguns in belt holsters, neither out. The woman held an M-16 in a two-handed grip closer to ready than the AK, and she didn't have the demeanor of a kidnap victim. Shadows moved in the stairwell, hinting that they faced more than four Lawless.

She aimed at the woman with the M-16—who jumped backward into the stairwell the instant she noticed the shotgun pointed at her. Cliff fired at the Lawless with the AK before he could swing it down into a firing position. Two rapid shots hit the man in the chest before one nailed him in the forehead. The man withered to a heap on the ground where he stood. Harper shot Talker in the chest at the same time Zach fired at him. The man clenched down on his Uzi, which barked a rapid burst, spraying the wall between Cliff and Zach with fragments of chipped floor.

Tegan screamed at the eruption of gunfire.

The other Lawless dove to the floor and belly-slid into a room two doors in front of Harper on the same side.

She shifted to cover the stairwell.

Zach aimed back and forth like a woodchuck on cocaine. He twitch fired a few shots at shadows; a scream came from the stairwell that sounded female and a little too young to have come from the woman with the M-16.

"Go!" shouted another man in the stairs.

Cliff aimed at the doorway the man slid into.

Two seconds later, a short, female Lawless in a denim jacket zoomed out of the stairwell in a stumbling run across the hallway. Harper aimed for the girl's head, but hesitated—the gang punk didn't look toward any of them, keeping her head down, arms up, stumble-running as if most of her forward momentum came from being shoved. She looked scared shitless. Disregarding her, Harper shifted her aim back to the stairwell the girl had come out of—right as a pudgy bald guy leapt out, raising two giant handguns.

Zach's .22 went off twice, but whether he hit the girl or not, she couldn't tell.

Harper blasted the bald guy in the face.

The gang girl disappeared into the same room where the man with the pistols went.

Baldy fired once from each gun, both painfully loud in the corridor, even louder than her shotgun, but had no time to aim at anyone before receiving a face full of buckshot. His head snapped back. Dead in midair, he collapsed flat on his side in the middle of the hallway, his copious stomach wobbling.

*Bastard threw that girl across the hall as a decoy.*

"Dave!" shouted the woman in the stairwell. Only her M-16 came around the doorjamb.

Harper retreated into the room, her back to the wall by the door, as the Lawless woman let off a wild, blind barrage. Somewhere under the roar of her weapon, Zach shouted several curses. A man roared in anger; rapid footsteps approached.

The Lawless who'd belly-slid across the hall burst into the room with Harper and Tegan. Being close enough to kiss him with her back pressed to the wall didn't give her enough room to bring the Mossberg to bear. He pounced on her, grabbing the shotgun in his left hand and pressing it into her chest, pinning her to the wall.

"Come with us, sweetie. This don't gotta be like that." He grinned, putting the tip of his pistol to her temple. "Now be a good little pet and let go of my shotgun."

"Don't!" shouted Tegan.

"If I was you," said the Lawless, "I'd drop that gun before I splat Red's brains all over the wall."

The snap of a .22 rifle firing four times fast came from the hallway, along with a woman's gasp of agony… and a loud *boom* from an AR15 or M16.

As soon as the man shifted his eyes toward Tegan, Harper smacked her left hand up, striking the bottom of the guy's wrist. His gun went off, hitting the wall a few inches above her head, momentarily deafening her in one ear.

Tegan fired, but missed. Harper rammed her knee into the man's groin while tightening her grip on his wrist, desperate to keep holding that gun away from her face. He doubled over from the nut shot, eyes rolling back into his skull. Growling, Harper head-butted him in the nose, knocking him back on his ass. Tegan fired again, hitting him in the low chest. He howled in pain. Harper recovered her grip on the Mossberg, stepped on his gun hand, and pumped a 12-gauge shell into his chest at point blank range.

With him clearly dead, she hurried back to the doorway and aimed out into the corridor, searching for a target like she used to do on the pop-up competition range. The woman with the M-16 lay dead halfway out of the stairwell door. No other Lawless appeared to be alive, at least anywhere in immediate sight. Cliff wagged his AR15 at a doorway two ahead from Harper, then held up one finger.

Harper shook her head.

He seemed to understand she doubted the remaining Lawless was a threat, and nodded.

She slipped into the corridor, advancing toward the next room, so close to the wall her arm brushed it. When she reached the doorjamb, she paused, then whirled around to aim inside.

The only occupant of that room had died months ago, hooked up to an army of fried medical equipment on carts. She backed out after two seconds to take in the scene, and kept moving up. At the second door where the Lawless had gone, she waited a few seconds longer, begging the universe that at least one of these idiots had the sense to surrender.

Harper whirled around the doorway, acquiring a tuft of mouse brown hair peeking up over a mattress where the punk hid between the two beds. "Don't move!"

The young woman cringed, ducking a little more.

"Do you have a gun on you?" asked Harper.

"Yeah," whispered the girl.

"Slide it away as hard as you can kick it."

A small, silver handgun came skittering out from between the beds.

*Boom.*

The gunshot went off in the hall behind her. Harper about crapped her pants, half a millimeter of trigger pull away from blowing the girl's head off.

A wheeze came from a ways farther down, then the *thump* of a body hitting the floor.

"Dumbass," muttered Cliff.

Zach rushed up beside Harper.

The girl behind the bed grabbed the edge of the mattress and peered over it.

Harper's jaw fell open at the sight of Renee Nichols... a girl she'd known since fifth grade... one of her friends she hadn't seen since the bombs fell. *Holy shit... I almost blew 'Nee's head off.* She lowered her gun as fast as she could without throwing it to the floor.

Recognition flashed in Renee's eyes. She jumped up. "Har—"

*Crack.*

"Look out!" shouted Zach.

Renee grabbed her chest and collapsed to her knees. She stared at Harper, gasping for air with a horrible, pleading look in her eyes, then fell over sideways.

Harper screamed, "Renee!" and ran to her, sliding to a stop on her knees and pulling the girl flat on her back. A tiny hole and growing red stain marked her chest.

"S-she charged at you," said Zach, edging closer. "She has a sash on. She's Lawless… she…"

Harper lunged to her feet, spinning into a strike that mashed the butt of the Mossberg across Zach's jaw, whipping his head to the side. He pirouetted around and crashed to the floor on his chest, his rifle sliding out into the corridor.

"She's my friend!" shrieked Harper, furious but crying. "Tegan! Help! Please!"

"Clear," yelled Cliff.

Dr. Hale rushed into the room, looking at Harper in search of an injury.

"No. Renee!" She pointed. "Please don't let her die!"

Tegan ducked past her and took a knee, pulling at the unconscious girl's jacket and shirt.

Zach moaned.

"You…" Harper whirled, aiming the shotgun at his head. "I swear… if she dies. If you killed Renee." She shuddered with emotion: fear, anger, sadness… wrath.

Something pushed the Mossberg aside. It took her a few seconds to realize Cliff had one hand clamped around the barrel, holding it away from the barely-conscious Zach.

"The girl fainted," said Tegan. "Bullet's probably in her lung. The wound doesn't look too bad. We have to get her to the OR. It's not gonna be perfectly sterile, but it's as good as it gets now."

Upon realizing she'd been so close to murdering Zach, she burst into tears at what he'd done to her friend. Cliff let go of the shotgun. Harper clamped onto him, sobbing on his shoulder.

"Easy, kiddo." He patted her back a few times. "She'll be fine."

She forced herself to stop crying and let go. They had to get Renee moved, fast. "Okay."

Zach moaned.

Harper glared down at him… and noticed a pool of blood spreading out from his thigh that hadn't been there before. "Oh, crap! Zach's hit."

"Help Doc Hale with your friend. I got him," said Cliff. "Don't want you 'gravity assisting' him down the stairs." He winked.

A humorless laugh escaped her throat. She swung the Mossberg over her shoulder on its strap and helped Tegan pull her friend up.

"C'mon 'Nee. You're gonna be okay."

"Are you hit?" asked Tegan. "Anything hurt?"

"My left ear is ringing like hell."

"Why is there blood on your face?" asked Cliff.

"I dunno. I don't feel anything. Is it even mine?" She helped carry Renee out into the hallway. "Where's the OR?"

"Ground floor... go to the stairs," said Tegan.

Harper nodded. "Okay. You lead, I'll follow."

"Been a long time since I tangoed," said Dr. Hale.

"Please don't make jokes now." Harper cry-chuckled.

Tegan elbowed the door open and guided Renee into the stairwell. "This isn't that bad an injury. Don't panic. If she didn't faint, she could probably be walking on her own. Your friend doesn't have much of a pain tolerance, does she?"

"Not sure about pain, but Renee is like scared of everything. We nicknamed her Rabbit." Harper snugged her friend's arm tighter across her shoulders. *Oh, no... What did those sons of bitches do to you...?*

# MOTIVES

Harper gnawed on her knuckle, pacing around in the hallway right outside the OR.

The downstairs corridor had little light beyond what leaked in from the far end, and the operating suite also looked quite dark. Firelight flickered on the walls of the operating room from an improvised lantern of gauze and isopropyl alcohol that filled the air with a strong odor. At least this corridor didn't stink like dead people.

Zach, clutching his left leg above the knee in both hands, sat on a bench not far away, waiting his turn. He'd broken out in a cold sweat and had been mumbling about a blue sash constantly for the past half hour. After bandaging the boy's leg, Cliff had run outside to give Rafael and Annapurna a status update.

She couldn't look at Zach without wanting to hit him again, so she didn't look at him.

*The Universe is cruel. Why Renee? She's so timid.* They all used to tease her when watching scary movies together, as even the not-really-frightening ones would make Renee hide her face and scream. Sometimes, she'd even scare herself into screaming. Like, she'd hang a coat up on a door, forget it, then notice it later and yell, thinking someone had snuck into the room with her. The idea of Renee running with the Lawless was unfathomable.

Worse, the thought of what they'd probably done to her.

Harper's blood boiled. She wanted to spend the rest of the day—the rest of the week—in Denver, roving around and shooting every single Lawless she could find. Those bastards had stolen Harper's innocence, forcing her to kill. They'd stolen Madison's innocence, murdering their parents while her kid sister watched. And now, they'd stolen Renee's innocence in... ways Harper didn't even want to picture. No way would her friend have willingly joined them and gone on looting/murder sprees. They would've abducted her, threatened her, and, no doubt, forced her to have sex.

Annapurna emerged from the stairwell and walked over. "Hey... you okay?"

"No." Harper shook her head.

"Where are you hit?" Annapurna grasped her head, tilting it to check her over.

"It's just a couple cinder block fragments. Tiny cuts. I'm fine. Bullet missed me by two inches, hit the wall."

Annapurna hugged her. "Cliff said you knew one of the thugs?"

"Renee's not a thug!" yelled Harper, then bowed her head. "Sorry... they kidnapped her. That one fat bastard threw her across the hall as a decoy. I nearly blew her head off *twice* today." She sank to a seat on the bench across the hall from Zach, shaking too hard to stand. "I don't know what I would've done if I killed her. We met in fifth grade. Renee's like my... it sounds crappy to say, but my second best friend. Only because I'd known Christina longer. 'Nee and I had the most in common. Both shy."

Zach lifted his head, giving her a *'you shy?'* stare of disbelief.

"Cliff told me she'll be fine." Anna sat beside her.

"Where is he?"

"Collecting guns and ammo from the dead. That big guy had a pair of Desert Eagles. Cliff thought it was hilarious. Called them 'movie guns.'"

Harper wiped her face. "More Lawless are going to show up soon, I bet. Hearing the shooting."

"Going as fast as I can," yelled Tegan. "Almost done. And... I'm sorry."

"What for?" asked Harper, paralyzed by sudden dread. "What happened?"

"I mean, for insisting we take this trip. Your friend..."

"Would have still been held captive by those goddamned savages!" yelled Harper. "It's not your fault. If you didn't bring us here, we wouldn't have found her at all."

"Sorry," said Zach with barely any sound to his voice.

Harper buried her head in her hands. "Holy shit... if he had a real gun..."

Cliff booted the stairwell door open and walked out into the hall, heading right over to stand in front of Zach. "Okay, kid. Listen up. I'll make you a deal. When we get back, you are going to resign from the militia... and I won't leave you here stuffed in a morgue cooler."

Annapurna blinked. "You're going to kill him? He's only seventeen."

"Eighteen," whispered Zach.

"Who said anything about killing him first?" Cliff smiled.

"Look. I'm sorry. I know I'm jumpy, but that girl had a blue sash on. We just had a bunch of people with blue sashes shooting at us. Yeah, I get it, I'm not a soldier. I just played hockey."

Harper lifted her head to stare at him. "And had a nice cushy life, got everything you ever wanted—except into my pants."

"Whoa, hey now..." Cliff looked back and forth between them. "Is that what this is about? You're trying to impress her?"

She narrowed her eyes. "I hope that's not why he joined the militia, because he's doing the exact opposite. Did you volunteer for this thinking I'd all of a sudden start respecting you, or were you just not Mexican enough to work on a farm?"

Cliff's stare bored into her. "What?"

"No, that's not what I mean at all. Zach's been picking on Logan for being Mexican and working on the farm. Called him a freakin' border jumper. This guy thinks he's like above farm work." Harper scowled. "For your information, Logan is not Mexican. He was born in Colorado. His parents were born in Colorado."

Zach shot a dirty look off down the hall.

"Kid..." Cliff folded his arms. "If you asked to be on the militia only to play big man, because you're 'too good' for farm work, I am going to make your life miserable until you resign. If by some cosmic craptangle of bizarre circumstance, you actually did this for the right reasons, you need to seriously sort your shit out and realize this ain't no damn hockey match. Someone stands down, you *don't* shoot them."

"Unless they go for a hidden gun," said Harper.

Cliff gestured at her. "Yeah. What she said."

Zach stared at the floor.

"You have a good long think about what the hell you're trying to do here." Cliff stepped closer to him, pointing at his face. "Because the next time you screw the pooch, someone who doesn't need to die is gonna die, and I ain't having that. You got a problem with Mexicans? You deal with that shit. There ain't enough people left on this little blue dirt ball to give a rat's ass about how much suntan someone has."

"I don't really hate anyone," said Zach in a somber tone. "Just thought it was some funny shit to say. My dad... they always said crap like that. Didn't mean anything."

"Maybe not to you. Bet Logan took it differently." Harper raked her hair off her face and tucked it behind her ear. "You shot my friend. There's probably no way I'll ever be even remotely interested in dating you. I understand she had on a blue sash, we'd been shot at, and you're jumpy. But, if you're looking for ways to try and salvage whatever respect I might have ever had for you, start by apologizing to Logan."

Tegan emerged from the operating room.

Harper jumped to her feet.

"She'll be fine, but she's a bit loopy from painkillers. Wound isn't as bad as I initially thought. Worst danger now is infection, but I've given her some antibiotics. Might as well leave her in bed while we grab the meds."

"Umm, Doctor Hale?" Zach pointed at his leg. "I've been shot. Cliff bandaged it but I think..."

"C'mon." Tegan took his arm.

Cliff grabbed the other, and they hauled him into the OR.

Harper went in after them, drifting left to the table that still held Renee. Her friend lay there topless, with a large rectangle of bluish paper covering her otherwise bare chest. The shredded remains of a T-shirt lay under her. Brown iodine antiseptic smeared her skin where it peeked out from under the paper. Fingertip bruises marked Renee's upper arm and neck. A dark spot on her left cheek appeared to be another healing bruise.

That sight made Harper shake with anger. *I'm gonna kill every damn one of... no... I can't. Some might be like you, forced.* She flashed back to Renee dashing across the hall, a one-second instant where Harper had made the choice not to shoot, a decision she would not have made if she had been lost to the blind rage of wanting to kill every Lawless she saw. Guilt at nearly killing her friend quashed the fires of vengeance burning inside her. She couldn't be responsible for murdering some other innocent person in the same situation.

She squeezed her friend's limp hand. "I dunno what to say. Everything sounds lame in my head. Holy crap it's good to see you. I'm so sorry you were..."

"Hey," whispered Renee. "I still have your *Firefly* DVDs. Gotta give them back."

"I don't give a damn about DVDs right now." Harper bowed her head, fighting tears. "I'm gonna bring you somewhere those bastards will never find you again."

# COUNTDOWN

Tegan worked on Zach's leg for an alarmingly long time. She'd given him something that knocked him straight out, and grumbled about him probably needing a transfusion… but any blood still stored here would be long spoiled. Minutes later, she complimented Cliff on his bandage, then resumed operating while complaining about the damage caused by 5.56 rounds.

"They didn't exactly invent those things to make fluffy bunnies," said Cliff.

"I know… just." She sighed. "Sick of seeing teenagers with these kinds of wounds."

"Yeah." Cliff shook his head. "But, this isn't the same sort of situation you're thinking of."

Tegan grabbed a tool from a nearby tray and stuck it into Zach's leg. "I'm aware of that. Doesn't mean it's not bringing back bad memories."

"You're here," said Renee in a daze. "Am I dreaming about stuff?"

"Nope." Harper squeezed her hand. "I'm actually here."

"Cool. I got kidnapped. That's not cool. I mean cool you're here."

Harper clenched her jaw. "You're un-kidnapped now."

"I'm not a virgin anymore." Renee waved her other hand around like an airplane.

*No…* Harper bowed her head, tears rolling down her face. "I'm so, so sorry…"

Tegan paused, staring at her with sorrow in her eyes. Cliff cringed.

"Brian Purcell," said Renee in a dazed voice. "I was at his house when everything blew up. We did it."

"Oh…" Harper stopped crying in an instant and exhaled. "Oh… Okay."

"He's dead. So are his parents. I haven't seen mine." Renee squinted at her. "I'm high. Feels weird."

Tegan wrapped Zach's leg. "This is about as good as it's going to get. I'm not sure Zach will ever walk without a limp again, but he shouldn't lose his leg below the knee."

"He'll have to quit the militia now," said Annapurna. "Unless he's a good enough sniper to sit on the buses all the time."

"Yeah, uhh, no." Cliff shook his head. "Guess he gets his wish. If he can't work on his feet, they'll probably just let him sit around doing nothing."

*Whatever. At least he won't hurt anyone that way.*

"Harp…" Cliff looked over at her. "You wanna stand watch over these two while we raid the pharmacy here? Shouldn't take us too long. Just in case more of those idiots show up."

"I'd rather get the hell out of here before you all die and I'm stuck here with two people who can't walk and forty-something shotgun shells, no water, no food. But… sure. I trust you."

He patted her on the shoulder. "Twenty minutes at most."

"We can pack everything in a laundry cart and wheel it up there in one shot." Tegan peeled off her latex gloves and threw them aside. "Wow. Tossing gloves on the floor in the OR. I could get written up."

Harper, Cliff, and Annapurna chuckled, then followed Tegan out.

"They're going?" asked Renee in a dizzy voice.

"Yeah. They'll be back in a little while."

Renee went off on an incoherent ramble about meeting Brian, deciding to date him because… something about Venus and Pluto, but he had a shih tzu, which she thought adorable. Also, Mrs. Green the English teacher said something about Zac Ephron, which meant Renee had to have peanut butter with bananas. And the gummi bears wanted to steal her teeth, so she needed to take them all out and hide them.

Harper laugh-cried while trying to follow along.

"Ow," said Renee. "I feel like someone shot me."

"Someone did shoot you."

"Oh. That would explain it. Did I die?"

"No?"

"Are you sure?" asked Renee.

"Yep. Pretty sure. I'm standing here talking to you, so you can't be dead."

Renee rolled her head toward her and smiled. "But what if you're dead, too?"

"No fair. I'm not high on… whatever she gave you. No discussion that weird."

"Sorry."

"It's okay."

"I think someone shot me," said Renee.

"Maybe the gummi bear exploded." Harper giggled.

"No. They want my teeth, not my tit." Renee poked herself. "Ow."

"Don't do that."

"I know. It hurt." Renee poked her chest again. "Ow."

"Stop!"

"I don't like coconuts. I don't wanna have coconuts. Whoever put coconut in chocolate bars needs to be slapped."

"Okay. I'll make sure I never give you coconut stuff." *That shouldn't be too difficult. Not swimming to Jamaica or whatever to get one.*

"Oh, hey." Renee gazed around. "Are we locked in here? Did they get us?"

*Grr.* "They're dead."

Renee looked up at her, bewildered. "How do you kill a door?"

"What? No… the people who kidnapped you are dead."

"Oh." Renee blinked. "That's good. Did I see it happen?"

"I don't think so."

"Good." Renee nodded—and evidently amused at how it felt to nod, kept on doing it. "Whoa. The world is tumbling."

Harper put a hand on her friend's forehead, holding it still.

"You fixed the room. You're an awesome friend."

"'Nee, you are *astoundingly* high right now." She sigh-smiled at her friend.

The girl looked too thin, and it bothered Harper that 'too thin' struck her as normal to see. Odd smears of purple and blue dye marred the last few inches of Renee's long mouse-brown hair, no doubt something the gang had done to her. Her boots, yoga pants, and skirt looked like normal 'Renee clothing,' but she'd probably been wearing them constantly for months. Her T-shirt had been sliced beyond usefulness, though the denim jacket appeared intact, draped over a cabinet nearby.

Harper always thought Renee 'pretty' and herself plain. Renee had the same opinion in reverse, always commenting how Harper turned heads but everyone ignored the plain brown-haired girl next door. She looked weary, exactly like Harper felt inside. For as long as she'd known the girl, Renee always had a personality like a little hamster that sensed an eagle right about to dive on her. That easily-startled nature had been the target of endless scare pranks. Renee usually laughed too, once she stopped crying.

"A whole bunch of Army people came and told us we had to leave. It was so loud and everyone yelled. Dunno what I did, but I got separated from the others when something blew up. I ran away like the big chicken I am." Renee laughed. "You know how you guys always pick on me for being scared of everything."

"Yeah. But that's why we love you."

Renee grinned vapidly. "Hey, there's a piece of paper on my boobs. Eep! Am I at the dentist?"

"Dr. Hale had to cut your shirt off to fix you. She put it there so you weren't hanging out."

"Oh. That's nice of her. It's nicer she fixed me." Renee touched the spot on her chest. "Ow."

"Stop poking it. You probably have stitches."

"How bad?"

"I dunno. I wasn't in here."

"Look?"

"Umm."

Renee turned her head. "I don't wanna see. Please look."

Harper gingerly lifted the paper, discovering a one-inch long stitched incision at the base of Renee's left breast. A smaller, L-shaped stitch marked the skin closer to the armpit above the breast. *What the heck? Two holes?* "Umm, just small cuts. Looks good." She lowered the paper.

"Those guys caught me. They locked me in a bedroom and—."

"I... don't need details."

Renee sniffled. "I gotta tell someone... and you're my best friend."

Harper cringed, nodded, and let out a long, slow sigh. "Okay."

Renee described being kept in a locked bedroom for the first few days with some other women. Eventually, they 'assigned' her to a husband and moved her to a different locked room she had all to herself. The whole time she'd been with the Lawless, they constantly pawed at her or taunted her with guns. Mostly, they left her confined in a room alone for several weeks until they decided she was too terrified to attempt running away, then only locked her in at night. They started bringing her along on 'exploration teams' during the day. Though they gave her a gun to carry, she'd never used it. Other than taunting her for being scared of everything, they didn't punish her for hiding whenever the shooting started. She described the gang as being 'relatively nice' to her since she'd been too chicken to do anything but what they told her to. Other people, men as well, had the crap beat out of them for attempting to escape or not following orders. Some died.

*She didn't say anything about being molested... She should be an absolute wreck right now. Did she repress it, or did she deal with it? No... no one can 'deal with' something like that. I want to wrap her in packing foam and keep her safe.* "You're gonna come back and stay with us, okay? You won't have to worry about anything." *We can probably squeeze another small bed into our room. She's not going to fit in ours.*

"Cool." Renee smiled. "Hey, there's paper on my boobs."

"Umm..." Harper looked off to the side, tears gathering to fall. "Did they... umm... Were you... assaulted?"

"You mean did they make me have sex?" asked Renee, her tone almost giggly due to the drugs.

Harper squeezed her hand.

"No. Almost happened, but I lied. Told them I was only fourteen."

"What? Are you serious?"

"Yeah. I told them." Renee nodded. "Darci always teased me for havin' small boobs. But they helped. They thought I was fourteen an' didn't make me sleep with anyone. One guy was going to, but this other dude Benny beat the hell out of him. I was scared Benny would find out I lied and be mad at me."

"Well, technically, we *are* underage..."

"Yeah, but I'm not fourteen." She counted on her fingers. "I'm only underage by five months, unless you're talking about drinking."

"I'm really... totally shocked—but thrilled—they waited." Harper fidgeted at the conflict raging inside her head... hearing that made it harder to arbitrarily hate everyone wearing a blue sash. More accurately, it made it impossible to arbitrarily *shoot* anyone in a blue sash. She still hated them to the last for what they did to her parents—or what they'd do to innocent people they captured.

Renee resumed endlessly nodding. "Yeah. Surprised me, too."

"Stop." Harper put a hand on her friend's head to hold it still again. "Don't do that. You'll break your neck."

"I'm already in a hospital. Why are the lights off? Oh... wait. I remember." She sighed, blowing the paper off her chest. "Oops."

Harper caught it and put it back.

"Thanks. So, yeah, they believed I was too young. They assigned me to this guy, and he even made this countdown calendar for the day I turned sixteen. He maybe wouldn't have waited the whole time. But he'd a' gotten in trouble if he didn't."

"Savages," muttered Harper.

"Why are you in Denver? You gotta get out. It's not safe here."

"I did get out. We came back for medicine." Harper explained her journey to Evergreen, meeting Cliff and Jonathan, having to join the militia, and so on. "The same bastards who kidnapped you killed Mom and Dad."

Renee burst into tears. "Harp... I'm so sorry. Your parents were really cool people."

They held each other for a few minutes, crying and reminiscing about some of the 'awesome things' her parents had done over the years, like going all out on a Middle Earth-themed birthday party for Harper when she turned twelve.

"Oh, shit!" Renee sat up fast, causing the paper to slide down into her lap. She stared at Harper with a horrified expression as though an axe murderer stood behind her.

"What?" Harper spun, saw nothing there, and whirled back to her friend. "What's wrong?"

"I forgot to study for that physics exam. I'm gonna fail."

Harper shook her head rapidly, unsure if she'd really heard that. "What?"

"What?" asked Renee.

Harper gently pushed her back down and pulled the paper back over her chest. "Study for a physics test? Are you serious or are you messing with me?"

"Neither." She laughed. "I'm high."

# WRATH

C lattering echoed in the hallway.

Harper swung the shotgun off her shoulder and pointed it at the doorway. She felt like a piece of crap for taking cover behind the surgical table with Renee on it, so stepped around it. Sure, that put her right out in the open, but she would rather use her body to protect her friend than hide behind her.

"It's us," said Cliff. "Please don't give me a buckshot enema."

*Whew.* Harper relaxed. "Clear."

Cliff pushed a gurney into the room and pulled another.

A trickle of gunfire went off outside, close.

"Crap. Is that what I think it is?" asked Harper.

"Yeah. Anna, Raf, and Tegan are lobbing slugs back and forth with some locals. We got a whole bunch of meds loaded, but it is time to go." Cliff picked Zach up like a rag doll and set him on one gurney with somewhat more care than moving a crash dummy. He scooped Renee up far more gently and eased her onto the second gurney.

The girl laughed when the paper flew off her chest.

Harper grabbed the denim jacket and covered her with it like a blanket.

"Lay your weapon on top of her and push from the end." Cliff dropped his AR on Zach and pushed him out into the hall. "Right there if you need it. Faster than straps. C'mon. Move."

Harper set the shotgun on the gurney beside Renee, grabbed the rail at the end and shoved, grunting from the weight. Once she got it rolling, keeping pace didn't take too much effort, but steering proved a challenge due to inertia. Renee caromed off cabinets, other gurneys, and the wall a dozen times as they went down the hall, around a corner, and down a long ramp to the emergency arrival area.

Rafael had the van backed up to the doors like an ambulance. He took cover behind the driver-side door, firing an M-16 at someone down the street to the left. Annapurna aimed around the nose end, also sending lead down the street. Tegan crouched low on the passenger side, pointing an AK47 to the right, but appeared to be watching for threats rather than actively engaging anyone in a shootout.

A giant mound of boxes, white bottles, and supply bags took up about three-quarters of the cargo space, packed to the ceiling.

"Think I can ram the van hard enough to throw him in?" asked Cliff.

"Umm..."

"Tempting, but I'm joking." Cliff pulled that gurney around to the side door, then shoved Zach onto the bench seat.

"Wow. What did Tegan give him that he's still out cold and Renee's awake."

"Gummi bears?" asked Renee.

"Not all the way awake," muttered Harper while pushing the gurney up to the rear bumper.

Renee sat up, gasping in pain. "Oh, ow. It hurts."

"Stop moving."

"I don't wanna get shot again." Renee rolled over onto all fours and crawled off her jacket into the van.

A loud *clank* announced a bullet hitting the van somewhere out of sight. Cliff recovered his AR, kicked the empty gurney away, and jumped into the van.

Harper grabbed the jacket and threw it at Renee before shoving the second gurney back into the hospital, climbing in, and slamming the rear doors.

Cliff leaned between the front seats, taking aim out the driver's door window. Three seconds later, he fired. The loud report of the shot pounded the air and made Harper's left ear start hurting again. Since the battle appeared to be spanning at least a 200-yard stretch of road, her shotgun wouldn't help. She curled up on the floor and covered her ears, hoping she wouldn't go deaf for good.

"Nice. Been tryin' to nail that slippery bastard forever," said Rafael.

"Time to go!" shouted Cliff.

Rafael scrambled into the driver's seat and wedged his M-16 between the seat and center console, pointing straight up. Cliff kept aiming out the window behind Rafael's head, popping off intermittent shots at the Lawless in the distance, keeping them pinned. Tegan jumped in the side door. Renee finally appeared to realize what the object in her lap was, and put her jacket on... though she forgot to zip it. As soon as Annapurna darted away from the front and leapt up to sit beside Zach, Tegan slid the side door shut and Rafael hit the gas. Hard acceleration into a right turn tossed Harper against the stack of medical supplies.

Once the shooting stopped, she let go of her ears and sat up. A huge white plastic bottle full of pills bounced off her head. "Ow. She rubbed the spot, raising her arms to shield from a few more that fell on the next turn. "Wow. This is a lot of meds. Surprised it was still here."

"Most of the stuff I expected would still be there was. Unfortunately, anything that required refrigeration is shot. Still, this trip was worth it." She chuckled. "We've probably got over a million dollars of medicine."

"That much?" asked Cliff. "Damn..."

"Well, not really." Tegan smirked. "That's just what they charge for it. What it *should* cost is quite a bit lower."

"Guys," muttered Harper. "There's no such thing as money anymore."

"Bummer," said Renee. "My bank account finally broke a grand."

A few stray shots came at the van, but between the vast numbers of wrecked cars they slalomed around, and Rafael's driving, nothing hit them—at least that anyone noticed.

When they reached Route 6 for the long run west past Lakewood, Harper briefly entertained the idea of asking them to stop at her old house again. She wanted to grab her and Madison's clothes. Maybe pictures of her parents or random keepsakes. Upon noticing that Renee hadn't closed her jacket, and the stitched wound seeped blood, Harper abandoned the idea.

She leaned over and zipped her friend's jacket.

*Nah. It would be stupid and selfish to ask them to stop. What if someone got killed or paralyzed? I can't ask them to get shot for me. Not for grabbing random crap. Besides, the only thing left in that house is bad memories.*

Harper fell into a pit of sadness, picturing her old home as if walking around in it. Every room, every door or cabinet. The bathroom sink, tub, rugs... Madison whined in her memory while rattling the bathroom door, yelling, *Harp, hurry up! You've been in the shower forever!* Never in a million years would she have expected they'd end up sharing a bath.

*Boom, boom.*

Cliff's AR-15 going off twice startled a shriek out of her.

An incoming bullet struck the middle window on the passenger side, shattering it and the one opposite it. Amid a spray of safety glass bits, wind blasted into the van, throwing Harper's hair around and toppling the stacked pill bottles, which rolled everywhere, rattling.

"That was nice of him," said Annapurna, taking advantage of the new opening to return fire.

An instant after she clicked off a shot, a distant cry of pain rang out.

"Wow, these bastards are persistent," said Cliff.

"They see a working van and go nuts." Rafael accelerated. "That's why they aren't shooting the tires or the engine. They wanna take our ride."

With a metal-on-metal *clank,* a bottle of pills burst open, showering Harper and Renee.

"Ack!" yelled Tegan. "Try not to crush any."

Harper stared at a haze of white powder in the air in front of her. "Little late. Is this bad to breathe?"

"Amoxicillin. Antibiotic," said Tegan, scrambling into the back to help pick them up. "Don't crush any more. One of these pills might make the difference between someone dying or not."

Leaving the doctor to play Pac Man with pills, Harper sat up and looked out the windows on both sides. Muzzle flare came from people hiding among the rubbled city, behind concrete chunks or flipped cars. None looked anywhere near close enough to engage with the shotgun, since the idiots tried to chase them on foot.

Content to sit this gunfight out—but terrified of catching a stray bullet—Harper flattened herself on the floor as much as she could.

Renee flopped next to her. "Ow."

"Stop moving so much," rasped Harper. "You just had surgery."

*Clank.*

Both girls twitched.

"I'd rather pull a stitch than eat a bullet. Well, another one."

"You had a .22." Cliff fired out the left side window. "That's barely an appetizer."

"Not funny." Harper huffed at the hair over her eyes.

Zach moaned.

"What did you give him?" asked Harper. "Horse tranquilizers?"

"Horse's ass tranquilizers," muttered Cliff.

Tegan stuffed handfuls of pills into an intact Amoxicillin bottle. "He was in shock. I don't know how he was able to walk on that leg. When he wakes up, he's going to be in a significant amount of pain. I gave him enough to keep him out until we get back to Evergreen."

Harper slid toward the front as the van decelerated hard.

"Why are you slowing down?" yelled Annapurna.

"Lot of junk in the road here." Rafael cursed in Spanish. "Unless you want I should crash into it?"

"No, no…" She fired out the window twice more.

Men screamed war cries outside, far closer than the ones plinking at them from the ruins. The van's rapid turning left and right pushed Harper into Renee, then Renee into Harper. Pill bottles bounced around, making her feel like she'd been thrown in a clothes dryer with a bunch of plastic balls. Footsteps clapped on paving, drawing near. Face down on the floor did *not* sound like a great tactical position. Harper pushed herself up, swung her legs forward, and landed sitting. She swung the Mossberg around, starting to point her weapon out the window at the runners, but stopped at the *whump* of a body crashing into the back doors.

Harper aimed to the rear. Thumping and banging came from a guy, no doubt standing on the back bumper, trying not to go flying as Rafael slalomed abandoned cars. She tried to figure out where to shoot at the closed doors to knock the guy off.

A wild-eyed face appeared in the small square window on the left.

Harper locked stares with him, a blue sash fluttering in the wind at his neck. He looked like the sort of crazy man who'd dabble in cannibalism if given the chance. In that instant, something deep in Harper's brain snapped open.

She stood in the living room of her house, unable to bring herself to kill the man charging at her from the front door. Dad swiveled, taking his attention off the deck to kill the guy seconds from shooting Harper. A man with a blue sash—the same man staring at her through the van's rear window—burst in the sliding glass door and shot her father three times with a handgun.

The scene replayed in vivid detail in the span of a half second. She had blocked it out, knowing someone had shot Dad, but refusing to remember the sight of it, or the face of the man who'd killed him. Harper had told people over and over what happened, but always said she never saw the man who murdered her father.

But she *had* seen him.

She'd stared straight into his eyes *while* he killed her father—and forced herself not to remember.

Having that same man five feet away broke down her mental fortress.

No trace of recognition shone in his eyes; to him, she'd just been some random girl to shoot or kidnap, no more memorable than dinner at a fast food place. A seam of light appeared between the doors. The man, the creature she hated most in the world, pulled the left door open and stepped one foot inside. His sinewy dirt-smeared chest gleamed with sweat, exposed by the tatter of a button-down shirt barely clinging together, flapping in the wind.

The greedy look in his eyes shifted to one of concern when he noticed the shotgun pointed at him.

Harper fired four times so rapidly that the Mossberg sounded like an automatic weapon. "Die you piece of shit!"

The man fell to the road, his scrawny body tumbling over and over like a sack of broom handles. About seven other Lawless jogged to a halt farther down the road, having given up on chasing the accelerating van.

She leapt to her feet and ran to the doors, shooting the bouncing corpse twice more, still shrieking in rage.

Tegan grabbed her from behind, bracing a foot on the still-closed right door. "Careful! Don't fall!"

Her father's killer slid to a stop on his chest at the end of a long, bloody smear. She fired again, not even caring if it hit the corpse.

Annapurna scrambled past them, caught a pill bottle before it fell onto the road, then stretched out to grab the swinging door, closing it.

"Harper!" shouted Tegan. "Calm down, honey. Are you okay?"

It occurred to her that her entire body shook. She let her arms fall limp. Tegan pulled her back from the open door, easing her to sit on the floor, still with both arms wrapped around her. Harper dropped the shotgun and buried her face in both hands, bursting into tears as if Dad had died all over again.

"Hon?" yelled Cliff. "What the hell happened back there? Is she hit?"

"No," said Tegan. "She's… just upset."

"Didn't think that thing had a full-auto setting." Rafael wiggled a finger in his ear. "Damn shit's loud, yo."

Renee crawled closer and hugged her. "Harp? What's wrong?"

"That's…" She sobbed. "That's the man who killed my dad."

"Damn," muttered Cliff. "If you want, we can turn around and go run him over a few times."

"That seems quite unnecessary as I am pretty sure he is dead," said Annapurna, peering out the square rear window.

Harper barked an unexpected laugh, tears still rolling down her face. "Nah... he's got friends who'll shoot us. I'd rather go home."

"I hear that," said Rafael.

# CLOSURE

Harper's hands still shook almost an hour later when they rolled back into Evergreen.

Coming face to face with the man who'd murdered her father had ripped the scab off the most painful memory her brain didn't want to confront. Trauma like losing her father all over again far outweighed whatever shock she may have felt at killing the guy.

Rafael pulled around the bus barrier, had a brief conversation with Cameron Black who currently had sniper duty, then drove into town and parked at the clinic. Cliff picked the still-unconscious Zach up and carried him inside. Harper helped Renee walk in, following Dr. Hale down a hall to an office that had been repurposed as a patient rest area. Nine twin beds, all taken from nearby empty houses, sat in fairly neat rows, one containing Fred Mitchell.

Renee sat on the edge of an empty bed, grimacing. Tegan tugged at the zipper of her denim jacket. Renee offered no protest to the doctor removing the jacket, leaving her bare-chested with Fred, Cliff, and Zach (unconscious as he was) in the room. Her friend's total lack of shame stabbed Harper in the gut with guilt and anger. *What did those bastards do to her?*

Cliff threw a blanket over Zach and walked out, keeping his eyes politely averted from Renee.

Tegan checked over the stitches, dabbing at the blood with a cloth.

Though the wound had seeped a little, she seemed satisfied that the stitches hadn't pulled loose and guided Renee to lay back in the bed before covering her with the blankets.

"How bad is she hurt?" asked Harper.

"Considering she was shot at close range, she's quite lucky." Tegan pointed at the larger incision. "The bullet entered here and struck a rib, ricocheting upward, passing under her breast tissue and exiting here." She indicated the smaller L-shaped stitching. "It tore some muscle, but didn't penetrate her lung."

"Wow," said Renee. "Lucky."

Harper balled her hands into fists. *I may just hug Walter for giving that idiot a .22 rifle and not a real gun.*

"Quite." Tegan smiled. "I'd like for you to stay in bed a couple days. Harper, why don't you head over and ask Liz about a couple shirts for her?"

Renee stared up at the ceiling. "Whatever you gave me is starting to wear off. I don't feel so high anymore and my boob's on fire."

"Okay." Harper patted Renee's shoulder. "Be right back. I'm sure you don't want to pull a Veronica."

Renee giggled for a second or two, then cringed. "Ow. And no."

Tegan muttered about needing Cliff—or someone to help her move Zach—and walked out.

They spent a few minutes reminiscing about the time their friend Veronica went topless at a party on a dare for about fifteen minutes. That led to Renee asking if Harper had seen any of the others, and a longer session of them both talking about how much they missed everyone. Eventually, they forced themselves to put their catching up on pause so Harper could go get her a shirt.

She hurried outside, intending to come back as fast as she could. Doctor Khan, Ruby, Darnell, Rafael, and Marcie helped unload the van, carrying the medical supplies in the door one armload at a time. Harper hurried across Route 74 to the quartermaster, ignoring the food pickup counter and going straight to Liz's desk.

"Hi. Got a sec?"

Liz looked up at her. "Oh, hey there. Sure. What can I do for you?"

"We found Renee—one of my friends—out there and brought her back. She was shot, and Tegan—I mean Dr. Hale—had to cut her shirt off. So she's got nothing on. Got any shirts or dresses left?"

"Sure we do. Renee, you said?" Liz grabbed a clipboard and wrote her name on a line. "Got a last name?"

"Nichols."

Liz nodded. "All right. Guessing she's only got the clothes on her back."

"Below the waist, yeah. So not even one full outfit."

"Go on through and grab her some things. Or just grab a shirt for now and she can come back later and pick for herself."

"Thanks!"

Harper entered the storage area via a door adjacent to Liz's desk and rummaged shelves for a few minutes until she found a couple T-shirts and a pair of jeans that looked like they'd fit Renee. Once Liz noted everything on the clipboard, Harper rushed back across the highway to the medical center.

Cliff waved her over before she made it to the door. "Hey… you still look pretty rattled. You okay?"

"Umm. Not really, but I'll deal with it."

"You're shaking." He grasped her hand.

"Yeah. Emotional as hell right now… That guy when I freaked out? He's the son of a bitch who killed my father."

"I heard." He patted her back. "I'm here if you need to talk."

"Thanks." She rested her head on his shoulder. "I guess they're right. Revenge doesn't make you feel better. Now, I'm all just sad and angry again."

"I'm not trying to replace your father, you know. Just… I dunno, kinda pick up where he left off and do what I can."

Harper hugged him. "Thank you. I think I about crapped my pants the first time I saw you in the mall, but I really don't know what I'd have done without you."

"Ehh, you'd have managed." He winked. "Maybe with a bit more scars and some mental trauma, but you're tough."

She raspberried him.

Cliff laughed, then resumed carrying stuff.

Harper brought the shirts and jeans to Renee, who rushed into one, a black T-shirt with an AC/DC logo.

"Doc said I didn't have to stay *here*, but I should mostly rest in bed for about a week." Renee held up a little paper slip. "And I passed her check. I'm clean enough to stay in town."

"Nice. C'mon. You're gonna stay with us."

"Cool."

With a grunt, Renee eased herself to her feet.

Harper supported her on the way outside. "Good thing is, the house isn't *too* far from here."

"That's good," rasped Renee. "Because I'm not gonna be able to take this for long. Holy crap this hurts."

"I can shoot Zach in the tit if you want."

Renee started to laugh, but stopped, cringing. "Ow. Please don't make me laugh. And no, it's okay. I *was* wearing a blue sash."

"So stupid… why would they do that? Everyone knows that means they're Lawless and they'll just shoot."

"I think it's mostly so they don't try to kill each other. And, they think people will be scared of them and run or give up."

"Is it true their leader took over the Mile High?"

"I dunno. They kept me in a house. We ran around that neighborhood, or into downtown. Never went to the arena or even heard anyone mention it. I think they have like different groups or something."

"Crap. That sounds organized."

"Those guys? No way. More like being stuck in a frat party where kidnapping isn't against the law. Half of them usually stayed too drunk to move. If I wasn't such a chicken, I probably could've jumped out the window and tried to run away."

Harper wondered if she'd have had the nerve to escape. Now? Probably. But if those guys had captured her and Madison months ago, maybe not. She couldn't blame Renee for being afraid. The girl who screamed and cried at B-grade horror movies didn't belong anywhere near the Lawless. She didn't really belong in a world burned to cinders by nuclear war either, but they didn't exactly have a choice there. However, she could do everything in her power to protect her friend and keep her comfortable.

Children's shouts and laughter came from the backyard, so Harper walked around the house, eager to see her siblings—especially Madison who had to be worried as hell.

Carrie Rangel from next door sat on a plastic lawn chair, babysitting. The warm late-March day had evidently encouraged the kids to all go barefoot, the girls to wear dresses, and Jonathan to put on the same khaki shorts he had on that day she'd spotted him swimming out of the pretzel shop. He'd lost enough weight that he'd had to tie a rope around his waist as a belt to keep them from falling off.

Jonathan, Lorelei, Becca, and Mila ran about, kicking a ball around between a pair of 'goals' defined by empty soup cans. Madison sat on the little slab porch behind the house, arms folded across her knees, head down.

The sight of her little sister too sad to play wracked Harper with guilt. *I had to go on that run. We needed that medicine. Can't just hide here in town.* She sighed out her nose. *I can cross my fingers we don't have to go scavving for a while, though.*

"Hey, Termite. I'm back."

"Oh, hey." Carrie smiled. "Welcome back. How'd it go out there?"

"I'll tell you later," said Harper. "Long story."

Madison's head popped up. She spun to the right, staring at Harper and Renee for a second before leaping to her feet and running into a hug. Surprisingly, she didn't burst into tears, just held on tight for a while in silence. Eventually, she leaned back, tears in her eyes, but smiled. "Har—oh, wow! You found Rabbit?"

"Heh." Renee laughed into a wince. "Yeah, she did."

"Her name is Rabbit?" asked Lorelei. "She's not fuzzy."

"It's 'cause she jumps at everything," said Madison. "She's easy to scare."

Jonathan emitted an 'evil mastermind' laugh while making weasel hands.

"Please don't," said Renee.

"Oh, he's kidding." Harper patted him on the head. "And if you're not, at least wait two weeks. She's injured. Making her jump could really hurt her."

"Ack! What happened?" asked Madison.

"Caught a stray bullet." Renee looked around. "Where can I sit?"

"C'mon…" Harper helped her friend to the back porch and inside.

Madison hovered clingy close, but didn't get in the way. After leaving Renee on the sofa, Harper went to scope out the bedroom for the addition of another twin bed. Unfortunately, her memory overstated the amount of free space between their existing bed and the dresser/closets. If Renee moved in here, she'd be on the floor or they'd be sleeping while stacked on top of each other.

*Dammit! I can't make her sleep on the floor. Can't ask her to share a room with Jonathan. It would definitely be too awkward for her to share a room with Cliff. Grr!*

"I got started on dinner already," said Carrie. "Wasn't quite sure if you'd be back in time. Will Cliff be here to eat?"

Harper headed down the hall to the kitchen. "Yeah, he should be. Not sure what's taking him so long."

"All right. Let me add some more then." Carrie plucked two cans from the cabinet. "Got it started with some of my provisions."

"Oh, you didn't have to do that. We have our own food."

"It's fine. I planned on eating here already anyway." She winked and headed out to the cinder block grill in the back yard.

Harper hovered in the doorway, watching her. The thirty-four-year-old with strawberry blonde hair looked noticeably younger than Mom who'd been forty-three. She had been flirting with Cliff for a while now, and though she didn't try to swoop in and play mother to her or her siblings, she did enjoy babysitting. With Harper, she felt more like a much older sister than a stepmom, but that worked. Maybe she hadn't quite coped with the loss of her husband enough to directly ask Cliff on a date. How many times would she have to make a comment about rattling around in that big ol' house all alone before he realized what the woman tried to say?

*Big ol' house...* Harper grinned, and ran outside to the grill. "Umm, Carrie?"

"Hmm?" The woman smiled at her while stirring an orangey-brown morass not quite stew but not quite soup either.

"That girl with me is my friend Renee..." Harper gave her a brief, okay-for-children-to-overhear explanation of how they found her. "She's hurt and... kinda delicate. After what she's been through, she's going to need people around to help her. I can't do it 24/7, but I was wondering if you might, like, adopt her? Or at least let her live with you? We don't really have any more room in here without a sleeping bag on the floor. Maybe seventeen is too old for adopting. Her parents might still be alive in Eldorado Springs. No idea."

Carrie smiled again. "Okay."

"Wow. That was fast. You didn't even think it over."

"What's to think about? I've got plenty of room. The house is too much for me alone. And with your friend right next door, it's easier for you two to spend time together."

"Cool!" yelled Renee from the couch. "I won't need a car to come over anymore."

Harper grinned at living so close to her friend, at having found her alive and—mostly—intact. She'd have to introduce her to Grace. Nuclear war had forced her life off the road she'd wanted it to take and sent it down a bumpy dirt path strewn with land mines and barbed wire. However, two friends, one old and one new, would help her cope. Maybe, some day, she could even pretend this existence was normal. True, she would never again feel carefree, never again enjoy a day where her worst worry was Starbucks running out of the sugar-free mocha flavoring, but what good would it do her to keep mourning that life?

*Well, Dad. I got the fu— piece of—.* She sighed, remembering how he'd always scolded her for swearing, even after they'd wound up hiding in their basement with most of Lakewood on fire. *Hah. Well, Dad... I got him. The guy who shot you.*

"What's wrong with me?"

"Do you want me to answer that?" asked Madison, right next to her.

Harper jumped. "Gah!"

"Sorry."

She looked down at her kid sister. "C'mere a sec, Termite. There's something I need to tell you."

# 35

## DESERVE

Harper led Madison out the front door and far enough down Hilltop Drive that none of the other kids would hear them.

"It's bad news, isn't it?" asked Madison, staring down at her toes.

"No. Not bad news."

She looked up, shocked. "You don't have to go on another ride?"

"Umm. Not that I know about. It's possible I will in the future, but I dunno. And no, that's not what I wanted to tell you."

Madison slouched in relief. "Okay. What is it? Spill."

"Ugh." Harper sat on a giant rock someone had put in their front yard for decoration.

"You said it wasn't bad news. Why are you sitting down?" Madison tilted her head, narrowing her eyes in suspicion.

"I'm gonna tell you something that maybe I shouldn't tell a ten-year-old, but you deserve to know this."

"Is it about sex?"

The unexpected—casual—comment caught Harper so off guard that she laughed. "No."

Madison furrowed her eyebrows. "It's not funny."

"Those guys with the blue sashes found us when we were at the hospital. We got into a shootout."

"Harp…" Madison grabbed and pawed at her, checking for injuries. "You're not gonna die, are you?"

"No, good grief, no." Harper hugged her. "I got thrown around a little, but I'm fine. We fought our way out of the hospital, got into the van, and drove off, but they kept chasing us. This spot of road had so many dead cars in it we had to drive super slow. One of the thugs jumped on the back of the van and pulled the doors open, coming in after us."

Madison gasped.

She hesitated. "Maybe I shouldn't…"

"Did he…?" Madison's lip quivered.

"No. I was riding in the back, and we stared at each other. He was… the same guy who killed Dad."

Tears ran down Madison's cheeks, but she didn't make a sound or move.

"I don't know what came over me, Termite. I shot him like six times as fast as I could pull the trigger. He was dead before he hit the road."

Madison stood there in silence, crying for a moment, then bowed her head. "Thanks for telling me. He deserved it."

"Yeah. He did."

"You didn't." Madison hugged her.

Harper wrapped her arms around her kid sister. "Huh?"

"You shouldn't have to kill people. We're just kids."

"Heh. I'm not really a kid anymore. Three months, I'll be eighteen. But… turning eighteen doesn't really mean that much now."

"I guess," muttered Madison. "You can even have beer, right?"

"Yeah."

"Can I have beer?"

"No. You're too small. Gotta be fifteen."

Madison cry-laughed. "Okay. Mom said drinking doesn't solve problems, it just makes them wait 'til tomorrow."

"I wasn't planning to get drunk over that bastard. Just because I *can* drink without getting in trouble now doesn't mean I'm going to get wasted all the time. That stuff tastes like crap."

"Then why do people drink it?" Madison leaned back from the hug, giving her a quizzical stare. "If it tastes bad."

Harper shrugged. "I haven't figured that out yet. Maybe it tastes good to them? I don't really know. Anyway, I just wanted you to know that the man who hurt Dad got what he deserved. He's dead and he'll never hurt us again."

"Can we go home now?" asked Madison.

A crack split down the middle of Harper's heart, threatening to break it. She stared into her sister's deep hazel eyes. *She still thinks we're going to go back there...* "Umm... Termite, we're... umm..."

Madison shook her head. "No. I mean"—she pointed at the house they'd been staying in for the past three months—"home."

*Oh...* Her referring to this place as home shattered the dam. Harper smiled, but couldn't stop crying. Perhaps her little sister wasn't as broken as she feared. "Yeah. Let's go home."

Mila's distant battle roar preceded the hollow thump of foot-on-ball, followed a half-second later by the deeper *thud* of ball-on-skull. Lorelei started to emit a squeal—but rather than evolve into scream-crying, she laughed like an idiot.

"Holy crap! She flipped over in midair!" yelled Jonathan. "Are you okay?"

"She's laughing," said Becca.

"She's bleeding!" yelled Jonathan.

"Just my node!" shouted Lorelei.

"Oops," said Mila. "Sorry. Didn't think you'd try to block it with your face."

"Uh oh." Harper jumped to her feet. "Sounds like we should get home like, right now."

# 36

# RATS

That night, Harper stood in her bedroom a few minutes before dark, frowning at the dresser.

She frowned because it didn't contain any of the clothes she'd left behind in Lakewood. Not that she had any urge to make a fashion statement, but what she planned to do tonight required a specific look. Unfortunately, she had only one option to wear black below the waist: yoga pants. She would've preferred black fatigues since those had pockets, or even camo. Alas, the Walmart raid had come up short.

She hadn't even chosen the yoga pants. They'd been wadded up and stuffed into one of the sets of jeans she'd claimed, probably by Marcie while trying to jam as much as possible into a shopping cart. Still, black was black. She pulled them on and added a black T-shirt, turning it inside out to hide the Metallica logo on the outside.

White sneakers, she couldn't do anything about. She didn't have darker shoes, and going barefoot would've been brighter. Her father used to joke that the crew of the International Space Station could see her from orbit whenever she went outside in a swimsuit.

She'd kept the handgun the guy had nearly shot her with, not at all concerned if anyone complained about her swiping it. The weapon had—albeit indirectly—drawn blood from her via itty bitty cinderblock fragments. It felt *super* weird to put a leather belt on over yoga pants, but she liked having a smaller firearm she could keep on her hip around the house. If she ever had to run out the door in a hurry, she'd never be caught unarmed. Even if she did have much less practice with a .45 than the shotgun, it beat nothing.

"I hate that you have to stay out all night," said Madison from the bed.

"It's not *all* night. Just four hours." Harper spun away from the dresser to smile at the girls. "It's my turn tonight, and it's just until we find who's stealing food. I'll try not to wake you up when I get home. Now, go to sleep."

"Not even dark yet," said Lorelei.

"Well… do something then before it gets dark." She kissed the little one atop the head, patted Madison on the arm, and headed out, Mossberg in hand.

So far, the militia who'd guarded the quartermaster's place at night had stood out in the open, an obvious deterrent. Harper got the idea to try something else and set up a trap by hiding nearby and watching the building so it appeared they'd given up guarding it. If the food thief thought they had an opportunity, she could catch them in the act. Since no one knew who had been stealing at night, she didn't say anything about that plan to anyone except Cliff. Not that she suspected people on the militia of being the thief, but the fewer who knew she planned to hide, the better.

A short distance down Hilltop Drive, she spotted Logan walking toward her. As soon as they made eye contact, he smiled. She did, too. He walked up to her, stopping almost close enough to kiss, but neither one of them moved or spoke for a moment.

"Hey," said Harper.

"What's up?"

"Working tonight. Militia stuff. Like, top secret." She winked.

He chuckled. "Cool. Hey, I was on my way to your place to ask if you wanted to hang out sometime. Just us?"

"No party this time?" She quirked an eyebrow.

"Well, maybe… but it would just be the two of us. Got a little surprise for you, and no it's nothing bad."

Harper grimaced mentally. She liked Logan, liked hanging out with him. He clearly seemed to be into her, but she had too much going on in her head to add worry about a boyfriend on top of it all. *After Tyler… I don't want… And, I don't feel that way about Logan, or…* She stared into his eyes, trying to consider how she felt about him without being preoccupied by the idea that *any* boyfriend would be a bad idea. A dazed butterfly orbited her stomach for a few seconds before crashing. *Okay... maybe something is there. And... any of us could die next week. Guess it won't hurt to at least try dating him. I'd go out with him if the war hadn't happened.* She bit her lip. *Well... if the war didn't happen, Introvert Prime would be screaming and running away right now.*

"Sure. Sounds fun."

"Great." He grabbed her free left hand in both of his, but didn't seem to know if he should shake it, kiss it, or just stand there holding it. "Umm... So, you said you're busy now?"

"Yeah. Militia stuff. Maybe tomorrow night or Thursday?"

Logan nodded. "Awesome. After dinner? I'll swing by and pick you up?"

"Yeah. It's a date then."

He grinned.

"But, I gotta go now."

Logan nodded.

She walked past him. A few seconds later, a soft, "Yes!" broke the silence.

Harper clamped a hand over her mouth to hold back a giggle.

An unexpectedly bright mood came over her for the rest of the walk to the quartermaster building. She even hummed to herself as if on the way to grab coffee or a new outfit, not sit in the bushes with a shotgun for four hours in the dark.

Seriousness returned when she approached the door on the side of the building, off the little approach road leading up from Route 74. Ken Zhang, who'd been watching the place on the previous shift, waved at her.

"Hey. Right on time."

"Wow, really? I just guessed."

"Yeah." He shouldered his rifle. "Everyone got used to using their cell phones for the time, no one has watches. So, whenever the relief shows up, they're on time. As long as it's not *too* far off."

"Right." She fist-bumped him.

"Who's on after you?"

"Uhh, Sadie or Marcie I think. Walter's handwriting is horrible, especially in dry-erase marker."

Ken gave her a knowing nod. "Yeah, I missed the first two nights thinking we had a Kim."

She laughed.

"Anyway, time for 'Kim' to go to sleep." He waved and walked off.

Harper stood guard by the door until he walked out of sight, then crossed the grass to the sidewalk corner at the northeast end of the building. There, she sat among the trees in a spot that gave her a view of the front entrance as well as the side door. The food thief had been careless a week ago, losing a pack of cookies in the hall near the side door. Evidently, they hadn't noticed it fall. Liz found it the next morning.

Due to that, the militia assumed the thieves made use of the side door along the north face of the building. It made sense, given that it had mostly open field across the road from it and that part of the building couldn't be observed from the militia HQ on the other side of the former kennel.

After arranging some low-hanging branches to conceal her pale face, she rested the shotgun across her lap... and waited. Normally, the militia guarding the quartermaster's at night had to patrol around the building every so often. Walter didn't want them standing still by one door the whole time. Harper figured the food thief made their move when the guard walked away, slipping into the building unnoticed, then leaving the next time they walked off. Or maybe they entered during the day, then made their way out unseen at night. That could explain how they managed to get in without breaking any windows.

At first, she'd hoped it had been the shadow men stealing food, thinking that they had camped out nearby or even used an empty house right in town while they waited for the opportunity to grab Mila or possibly scouted out other children they could abduct and brainwash. Whether by morbid curiosity, sheer random oddity, or what, someone had decided to give Mila a set of throwing knives they'd confiscated from the dead. Hell, why not? The girl was *damn* good with them, even if the weapons themselves didn't have the killing power of a gun. If she kept practicing with them, by the time she even reached Harper's age, she'd be damn scary.

Of course, Mila wasn't allowed to carry them around all the time. Not yet. Her mother let her practice with them in the backyard of her house for now, if she wanted to. Harper suspected she probably carried one, hidden, just in case.

She shook her head at the thought of a girl younger than Madison who could nail a kidnapper in the eye with a throwing knife. If not for her noodle of an arm, she probably would've killed the guy. Then again, her sister had shot a man. Admittedly, it hadn't been fatal, but still, Madison had put a bullet into a man trying to kidnap Jonathan. She'd never spoken of it since, nor did she have any interest in carrying a gun around. That Mila wanted to carry at least one knife around, just in case, worried Harper.

*Oh, please let her cope and be normal. As normal as anyone can be now.*

One hour dragged into the next. The moon kept vanishing and reappearing behind fast-moving clouds, making it difficult to see. Harper tried to hold as still as she could, only turning her head a slight bit to keep scanning the two doors.

Roughly two hours into her shift, the soft crunch of multiple footsteps on dirt came from her right. Harper froze, listening. Faint whispering followed, but she couldn't make out words. Inch by inch, she turned her head toward the voices.

Minutes later, three forms emerged from a cluster of trees at the south end of Elk Meadow Field, crossing the road in a rapid shuffling walk toward the quartermaster's. A trio of tween boys, all on the heavyset side, hurried up to the door. They wore oversized jackets and expensive sneakers, looking as if they'd come straight out of inner-city Chicago. One kept pulling at his pants, which wanted to fall to the ground. Though he remained quite overweight, he'd clearly lost enough to drop a pant size or two.

The tallest—and widest—of the boys had a mocha complexion and a red bandana over his hair. He sidled up to the door, pulled something out of his jacket pocket, and huddled close to the lock. The other two boys, both slightly younger, one dark-skinned, one white, turned their backs to him on lookout for danger. The white kid stuffed his hands into the pockets of his starter jacket. A bundle of gold chains around his neck hung down to the middle of his chest.

*Crap. They're like twelve-year-olds. Dammit.*

Harper mentally grumbled to herself for sitting on the ground, but she'd never have lasted long squatting before her muscles gave out. As quietly as she could, she shifted her weight onto her feet. The black kid looking in her direction turned his head, evidently having heard the rustle of the tree branches around her.

She jumped out from her hiding place, holding the shotgun sideways, unable to make herself aim at *children*. "Hey! What are you guys doing?"

"Oh, Laird Jesus!" shouted the one who'd been picking the lock while leaping away from the door and grabbing his chest.

His friends also jumped, though neither yelled.

Harper took a few steps closer. "Sorry for scaring you, but what are you doing?"

The big kid kept pressing his hands into his chest, wheezing. "You scared the shit outta me."

"We ain't want no trouble," said the dark-skinned boy, still holding his pants up. "Just need something ta eat."

"Where are you guys from? We've been thinking someone in town's been raiding the pantry. I don't remember seeing you guys. Are you from the south half?"

"Uhh, no." The lock-picker pointed a thumb back over his shoulder. "We got a camp little bit up in the hills. Natural walls. Good place to hide. Just comin' down here for food."

"Come on. You guys can stay here in town. Just gotta stop stealing. There's no need for you to keep hiding out in—"

The white kid yanked a hand out of his jacket pocket and pointed a smallish handgun at her. "Yo. We're leavin'. Gimme that shottie, nice an' easy, an' we gone."

"Jimmy, what the hell, man," whispered the lock-picker.

"Shut it, Darius," said Jimmy.

Harper swallowed hard. Not that she wanted to shoot a twelve-year-old, but if she tried to pivot the shotgun at all, he'd probably kill her.

"Ju hear her?" asked the black kid. "Dude, chill."

"I ain't chillin' T-Bone." Jimmy took two steps closer to Harper, holding his gun higher, tilting it sideways. "Gimme the damn shottie."

*That's the gun they stole from Kathy Bowden.*

"Drop the gun or I'ma blow your nuts off!" shouted a small voice behind the boys.

The color faded from Jimmy's cheeks. His fingers snapped open, letting the gun fall to the ground with a *thump.*

Harper trained the Mossberg on him. "Okay. All three of you against the wall, hands apart."

"Aww, man," muttered Darius.

The boys stood there grumbling in protest for a few seconds, but it didn't sway Harper. They begrudgingly complied, shuffling up to the wall. As soon as all three had assumed the position, she looked for the child who had yelled.

Madison, wearing one of Cliff's black T-shirts for a dress, still barefoot, stood on the curb behind the boys, holding a plastic flashlight in the manner of a gun.

"Dammit, Jimmy," said T-Bone. "Now we f—"

Harper blared the air horn to call for backup.

All three boys yelled.

Darius lost his balance and fell on his butt. "Girl, you tryin'ta give me a heart tack? Dayum." He fanned himself.

"Relax. I know you two told him to knock it off, but your friend there just pulled a gun on me, so I'm being careful. We don't have cops anymore, just militia. You're not going to jail, so calm down. This is a safe place, and the three of you should stop sneaking around at night and just move in, okay? There's no reason for you to stay out there alone."

Madison scurried over and picked up the gun Jimmy dropped in two fingers, holding it like a turd. She hurried over to stand next to Harper.

At the sight of the ten-year-old with a flashlight, not a gun, the boys all groaned. T-Bone lost it a few seconds later, laughing and pointing at Jimmy.

Answering air horn pips came from the distance.

"What the heck are you doing here?" Harper glanced at Madison.

"You were just away on a scary scavenge trip." Madison edged closer, leaning against her. "I have separation anxiety."

Harper almost laughed at the matter-of-fact statement, until it made her feel too guilty.

"Cliff's flashlight doesn't work. I got lost trying to find you."

Dennis Prosser and Roy Ellis jogged up Route 74. With his longish squiggly hair and already-thin frame, a couple weeks of lean rations had left Dennis looking almost like the grim reaper. Somehow, Roy still appeared muscular, though his sunken cheeks gave away that he had, in fact, also dropped some weight.

"Here," shouted Harper.

The men jogged up the driveway.

"Aww, shit, yo," said Jimmy. "That one looks like a real cop."

Roy almost smiled, then put on 'cop face.' "What's going on?"

Harper lowered the shotgun. "Found who's been taking food. These three are living in some kind of camp nearby. I think they're on their own. That one"—she gestured at Jimmy with the shotgun—"pulled a gun on me, but he's only like twelve, so I'm willing to forget he did it if he loses the attitude."

"Walter starting them off a bit young huh?" Dennis smiled at Madison.

She held up the little gun, still pinched between two fingers. "You should take this."

Dennis clasped his AR under one arm and took the pistol. He popped the magazine out and looked it over. "Cripes, this thing is tiny. What is it a .32?"

"Nah. Looks like a micro-9," said Roy. "Okay, you boys carryin' any more hardware like that?"

"No sir," said Darius.

"Nah." T-Bone shook his head.

Jimmy also shook his head, but didn't say anything.

Roy proceeded to give the boys each a brief pat-down. Satisfied, he nodded to the side. "All right. C'mon with me. You three all need a bath and a change of clothes."

Jimmy glanced at Harper as the boys filed past her, his expression somewhere between apology and annoyance. Dennis brought up the rear.

"Hey, Dennis?" asked Harper.

"Yo?" He paused.

"This is maybe a stupid question, but since we found who's been taking food… do I still need to sit here all night? Maddie's up way past her bedtime."

"And I have separation anxiety," said Madison.

"Aww…" Dennis smiled at her. "She's adorable. Yeah, go on home. Doesn't seem any point to it now."

"Sweet." Harper took her sister's hand. "C'mon. We're both up past our bedtime."

A short walk later, they slipped quietly inside the house and went to their room. Harper changed into one of her nightgowns. Madison pulled the black T-shirt off, which she'd put on over her nightie. Lorelei remained asleep, not having realized she'd had the bed to herself.

Harper hopped in bed and held the blanket up for her sister to jump in. Madison cuddled up beside her, clinging.

"Night, Harp."

"Night, Termite."

"Night, John-Boy," said Cliff from his room.

"Huh?" asked Jonathan.

Cliff chuckled. "Never mind. None of you are old enough to get that."

"Why is everyone awake?" asked Harper.

"Lori's not," whispered Madison.

Harper chuckled.

"Go to sleep," said Cliff, from his room.

Grinning, Harper closed her eyes. For once, she didn't think she'd have trouble falling asleep.

# 37

# SUNSET

After dropping the kids off at school the next morning, Harper swung by the medical center to visit Fred Mitchell.

He looked better, having regained color. The doctors still didn't want him doing much, so he had been staying in the patient room. She filled him in on the food thief situation, which made him laugh. He mentioned that Zach had hobbled out of there on a crutch the previous night, and would likely be resigning from the militia due to his leg. Tegan and Dr. Khan both predicted he would have a permanent limp, though hadn't been sure of the severity. In some way, she felt bad for him having an injury like that at only eighteen. But, it wasn't as though it cost him a chance at a promising career with the NHL.

The war already did that for him.

Harper left the med center after a short visit, citing her need to get back out there. She crossed the street to meet with Walter Holman and give him her official story regarding what happened at the quartermaster's last night.

He listened to her explanation, then grinned. "Excellent work, Harper."

"Ehh... I didn't really do anything but happen to be there at the right time."

"That staying hidden and watching thing... we should've tried that. Like using a deer blind. Let the prey walk right up to you."

"What's going to happen to them? They're just kids. Oh, I think the gun they had is the same one stolen from Katherine Bowden's place."

"Doctor Khan cleared them, though the oldest boy had some rash issues in a sensitive place... they hadn't changed clothes or bathed since the bombs fell."

"Ick."

"The one needs a smidge of an attitude adjustment, but for the moment it looks like they'll be staying here. Anne-Marie's looking for volunteers to take them in. Oh..." His expression fell grim. "Bit of somber news."

"Uh oh."

"We lost one of Janice's people. Kam McFadden. That weird bastard who tried to grab Mila attacked him last night when they tried to bring him food. Got Kam's weapon away from him, but he didn't have the keys to the cell. Hostage standoff ended with both Kam and that freaky son of a bitch dead."

"Oh, no..." Harper sagged on her feet.

"Don't go feeling guilty about anything here. None of that was your fault. It's making us reconsider the policy of using the jail for prisoners."

She cringed. "We can't execute everyone."

"Well, in most cases, exile should work unless we think there's a strong reason they'll come straight back to cause problems. But, that's not your thing to worry about."

"Oh, Mr. Holman, there's one more thing."

He tilted his head, a note of worry in his eyes about what she might say... like he suspected she might resign.

Harper walked around his desk and hugged him. "Thank you for giving Zach a .22."

"Umm..."

"If you issued him a real weapon, he would've killed my friend, Renee."

He winced. "Yeah, I heard the story. I had a feeling that boy needed an evaluation period. How are you holding up?"

"Fine." She smiled. "Gonna head back out and keep an eye on my, umm, district or whatever unless you need me for anything else."

He chuckled. "All set. Stay safe out there."

"Will do."

Harper waved and walked out.

THE KIDS ALL KEPT GIVING EACH OTHER WEIRD LOOKS OVER DINNER, THEN smiling at Harper and giggling.

Somehow, everyone appeared to know she had planned to go out with Logan tonight. Then again, knowing Cliff, he'd probably heard the two of them talking last night. He pretended nothing weird went on the whole time they ate box macaroni and cheese, which surprisingly came out okay when cooked over a wood fire. Watching the kids lick every scrap of cheese off their bowls had been surreal.

Cliff collected the dishes afterward while the kids headed to the living room to play Uno.

"Want help?" Harper leaned against the counter.

"Nah, you go and have fun." He didn't look up from the bowl he scrubbed, adopting a note of comic aloofness.

"Really? Wow, no like 'dad talk'?"

"You're seventeen, few months from the big one-eight. That's as good as an adult nowadays. But, I will say one thing." He glanced sideways at her. "If you decide to let him stab you, it could kill."

She gasped and blushed. "Umm, wow. Not sugar coating anything I guess."

Cliff grinned. "Real talk. Besides, I trust you. If I didn't, you'd spend the night handcuffed to a chair in my office."

"Hah!" She snickered, remembering how terrified she'd been of getting in trouble when 'Cliff the mall security guard' had busted her for shoplifting. She leaned against him. "Thank you for being concerned. I have no intention of doing anything even close to that with Logan… at least yet. Probably not for a while if ever."

He leaned his head against hers rather than hugging her with wet hands. "Go have some fun. You deserve some for once."

Her limited wardrobe didn't allow for any sort of 'prettying up' beforehand, so she decided to go with the same white T-shirt and jeans she usually wore. Since she had the .45 on her belt, she left the Mossberg in the bedroom closet. It absolutely terrified her to have a weapon sitting out with three children in the house and no gun safe in sight. Her father would probably reanimate as a zombie and walk all the way to Evergreen to yell at her for that. But, they didn't *have* a gun safe, and after everything they'd all been through together, she had a reasonable amount of trust that neither Madison nor Jonathan would dare go near it unless an extreme emergency happened.

Lorelei, she didn't feel as confident about, but the girl had shown zero interest in guns and the older kids wouldn't let her touch it. Plus, Cliff was here to watch them, and she'd be back before he had to go out on night patrol.

As she didn't have to change, owned no perfume or makeup, and had no idea what to expect, she simply paced around the living room.

"Have fun on your da-ate!" singsonged Madison.

Harper put a hand on her gut in a futile attempt to calm her nerves. "I'll try."

Madison got up and ran over. "I still have separation anxiety, but you need to do something fun. It makes me sad that you don't really smile anymore."

"I'm sorry, Termite…" Harper hugged her.

"I'm sad, too. And scared. But, it's okay for you to do fun stuff sometimes." Madison squeezed her, then poked her in the side. "You'll be back in an hour or two anyway. I can cope." She stuck out her tongue and made a silly face.

Harper ruffled her hair and went out to sit on the front porch. Evergreen at a half-hour from dark had become peaceful and serene. Few sounds other than birds intruded on the gentle rustling of trees in a mild breeze. She'd never simply sat outside alone with her thoughts before the war, always at school, work, with her family or friends—or plugged into the internet. Still, sitting there doing nothing made her feel restless. Her life had been a speeding car, the world outside a total blur, and now she'd found herself walking.

"Mom, Dad?" she whispered. "I found Renee. She's kinda okay. It could've been *way* worse, but she's still freaked out. Yeah, I know what you're going to say. She's always been jumpy. Renee met Grace today, and I think they're gonna click with each other. They spent the afternoon here. I'm still not sure if I should feel guilty for enjoying hanging out with them while my other friends are possibly dead or… with those bastards. Renee didn't see any of them, so maybe they made it out. We talked about how we're all gonna look like something out of a sci fi movie in like ten years when all our clothes fall apart and there's nothing modern left. One of the scavenging groups found that someone nearby had a bunch of pet alpacas, so they brought them here. They might produce wool. No one knows how people way in the past made clothes. Like, we're all so used to just going to the store, how do you get cloth after you shave a farm animal?

"Anyway, someone's gonna have to figure it out again or we're gonna be wearing plastic bags. Renee was always making cosplay stuff, so she can make normal clothes, but she has no clue how to make cloth from scratch. Grace is gonna become the closest thing to a doctor possible now. Not like there's any med schools left now that the world has gone completely crazy."

Harper looked up at the darkening sky, mesmerized for a moment at the sight of both sun and moon visible at the same time.

"I dunno if you guys can hear me or if ghosts are nonsense, but... I'm starting to think we might be sorta okay here. Miss you guys so much."

She bowed her head, choking back tears, and sat in silence for a little while before the scuff of sneakers on pavement came from the right. Someone walking by on Hilltop didn't interest her enough to look up—until they entered the yard and came to a stop right in front of her.

Logan, also in a white T-shirt and jeans, smiled at her, his hands in his pockets, his long, dark brown hair draped half over his face. "Hey. Hope you're still free tonight."

"Yeah." She stood, taking a deep breath or four, hoping her eyes hadn't gone too red that he noticed. "So, what's this thing you wanted to show me?"

Cliff coughed from inside the house.

Harper blushed.

"Umm, it's not what your dad thinks it is." He offered a hand. "I promise."

Laughing, she took his hand and let him lead her down the road. They walked to Route 74 and north, randomly talking about life in Evergreen. He didn't mind working on the farm, even though it wound up being quite far from what he'd expected to do with his life. She rambled about how she couldn't believe she'd become basically a cop, and admitted that she sometimes felt like an actress pretending to be someone she wasn't.

They crossed the field into the southern end of the farm area, Logan apparently guiding her to a hand-built storage shed made from metal sheets and plywood. Seeing that reminded her of catching Beth and Jaden in the house, and of her father giving her 'the talk' the first time he'd caught her with a boy in her bedroom. She'd been fifteen, as had the boy. Her father had walked in on them kissing, chased him out, then spent the next two hours rambling about how she had to be careful because her whole future—school, job, career, and so on—would be threatened or ruined if she 'made a mistake' and got pregnant.

She rolled her eyes at the idea of any future she might have being ruined now. School, advanced degrees, a career... all of that had gone down the drain at a few minutes to six in the morning one day last September. Getting pregnant might not force her to drop out of school, but it *could* be dangerous. Some women died during childbirth even with modern medicine. In the aftermath of such a devastating nuclear war, the odds of that had to be almost medieval—or at least 1800s-ish.

Logan smiled back at her as he reached for the door. His expression had a degree of amused innocence to it that allowed her to trust him. He didn't at all give off the sense he wanted to bring her somewhere out of sight to do anything inappropriate.

He stepped inside, pulling her in by their clasped hands.

Nothing triggered her gut about him, not like Tyler. If she forced herself to forget the state of the world—that they could be killed at any moment, something might happen to Madison, Jonathan, or Lorelei at any time—she could see herself dating Logan. However, being open to the idea of romance and ready to do *more* with him weren't the same thing.

Two folding tables stood against the wall on the right, barely visible in the dark, windowless shed. Straight ahead, the darkness felt almost solid, like something big occupied most of the space. Faint hissing came from that direction.

"Umm. I can't see anything."

"Hang on." Logan let go of her hand and stepped deeper into the murk.

She fidgeted. "Be careful. Do you even know what's in here? Don't step on anything sharp."

With a soft *click*, a single bulb came on overhead, flooding the shed with painfully bright light.

A maze of thick pipes took up most of the back end of the room, weaving into progressively smaller pipes before going out through the right side wall as thin copper tubes. The folding tables held an assortment of pipe fittings, tools, and hose bits. Logan stood by the tables, fiddling with something.

"You wanted to show me... the irrigation system?" She gazed up. "Or a working light bulb?"

"Not exactly..."

"So...?"

He turned to face her. Music started up behind him, coming from a small speaker connected to an MP3 player. He slow-walked up to her as the first notes of *Everything Has Changed* by Taylor Swift and Ed Sheeran filled the cabin.

Her throat tightened.

Logan raised a hand toward her. "I was hoping you might want to dance."

She stared at him, too choked up to speak. This moment at once felt too surreal to believe and too unbelievable to process. Hearing music for the first time in months... and *that* song, having him stand there, arm out, expectant, hopeful look glimmering in his eyes... she had all she could do not to burst into tears.

Mutely, she accepted his hand.

He stepped in, the warmth of his body close. She rested her other hand on his shoulder and tried to remember how to slow dance. Taylor Swift's voice filled the shed. Harper found herself agreeing... she wanted to know him better.

They danced somewhat awkwardly for a few minutes, her emotions a weird tangle of tentative love, hope, and sadness. Whenever the chorus said 'everything has changed,' she thought of the world burned to cinders. Logan grinned, no doubt aware of her graceless attempt to dance, but unbothered. He seemed much more practiced and guided her until she relaxed into the motion. As the song started to wind down, it hit her that 'everything has changed' also applied to her: the timidity she'd shed, the safety she had to provide for herself, and... how she felt about Logan.

The song stopped far sooner than she wanted it to.

She looked up at him. "I, umm... haven't danced since junior prom."

"You're pretty good."

"You're a pretty bad liar."

He smiled. "For someone who hasn't done this before, you're pretty good."

"Didn't picture you for a Taylor Swift fan."

"I listen to a lot of stuff. Never thought I'd hear music again."

She broke eye contact, staring at his chest. "Yeah, same here. Wow... I'm crying."

"Sorry."

"Don't be. This was... wow. Umm. Magical." She bit her lip.

A moment of silence passed.

"I can put something else on if you want."

"Maybe... later? I... don't want to ruin that. It's a memory. The first good memory I think I'm going to have after..." She looked up. "I think I need a little air. It's getting warm in here."

Logan took her hand and led her out of the shed and across a short distance of field to the creek the pipes fed from. "How's this?"

"Good." She smiled, then lowered herself to sit cross-legged near the bank.

He sat beside her and gathered a few small rocks, tossing one into the water. "It really is beautiful here. Sometimes, when I'm working on the farm, I think about the people who lived on this land back before technology. Native Americans, pioneers... they found a way to thrive."

Harper leaned back, staring up at the sky. "We forgot everything they learned. Like, I was talking about that earlier. No one here knows how to make fabric. Or furniture. Or most of the stuff we used to just buy."

"Yeah. People used to make everything by hand, then machines and factories happened so everyone forgot how to really do things."

"Not everyone. There's YouTube—*was* YouTube videos of people making stuff by hand. But none of those people happen to be here in Evergreen. How far back do you think we'll go? 1800s? Medieval days?"

Logan tossed another rock into the creek, causing a tall, narrow splash. "Probably closer to the 1800s. If the Third World survived, there might still be factories and stuff left or real schools."

"I was so worried about getting into a good college, but I still hadn't figured out what I wanted to do. Might've gone for veterinary medicine. My dad suggested psychology, but I chickened out. Dealing with people with super sad issues would've broken me. I couldn't sleep because I had no idea what to study for or what to do with my life. Could be worse, I guess. This woman who walked here with us, Summer, studied business, got a degree... and like months after she got her first real job, the war happened. Me stressing out over what to do doesn't seem that bad. At least I didn't waste four years learning stuff that won't do any good now. So, Logan Ruiz, what were you gonna do?"

He threw another little rock. "Same thing. Trying to figure it out. I was going back and forth between a trade school—like for welding or electrician work, joining the Navy, or maybe going into teaching."

"Trade school?" She blinked at him. "Really?"

"Yeah. My dad said there's a lot of money in those jobs, but it can be dangerous ass-busting work. I was kinda leaning toward joining the Navy and getting into something science-based that I could've used in the civilian world after. 'Course both of those options are kinda shot now." Logan shook his head, throwing another rock, harder. "I can't believe people actually fired the damn nukes. So many dead... so damned pointless."

"Yeah." She looked down at her lap.

He hesitated, then exhaled. "That Taylor Swift song... Luisa sometimes got a hold of my stuff. She put it on there, probably as a joke. I was gonna delete it, but now I can't. It'll always make me think of her."

Harper choked up.

"And, it'll always make me think of you." He wiped a tear, managing to salvage a smile.

She leaned against him. That he'd played that song for her felt as though he'd opened up and bared his soul to her. As long as she'd known him—which, admittedly hadn't been that long—he'd never much spoken of his family or seemed anything but happy, rolling with the giant punch life dealt him. Seeing that vulnerability in him clicked with her. She sat there for a while in silence, just being with him in their shared grief.

"I hate the war." Harper scowled. "How could anyone be so stupid and cruel to use weapons like that?"

Logan exhaled. "I don't know."

"Do you have any idea what started it?"

"Nope. Everyone's too busy trying to survive to ask why it happened. I figure by the time civilization recovers, no one will care."

She pulled her hair off her face and peered over at him. "Do you think it'll recover or are we all going to wind up tribal and crazy... running around half naked with spears and stuff?"

"Nah. I don't think it'll go *that* far. We'll be okay." He threw his last rock, which vanished into the creek with a melodic *ploink*. "It's just like living in the Old West again. Lack of tech didn't turn them into *Mad Max* back then, right? Why would it do that now?"

She smiled down at the grass between them. "Yeah, I guess. Maybe I shouldn't give up hope yet."

"I haven't given up hope."

"Oh," said Harper. *Wow. He lost his family and he's still optimistic? Is he too full of life or am I an emo queen?*

"But, I have much bigger hopes than society merely surviving."

She sat up, giving him an 'oh really?' stare. "Like what? A green new world like from *Star Trek* rising out of the ash?"

Logan rested his hand atop hers. "Well... I was kinda hoping you might want to kiss me."

Butterflies swarmed around her gut. Part of her wanted to, but even the few glimpses of feeling happy she enjoyed recently felt like she somehow disrespected the world that had died. "I dunno if I'm ready for that yet."

"Okay. No problem." He smiled, though disappointment flickered across his eyes.

"I like you, Logan." She took a deep breath to still the nerves exploding throughout her body. "I think I maybe *do* want to kiss you, but I can't yet. I'm too messed up. I need to know I'm really into you and not just pulling a Lorelei and clinging to the first guy who's nice to me. It has to be real. Will you give me a little time to let the dust settle? Can we maybe start by holding hands and watching the sun go down together?"

Logan slipped his hand under hers and laced fingers with her. "Yeah. That sounds romantic."

She grinned and leaned against him, gazing up at the sun slipping into its mountainous bed. It tinted the undersides of clouds pink, spreading a wide band of orange along shadowy peaks beneath a blanket of indigo.

He hummed the song they'd danced to.

A tear slipped out of her eye. Taylor Swift had been right.

Everything *had* changed.

~⦿~

*fin*

# ACKNOWLEDGMENTS

Thank you for reading *The World That Remains!*

When I wrote Evergreen, I hadn't been prepared for the overwhelmingly wonderful response it received. In truth, I'd planned that book as a one-off. However, so many people asked for a follow up novel that no real choice existed for me. I had a great time getting back into the heads of these characters, and I hope you enjoyed the trip along with me.

Additional thanks to Lee Sheridan for editing.

Also, thanks to Alexandria Thompson for the wonderful cover art!

# ABOUT THE AUTHOR

Originally from South Amboy NJ, Matthew has been creating science fiction and fantasy worlds for most of his reasoning life. Since 1996, he has developed the "Divergent Fates" world, in which *Division Zero, Virtual Immortality, The Awakened Series, The Harmony Paradox, and the Daughter of Mars series* take place. Along with editing for Curiosity Quills press, he has worked in IT and technical support.

Matthew is an avid gamer, a recovered WoW addict, developer of two custom RPG systems (paper & dice), and a fan of anime, British humour, and intellectual science fiction that questions the nature of reality, life, and what happens after it.

He is also fond of cats, presently living with two: Loki and Dorian.

Visit me online at:
    Facebook: https://www.facebook.com/MatthewSCoxAuthor
    Pinterest: https://www.pinterest.com/matthewcox10420/
    Goodreads: https://www.goodreads.com/author/show/7712730.Matthew_S_Cox
    Twitter: https://twitter.com/mscox_fiction
    Instagram: https://www.instagram.com/mscox.author/
    Email: mcox2112@gmail.com

# OTHER BOOKS BY MATTHEW S. COX

Divergent Fates Universe Novels

Division Zero series

- Division Zero
- Lex De Mortuis
- Thrall
- Guardian
- Harbinger

The Awakened series

- Prophet of the Badlands
- Archon's Queen
- Grey Ronin
- Daughter of Ash
- Zero Rogue
- Angel Descended

Daughter of Mars series

- The Hand of Raziel
- Araphel
- Ghost Black

Virtual Immortality series

- Virtual Immortality
- The Harmony Paradox

Divergent Fates Anthology

(Fiction Novels - Adult)

The Roadhouse Chronicles Series

- One More Run
- The Redeemed
- Dead Man's Number

Faded Skies series

- Heir Ascendant
- Ascendant Unrest
- Ascendant Revolution

Temporal Armistice Series

- Nascent Shadow
- The Shadow Collector
- The Gate to Oblivion

Vampire Innocent series

- A Nighttime of Forever
- A Beginner's Guide to Fangs
- The Artist of Ruin
- The Last Family Road Trip
- The Phantom Oracle

Standalones

- Wayfarer: AV494
- Axillon99
- Chiaroscuro: The Mouse and the Candle
- The Spirits of Six Minstrel Run
- The Far Side of Promise anthology
- Operation: Chimera  (with Tony Healey)
- The Dysfunctional Conspiracy (with Christopher Veltmann)

Winter Solstice series (with J.R. Rain)

- Convergence
- Containment

- Catalyst

Young Adult Novels

The Eldritch Heart Series

- The Eldritch Heart
- The Cursed Crown

### Evergreen Series

- Evergreen
- The World That Remains

### Standalones

- Caller 107
- The Summer the World Ended
- Nine Candles of Deepest Black
- The Forest Beyond the Earth
- Out of Sight
- Evergreen

## Middle Grade Novels

### Tales of Widowswood series

- Emma and the Banderwigh
- Emma and the Silk Thieves
- Emma and the Silverbell Faeries
- Emma and the Elixir of Madness
- Emma and the Weeping Spirit

### Standalones

- Citadel: The Concordant Sequence
- The Cursed Codex
- The Menagerie of Jenkins Bailey
- Sophie's Light

www.ingramcontent.com/pod-product-compliance
Lightning Source LLC
Chambersburg PA
CBHW032152190626
46814CB00005BA/1951